# The Illumination of Ursula Flight

For my mother, Rose,
who took me to the theatre

# The Illumination of Ursula Flight

Anna-Marie Crowhurst

ALLEN&UNWIN

First published in hardback in Great Britain in 2018 by Allen & Unwin
This paperback edition published in 2019

Allen & Unwin
c/o Atlantic Books
Ormond House
26–27 Boswell Street
London WC1N 3JZ

Phone: 020 7269 1610
Fax: 020 7430 0916
Email: UK@allenandunwin.com
Web: www.allenandunwin.com/uk

A CIP catalogue record for this book is available
from the British Library.

Paperback ISBN 978 1 76063 202 1
E-Book ISBN 978 1 76063 879 5

Designed by Carrdesignstudio.com
Printed and bound by CPI Group
(UK) Ltd, Croydon, CR0 4YY

10 9 8 7 6 5 4 3 2 1

*being the*

# TRUE TALE

*of*

# THE
# Illumination
## — *OF* —
# URSULA
# FLIGHT

WRITTEN
— *by* —
A LADY

PART

*The*

*First*

# I

# BIRTH

*In which I am born under inauspicious circumstances*

On the fifteenth day of December in the year of our Lord 1664, a great light bloomed in the dark sky and crept slowly and silently across the blackness: a comet. The prating in the coffeehouses was of the evil the fiery star portended. Such astrological phenomena, it was known, brought war, famine, disease, fire and flood; the fall of kingdoms, the death of princes, mighty tempests, great frosts, cattle-plague and French pox. Every evening afterwards, though snow lay on the ground and the air bit with frost, men across the land threw open their windows and went out of their doors in cloaks and mufflers to gaze at the heavens, necks stretched up, hands shielding eyes, crooking long fingers to trace the burning thing that flamed across the night, while dogs moaned in their kennels and wise women chanted incantations against bright malignant spirits.

My mother, then in her fourth lying-in for childbed, had heard the tattle, by letter, from her sister, and begged her lady to open up the chamber curtains, the windows being tight fastened against ill winds. A fire blazed in the grate and bitter herbs got from the apothecary smoked in pots. My mother, taut and swollen, sweated in her night-shift.

It was hard to see at first, my mother said: that night the sky was so pricked with stars, the air so thick and dark. But as she gazed, wet-faced, propped full-bellied on her pillows, there broke out from under a cloud a great white star with a flickering tail. At the sight of it she cried out in wonder, and, I think, in fear, and doing so broke her water: her agonies began.

Thus began, too, my journey into the world: she, crying and clawing, as I strained, sightless and bloodied, to meet the wonder which that very moment was bursting through the empyrean. With a wrench, I was born, into the deepest part of the night, blinking, kicking, then so strangely silent they thought me dead, just as the comet ended its glowing travails and disappeared from earthly sight.

# MOTHER

*In which I assert my independence at three years old*

'Mother! Mother! Motherrrrrr!'

I liked to call my mother, just to see if she would come. I had copied it from the way she called out to Joan, her lady, who always came a-scurrying and tripping on her skirts, before taking her orders with a heaving chest and a reddened, funny face. I wanted my mother to come and make me giggle. She could tickle me and it would be a game.

'Mother!' I yelled again, making my voice go up and down and twisting my face into a few silly grimaces for good measure. I liked the different things I could do with my voice, and it was funny because shouting was naughty. I put my hands to my face to feel it move. There was goat's milk crusted on one of my cheeks. I scratched at it.

My mother did not come. There was silence in the parlour, save for the faint whistle of the wind down the chimney. I lolled against the wainscot, sniffing at the grown-up smells of wax and wood-smoke. I was afraid of the vastness and emptiness of the room when I was in it all alone, but I pushed at my stomach, feeling a bubbly thrill creeping up to my chest despite my fear at being in a place that was kept for visitors, and mostly forbidden to me. I had stolen in when everyone was busy. Now I could explore. I held my breath as long as I could then let it out in a great gust. If I did it three times then my mother would come.

I went around the room, holding out my arms, stretching my fat child's fingers to touch each object. I stroked everything a little in turn, touching the precious things, as I was never allowed to do when there were grown-ups around. It was different from the nursery, where everything was brown and wooden and could not break. Here there was a great black cabinet, painted with sea gods and mermaids, topped by two knobbly silver candlesticks with burned-down wicks; a glossy table with stout, spiralled legs, and in the corner, resting on a stand, my mother's mandalore, with the fat face of a cherub carved into its neck. The tale of the mandalore was one of my favourites; I made Mother tell it to me at bedtime. Then she would whisper in her story voice of how it had been carved from the wood of a little pear tree by one Signior Testore, a gentleman from Venice with flowing black hair and shining eyes like conkers. It was given to her by my father as a present on their wedding day and she would treasure it for evermore.

The sunlight from the window threw bright oblongs onto the floor. I went over to the shapes and jumped onto them with a 'Ho!', hoping I might be transported to a faraway land, as in the stories told to me by Goodsoule, my nurse, who was a wise woman – but that must not be spoken of in company, lest somebody hear, and put her in the pond.

I jumped in and out of the squares, liking the way my body turned from light to dark as I moved. Singing a song about fairies, I hopped up and down on the spot and then stood stock still in an oblong and stretched out my palms, watching the light make them golden. I stayed there breathing in and out, watching the dust rise up, then lay down in the sun, as I had seen our big dog Muff do, and kicked out my arms and legs in a star shape. I was hot and bright all over.

'Muuuuuuu-ther!' I called, sliding my legs open and together on the floor. The swishing of the skirts of my gown as I kicked. 'I am here, Mother! Oh Mother, won't you come to me? Here I am in the parlour, Mother!' I sang.

I held my body still for a moment and waited. 'Mother!' I screamed it as loudly as I dared, then caught my breath, frightened at my own naughtiness. I listened for the squeak of the stairs, the tip-tapping of running, angry feet... The clock chimed the hour in the hall, but nobody came.

I lay in the light-shape with my eyes closed. The sunlight was under my eyelids: there were purple spots and green swirls. I sat myself up and gazed out of the window. The sky was pale blue peppered with wisps of white. My father liked his turnips peppered and it made my mother sneeze. Children did not like pepper, as a rule, Father said.

I should have liked to go and play outside. It had rained in the night, but now there was only the whistly wind – and the sun looked as if it might be hot. There were birds' nests and the drays of squirrels in the gnarled old oak, and I could make daisy-chains with Goodsoule and wear them as necklaces. We had a squat little crab-apple tree with low branches that could be climbed, if somebody helped, and stood by in case you fell.

The door creaked and Father's wolfhound trotted in, making a noise in her throat when she saw me on the floor. 'Come now, Muffy!' I said, and threw out my arm as I had seen my father do. She came over with a solemn face and lapped at my nose and the salty place behind my ear. I tipped backwards, giggling, and Muff barked joyfully and began to worry at my shoe. I lay back in the oblong, laughing and tugging my foot away, while she nipped at my shoe leather, letting out little excited yips between each bite.

'Oh Muff,' I said. 'You are a very naughty girl.'

The dog had got my shoe off and was joyfully eating it in a corner when Mother came in with a rustling of skirts, a stiff look about her face. I wiggled my stockinged toes and waved at her from my place on the floor. She might lie down in the bright square too, if she knew how warm it was.

'Ursula, you naughty child,' she cried, seizing my arm and dragging me upwards and giving me a few sharp pinches. She set about brushing the dust from my back and rubbing it out of my hair. When she got to the stuff on my skirts it felt much like smacking. But I stood still and leant my weight against her, as much as I dared. I liked being close to my mother and breathing in her mother-smell, which was roses and cloves and lavender, from the pomander she wore about her neck.

'You are not to lie on the floor and get your smock dirty,' she said. 'And you should not be in the parlour, besides. Where is Goodsoule? Is it not time for your nap? Muff! Bring that here at once.'

Muff eyed my mother balefully, then, dropping her woolly head, spat out a piece of leather.

'I wanted to see if you would come, Mother,' I said, in a small voice, for I hated to be scolded. 'And – and...' I was thinking up a reason as quickly as I could. 'And to tell you about Muffy who has been so good and sweet. We had a game and she took my shoe. I think it smells of dog-dinner to her, for she licked it most thoroughly.'

My mother had wrested the remains of my shoe from Muff's jaws and was now fastening it back on my foot.

'It is wet,' she said. 'But 'twill serve you right.'

'Yes, Mother,' I said.

She took my hand and dragged me from the room. Muff, watching me go, started up a moaning, which echoed around the house and made the kitchen maids take fright.

# III

# FRIENDSHIP

*In which I make my very first bosom friend*

The drifting scents of spring were in the air. Bluebells and honeysuckle and sun-dried hay mingled with the piles of manure from the farm horses, who had carried the King and Queen of the May, but then forgot themselves and been naughty.

I spread my fingers out and felt the sharp stalks scratch against my palms. I had been allowed to join the cottage folk on their hay bales on the green to watch the maypole dance. After a week of being trapped indoors, I was mightily happy to be outside – Goodsoule had been busy with my little brother Reginald, who had suffered an attack of the mumps and was much given to screaming, and I had grown bored of wandering about the house in search of amusement. It was good to be basking in the sun, which was high and hot, though it was not yet noon. I touched my nose, feeling it might be getting pink, despite my bonnet. The admonishment of Mother to *stay in the shade* still rang in my ears; I knew she would scold me for sun-burn. In imitation of the village girls, I unlaced my bonnet and tipped it further over my eyes, loosening my linen collar which was high against my neck.

I liked the way the villagers clapped and smiled as the fiddler made merry. He had played 'May Morning' and was onto 'Come Lads and Lasses', bowing and taking a few jaunty steps in time. I followed the bright-haired dancers with my eyes as they circled the maypole in their white gowns, which had great sleeves and full skirts. I should like to be one of them, one day, if Mother would allow it. She liked me to learn dancing, at any rate, and was teaching me the gavotte. I loved to hear music and skip around the room, but could not point my toe high enough, though I practised stretching it each night in my chamber.

Mary Goodsoule came over to the hay bales, a bunch of daisies in her hand. She was taller than me by half a head and had light red hair the colour of the stable cat. I had seen her waiting at our garden gate for her mother to come home – I often knelt on the window-seat of my chamber to watch Goodsoule leave us for the day, for my night-times were lonely and I was loath to see her go.

'Do you want one?' Mary said, opening her fist to show the fuzzy stalks, warmed and wilted in her palm.

I hesitated. I felt shy of speaking to the child of a servant.

'Go on,' she encouraged, pushing back a lock of hair that had fallen over her face. Her cheeks were round and rosy as her mother's, and she had the same kindly sweetness about her face, the same wide-spaced eyes.

'Have you been dancing?' I said.

'Oh no,' she said. 'My sister Kitty wouldn't have it, for nothing is to spoil her day of being Queen. That's her, with hair like me, threading ribbons on the maypole. I have been up over yonder' – she flicked her arm behind her – 'gathering blooms to make a perfume. My ma teaches me. Mayhap she will teach you, if you ask her. You crush up the petals and put them on your bosom for the gentlemen to sniff, and then they come a-wooing.'

'Oh.'

'Take a daisy,' she said. 'I picked them in a waxing moon, and that means goodness.'

'Oh,' I said again, feeling foolish. But I took a flower from her, and held it between my fingertips. I twirled it a little in the air, uncertain of what to do.

'How old are you?' said Mary. She had fair, freckled skin and the same long nose as her sister, which gave her an elegant air, child as she was.

'Seven years and one-hundred and thirty-eight days. I counted yesterday.'

'I'm nine,' she said. 'I'm Mary.'

'I'm Ursula,' I said.

And that was how I made the very first bosom friend of my life.

❦

One bright day in early summer, Mary came to me while I was playing a boisterous game with the dog in the orchard – Muff had a stick in her mouth that she would not let go of and it made me laugh 'til my belly hurt when I hung onto its end and let her pull me along the ground, she shaking her head and growling all the while; me kicking my legs and feeling the damp grass slime across my arms as she dragged me, the warm huff of her breath on my hands.

'Ho,' said Mary. 'Where's my ma? You'll be scolded later, for you have covered your second-best gown in grass stains, and they are harder to get out than blood.'

'What do you know about it, Mrs?' said I, letting go of Muff's stick, so that she flew backwards with it, and danced about by a tree.

'A great deal,' said Mary, sitting down daintily beside me, 'for Ma has been teaching me the work of the household, and that includes washing.'

I turned up my nose at this. 'I do not need to know about it,' I said, pulling up a fistful of grass and letting it shower upon my head. 'For the servants do it, I think.'

'Aye,' she said, 'but not for us, for we *are* the servants and must do it ourselves.'

'I suppose that is true,' I said, looking at her, for in truth I had not thought much about my Mary's lot in life. We were both quiet then, I tugging evermore vigorously at the grass. Muff had seen a squirrel, and dashed off after it with a volley of joyful barks.

'But do you not want to know why I am come to visit you?' Mary said.

'No,' I said, which was often my instinctive answer to questions. She pursed up her face in the cross way she had. 'Yes, yes of course,' I said quickly. 'For who is looking after your brothers and sisters while your father is in the fields?'

'Old Mistress Claxton is with them, and I have come to be your companion,' said she, peering at my face. 'I am now old enough to earn my living. Your ma asked mine to see if she might set about finding a village girl to keep you company and be your playmate, for she is afeard,' – here she jabbed me playfully in the ribs – 'that you are growing up strange and wild...'

'Wild!' I cried.

'You cannot argue with it,' said Mary. 'And you are lonely – so here I am come to play with you and to keep by your side.'

'Faith, can it be true?' I cried, getting up and pulling her with me into a stumbling sort of passepied about the orchard, and kissing her face. She pretended to push me off, and we romped about between the trees then in a topsy-turvy game of tag.

Goodsoule came out and I ran to her and put my head in her skirts, and she patted my back with her rough hands, the hands I knew and loved, though they had slapped me when I was naughty. I lolled in her embrace feeling the fabric of her apron on my cheek. 'Now, now,' she said in her deep voice, and bade us both smooth our hair and come into the parlour, where my mother was waiting by the window, stiff-backed on her favourite chair. Goodsoule pushed me forward and I stepped reluctantly away from the comfort of her nearness.

'For shame, child – can it be that you have mussed your gown again?' said Mother, darting at me and flicking at my skirts, smeared irrevocably with green. 'Lo, 'tis all up one sleeve, and your bodice too.' She slapped at my arms, and I tried to dodge her hands.

'Ow! It was a game with Muff, who...' I began.

'Goodsoule,' Mother said, 'see that Ursula does not drag herself along the ground, for it makes too much work for Lisbet – and you besides.'

'I beg your pardon, mistress,' said Goodsoule.

I turned my face to look at her. ''Tis not her fault,' I began, but seeing Goodsoule's eyebrows rise, I kept my peace, and went and sat on the little footstool my father liked to rest his feet upon in the evenings.

'Come here, child,' said my mother to Mary, and my friend went to her, and was turned around by her shoulders, and peered at by my mother in a way which made me feel strange. I wondered at Mary being able to bear it.

'Are you a good girl?' said my mother.

'Yes, mistress,' said Mary in a docile voice, so different from the one she used when we called to one another, which was high and light as a bird's.

'And will you work hard and be a helpmeet to my daughter, and keep by her side, and see that she is safe?'

'I will, mistress,' said Mary.

'Very well,' said my mother, in a cold sort of way which made my belly churn. 'Your mother is run off her feet, what with Reginald and his maladies and the nursing of the babby. So we will try it and see how we fare.'

'Oh thank you, sweet Mother!' I said, jumping off the footstool and rushing at her, at which she put her arm around me, quickly bent her head towards mine then straightened it again, before releasing me and pushing me off.

'You must be a very good girl now, Ursula, or Mary will be sent away.'

'Yes, Mother,' I said.

'Thank you, mistress,' said Goodsoule.

# IV

# HOME

*In which I meet an actress and get a head pain*

Viewed through the eyes of the approaching traveller, our village of Bynfield, in the southerly county of Berkshire, is a pleasant and countrified place, with its rolling hills, gurgling stream and wild moors of waving grasses, which are dotted with the oak and beech trees characteristic in those parts. It was then, and is now, bordered by a forest to the west, and by a small wood to the north: a shady place carpeted with needles and bracken, which turned orange in autumn and gave camouflage to deer.

This place was known to Bynfield children as Bear Wood, which, we told each other, was on account of the wild and hungry creatures that roamed there. I passed many happy days here as a child – there were fleshy fairy rings of toadstools which sprang up in the shade and wildflowers to gather and weave into our hair. I never did see a bear, or anything more frightening than a vixen, but the older children knew stories of the ancient days and told them to us in such whispering tones, I had strange and unquiet dreams: of dark, waving branches and outstretched, catching claws.

Few travellers, in truth, came to Bynfield for its own sake – its inhabitants were mostly farmers and a few handy folk who made stockings on looms. The place comprised but a dozen scattered dwellings, some cottage farms, a church, and a few heaths and copses on which cattle roamed. We therefore saw few strangers, save for the summer months when the Court was at Windsor. Then, a few courtiers travelling eastwards to the castle came to the inn, which perched on the edge of His Majesty's Great Park and, being just behind the eight-mile stone to that royal town, was convenient as a stopping place.

My family had a good sort of house, for we were the nobles of that parish, and kept Bynfield Hall, a sprawling brick and timber manor which was built by my great-grandfather who had had a sickly wife in need of country air. It was a godly sort of place, with a pleasing aspect across the bright fields of corn to suit the invalid, and fresh water from the spring that flourished just beyond the garden wall.

When my grandparents went to God, my mother and father took it up and, because Mother was rich and brought a great dowry, added a wing, and a stable block, and a kitchen garden that grew thick with thyme and lavender. They were young and true sweethearts when they married (or so my mother said) and so they were merry as the day is long at Bynfield, or as they could be, for the age was a hard one under Cromwell.

My father had been a loyal supporter of the King and, through all the misery and the darkness of the time, kept himself strong and true and proud, being part of a sworn-secret faction with a band of other local men, who had vowed a lifelong allegiance to the Crown. To this end they met every Thursday at the All Saints church, where they whispered morsels of news from the Continent and drank the King's health out of earshot of the vicar.

When Old Rowley was Restored, my father prospered, being rewarded with a contract to build His Majesty's ships, for he had grown up near Norwich, and had spent many years inland, dreaming of the sea, which had got to the King's ear and tickled him. How pleased my mother was at my father's frequent absences I never knew, but she was kept busy enough in the bearing of children, for every time he came home he got a babby on her, and she had given birth to three that did not live, before I came, with the comet.

Having been released from chores and sewing, and not inclined to begin one of our woodland games – for though it was an unseasonably fine day in March, it was not yet warm – a group of us children – Grisella and Nicholas and Mary and I – were sitting on the tumbledown stone wall that ran opposite the inn, hoping to catch sight of a stranger. We had all but given the game up for lost, and were debating Nicholas's suggestion that we make for Bear Wood to look for nightjars' eggs (it was ever our ambition to raise the chicks of wild birds, which could then be tamed and taught to do tricks and carry messages) when Mary heard the tell-tale thumpings and clatterings of a carriage coming down the way, and we stood up to better catch the first glimpse of the finely dressed lady or gentleman.

It was our habit on such occasions to clutch at each other as the approaching traveller pranced up on horseback, at which the boldest of us might call out a saucy greeting, which was usually ignored. Then we would watch agog as the mud was brushed from cloaks and Mr Sprogget the innkeeper was bidden to water the horses, tarrying until the travelling party had retired to their chambers to fortify themselves with sack in preparation for Mrs Sprogget's cooking. In the morning they would primp their hair with sugar-water and ribbons, so that they could go before the King looking their best – all the better to get a royal favour or a pardon for a misdeed. And we would never see them again, but go home very well satisfied that we had had a peek at another sort of life.

On that particular day, the sound of approaching hooves was accompanied by the jingle of a carriage, and a coach and four drew up in a cloud of dust. Mary clutched me and Nicholas gave a whistle as a foppish gentleman in velvet emerged from within, and supported a masked lady in a shell-pink gown, who seemed to be weeping and dragging her feet. That the man had the lady by the elbow as he led her into the house, and that the lady was twice prevented by him from removing her vizard, caused a rumour that ran the breadth of the village that she was an heiress and kidnapped by a scoundrel with designs on her portion.

By eleven o'clock the bruits reached Rector Thistlethwaite, who, feeling it was his Christian duty, if it was anyone's, went to enquire, while we children crowded round, chattering. Presently the slamming of a door was heard, and the rector came down the front path with a face as red as roast beef, stuttering that she was a married lady after all, and all was as God would wish it. On further questioning by Nicholas, who hung on his sleeve and worried at it, the rector said that it was his own belief that the lady was an actress, which was not godly, but he did not make the rules.

After he had gone off in the direction of the rectory mumbling about the whimsies of the gentry and the liberties of the age, my friends challenged me to go and enquire after the lady and see if she was an actress and to discover, if I could, what an actress might be.

I could hardly get out of the dare, as Grisella had thrice turned around and touched the ground, so to go against it would mean seven years' bad luck. And so, after some argument, I consented.

'That's the spirit,' said Nicholas.

Mary cried: 'Good luck to ye, Urse!'

I could hear their giggling as I crossed the path, approached the inn, lifted the latch on the door and passed inside it.

It was dim and cool in the inn, and the yeasty smell of hops rose up to my nose; my feet kicked the straw that lay strewn on the ground in readiness for spillages. There was a fire blazing in the large and oft-blackened hearth, but no one warming themselves by it, or tending the bar neither, so I swiftly crossed the room to a stout-looking door and turned the iron handle as slowly as I might.

A staircase lay behind the door, with a high-up mullioned window casting a dim pool of light that fell in a scatter of shapes across the steps. 'Hello?' I whispered – I half wanted to be found and sent back to my friends with a twisted ear.

No reply came, so, remembering the challenge, I crossed my fingers and stepped slowly up the stairs, going mighty carefully to avoid squeaking, and pausing on each step, my ears pricked for the coming heavy tread of furious grown-ups. I heard nothing to frighten me but the groan of boards overhead, higher up in the house.

I had almost got to the top, and was wondering what to do next and whether I might in all conscience go back outside and pretend the inn was empty after all, when I caught the sound of laughter: a woman's voice, bright and pleasantly musical. It floated out to where I stood, one hand on the newel, one toe pressed on the very top step.

'Confound thee, Mistress Minx!' came the rumbling voice of a man, and with it more laughter, and muffled sounds, and the creaking of a bed.

'Nay,' came the woman's voice. 'Not until we are wed, Felix. For I did not miss two performances to hole up in a low tavern and act as your concubine.'

'Hush, madame!' was all I heard before the voices dropped to murmurs that were beyond my hearing. I stood stock still on the landing knowing not what to do, for I knew ear-wigging to be a wrongdoing that was often punished with a spanking. I had turned back towards the staircase once more and was stealing my way down the first of the steps, when the door was flung open and the man emerged, still wearing his velvet breeches, his periwig askew.

'What's this?' he said, sweeping past me as I pressed against the wall, but took no more notice of me, and went down the stairs, banging the door behind him, so that it sprang open again with the force. I stood not knowing what to do, but then the woman's voice came.

'Who is there?'

I could hardly disobey a grown-up, and so I went meekly to the open chamber door and dropped one of my best curtseys (I had been practising but was still unsteady about the knees and very much given to leaning).

''Tis I, mistress,' I said, with my eyes politely pointing floorwards. 'Ursula Flight. But I did not hear a thing I oughtn't and will be on my way now, if it please ye, mistress.'

'Strange, bold child!' said the lady, coming towards me, and I saw she was very pretty, with a coil of chestnut hair and pearls at her ears and throat. She looked me up and down, with her painted lips twisted into a queer little moue. 'What do you mean by lurking there? Do you live here, at the inn?'

'Nay, but at Bynfield Hall and I do beg your pardon, mistress. For it was a challenge by my playmates,' I said, knowing now the fat was in the fire. 'And I am very sorry for troubling you.'

''Tis no trouble,' said she, with a toss of her head, which rattled all the pearls. 'Come in and tarry awhile, for I am apt to grow bored, and you amuse me with your strange, fierce face, child.'

I went in as she had bidden and stood with my arms crossed behind my back.

'What do you wish to be when you grow up, Ursula Flight?' said she.

'Why, a dashing adventurer, and if I cannot be that, a nun, and if I cannot be that, a mother to ten children, all of them twins and with bright golden hair.'

'Is that so,' said she, with a twisted sort of smile. And then she looked at me. 'Tell me, child. What age do you think I am?'

'Why, I do not—' All grown-ups looked famous old to me.

'I am three-and-twenty, but I am a fool,' she said, going over to the window and looking out of it, running her white hands up and down on the window-sill all the while. 'And that man you saw just now is not my husband,' she said, watching my eyes. 'Does that amaze you, Ursula Flight?' She had a pink look about her cheeks, and a restlessness about her person.

'A little,' I said. 'For the rector said so and that you were not kidnapped after all.'

'Nay, I am not kidnapped,' she said. 'But I am not wed. I told that man a falsehood when he came, and do you know why, little maid – aside from the fact he is a great sticky beak and should not be poking it hither and thither?'

'Nay,' said I, being mightily confused by the conversation.

'Because I am an actress 'pon the stage in London, and 'tis not respectable. At Court I am much admired by the King – and, ooh, well everyone admires me, in truth. I am a great beauty, you know. I have silks and jewels and a little servant boy called Peregrine and a green parakeet in a golden cage brought from foreign lands, and I dine with duchesses and make merry all my days.'

I shuffled in my place. I was growing troubled that my friends would by now have run away and Mother would surely be cross at my staying out past dinner-time.

'Forgive me, mistress,' I said. 'But what is an actress?'

'What is an actress!' cried the lady. 'Are we that far from Court? But I see we are,' she said, looking at my face. 'An actress is a lady actor, who goes 'pon the stage and acts in plays, taking the parts of ladies – or of gentlemen if it is required – and in truth my own performances in breeches get the most applause of all. But never mind about that.'

'The rector said 'tis not godly,' I said.

She laughed at this and twirled at a lock of her hair. 'I can find nothing in the Bible against it,' she said. 'And I have read many books, for I greatly delight in the written word as much as I do the spoken. But there are those that cannot abide change, nor the freedom of women neither, and will do anything to keep us down, and the whole world caught in the Dark Ages besides. And it is for us as women to put them in their place, and do as we will, though many would prate at us for it.'

'I see,' I said, though I only half did.

'Acting is a wondrous career for a woman, in faith,' said she, a brightness coming into her eyes. 'For it means applause, and wages, and fame and flirtation – and if you play the thing right, jewels and marriage, for there are always noblemen who will call 'pon the 'Tiring Room, and are spun about the head by a cream-skinned wench half out of her shift. Such as he . . .' She tossed her head towards the doorway. I followed her gaze.

'But I gave it all up to let myself be driven in a draughty, rattly coach to this ghastly backwater because I thought by the end of it I would be a Marquess. Now it has become apparent that I have not got him by the nose as I had thought.' She began to walk up and down the room a little, with a dainty, light-footed tread. 'Unless I can get him to the church I have wasted my time, and have lost my career and my place besides.'

There did not seem to be much to say, and I did not understand the half of it, but I knew enough to say: 'I am sorry, mistress.'

'Aye,' she said. 'Aye.'

We stood still like that, her eyes fastened on the window, mine on the floor, waiting on the moment when I might make my escape. I was growing evermore uncomfortable that the man who was not her husband might return at any time, and cuff me for my intrusion, or worse.

I coughed.

'Go now then, child,' she said, turning to face me again and waving her hand at me. 'But remember this. Ware the man that says he loves you – for it means nothing without the marriage contract. Nothing but tears.'

I ran then, caring not who heard me, but that I got away from the sad, beautiful lady and dark inn. Nicholas was the only one still waiting on the wall and he let out a low whistle when I told him what had transpired and that I had met the lady and gone into her chamber, though I did not say she was not married after all. I ran home wishing with all my might I was an actress 'pon the stage in London with a shell-pink gown and a green parakeet. I scrunched up my eyes so many times in my imagining, I woke in the morning with the first head pain of my life, which Goodsoule dosed with a posset made of nutmeg, orange peel and the burnt foot of a rabbit.

⚜

# V

# LESSONS

*In which I begin my education*

I had got what I had prayed for on so many nights, on my knees, in my chamber. I had promised the Lord our God in heaven to do many things in the getting of it too: I would not chatter at dinner, I would put away my toys (the peg dolls *would* get out and roam about the house), I would practise my scales at the spinet and I would be obedient for my mother.

How fervently I had murmured with my eyes fast shut, my hands clasped together over my head: *O Christo Jesu in caelo, da mihi sororem*. I had a brother already – Reginald had come along when I was two – but I knew I needed a sister too: I wanted someone to play with, and to tell my secrets to, and she would look well in the pudding cap I myself had worn which had been sewed by my mother in her confinement and was trimmed with gay yellow ribbons.

My sibling-lack was not for the want of my mother's trying. She oft grew stout and round about the middle, and went about in a loose-laced gown, groaning when she got off the couch, and grumbling at my father about the pains in her back – but she could not get a babe to live. Every twelvemonth or so there would come a time when I was hushed in the parlour or bade to play in the nursery, from where, roused by the strange sounds that echoed in the house, I would slip out to see a white-shrouded little bundle laid out on the table by the servants, which would then be taken off and put into the ground with the others while my mother wept and my father prayed to God in heaven, send me another son, O Lord, amen.

By the time I got my sister, Reginald was a burly little boy of six; a whiny child who could never lose a game and was only sunny when being praised. I had given up trying to play with him, for he would not charade at prince and princess, or cruel king and pretty maid, or any of the other entertainments I devised for us with costumes. Neither did he like to stay out of doors and roam about Bear Wood, as I did. I cut us both branchlets for swords and tried to make him have a duel (he was supposed to be the Dutch, and me the King's man waiting to run him through at Lowestoft), but he went off and cried to Mother that I beat him, so I gave the whole thing up for lost, leaving him to lurk about the stables with the queer gleam in his eye that usually meant he was about to do a mischief to the cats.

My sister finally came, at the end of a mighty storm that tore the roof tiles off the stable and uprooted three saplings in the orchard. What I first took for the moaning of the wind around the gables was in truth my mother's wailing, a strange unearthly noise that lasted all the morning and frightened Muff, so that she leapt about the house, knocking over with a clatter the silver candelabra that my parents had got as a wedding present. I crept about the corridor, listening for the usual sound of women's tears and the appearance of the midwife with yet another tiny bundle – but the weeping did not come, and the midwife neither.

I tip-toed up to the door of my mother's chamber and pressed my ear to it. Through the thickness of the oak I could dimly perceive the tap and creak of several pairs of feet moving rapidly across the floor, and the rise and fall of voices, the cries of my mother, and then – oh wonder! – there started up a set of lusty infant yells which seemed to shake the very door and made me step quickly away from it. My father must have heard the crying too, for he came bounding up the stairs two at a time on his long legs, and crashed open the door.

An exclamation. The sound of voices. More footsteps.

My father came out again, ruffling my hair as he went. I knocked and was admitted by Mistress Knagg the midwife, a stout lady with burly forearms beneath her rolled-up sleeves and a kindly looking face. My mother's complexion was wan and her hair stuck fast to her cheeks with sweat, but she whispered that God be praised I had a sister, and showed me the babby, who was dark haired and fiery red all over, with a slimy, scrunched up face that could not be called beautiful and looked somewhat like my father, with the same bulbous nose and cupid's bow lips that he had, in miniature. She slept soundly while I kissed her hot little head and whispered in her ear that though she was ugly, it did not signify, for I was her big sister and would love her all my days.

❀

Catherine was still a babe in arms, and become quite bonny, when I was told I should begin my education at last. We were playing cribbage after supper and my father handed me a hornbook on a thin leather strap. It was a thing of great significance, for he had decided – here he looked up at my mother, but she was chucking the babby's face, fussing and scarlet-cheeked in her swaddling – that at eight years of age I was old enough to begin my schooling. Today would be our very first lesson.

How I clapped at this! I had often wandered into my father's study and run my fingers along the leather-bound volumes on his shelf, before leafing through their pages and wondering at the meaning of the black letter-shapes, which I knew would be greatly interesting, if only I could make them out. My father was a very learned man who had taken a degree at Cambridge before marrying my mother, and it pleased me to be following in the family tradition. I had also been musing on my duties as an elder sister and it seemed fitting that I would be educated and could teach Catherine in turn.

Father's quill was too long for me; I could not get hold of it and flicked ink in a great arc that landed as a long dark spray across his face, his shirt, and the table. He said an oath, and the next lesson he had cut me my own quill. I liked the dipping of it into the ink pot and the clicking, liquid sound as the nib hit the pot.

The first task my father set me about was to write my name and the name of our family, so that I would always be able to sign documents and contracts, such as the one pertaining to my marriage portion, when I was a grown-up lady. He drew my name out for me in a fine hand, with a flourish on the end, and set me about copying it, which I did painstakingly, but making many mistakes, and sighing over them, my lower lip caught between my teeth all the while. My childish blunders were many: I pressed the nib too firmly into the paper, and tore it, my hands grew clammy at the effort and I dropped the quill, and the shapes I made looked crude and ill-formed against my father's, but by Ascension Day I had mastered the thing at last.

I discovered, too, that there was nothing I liked more than to see my own name drawn out by my own hand, and so I wrote it everywhere I could, including places I knew were forbidden:

*Ursula Flight*

*Ursula Flight*

on the end papers of my prayer book, the inside of my left arm (it lasted for six days), and behind the door on the wall of my chamber (where perhaps it may be still, for I do not believe the current owner would distemper it).

'Mary cannot spell out her name as I can,' I said to my father at the end of a lesson – we had started on the counties of England, and the dukedoms and the Kings and Queens of England too; these I was to chant and scratch them over and over in my hornbook, to better commit them to memory. It gave me great pride to do what I knew none of the village children could and the tools of my trade were precious to me: I sewed my own quill-case and, after carefully wiping the nib, stowed it there safely after every lesson.

❦

It was coming on for summer; the windows were pushed wide open, and the scent of the lavender bush floated in. There was a bee buzzing near the top of the plant; he went from flower to flower, clinging onto each one and humming there for a while.

'Is he making honey?' I asked.

'He is,' said my father. 'And next week we shall drink it in our honey wine.' He moved around the things on his desk – sticks of sealing wax and the stamp with our family crest, a silver candle-snuffer, and books and scrolls, held open with weights. I liked to watch his hands, with their moon-shaped nails bitten down to the quick. I had started nibbling at my own nails, but Mother slapped my hand away and threatened a whipping. Hands were important to a lady – not so much to a man.

'Mary could have lessons with *her* father,' I said, returning to my original topic. 'And then she might write her name out too. And we could write other things and send each other secret messages in invisible ink, such as ladies and gentlemen do in an intrigue!'

'Perhaps,' said my father, moving his books about.

'But is it not a good idea, Father? I think it is. I shall run and tell her now and she can ask Mr Goodsoule to begin. He is not often at home as he works in the fields, but she will have to ask him nicely.'

I got down from my stool and began to wipe my inky hands. I was always being scolded for it.

'I do not think Mary's father will be able to give the lessons, as I do. He is in the fields all day, for his duty is with the cows.'

'Oh,' I said. 'But p'raps it would do no harm to ask him. He might spare an hour, after supper, as we do when we swap verses. Even Mother likes that game.'

'But I do not think Mr Goodsoule can make the letters himself, child. So he cannot teach it.'

'Oh,' I said, digesting this. 'Well, then Mary must join in our lessons. Could she not do that?'

'She might.' He had moved over to the window and was watching the bee as it zig-zagged over the lavender. 'But I do not think she would want to. Book-learning is not the thing of servants, for they do not need it. You will comprehend it better when you are older, child.' He came back to me and put his hands on my shoulders. 'Next lesson we will learn the habits of the honey-bee and his ways of making honey for our puddings.'

'Aye, Father,' I said.

❧

## IN THE NAME OF GODDE,
## HERE ARE THE RULES
### *of*
## OUR *CLUB*
### *(If you are Reggie GO AWAY)*
## Written down by URSULA FLIGHT
### &
## helped by MARY GOODSOULE to do it

## On the 15th day of JULY, in the year 1673 A.D.

Rule the 1st: Do not tell about the S E C R E T S, on pain of a grisly, lingering death at Tyburn!

Rule the 2nd: Practise the dance steps and song every morning, even if your mother scolds you for it.

Rule the 3rd: Reginald and Johnny are the enemy!!! They smell of dung!

Rule the 4th: Our motto is Singulare Aude.

Rule the 5th: Our pass-word is 'Blue Boy'. (For he is our favourite horse!)

Rule the 6th: Our uniform is bonnet straps undone and the nut-shell necklaces (to be kept in the secret box – shhh).

Rule the 7th: On _washing day_ we meet in Bear Wood by the great twisted root and speak the _solemn vow_ and wear the vizards and when we do this we bring great luck upon us and we will be happy all our days and be rich and marry well and live next door to each other for ever when we are grown.

Rule the 8th: We are best friends and Grisella cannot speak to us.

Rule the 9th: Huzzah for Muff!

Rule the 10th: Huzzah for the King and Queen of England!

❦

I soon began to take such pleasure in my expanding knowledge that I grew to anticipate my lessons as I once had my mealtimes. I remember now too well the feeling that my young mind was opening up and enlarging with each new subject we began. I developed a craving – to read more, to absorb more facts, to memorize more verses, and to understand mathematics, which we had started with an abacus, and which was a great puzzle to me, though I slaved at its understanding and spent nights after bedtime wondering aloud over complicated subtractions and the great eternal mystery that was algebra.

My father had started me on the Classics as soon as I had got my reading and writing to a standard that he was pleased with, and this I greatly enjoyed. The Greek myths were my greatest discovery – I begged my father to read them to me aloud, for listening to his low, measured voice was another pleasure of my lessons: he was a great story-teller, and could speak well, and so had the knack of making things seem diverting. During the telling of these tales I liked to creep up to him and lean my head on his arm, enjoying the vibrations of his voice and the comforting heat of his nearness while he told of the cyclopes and the Titans and the Argonauts. I shivered to hear of the horrible minotaur burrowed deep in his underground lair, and Medusa with her undulating snakes'-pit hair that was cut off by Perseus. I liked to draw as he told me these stories, filling my hornbook with strange gods, coiled serpents, and armoured warriors in golden winged sandals. We moved from myths to the languages of the ancients, reading Homer and Ovid and Virgil together, my father patiently correcting me as I traced my finger over the unfamiliar characters and recited my verbs aloud: *amo, amas, amat, amanus, amatis, amant.* We began to use Latin as a private language between us, to my mother's irritation, for she had never learnt it beyond her prayer book, and though my father offered to teach her, she did not have the patience to try.

'*Salve pater. Quid agis?*'

'*Bene. Esurio.*'

'*Mihi placet lingua latina!*'

At my father's encouragement I spent much of my time roaming about his library finding books to devour – even when he was away, I had his permission to take what I would, though my mother was always calling me to come to her to do some task I thought very dull – for in comparison to reading, there was no joy in mending my stockings or practising my music.

It was with great joy one rainy morning that I came upon a high-up shelf near the window which was stacked with volumes of plays bound in calfskin and, opening their pages, found tales of other worlds, of pretty maids and fearsome kings; of enchanted islands and avenging wizards – I took them one by one and read them at a fevered pace. It was my habit to creep off into corners of the house where I could not be disturbed: on my chamber window-seat, half-hidden by the curtain; under the vegetable store in the scullery; in the low crooked branch of the apple tree. It was here I had Shakespeare, and Fletcher and Jonson and Marlowe and, when no one was watching, Dryden. I copied out great speeches and committed them to memory, reciting them for the assembled company after supper, with my hands clasped behind my back and my voice rattling a little in my throat, for I was nervous at first, before I grew used to the thing and became bolder. All the while the actress at the inn floated into my mind, and as I declaimed and struck poses or when I took my curtseys in the parlour, I did it all as I imagined she would do it, with pearl drops in my ears, a toss of my head and a bright, pleasant voice that floated on the air.

As I grew in confidence at these charades, it seemed natural to include Mary in my games, for as my ever-constant companion, she was the loyal audience to all my recitations, and, I soon realized, could play the parts I could not. There was the difficulty that she could not read to contend with, but she was as good a mimic as any child and, after diligently learning her lines with me by rote, spoke her part as well as any I had heard.

We had the orchard as an outdoor stage when it was fine, and when it rained we had the parlour, if we pushed back the side tables and set the vases on the floor against destruction. On these occasions it was often the habit of my brother and sister to creep in and be our audience, and for their sake we began to costume ourselves.

We gave performances of *Tamburlaine* in which I strode about in Father's cloak making extravagant heroic gestures which seemed to increase twofold at each playing – for I well enjoyed my part as the Scythian shepherd who seemed to me a bold and dashing fellow. We acted *The Alchemist* and *The Maid's Tragedy* and *Cymbeline* and *Macbeth*, though we had to get Muff to stand in as Third Witch, and she would not keep still, and barked. When we had run through all we had and the children clamoured for something new, I began to devise us our own little scenes, which I scribbled down in my hornbook. To encourage Mary's involvement – for at first she was wont to say that my mother would not like the playing – I let her be the princess or the queen or the chaste and pretty maid, while I took the roles of nursemaid, tavern keeper, rake and hobbling serf. I discovered in these roles that I had a flair for comedy, and the thrill that came from making people laugh; there was no greater reward for my scribblings than my sister Catherine's shrill little peals when I crept out in disguise as a washerwoman, and even Reginald's scornful yelling at the sight of me in breeches and a turban was a paean to my endeavours.

# VI

# STARS

*In which I watch the sky at night*

'Pssss. Ursula. Wake, child!'

I flicked my eyes open and felt my dream, of riding Blue Boy backwards in a thunderstorm while trying to eat a great sugar-pudding, float away. My chamber was still in darkness, save the fuzzed triangle of light which came from between the curtains. They had been hastily drawn together at bedtime by Joan, who had been in one of her tempers, because her sweetheart had grown disdainful and was not like to ask for her hand.

'Ursula!'

My father was pushing at my shoulder. I sniffed his leathery father-smell. Blinking, I felt for his arm; touched the sleeve of his nightshirt.

'Wha'?' I said thickly.

''Tis time,' he said, patting my arm. His voice was merry-sounding.

'Father?' I was still groggy with sleep. I flung out my arm. 'What time is it?'

'Past the witching hour, so you are quite safe from ghouls and goblins. Mother slumbers and will not disturb us. Get up now, child. We are to have our lesson. In astronomy.'

'Now?' I cried, sitting up. 'In the middle of the night?'

'But of course, child – 'tis the middle of the day for the stars, and we shall catch them at their business. I will go before you now and find a suitable spot for our observations.'

He crept away and was disappeared into the darkness of the house.

I pushed the sheets back then and got up and clad myself in what I could get on quickly – woollen hose under my nightgown, and my cloak over the whole – and stepped quickly down the stairs, my shoes in hand, so as not to wake the whole house. I stole into the hallway and paused a while to get my bearings – in the thick dark of the house everything looked different, and I was afraid to fall. I felt for the bannister and then for the smooth wood of the panelled wall. The clicking sound of claws on wood and Muff was brushing against my hip, nosing my hand for treats, her breath wet-hot on my palms. I was glad to have her, for though I was too old to be much afraid of the dark, I did not like ghosts, and it was hard to make out what was in front of me, or behind me, or what lurked in the recesses of the hallway.

'Hush, my sweet,' I whispered. Muff made only a little whine in answer, and followed close on my heels as I stealthily trod my way to the backstairs, my arms stretched out for obstacles before me as in a game of blind man's buff. Upon reaching the backstairs Muff moaned a little, knowing she was forbidden to descend them after an episode in which Eliza's joint had gone missing from the sideboard, and Muff was suspected but never proved (her lack of interest in supper being held in very great suspicion). I scratched the soft tufted place around Muff's ears and went downstairs, leaving her whimpering behind me. I stopped to listen to the night-time sounds of the house. The brief peal of the grandfather in the hall above, and then, closer by, the screeching of a mouse. The flagstones of the kitchen were cool beneath my stockinged feet, so I put my shoes down and stepped into them. I pushed open the scullery door.

It was a blustery night with a high wind that tweaked the leaves off the trees and threw my hair about my face, for in my sleepiness, I had come out without my nightcap. I stood in the doorway squinting to make out my father. Though the moon was waxing full, the blackness was fuzzy and strange about me: there were violet shapes that shifted and moved the more I peered at them and all around me rolled the hills that in daylight were friendly green things and now were dark places where I was afraid to go. Slowly, the lumpen outline of the privet hedge merged into focus. I wrapped my cloak tighter about my neck.

'Ursula! Come here!'

My father held a lantern up, above his head; he was beyond the hedge, in one of our nearby fields. I went towards him slowly, my arms outstretched, pushing through the gap in the bush he had gone through, stumbling a little in the mud, which was dry and soft with recent ploughing and rose up over my shoe with every step. My father put out his arm and drew me to him. He had on his old long leather coat that Mother said made him look like a highwayman, and breeches under his nightshirt. I felt down his sleeve for his hand and pressed my soft hand into his rough one.

'Cold paws,' he said, and chafed them a little. We stood like that, a little while, and then he suddenly snuffed out the lantern and set it down, plunging us both into darkness. I caught my breath. 'Now,' he said. 'Look up.'

I twisted my head upwards. The ink-black sky was speckled all over with tiny silver dots and flashes, stretching out in spools of broken light as far as I could move my neck. I swivelled my head this way and that, all the better to take it all in.

'Why, I've never seen them like this afore, Father,' I said. 'Are they always this bright?'

'Aye. But I have been waiting for a clear night, so that we might see them well enough. We shall make out what we can from here, and on the morrow we will make a star map. Look, what see you up there?'

He held his finger aloft and traced it along the shape.

'That bright star there, where my finger points, is the beginning of the Lynx. See where his head meets his body, and then along his back leg?'

'I see him, Father. But he does not much look like a lynx. More like a snake.'

'True, child.'

'What is that below him, over yonder?'

'That is Pollux and that is Castor, the bright stars which are the heads of the twins – see how they hold hands and dance across the skies.'

My head was twisting about on my neck, following my father's pointing.

'That burning orange dot is the planet Jupiter, discovered afore you were born by an Italian and his telescope instrument, which is a sort of spy glass for the heavens.'

'Oh!' I said. 'I am ruled by Jupiter. 'Tis in my horoscope. But I did not know you could see it from Earth, nor any planets neither.'

'There are six planets in the universe,' my father said, in his lesson-voice. 'We all of us revolve around the sun, so that we might be warmed by his rays, in turn. But we cannot see them all, from here.'

I gazed at Jupiter in wonder. 'And do other people live, on all the planets, as we do on Earth? Do men live on Jupiter?'

'Very likely, child, for God made the universe, and he gave us curious minds. Now Ursula,' he said. 'Look up, straight up.' He crooked his finger.

I craned my neck back so far that it started to ache.

'What see you there?'

'White sparks, Father. Is it another creature?'

'Yes, child. That is the star Muscida, which is the creature's nose, and over there is the tip of his tail which is Alkaid. And his feet are there and there – Alula and Tania Borealis.'

'They have strangely beautiful names.'

'But see, trace the shape, child. Do you see it? The head, the feet, the tail . . . 'Tis a bear. A great big she-bear that prances through the galaxy for all to admire her. Ursa Major is her name. For it is your constellation, Ursula.'

I clapped my hands at this. My own constellation!

'And bend back further, or better still turn around completely, before you snap your neck in two . . . above it, the biggest brightest star of all – that is Polaris – the North Star.'

'I see it. That is how we can always find our way home.'

'Aye,' said my father. 'The night you were born, on the night of the great comet, I walked out here, as we are doing now. I cast my eyes up and aloud thanked God in heaven for your safe delivery and your mother's great fortitude and strength. And there above me was the Great Bear herself as brilliant and dazzling as ever I'd seen her, and I knew her come out to greet my child and make her welcome. And so I named you for the stars, Ursula.'

Here he reached down and ruffled my hair.

'I did not know that,' I said. 'I had thought myself named after the saint, who did good deeds and was killed and so became a virgin martyr, for Mother said . . . But this story is much the better one! My own star bear in the heavens! Mary will be green, I think.'

My father chuckled at this.

'How long have they been there, Father? The stars?'

'Oh hundreds of years, perhaps thousands. Perhaps since the Earth began. Ptolemy saw them, and Aristotle too, and that was before our Lord Jesu was born.'

'It's a famous long time ago,' I said.

'Oh famous,' he agreed. 'And we may learn more of them 'ere long, now the King has said we are to have our Royal Observatory at Greenwich, where scholars shall study the stars and the planets, so that the knowledge may benefit the navy – the seas are controlled by the heavens, you know.'

'And people too,' said I. 'For I am unlucky, being born under a comet, and choleric, being born under Sagittarius, which rules the ninth house, and so I have good, broad hips, and so shall be much given to childbearing, but a weak liver, and must not drink ale,' I recited. I had been recently at the Goodsoules'.

''Tis true,' said he, taking my small hand in his large one. 'Many believe that the wellness of the body is written in the skies. They say the moon has many powers over us mortals, too. Choleric children' (here he prodded me in fun) 'must ware the eclipse for it greatly distempers their bodies.'

I held his hand tighter.

'Each body part is governed by the zodiac, and each illness augured by the positions of the stars. Ah yes, it is all writ above us,' he said. 'My earth-sign means I will walk always on the ground. Your mother is governed by the crab, and so she feels things deeply, though she may not speak them. Your centaur governs you and he is the archer. You shoot for far-off purpose, child. And one day you will strike home and true.'

The stars speckled the sky in all their mystery. I was born under a comet and was destined for greatness. I was ruled by Jupiter and would have good fortune all my days.

My father clasped me to him. 'Let us go in, child, for you are chill, and must get your sleep. Tomorrow we shall make our star map – and a model of the planets.'

# FACE

*In which I become aware of my appearance*

I was not a particularly vain child, but once I had grown into consciousness of it, the slow changing of my appearance from childish to something approaching womanly began to fascinate me. I was a sallow-skinned little thing with the sort of complexion called 'bloodless' by some: as I came to know what it meant to be a beauty, and hear snatches of conversation about women who were considered so, I spent a great deal of time at cheek-pinching, and later became a slave to rouge, for I could not blush and looked wan and ill in the winter months.

In my thirteenth year I spent every spare chance I had gazing at myself in the looking glass in the parlour (the only useful one in the house besides that in my mother's chamber, which I could not often get at without arousing her attention). When I could slip away from my sewing or steal a moment between my lessons and dinner, I liked to get my face close to the glass, and slowly turn my head this way and that, observing the sharp planes of my cheek-bones, the slow spread of freckles on my cheeks, and the small pink birthmark on my chin which, once I learnt how, I tried to lighten with a paste made from crushed chamomile flowers which I wore in the sunlight. On bright days, I liked the way my cheek and throat and ears caught the light; slowly batting my eyelashes I marvelled at how the sun went through them and turned them colourless.

I had also become interested in the transformative power of a hairstyle, and so it was also my habit to push at my hair and admire the effect an arrangement had on my broad forehead, and to see what it might look like piled up from a sideways view. To counteract the strange scowl I realized I put on when scrutinizing my features, I also liked to see what I might look like animated by conversation. I tried a few 'How do ye do's and 'You compliment me greatly, kind sir's and, on one dull afternoon a long while from supper, acted the part of a fine lady embroiled in a scintillating flirtation, which involved much fluttering of an imaginary lace fan, but as ill luck would have it my father came in in search of the dog and caught me in the middle of throwing my head back in a particularly trilling laugh, and I blushed to the roots of my hair; he then with very twinkling eyes bade 'My Lady' to go to my mother, who was calling for me to wind her thread.

As Mary and I began to appreciate girlish sorts of things, we played at being fine ladies. Patient Mary was mostly happy to be hair-dresser and we spent many rainy days teasing my hair into puffs and sticking it into kiss curls on my forehead with sugar-water, which had the unfortunate advantage of attracting wasps. These endeavours were never wholly successful and I often went off in a temper to drag my comb through it before I could be teased by Reginald, who was fond of bursting into my chamber, and trying to catch me at some sort of disadvantage.

The difficulty with all our endeavours soon became apparent: it was plain fact that my looks were not of a fashionable type, for then a 'beauty' was as black-haired as the sovereign – and my hair was that fairish colour that I have heard described as like the fur of a field shrew. In the summer it was dark gold, but in the winter it was dull-looking and did me few favours. It was unlucky, my Aunt Phyllis was fond of saying, that I didn't turn out dark, white-skinned and apple-cheeked like my mother and Catherine, for then I could grow up to be as admired as Barbara Castlemaine, who was ample of figure and fair of skin with a rippling lake down her back of raven-coloured curls.

Mother had been such a beauty in her day and, though she now had retired to married life and the country, was still quite striking in her middle age (she was then one-and-thirty years or thereabouts), her large brown eyes and dark lashes and plump hands and arms giving her an elegant look that had made rakes write verses and my father ask for her hand at their very first meeting. My arms were thin, my eyelashes were the sparse kind that could not be batted, and my eyes were the unfashionable light grey-blue of my father's.

I was a sharp little thing when I was small; my mother was relieved when my face softened out and grew round and almost heart-shaped. That sort of face, she said, was much admired by ladies and gentlemen of fashion. The birthmark I could do nothing about (the chamomile proved unsuccessful), but later I covered it with patches, and as to my hair, after much trial and error, I worked up a system of overnight curling that gave it a more pleasing and, I hoped, voluptuous wave. I ran away from Mother's scissors and grew it down past my waist and wore it with curls crimped on top to give the illusion of height – for I never did get particularly tall.

By the time I was almost fourteen I had got the figure that would last me most of my life, for though I would spend some years trying to fatten it up with puddings and sugar-flowers, in those days I liked to romp about the countryside, and could not easily get plump. My hollow child's body slowly bloomed out into a thing with soft curves, but I kept my narrow shoulders and ordinary sort of neck. My breasts and belly had a few scattered beauty marks but were of a tolerable sort, and I thought my waist a good one, the span of which would eventually be further reduced by tight-lacing. I have not much to say about my legs, but my mother was oft to remark on the daintiness of my feet and so I supposed that a good thing. Though most feet looked the same in slippers, I supposed it was prettier to have a little shoe rather than a great one.

# VIII

# KISS

*In which I put on a play and meet a handsome fellow*

Bear Wood was a pretty place in summer. The weather that year had been fair and hot since Whitsun and our splashing romps around the stream and hide-and-seek in the tumbledown barn left us children scarlet-faced and panting in our aprons and jackets. When the sun reached its zenith, we retreated to the shady bower of the wood and crept deep into its heart where the tree branches grew thick and tangled together. The grown-ups, we knew, would not trouble to follow the meandering tracks to find us there, and so we had respite from lessons and chores and unwanted meals, though we might suffer for it afterwards, with a birching.

We each had a favourite path that led to one of our special places. Mary liked a sunlight-dappled dell that was found by scrambling along the hollow of an old and dried-up brook. Nicholas had a way which wound around a mound to a dark and boggy place with a knot of broken trees, caught, we supposed, in a lightning-storm. Upon arrival at this spot he was inclined to make strange gnomish faces and begin throaty chantings that we did not much like. Grisella preferred an open clearing quite close to the main path; a bare sort of place with a large fallen log and not much else to recommend it, save that her mother was likely to come for her if she stayed out past dinner-time, and from there she could hear the shrieking.

I thought my chosen way the best of them all. It was found by passing through a bank of holly, to arrive at the lip of a great ditch, which was at least thirty feet across and had walls at least a man and a half high – my father said this was part of a hill fort put there by the Atrebates, then used by the Romans as a camping ground. Slithering down into this ditch was to discover my little glade: carpeted with bluebells in spring and foxgloves in summer, it was slightly risen at one end; the higher side topped with bracken. Sheltered from intruders by want of the earthen walls around it, and from the vagaries of the weather too, I thought it the perfect spot in which to act out plays.

On that particular day, we stopped at the edge of the wood, near a great oak which was the marker for the beginning of the path to Billingbear. After joining hands and renewing our continued oath to keep the forest secrets, we pulled straws from a clutch brought by Mary, to decide whose path would be chosen. For once it was I who was the victor.

'Fie!' I said, waving my straw stalk aloft. 'You all lose and we shall go to Bluebell Glade.'

'Baw,' said Nicholas, throwing his straw to the ground. 'I had thought to make a mud pie in Goblin Hole, for it has rained these last two nights and the conditions are favourable.'

'Nobody likes your mud feasts, Nicholas,' said Grisella. 'We are pretty maids who care not for dirtying ourselves up to the elbows in filth.'

'Pretty, my eye. But that is why I invited two fellows to join us,' he said, brushing his hands. 'Jasper and Samuel will be along soon, and they may well have a real pie with them, for Jasper has a fine cook, who is forgetful about leaving things about, and it might very well be pork, for they have a dozen swine with speckled backs.'

'Boys!' cried Mary. 'But they are not in our band, and have not sworn our secret oath.'

'I'll make 'em do it and spit on the stump,' said Nicholas. 'And you've no need to fear 'em. Jasper and I have the same tutor, so I know he's the finest sort a fellow can be, though I hope he's better than me at arithmetic. When it comes to counting I've a wet sort of lump where my brain should be.'

'We know it,' said Grisella.

'I'll warrant his Cousin Samuel is a fine fellow too,' he continued. 'He has come to stay with Jasper because his mother has died and he is too much trouble for his father, who is a great man of business and very lusty, so my pater says.'

'I know I shall not like them, despite their pies,' said Mary, a great scowl screwing up her freckled face.

'Well I do not mind,' said I. 'I have written out a play for us to act, and the more actors we have, the better, though I have made only four copies and so we will have to share.' I got the folded roll of papers out of my pocket and waved it.

Mary clapped her hands saying, 'Egad I do like a play,' just as Nicholas scuffed at the ground with his feet and muttered: 'Not again.'

Grisella said: 'If you think to get a sweetheart, Mrs Mary, ware you well, for you have not seen them yet.'

'Shush, Grisella. I do not need a sweetheart, for I am promised to Malcolm Longfoot, who is sixteen years old, and handsome.'

'He has pimples and a squint, or I'm a stoat,' said Grisella. 'And I expect, like you, he doesn't have a bean.'

'Aye, I am poor – and what of it?' cried Mary.

'For shame, Grisella,' I said.

'Well,' she said.

The squabble was broken by the arrival of Nicholas's friends, who came towards us out of the sun, blinking their eyes to make us out in the gloom.

'How do ye do,' said Jasper, who was a large sort of boy, with fair hair scissored straight across his forehead and a round face that looked like the product of puddings. 'This is my cousin Samuel Sherewin. We're here to follow the secret paths. Nicholas has told us all about it and we want to join your club.'

'How do ye do,' said Samuel, with a roguish sort of smile that twisted his face up to one side, the way Joe the cowper's did – only Joe was very weather-beaten, and married. Samuel was a tall, well-formed boy with broad shoulders and, I thought, a manly way of standing, with his hand on one hip. He had dark brown eyes and light brown hair that curled pleasingly at his neck. I found that I thought him very handsome, and busied myself with my pockets to cover it.

'Nicky said you might be testy, so I've brought a bit of a wench-sweetener,' said Jasper. Here he winked at Nicholas, folding open his knapsack to show us a dun-coloured cake trussed up in a white linen cloth. 'It's an orange pudding,' he said. 'Wenches love a pudding.'

'Oh do we?' I said.

'What have you done to it?' said Grisella, peering in. 'Why, it's all squashed – and half of it is crumbs!'

'And,' said Samuel, getting a flask out of his belt with a flourish, '*I* have brought cordial that I topped up with sugar when my Aunt Margaret was at her devotions.'

'You'll have to swear,' said Mary quickly. I knew that she had a very sweet tooth, on account of not having sugar at home. 'It might be well, mightn't it, Ursula?'

'Well, you shall have to agree to be in my play,' I said, in what I hoped was a lordly tone. 'I have written one and we are to act it in my glade. I won the straw to choose the path.'

'I am your servant, madame,' said Samuel, giving me a bow, and then looking at me for such a long time that I smoothed down my hair and fiddled with my collar.

'I have always wanted to act, and I think I shall do quite well at it,' said Jasper. 'Mama says I have a carrying sort of voice, and I believe I can recite quite as well as the next boy, if not better.'

'Tis true,' said Nicholas, who had been lurking near the oak, looking sheepish. 'Well you better swear the oath then,' he said, and told them it, and they held their hands aloft and repeated our rhyme.

*I do solemnly swear by the cloth of my hood,*
*to keep the dark secrets alive in Bear Wood;*
*If I do prattle, or if I do prate,*
*I know that I'll meet me a terrible fate;*
*so I swear by my spit on the mystical tree,*
*that I'll always keep mum, by my eye, verily.*

'And now you spit,' said Mary.

We spat.

I led the way, the others in a straggly line behind me, Nicholas, as usual, bringing up the rear. The new boys seemed much excited by the journey into the deep part of the forest, declaring that they had never been so far in, and wondering at everything they saw. I turned at the top of the ditch to watch them catch their first sight of my glade.

'Faith, 'tis a famous pretty place,' said Jasper, taking off his hat, and wiping his brow.

'You are clever to find it,' said Samuel, his eyes fixed on mine in a way that seemed admiring.

Nicholas and Mary set about busying themselves in tidying the place up, for it had been many weeks since we had been there, and there were broken branches that had come down in a storm.

'Which is the stage?' said Samuel.

'That high part yonder,' I said. 'And those not acting may sit down there, when not called for – that part is the pit.'

'Do we have costumes?' said Jasper, striding about in a territorial sort of way that I did not like.

''Tis what I am always saying we need,' said Grisella. 'It is devilish hard for me to get into my part without some sort of trifle to help, especially if I am to play a man, or a serving wench. I have asked Ursula for a dairy maid's bonnet, or a tricorn, or a cloak of purple satin, oh an endless number of times, but will she bring 'em? No she will not.'

'I'm the author, not the mistress of the wardrobe,' I said, 'but what is to stop you bringing a hat or two with you other than your own indolence?'

'It's her nursey, Mistress Marigold, who has a spanking paddle and an itchy hand to use it, is it not, Grisella?' said Mary, with a smirk at me.

'Aye!' called Nicholas. 'And 'tis why ye will never see Mrs Griss sit down. She cannot do it, for her back-cheeks are blistered all over.'

'Indeed they are not, horrid boy!' shouted Grisella, but her face had coloured up, and she turned her back on us and began to hum a ditty.

We settled to eat the picnic, then, before the pudding could disintegrate further, and though it was as crumbly as Grisella had first thought it, and we had to pass the cordial around and take a great gulp each before wiping the bottle neck for the next child, there was something about the twittering of the birds all around us, and the spots of sunlight on our arms, and the greenish glow of our faces, that made the whole thing quite magical. After some discussion over the parts, we began our playing.

# THE *ENCHANTMENT* of LADY CASSANDRA

---

*WRITTEN BY*
A PERSON *of* QUALITY

---

THE PLAYERS

LADY CASSANDRA, *a gay young gentlewoman* – Mrs Grisella Shadforth

MAUDE, *her maid* – Mrs Ursula Flight

ROVER, *Cassandra's faithful mutt* – Mr Jasper Rackwood

DUKE JOHANNES, *a handsome young duke* – Mrs Mary Goodsoule

TOBIAS, *his servant* – Mr Samuel Sherewin

OLD CRONE, *a wise woman* – Mr Nicholas Danbye

ACT II, SCENE I

> *A magical forest in England, the stroke of midnight on Midsummer's Eve. The moon is full: its gleaming light makes soft white shapes which dapple across the leafy earth and the banks of bright green bracken. The sweet scent of honeysuckle drifts across the warm night air. In the distance, the faint and eerie keening of wolves.*

> *Enter* CASSANDRA, MAUDE *and* ROVER, *at their heels.*

CASSANDRA: How dark it is in the forest tonight and such a perfume that floats on the very air! Methinks this glade alive with enchantment. Ah, such strange things I do to meet my true sweetheart, the Duke, in secret.

MAUDE: Hark! [*They listen*] The howling of wolves! I pray they will not come close, for I am a simple girl and am much afeard of the beasts. 'Tis said they are the servants of the Devil and do his bidding, on scurvy nights like this.

CASSANDRA:    'Tis the moon that makes them howl so, it is like
              a strange sort of music on the wind. But do not be
              afraid, my Maude: we have our faithful Rover with
              us. He will protect us.

ROVER:        Woof!

CASSANDRA:    [*Petting him*] There now, my good boy.

ROVER:        Woof!

MAUDE:        Hark, what is that? Methinks I heard a twig snap.
              The crackle of broken leaves underfoot! Someone
              this way comes.

ROVER:        Woof!

CASSANDRA:    [*Crossly*] You must not keep saying 'Woof,' Jasper;
              you'll ruin the suspense.

ROVER:        But I have no cursed lines! I thought perhaps the
              doggie could have a bit of a chat with Samuel – I
              mean Tobias – when he comes on.

MAUDE:        You're ruining it, Jasper! Just be quiet, and act your
              part, like a real dog, or you'll have to sit it out.

OLD CRONE:    [*From off-stage*] Button it, Jaspie, there's a good
              fellow.

CASSANDRA:    Let us go behind this blessed oak tree and wait
              for the handsome lover I pray will soon be mine.
              And remember, Maude, we must play it as we have
              schemed.

MAUDE:        I am ready, mistress. [*They step behind the tree*]

                        *Enter* THE DUKE *and his* TOBIAS.

THE DUKE:     This must be the place; it is a mysterious and
              magical glade, just like my Lady Cassandra. How
              like her to choose it for our tryst. Look, there are

|              |                                                                                                                                                      |
|--------------|------------------------------------------------------------------------------------------------------------------------------------------------------|
|              | fairy rings. We may yet be set upon by elves, for I feel their hypnotic presence even now... Hark! Is that the sinister whining of wolves I hear, Toby? |
| TOBIAS:      | Yes, master, but have no fear. I have a big blunderbuss in me kecks that I'll not hesitate to set off at the first sign of any such abominable beast.   |
| THE DUKE:    | A good fellow, you.                                                                                                                                   |
| TOBIAS:      | Aye.                                                                                                                                                 |
| THE DUKE:    | Stop! There goes one of the foul canines now! Prithee, blow its guts out before we are all ripped to pieces by its loathsome yellow fangs.             |
| TOBIAS:      | [*Pulling out his gun and pointing it*] Ware, evil dog, for I shall send you straight back to the fiery hell from whence you came!                     |
| THE DUKE:    | What is it doing, pray?                                                                                                                               |
| TOBIAS:      | Why, it's cocking its leg, master.                                                                                                                    |
| THE DUKE:    | Curious creature!                                                                                                                                     |
| TOBIAS:      | Now it lays on the ground and begs for its belly to be rubbed, master.                                                                                |
| ROVER:       | Woof!                                                                                                                                                |
| TOBIAS:      | Faith, 'tis only a mangy old dog. It looked like a wolf in the moonlight.                                                                             |
| THE DUKE:    | Ah, Lady Luna. Such fiendish tricks she plays on us mortals.                                                                                          |
|              | *Pause.*                                                                                                                                             |
| MAUDE        | [*Stepping out from behind the tree*] Pray, gentlemen, do not hurt my dog, my faithful mutt, Rover.                                                   |
| ROVER:       | Woof!                                                                                                                                                |

| | |
|---|---|
| THE DUKE | [*Stepping back into the shadows*] [*Aside*] The game was almost up! Thank Jesu for the moonlight, for I know its artful cunning will conceal me, and with it, my true purpose to trick my Lady Cassandra. |
| TOBIAS: | [*Disguised as* THE DUKE] Lady Cassandra, is that you? I cannot make out your pretty visage in the dark. The moonlight plays such artful games. Is that my fairest love or else is it a wondrous mirage step't from my deepest dreams? |
| MAUDE: | [*Disguised as* CASSANDRA] My love, 'tis I! Is that my dear heart, the Duke Johannes? I cannot see you well, for the light is bad and this forest casts a strange sort of spell to muddle me. |
| TOBIAS: | 'Tis I, my lady love. [*He sweeps a bow*] |
| MAUDE: | We do not have much time, my Lord. I am come to tell you that my father will have me wed to the evil Count Bonbon and I am to go to his mother's house tomorrow to prepare for our conjugation. |
| ROVER: | Way hey! |
| TOBIAS: | The scoundrel! The knave! Why, I'll kidnap you 'ere long and carry you off. |
| MAUDE: | My Lord, you cannot, for I have crept out of my chamber under cover of darkness and will soon be missed. |
| TOBIAS: | I must embrace you then, for your beauty overpowers me. |
| | *They kiss.* |
| ROVER: | Woof! |
| TOBIAS: | Hold your tongue, dog. |

| ROVER: | That's not in the script! |
| TOBIAS: | Shush. |
| | *Enter* OLD CRONE, *with a bent back and creeping gait.* |
| CRONE: | A word in your ear, Lady Cassandra. |
| TOBIAS: | What? Are we discovered? |
| CRONE: | Nay, be not deranged, my Lord. 'Tis I, Mistress Grundle, who lives in the forest, casting spells and healing the poor souls who stray too far from the path. The Lady Cassandra knows me, for I dandled her on my knee and, like a mother, fed her from my very teats. |
| ROVER: | Oddsfish! Now I've heard it all! |
| CRONE: | I'm just following the script, Jasper, so shut up. |
| MAUDE: | My nurse! I can hardly make you out in this flickering and watery gleam. |
| CRONE: | 'Tis I, my Lady. And I am here to warn you, by my dark arts and my cunning. Ware the Duke Johannes! For he is not what he seems. |
| MAUDE: | [*Aside*] Neither am I, in truth – Oh no! |
| TOBIAS: | Thou lieth, crone! |
| CASSANDRA: | [*From behind the tree*] Woe, it cannot be! |
| DUKE: | [*From the shadows*] What devilry is this? |
| MAUDE: | And that's as far as I've got. |
| DUKE: | But it was just getting good! |
| ROVER: | The dog wasn't. I was quite under-used. |

| | |
|---|---|
| CRONE: | Do shut up, Jasper. |
| ROVER: | And why were the servants in disguise as the quality? If they were in a wood and no one there to see them? It doesn't make sense. |
| MAUDE: | I haven't got that far yet. |
| TOBIAS: | I thought it was monstrous good. |
| MAUDE: | Thank you, Samuel. |
| CRONE: | I know what he liked! |
| ROVER: | The conjugation! |

*Exeunt.*

# IX

# MALADY

*In which I take a head-cold and pay a call*

As the astrologers and almanacs had predicted, the winter of 1678–9 was a hard one – it had snowed straight through from November to February, and we had all of us forgotten what the sight of a blooming flower or green field looked like. My fourteenth birthday passed in a flurry of snow showers. Up and down the country, the endless winter was all anyone talked of – some saying that it showed the Lord Jesu's displeasure with the liberties of the age – and though I did not quite comprehend what this might mean, my father said that the King was a man who loved beautiful things and to be merry, and the Court become a place of pleasure rather than prayers, and some did not like it.

I wondered at this, and how merriment might be wrong, and how at Bynfield we children were the opposite of merry, for we had become irritable and mischievous with being shut up in the house. We played at hide-and-seek, but it often went on until nightfall, for Reginald was inclined to make his hidey hole so difficult, he could never be found, and the rest of us vexed and exhausted in the hunting for him. We tried to get the little ones to act in a play, but they could not read, and the lines were too long for them to learn by rote, and so the attempt ended with everyone in a disagreeable temper. Hunt the Thimble entertained us for a while, but Catherine was too little to spy it, and Reginald began to grow irked at my helping her, and made a great fuss, which ended in a row, and with everyone weeping, even Mary, who was usually so placid.

It was a bitter Thursday in February and the room grey with early light. We three children, who had been up since daybreak, clustered about the fire, watching Father eat his morning meal, while my mother sat, ready to come to his aid, should he need the salt-cellar, the milk, or a napkin – it was my mother's great grief that Father was given to using his kerchief, or in real moments of absent-mindedness, his sleeve.

'They say the frost is still not like to melt for some weeks,' said my father, tearing at a piece of bread and dipping it in his ale.

'Who says?' said my mother, in her sharp way. In the morning light, the wrinkle on her forehead was a long dark crease. Her hair was caught up in two pretty combs but below it, her face was pale, and I wondered if something ailed her.

'Oh, the astrologers,' said my father, winking at me. 'It is said when the snow melts, the Queen will be with child.'

'The astrologers or the old men at the coffeehouses?' said my mother. 'Why, 'tis none of our business whether the Queen is with child or nay. A small wonder the poor woman cannot get a babby when all the men in England have been prating of it from morning until night for all these years.'

''Tis everyone's affair when we need a boy-child for the succession,' said my father. 'Else we shall all be cast at sea again. But King Charles knows his business as well as we do. So let us not quarrel of it, wife.'

My mother made a muttering sound, and folded her hands in her lap.

'What are the coffeehouses like, Father?' said I. 'I imagine them full of wise men with deep thoughts, having very learned conversations. I should like to go there, I think.'

'Papa goes to the coffeehouse and he comes back very smelly,' said Reginald, lolling against the table, his fat hands slimy with oyster juice. 'When I am grown up I shall not smoke tobacco or drink a dish of coffee neither.'

'Oh no?' I said. 'Will you drink cordial and fortify yourself with sugarplums, though you are aged and lean on a stick?'

While Mother looked the other way, Reginald thumbed his nose at me, then stuck out his tongue for good measure.

'Papa,' said little Catherine, 'is a plop.'

'Shush,' said my mother.

'Botty,' said Catherine.

The little ones giggled.

'Your manners are very ill, young lady,' said my father, scooping Catherine onto his lap. 'But no more of this gutter talk or your mother will spank you until your *botty* is red as a radish. I see her fingers itching to do it now, look.'

'Providing the discipline in this house is something I never itch to do,' said my mother, and her voice sounded brittle. 'But one of us must do it, or else everyone run wild.'

I held my breath for the argument that must come.

'That is so, wife,' said my father, but his smile was gone, and though he made no further reply, there was something in his eyes that I did not understand.

❦

I had grown bored of drifting about the house. Even my books did not console me. I felt the frigid temperature keenly and, once away from the fire, was ever blowing my hands to warm them; though I tried all sorts of tricks to warm myself, such as hopping on the spot and clapping my hands, the thawing did not seem to last. I had caught a cold, too; the sort that filled up my ears and nose, so I was cross that day, as well as chilled, for I had had a bad night's rest: the flux from my nose would keep running down my chin, and waking me up, and that morning it had moved to my chest, and I had started wheezing and barking like Muff.

When I was certain that Father was gone, and Mother had bustled off on some mysterious household errand or other, I wrapped myself in my woollen cloak and boots, and slipped out of doors. The world outside was silver-white and very pretty-looking, and after feebly kicking at a snow drift, I took the winding little track that led through the fields behind our house and stamped down the snowy lane. The Goodsoules' cottage was set off the road and had a sloping, thatched roof. A great brown tangle of briars grew up against the house; under the snow it looked queer and misshapen.

I went through the gate and around to the back of the house, lifting up the latch on the door and pushing it open to find Goodsoule kneading a great slab of dough, her broad freckled arms dusted all over with flour, and Mary vigorously sweeping the floor with a besom. I stepped over the threshold, dropping snow all over the floor, feeling the heat from the great hearth on my face. The fire was spitting most merrily, and the little cottage quite warm. Instantly I had a great fit of coughing.

'What's this, Ursula? Why, you'll catch your death!' cried Goodsoule, coming to me and brushing the snow from my legs and shoulders. 'We thought not to see you, for your ma sent word you had took bad, and could not be with my Mary today.'

''Tis true I have got a cold,' I sniffed miserably, 'but it is so dull without you, I thought to come here.' I coughed again. I hated to go to my bed and be bored.

'Well,' she said. 'You have come to us at a godly time. The babes are asleep, Johnny and Harry are helping their father, and Mary and I are all but done in setting things to rights.'

She nodded at the little stool by the fire and I took heed of her and drew it up to sit upon, holding my limbs out to thaw them, in turn, while they busied at their work. It gave me a rosy sort of feeling to watch them occupied thus, letting the cottage smells – the wood-smoke; the baking bread; the drying herbs which dangled in stiff little bunches from the rafters – float over me. Then I leant my head in my hands, for the effort of coming out of doors had caught up with me. I sneezed, and groaned a little.

'I think the fresh air has done me ill,' I sniffed.

Goodsoule came and felt my head and neck and cheek. I wiped my hand across my face, for the flux had started running down my lip again. 'I beg your pardon, Goodsoule,' I said. 'I cannot stop it issuing forth, for my head is full of the stuff to overflowing. Some of it is green.'

'Horrid girl!' said Mary.

'I will make a posset and you will drink it off like a good girl and be cured,' said Goodsoule. She went into the larder and came out of it, and set about plucking things from the herb bundles, and setting a copper pan of water to boiling, giving instructions to Mary all the while.

'What is it?' I said, when she set the little pot before me, which had steam coming off it and a sweet, poisonous sort of smell that was sharp in my nostrils.

'Mistletoe, which is a plant of the sun in Aries and being hot and dry treats cold and wet illnesses of the head,' she said, knowing I liked to hear her wisdoms. 'And there is comfrey to cure what ails ye. And rose to keep ye calm and fair.'

'Thank you,' I said, drinking it down and spitting at the taste. 'I would like to know how to make ill people well, for it seems a great art.'

'Aye, though you would not think so, to hear it in the village,' said Goodsoule, taking up a stool beside me. 'Bless you, child, you must not repeat what you have heard in this house. For there are those that think any curing done by a woman is witchcraft, and any herb gathering is spell casting, and any chanting is the Devil's lore.'

'But that's mighty foolish,' I said, crossing my fingers and swearing my oath. 'Do people want to die?'

'No, they do not – but they are more afeard of the black arts than they are of dying and going to see their God in heaven, which is why they hanged poor Mistress Purvice last winter.'

'She tried to cure the baker with a toasted toad,' said Mary. 'But she only gave him warts.' Goodsoule hushed her.

'I would hear of your learnings, Goodsoule,' I said. 'For they are different to the ones I get from Father, and would distract me from my cold,' guessing rightly that she could not help but indulge me.

'You have a cool complexion,' she said, holding up my chin and gazing at my face. Her fingers were rough on my cheek, and I thought then how different they were from the soft hands of my mother, which were smooth and white, but rarely touched me. 'The right sort of fare can remedy a troubled set of humours, and stop the body yielding to agues and distempers. So you must eat up all your viandes and drink down your milk, every day.'

'I will,' I croaked.

'You must avoid winds, for they carry miasmas and so are treacherous,' said Goodsoule. 'And changeable weather, too, is bad for a body. You know that snow and rain are the worst, for the wetness brings rheums, dropsies and quotidian agues – and colds.'

''Tis no wonder you took ill, Ursula,' said Mary. 'The way you tramp about the countryside in the snow with your gown and cloak wetted right up to your waist.'

'Aye,' I said. 'I rue it now.'

When I had had my posset, Goodsoule returned to her chores and Mary and I retired to the corner of the kitchen near the larder, so that we might whisper our secrets, and be warmed by the smoky hearth.

'You will not guess who I saw down at the green, when I went by there the other day,' said Mary, as soon as her mother was gone. Her eyes were lit up and dancing.

'Who?' I said. 'Tell me!'

'Well, 'tis someone you know,' she teased. 'A boy... a handsome boy... that you know... well... very well indeed, I warrant.'

'I do not know,' I said priggishly, though I could feel my colour rising in my face.

''Twas your kissing-fellow, Samuel!' she said. 'And I called out to him and, being with some bigger boys he put his head down, and pretended not to know me.'

I knew that I blushed rosy red and she laughed to see it and prodded at me in fun.

'Tell me again what it was like to feel his lips on yours,' she said.

'Well,' I said, 'there was a queer sort of thrill in my belly all the while and something that fluttered and leapt in my chest... it flared up when he put his hands about my waist, and warmed me... all over – do you remember him doing that?'

'Aye!' said Mary, her voice rising. 'And I saw him bend you backwards – and press his body on yours!'

'Hush,' I hissed, poking her. 'Your mother will hear and then where will we be?'

'Oh, Ma understands lovers' secrets, I am sure,' said Mary wisely. 'Besides, you have done naught but acted in a play.'

'Imagine if my mother were to know we played with strange boys, when we do not even know who their mothers and fathers are or where they are from!' The thought of it excited me, in truth.

'They are from good families, that much was plain,' said Mary in her sensible way.

'I thought him a very nice boy,' I said, the image of his twisted-up smile suddenly in my head. 'Though I was not so sure of his friend, who seemed very idle and given to preening. I cannot see why we may not play with them again for this winter. It is so cold and dreary I am of a mind to take up *Lady Cassandra* again and write more of her, and I am ever in need of actors. I did think Samuel good at being the manservant, and so for that reason I should like him to play with us again.'

'Oh aye,' said Mary. 'Well 'tis all for the good, for I did not tell you what happened next.'

'Next?'

'After he – Samuel – put his head down. I thought he had gone away with his playfellows, and paid him no mind, but then he came loping up to me.'

I clutched at her. 'He did not!'

'Did so. And he says, pinching me at the elbow, "I am gone from my aunt's house tonight and cannot tarry, but I will return afore Easter." Then he says: "Tell Ursula, if she may slip away, to meet me at the Rhyme Tree at noon on Ash Wednesday, for I would *dearly like to see her*."'

'Nay!' I was red again.

'Aye!' said Mary, her voice getting evermore bird-like with the excitement of it.

'Oh,' I said. 'What shall I do?'

'Why you must go to him, Ursey, for I think he wants to be sweethearts.'

'It is not 'til April though...'

'Oh, *Samuel*,' said Mary then, in a slow, exaggerated sort of way. 'You are such a good *actor*. How well you speak the lines that I crafted *'specially for ye*.' She flicked up an imaginary fan.

'Stop it,' I shouted. 'That is not what I did, not at all!'

'Will we be tenderhearts, *Samuel*?' she lisped and, when I protested, began tickling at my armpits until I screamed out and we fell onto the floor in a rough-and-tumble and Goodsoule came and scolded us for waking the babby, but all we could do was laugh helplessly. The talk of romance had lifted our spirits right up to the rafters, and we did not want to come down.

# X

# TRYST

*In which I am distracted by thoughts of flirtation*

Though I tried to distract myself with reading and my lessons, I found
that my thoughts had begun to turn to Samuel and his long-ago
kissing. I mused on what might happen if I went to meet him as he had
asked and found myself thinking of his mouth, which set me to blushing,
and my father asked why I was staring out of the window, instead of
working at my arithmetic. Goodsoule wondered at my inability to thread
the buckles on my shoes.

'I have been a-pondering,' I said to Mary, one wet afternoon, when
we had finished an energetic game of Lanterloo, which had made us
both hungry, and so we were feasting on currant-biscuits, discovered
under a cloth in the larder. 'I think I will try to discover what Samuel
is about, for if I *must* marry, I would not mind if it were Samuel. Or
someone much like him.'

'Well now, Mrs!' she said, letting some biscuit fall out of her mouth
and onto her smock. 'He might not ask you though,' she said, chewing.
'For you are not even sweethearts and he may have found another in the
months it has been. You must be sweethearts first, if ye are to marry.'

'Must we?' I said.

'Oh yes,' she said. 'A boy may ask a girl to be his sweetheart and then
they will promise to keep only unto each other. Well, until a handsomer
one comes along and then she may pretend she never said it at all. Kitty
did that with the ostler's boy, and weren't he scowling every time he laid

eyes on her in church, and didn't she hold her head up proud, for she had already been asked by Jack Browning if he could court her and he has five pound a year, and so she didn't give a fig.'

'Kitty is so beautiful,' I said wistfully.

'Yes,' said Mary. 'But she has a devil of a temper. It is well she keeps with my aunt, for I cannot abide her screaming.'

'It does not matter if you are the biggest crosspatch that ever lived, if you have fine eyes and a pretty face,' I said.

Mary poked me at this. 'You are a pretty enough maid yourself and *you* are of noble family besides and so shall make a good match when the time is right, my ma says.'

'Your mother is kind to me,' I said. I thought of Father and Mother and the babbies. 'I do not know if I should want to wed for a good while yet. It seems a famous lot of work and there is not much making merry.'

Mary laughed. 'We all have to wed!'

'I do not see why,' I said. 'My Great-Aunt Pomfrey never did, and she always seemed a very happy woman, for she was always riding horses and sketching and doing a great many things, until she died.'

'Of drink!' said Mary. 'For Kitty told me she was an old maid with a shrivelled womb and a coddled mind – and she drank herself to death.'

'Oh,' I said. 'Oh.'

'Mayhap you shall marry Samuel,' said Mary, clearing away the crumbs, lest Eliza should notice and give her a slapping. 'And be happy all your days.'

'Mayhap,' I said. 'But I would rather have a horse.'

❀

Spring had come to us at last, and it was the sort that was made of all weathers. In any one day it might be ice-cold and windy – and then the sun would come out, as if naught had gone before. On the appointed day of my meeting with Samuel, it had rained heavily all the morning, me peering out of the window wondering how I might slip out to the wood in such weather, for it would look mighty strange to be heading away from the house on such a day. Catherine, momentarily escaped from Goodsoule, came to stand with me by the window.

'We cannot play while it rains, Ursey.'

'No we cannot,' I said, putting my arm around her still fat child's body, 'for it would wet us most thoroughly and we should grow ill.'

'And then we shall take to our beds and expire,' she said, her little round face screwed up into a scowl. 'For Reggie told me so.'

'For shame, do not listen to him!' I said, dragging her up into my lap and petting her head, for she had now begun to whimper. 'He is a naughty boy and a terrible tease, besides. You shalt not catch cold nor die neither, but live long and merry, as all we Flights shall, for we are hardy stock and not like to succumb to maladies.'

That seemed to soothe her, for she quietened, and got down, and went back to the nursery, her little thumb hooked in her mouth, her soft leather booties scuffing the ground. I saw that the rain had stopped, and the weather began to brighten. Though it was still but eleven of the clock and I would be early, I threw on my rain-cloak and stepped out of the house as quickly as I might, in sudden fear that somebody might call for me and I miss Samuel altogether. It was almost warm, now the sun was out, and I squelched across the meadow towards the path to Bear Wood with something lifting in my heart, for the almanac had foretold today an auspicious one, and a thrill was running through me at the thought of what may come.

In the distance, a flash of blue picked out by the sun, the dark shape of a figure coming over the hill and across the field, from the village. As the figure neared, I saw with a panic that it was my mother, with her basket. I did not turn a hair (though I had thought her safely in the house) but slowed my step and, affecting a careless attitude, bent down to pick a few of the meadow flowers that clustered here and there.

'What do you do out of doors, Ursula?' she said, sounding cross, her cheeks rose-red with the exertion of walking. 'Dawdling about the meadow when there are instruments to be practised and linens to be tidied? 'Tis not what I expect of my eldest child.'

'I – I just thought to get myself a posy. And one for you, Mother,' I said, holding out what I had hastily wrenched out of the earth, which had a dandelion in it, and soil clinging to its stems.

'Not now,' she said, pushing my hand from her. 'I am expecting visitors and have been walking about trying to find Lisbet, who had gone off to get a shoulder from the butcher, but has not come back, and so we are all in a quandary.'

'I can go after her!' I said, gazing at her with my eyes very wide.

'Nay, nay,' she said. 'You must come inside and change your gown, for you are not fit to be seen in that one, and there's mud on your shoes.'

Brushing the soil from my palms I followed her into the house, with a drooping head, wondering if, even as I did so, Samuel watched me go from the shade of the tree, and wondered why I did not come.

But the luck the almanac had predicted held, for no sooner had Goodsoule wrenched me into my gown, then came a message from the visitors saying one of them was took ill with a dropsy and, fearing it contagious, would rest themselves indoors. The clock had rung for half past twelve by the time I had extricated myself again, for my mother was going up and down the house, shouting at the waste of food. This time I took no chances, and broke into a run when I came to the patch of open meadow I must cross, my skirts held high above my ankles, my best shoes throwing up a spray of earth as I sprinted, for I had not had time to change them.

I crashed into the wood, heeding little that my cloak caught on branches, and was pricked by a holly bush as I ran down the caked mud path, slowing as I came to our wishing tree, pawing at my hair, though I knew it was hopelessly disarranged. I stopped a little way off, so that I might catch my breath, and, having done so, walked briskly into the clearing.

He was not there.

I walked over to the tree and pressed my hand against its bark. It felt warm to the touch. Had Samuel lingered here, while he waited all this while? Misery invaded my body, for now what would I do for a sweetheart? And how would I see Samuel again? It was not fair. I kicked the tree.

'Don't blame him,' came the voice behind me. 'For it is not Monsieur Oak's fault you are late and left me tarrying here all afternoon.'

I could hardly turn around, before his hands were about my waist, and he twisting my body around to meet his, so that his open mouth met mine sideways on. I tried to push him away, for his hands were wandering upwards and I was afeard of my bosom being felt (it was not yet full-grown), but I forgot myself, and allowed him to push me gently back towards the tree, which he pressed me against with his hot, hard body; before touching his lips on mine, and trailing his mouth along my jaw. It seemed very advanced for a boy of his age, and I wondered at his boldness.

'Mmm,' he said. 'Ursula.'

I closed my eyes.

We kissed and clutched at one another for what felt like an age, and though he kept trying to pull me downwards to lie on the floor, remembering my various talks with Mary on the topic of bundling, I kept my wits about me, and would not be moved from my safe spot against the tree. When he saw that he could not coerce me into romping, I felt his hands begin to wander downwards, and he trying to get under my skirts, though I murmured that he must not, and at the same time arched my neck back, and he brought his leg up under mine, and slid his hand under my skirt, stroking slowly right from my stockinged ankle to the top of my hot bare thigh, and as his fingers brushed downwards against my flesh I woke up a little from my stupor, and knew I must put a stop to things, before they got any more out of hand.

'Nay,' I said, twisting out from his embrace and stepping a few paces away from him. 'I like your kissing but I cannot... I am but fourteen years old.'

'Come, now,' he said, taking my hand. 'I will not hurt you. Forgive me,' he said, seeing that my face had grown serious. 'I forgot myself, as all men do, but I would not anger you, Urse. Let us talk awhile.'

We stood then, and told each other all about our lives. I learnt that he was of a good family, but was not noble, and lived up at Gloucester when he was not with his aunt, and had four brothers and two sisters, and missed his mother more than he could say. He liked to make merry with his brothers, and run races, and to play other games, and had a tutor for schooling and enjoyed reading his atlas and his history books too. At this I exclaimed, and told him of my studies with Father, and our latest studies of the heavens, and how I was named for the Great Bear, and he was greatly pleased with this, and the tale of my learning too, for he said he liked his women both pretty and clever. The conversation tailed off.

Samuel picked up my hand. 'And now, may we kiss,' he murmured, 'a little more. Just a bit... more?'

His hand slid up my arm and around my back. He pressed me to him. We embraced again. I began to feel a trembling in my knees. My resolve to stay upright was weakening.

Something, a swishing, forest sound, disturbed us. The tell-tale snapping of boots on twigs. We jerked apart.

'Ursula! Ursulaaaaa!' came the twittering call. It was Mary.

'She has come to bid me come for dinner,' I said. 'I must go now.'

'Ah,' he said. 'Shame.' His dark eyes were dancing. 'I will miss you, Ursula, named for the stars,' he said. 'But I know that I will have the sweetest of dreams.' Here he closed his eyes and let a stupid smile creep across his face.

'Impertinence!' I said, smacking at his arm. 'But I will... think of you too.'

We said our goodbyes, he promising to send word to me of his next visit to Berkshire, and I went to find my Mary with a song in my heart.

'Oddsfish, Ursula!' she cried, upon seeing my mussed-up state. 'Your hair's all askew and your chin red enough to tell all what you've been doing.'

I put my hand to my mouth, which was admittedly sore. 'He kissed me,' I said.

'I can see that,' she said. 'And by the look of it, more than once.'

❁

For the next few days, I hid myself away from my mother as much as I could, and kept hard at my books, for I felt sure she would see the change in me, and know that I had been with a boy and been kissed and felt against a tree, but my father only exclaimed at my new application and praised me for my endeavours, little knowing that though I turned the pages of my book, I barely read the words printed there, for my mind was far away, in the shadows of the wood.

How I waited in hope for word from Samuel and how I began to grow disconsolate with every day that passed in silence. I dawdled in the hallway every morning for a sennight, for I hoped that Samuel might get another message to me as he had said he would, but it was not to be so. The weeks wore on, and spring had become early summer when a little cloth-bound bundle, with a brown paper tag addressed to me, appeared in the entrance hall, and no one could say how it had arrived. My luck held again, for it was only Lisbet who had come across it, and I tugged it out of her hands, and ran away with it, calling that it was from Mary and one of our games, lest she took it into her head to tattle on me.

Hastening into my chamber, I dragged the chair up against the door to hold it, and sat myself on my bed, the bundle before me. It was tied with a sky-blue ribbon in a strange, clumsy sort of knot, and I picked at it a while before it would loosen, then tugged the bundle apart. Inside was a little wooden box. I stroked it with my fingers at the novelty of such a gift. I hoped it was not one of Reggie's tricks and I would find a great hairy spider inside. Holding my breath, I slid the lid open.

It was something, not a spider, an object, made of wood. A figure or creature of some sort I knew, for I could see the top of its rounded back, with little marks all over it, where the woodcarver had positioned his chisel. I picked it up and placed it in my palm.

It was a carved wooden bear, a little dancing bear, in miniature. I stroked my fingers along the hard planes of her long sweet muzzle and curving, upright ears, and turned her over to marvel at her paws, lifted up as if in motion with their chisel-nicked claws. The bear was unpainted, save for the grass-green collar she wore, as if at a fair, with a gold link of chain picked out in gold leaf. I peered at the collar. There, also picked out in gold, were initials painted on in a very neat hand:

S.S. ~ U. F.

A love token! I gave a little high-pitched yelp of excitement. The bear was dainty enough to hold in my fist. I closed my fingers over it and clutched it to me. I looked in the box again and spied a folded note that I had missed, pressed against its bottom side. The softness of the paper under my fingertips as I unfolded it to read:

> For my sweetheart Ursula Flight
> Until we meet again.
> From your Samuel,
> *sic erit; haeserunt tenues in corde sagittae* ANNO 1679

I grasped the little bear in my hand and held it aloft in my jubilance. 'Yes!' I cried.

❦

My love-happiness was not to last, for though I kissed the bear and put it under my pillow every night, including with my prayers the secret wish that my sweetheart might come to me again, no more notes ever came for me from Samuel, and I heard no word of him in the district, though I sent Mary to tarry by the green as often as I dared; Jasper said he did not know where his cousin was, or when he would be visiting him again. My love cooled a little then, though I held onto the secret wish that all was not done with him.

It was coming on for harvest when I had it from Grisella that Samuel's aunt was gone away back to Gloucestershire for good, and Samuel not like to visit Bynfield again, and I wept a few hot tears for the loss of him, and all that might have been, all the while the little wooden bear clasped tightly in my fist.

# XI

# CONVERSATION

*In which I have dinner and am mischievous*

The Blacklocks and the Ditchbornes were coming to sup with Mother and Father and as a great treat I was being allowed to sit up with them for the evening. Since I had turned fourteen, my mother had begun to let me do this now and then – dining in company would help my manners, she said, for she was keen that I learn the skills I would need when one day I played hostess myself. Father said at my stage of learning Italian, it would do me good to converse in that language with Lord Ditchborne, who had used it in his days as a travelling merchant, before he was risen up by the King. We rehearsed a few little phrases together, that I might politely insert into my conversation.

It had been a dull sort of day, and to distract myself from thoughts of romance I had roamed restlessly about the fields – Mary had been confined to her cottage, made prisoner by her mother amongst the hurly burly of her many small brothers and sisters, and I had no luck getting any sort of cake from Eliza, who was in a fluster at the coming of the guests and much given to smoothing down her apron.

I banged the gate as loud as I dared and stamped about, looking for the countryside treasures I liked to collect: bright coloured pebbles, speckled feathers, the dried skulls of dead birds (I had found one of a crow, turned it upside down and used it as an ink pot). I stood by the pig-pen and watched the sows sleeping all in a row. Their bristled bellies rose and fell, their snouts hanging open and issuing sonorous snores: they were very sweet indeed. I went inside and tried to write a sonnet about them (Father and I had been reading Petrarch and I had been experiencing poetic urges), but I could not get the sound of their grunting, nor the look of their soft little snouts into the rhyme, which was restrictive in its rhythm and form.

By the time I had emerged from my hiding place in the scullery, and allowed myself to be found drifting about near the parlour, Mother was in a great pet at my disappearance, her hair escaping from its combs. Her voice was a taut shrill thing as she bade Joan chaperone my washing, before hurrying me into a better gown that did not have mud on the hem and ink blotches at the sleeves.

# THE
# SIEGE
## *of*
# BYNFIELD

*a*

## COMEDY

---

*Acted by*

## THE DUKE'S PLAYERS

*at*

## THE THEATRE IN DORSET GARDENS

---

*WRITTEN BY*

## MRS. U. FLIGHT

*Late afternoon, the dining room. The low
sunlight slants in the window, picking out
the ears of a suckling pig, the glistening
tip of a great blancmange, the handle of a
silver spoon. A grey-blue-eyed maiden with
the sort of hair that was the admiration
of five counties stands by the window
with her arms folded. Enter: LORD and
LADY DITCHBORNE, MR and MRS
BLACKLOCK (she leaning heavily on his
arm, with gout); FATHER and MOTHER.*

MRS BLACKLOCK: Ah what a fine spread indeed. [*To* MOTHER]
You compliment us greatly, Cecily, indeed
you do.

MOTHER: 'Tis nothing, Winifred.

URSULA: Lisbet and Eliza have slaved for many days
in the kitchen to make this for us and are
themselves this moment making do with
lumpy potage.

FATHER: Hush, Ursula.

MOTHER: Shall we be seated?

FATHER: It is so very good to see you, Henry,
Godfrey, Ebbaline, Winifred.

LADY DITCHBORNE: [*Her eyes swivelling around the room and
alighting on me*] Ah, Ursula. I did not know
you would be joining us. How grown-up
you are. A new gown? I did not know green
was the mode, but as my dear little Lettice
says, I am quite behind the times. We are all
getting older, are we not? Well now.

| | |
|---|---|
| MR BLACKLOCK: | Is that a black pudding? How charming. |
| MOTHER: | Thank you, Henry. Clifford, will you call for the girl to fill the glasses? Winifred, dear, will you have wine or a dish of tea? |
| MRS BLACKLOCK: | Tea! |
| LADY DITCHBORNE: | You look bright today, Ursula, and I am pleased to see it. Your blessed mother worries about you growing pale with your studies. And as well she might, for 'tis well known that book-learning can bring on the ague. Why, I heard of one poor learned lady who lived at Oxford who was in the habit of attending lectures (not, I hasten to add, with the sanction of the college for they would not have allowed it if they'd known. She got in with the help of her brother, who must regret his actions to this day – foolish man!). This lady was prone to fainting fits – the great strain, I believe, of study was too much for her female mind. After a full day of reading some very large tomes, she went into a stupor and died in the very library where she had got the books. They opened up her body after she was dead and were amazed to discover that her very brain was shrivelled and wrinkled as a walnut – for it had soured in her head from too much reading and that was the thing that carried her off. |
| MRS BLACKLOCK: | Pickled! |

LADY DITCHBORNE: Do you feel quite well, Ursula? For I know I should worry if Lettice were at the same thing, but she takes little notice of study and is instead much given to Court tattle and her drawing, which I believe is coming on very fine. Yesterday she finished a sketch of the donkey, and it was, I believe, very like the life, except that it had not enough legs, but that is easily remedied. We are minded to get her a drawing master, are we not, husband?

LORD DITCHBORNE: [*Spooning at his pie*] What?

URSULA: I am very well, ma'am. Father and I have been translating *Utopia* and I am learning of the many wondrous things in the world.

LORD DITCHBORNE: Excellent! I have never set any store by the talk that women have inferior sorts of heads which are not adapted to the rigours of academia. Indeed I would say it suits you very well, young lady. Though whether it suits me own children, I'll never know, as they're very stupid, every one.

FATHER: Ursula is making great progress, though, like all children, she is oft to get distracted and end up staring at the window-pane. Do you not, Mrs Ursula?

URSULA: It can be most diverting, watching the clouds floating on. [*Aside*] And thinking about plays and books and boys!

FATHER: Her Italian, especially, is improving, I think, which will interest you, Ditchborne,

with your linguistic talents! Pray, Ursula.
Tell Lord Ditchborne the phrases we have
learnt together.

URSULA: [*Coughs*] *Piacere di conoscerti, Ditchborne, amico mio.**

LORD DITCHBORNE: *Salve*, Ursula.

MRS BLACKLOCK: [*Clapping*] There now!

URSULA: *Mi chiama Ursula. Ho fame. Chi non risica, non rosica. Ho un cane di nome Muff assomiglia un po a sua moglie, forse.*†

LORD DITCHBORNE: *Mi scusi?*

MRS BLACKLOCK: What a magical sound that language has. It's wonderful to hear it. Wonderful.

URSULA: *Grazie.*

LADY DITCHBORNE: I'm not certain I favour this course you are taking with Ursula, Clifford, and believe you may come to regret it. For what can an education do for a young woman but give dissatisfaction when she is married? The natural concerns of a girl should be hearth, home and husband, and nothing more, for as I always say, women get spoiled by wandering. 'Tis my belief that those misses who have Latin and Greek, and stride about declaiming in all manner of outlandish tongues, are not the ones that get the husbands.

MRS BLACKLOCK: Spinsters!

---

\* Pleased to meet you, Ditchborne, my friend.
† My name is Ursula. I am hungry. Nothing ventured, nothing gained. I have a dog called Muff who looks a bit like your wife, perhaps.

MR BLACKLOCK:        [*Chuckling*] Just so, Lady D. My Winnie
                     came to me with not a single mite of book-
                     learning in her head and God has seen fit
                     to bless us with many happy years together.
                     [*Pats her arm*] I daresay I'm quite hare-
                     brained myself. Only yesterday I put two
                     feet in one breech-leg and toppled right
                     over. There's a bump on my noggin as big
                     as an artichoke and I had a mustard plaster
                     for it, which made me sneeze seven times in
                     a row, which augurs very ill indeed, and I
                     expect I will drop down dead tomorrow.

MRS BLACKLOCK:       Oh!

URSULA:              Mother can read and write, and speak French
                     too.

MR BLACKLOCK:        She has other wifely skills too, I'll warrant.
                     Is that not right, Clifford? Is it not right?
                     [*Pinches at his arm*] There. What a good
                     fellow.

MOTHER:              Ursula is also working very hard at her
                     needle and music and her drawing is
                     improving most steadily. She can write a
                     receipt and order a meal from Cook and
                     take stock of the linen, and make out the
                     household accounts besides.

URSULA:              And I have been writing a play-script.

LORD DITCHBORNE: Excellent!

LADY DITCHBORNE: What did she say?

LORD DITCHBORNE: I propose somebody passes me the trifle.

| | |
|---|---|
| URSULA: | Mary and I act it out in the barn, away from prying eyes. It is about a very dashing girl with a large fortune and hundreds of jewels who gets kidnapped by a poor but handsome duke with a very fine calf and is taken off to London, but when she gets there he takes all her fortune to the gaming tables and decides not to marry her after all, and so she goes off in a great pet, but then decides not to bother too much, and goes to see the King, and he likes her, and she becomes quite infamous at Court, because she is quite the prettiest woman there, quite a lot more than Mrs de Keroualle, even though she is not French in the slightest, and she goes out wearing a picture hat and the gauziest veil which sets off her waist, which is very trim, to ride most days on Rotten Row, where she is admired greatly by all the young blades, who ask for her hand, but she turns all of 'em down and buys a tame monkey and lives happily ever after, in a grand mansion with red-and-yellow-striped window silks and a faithful manservant who turns away all of her unwanted callers and entertains her with rollicking tales of faraway lands in the evening while she never eats boiled fish, but instead feasts on macaroons and ginger-bread and raspberry wine all of her days and the manservant becomes her lover and it turns out that he is a marquis who had been in ignorance of his noble birth. |
| MRS BLACKLOCK: | Ooh! |

> *LADY DITCHBORNE is observed to be*
> *fanning herself.*

MOTHER:             Ursula, enough.

FATHER:             Ebbaline, are you quite well?

LORD DITCHBORNE:    'Tis the mention of lovers, she can't abide to
                    hear of them at her age.

> *LADY DITCHBORNE, whose skin has*
> *turned the colour of cold gruel, goes limp,*
> *and with a roll of the eyes, suddenly lurches*
> *forward. A clatter of silver.*

MR BLACKLOCK:       Allow me, Lady D. [*He supports her*]
                    Ho, too late, she has put her hair in the
                    pudding.

MRS BLACKLOCK:      Dear me.

> *MOTHER goes to her, with a handkerchief.*

LORD DITCHBORNE:    As I always say, there's nothing quite like a
                    trifle.

MR BLACKLOCK:       She's opening her eyes!

MRS BLACKLOCK:      There's pudding on her face.

URSULA:             But pray, I did not tell you what befell her
                    sister!

MOTHER:             Not another word.

> *Curtain*

# XII

✤

# CURSE

*In which I become a woman*

❦

My mother liked me well enough, I think until I attained my fifteenth year, when a quite commonplace event occurred that seemed to change me in her eyes.

The curse began.

It was early morning on a bright cold day, and most happily and toastily abed was I, still drowsing in the deep, untroubled sleep of childhood, when an onerous sort of twisting in the foot of my belly broke me from the haze of a dream. As I lay there, groaning a little to myself, I felt a strange sensation; the result of investigations under my night-shift was that my fingers came away bright crimson.

'Lord help me!' I cried, my mind tumbling over with thoughts of dark magic, ill humours and quickly-fatal plagues – I could be dead within the hour, there was no time to waste. I pounded, bare-footed, into the corridor, screaming for Goodsoule, who came upstairs tripping on her skirts, worry creased across her face.

On hearing my complaint – I stammered it out through tears; I trembled, unready for the hour of my death – she took me gently by my now-perspiring hands and drew me back into my chamber. As we sat together, gazing out of the window – it was snowing – she told me that it was just the woman's curse that had come to me at last, petting my hair as she spoke and sometimes breaking off to hum the lullaby of my cradle.

'There now, sweetheart,' she said. 'It must come to us all, alas.'

A film of sweat broke across my back – I was not gravely ill with a lethal bleeding; I would not burst out in pulsing buboes and end the day consigned, by my elbow, to a plague-cart. Nay, it was much, much worse: I was become a woman and could now bear children!

*Salva me Domine!*

I felt as afraid then as I did foolish – for I had heard snatches of Mary and her mother talk of a woman's courses, and vaguely knew what the coming of them meant, but I had thought it a thing for full-grown women, and had not realized that it would pain me so and make me feel so strange or that there would be so much blood. I felt a surge of anger at my mother then, for she had said not a word to me of what was to come and had only talked vaguely of my 'growing up', thinking perhaps that I knew it all already. I wondered if the time I had spent with my nose pressed in a book was partly to blame for my ignorance, and cursed myself for not paying more attention to the chatter of others, and the workings of the world about me.

To staunch the flow of my bright blood, which now seemed to be dripping from my body, and made me feel quite faint (I swooned), Goodsoule helped me to make a napkin out of cloth and tie it onto myself, with the help of a waistband, which did not feel comfortable, but Goodsoule said it was one of the many crosses we women had to bear. Then she got me into a fresh shift and took away the other, before bringing me a cup of steaming posset.

I drank the potion off, which was fragrant with flowers and delicious, though I could not enjoy it for I felt famous bad and said so. I wept a little then, and Goodsoule stroked at my back, but I could not stop my weeping, and so she went away. Mary came up then, and tried to soothe me and pet my head, but I was angry that she had not warned me properly of this affliction, and I would not speak to her, and she, too, went away. I crept back into bed, where I stayed deep under the coverlet, in a clammy sort of doze, while the beating and pulsing of my womb kept on, the pain dragging at my innards like nothing I had ever known. I lay there, twisting about, until the windows glowed purple and the scent of meat-broth seeped up through the floorboards.

When I went down to supper – for I had realized I was monstrous hungry – it was Mary who asked me how I did, and sat down next to me, and took my hand and stroked at it, under the table. My mother only stared at the pinkish rims of my swollen eyes. She stirred her dish of oysters and bade me pass the pepper.

I did it.

It was a waning moon that night.

❀

The ending of my childhood seemed to harden my mother's heart towards me, for from that day hence, she never glanced on me with smiles, or clasped me to her side, but gave me such strange looks I could not fathom. She would not comb my hair, nor read to me aloud, as once she had. Instead, she peered at me with sharp and narrowed eyes, as I bound nosegays in the garden with Catherine, or danced about the house and teased the dog, or embroidered the cover for a jewel-box, a tangle of threads and beads upon my lap, humming 'The Lunatick Lover' half under my breath, innocent of the forbearance which must come to women; the things which must be borne with a smile and a 'Yes, husband, dear.'

Perhaps the recent birth of her ninth child (and only fourth living, poor mother mine), my brother Percival, took me from her thoughts, for he was – oh miracle – the second breathing boy. A whey-coloured, sickly thing at first, he howled into the house on St Swithin's Day: they rang the bells. He grew to be most lovable, a fat-legged and bonny babe, who easily usurped my warm place on her lap and later was always at my father's side, trailing a dolly in his wake.

He died, at twenty-three, of typhus, contracted at a low tavern in Hounds-ditch that had bear-fights, brawls and pox-addled whores.

# MY MOTHER AND I,
## A CONVERSATION

*Late December 1679, night, upon the staircase.*

MOTHER:  Ursula! You have dropped your bead box. Do you have eyes in your head? They are scattered on the floor.

URSULA:  I am sorry, Mother. I was called in to dinner and forgot.

MOTHER:  Pick them up at once and get yourself to bed.

URSULA:  Yes, Mother. I was going up now, I—

MOTHER turns her back.

URSULA:  Mother, tomorrow can I see the kittens in the barn? Grisella has been and says they are so sweet. There is one with a black face, she says, and—

MOTHER:  Have you learnt your scriptures?

URSULA:  Yes, Mother.

MOTHER:  Have you tidied your shoes?

URSULA:  Yes, Mother.

MOTHER:  Have you mended your collar?

URSULA:  Not yet, Mother. But the kittens are to be drowned and Johnny said if I were quick I might—

MOTHER:  You can see the cats when you have mended your collar and not before.

*Ending: Ursula, A fit of sulks. Mother, Forbids me fish at dinner. The kittens, Drowned every one, in a sack, at noon.*

Perhaps my mother was cruel to me against her secret will, to better ease the wrench of our future parting, but at my tender age my senses were keen, and I fretted, daily, to myself, that I had done her some unknown, awful wrong.

I put her in my night-time prayers, and was obedient and docile at table, and played with the little ones when she had an ague, and said 'Yes, Mother' in the gayest voice I knew. But she would not catch my eye and her voice to me was brittle; thin. I tried one day to take her hand; she shook it off. I could not make her love me.

# XIII

# CONTRACT

*In which I am informed my life is to change*

My woman-pains were gone, when two weeks after the curse first came to me, my father bade me, before dinner, to see him in his library.

The weather had reached the stubborn phase of deep midwinter when everything is white and still. Snow lay in great banks against the house and ice-shards dropped from the rafters; the windows were all but frosted over. Father always had a merry fire spitting in his grate – he had no taste for saving firewood – and I was glad to go to him and be warmed. I would sit on the footstool that perched beside his desk and smell the linseed, ale and ink. Though it was not Tuesday or Wednesday, I thought he might bid me read my lessons, and I had my hornbook in my hand, in which I had translated the Venerable Bede into Greek, painstakingly scratched out on winter nights, to please him.

He was working at his papers, his familiar hands with their long fingers moving across the parchment, a dish of his precious tea at his elbow (he had got it, in the autumn, from a sailor). I drew up my stool, to lean on my arm and watch him as he worked. We had the same fair-coloured hair – our ancestors were Danish – same teeth, woven close together on one side of the mouth, and the same half-twisted little toes. I felt sure I was the one of his children who in character was most like him: spirited, stubborn, strange.

'May I try the China drink, Father?' I said. The tea was growing cold, it seemed a famous waste. 'It's said they live off it at Court and the Queen has naught else – and she has never had the plague – and has dark and lovely hair.'

He laughed and let me drink it; it was cool and bitter in my mouth. I swilled it round my gums and swallowed it with a sigh.

'Child,' he said, putting down his pen and twirling its feather in his knuckles. 'What think you of Lord Tyringham?'

I was, I think, quite taken aback to be asked for my thoughts on any subject, and, shifting on my seat, floundered a while.

I knew I should try to speak most honestly, as would please my father. *Et cognoscetis veritatem et veritas liberabit vos*, said my mind – that phrase graven deeply on my memory since I was six years old, after a long and thorough thrashing because of a stolen sugar-cake.

(Confession: I ate it.)

I breathed in. The fire snapped.

'He is the pale-skinned man who helps you in your work, and comes oft to dinner and is kind to me,' I falteringly began. 'A nobleman of rank... Mother says he owns half the county and is rich and we must be most civil to him, to help you build your ships.'

My father's eyes were merry now.

'He knows the Duke of York, I think, and can get favours and commissions.'

'Well, child, I am glad you think him kind,' said my father. 'For he has made our family the godliest of compliments. Far beyond, I think, the ones he makes to me on business matters.'

He talked then at length about the politenesses which were due from our kind to his, and the need for money to carry on our estate, and the hardness of the age, and the war against the Dutch, and the boats that must be built to see them off, and those that held the choice of shipbuilder in their fist.

Then, picking at his cuffs – a little lace had come undone – he spoke of the great unbroken line of our family name, and whence we came, and of filial duty and (here he fell somewhat to coughing) the great rituals of life and the mysteries of nature, which we were all bound to follow, though sometimes we knew not why.

The snow had begun again: it was falling thickly, the world a blur of white behind it. I watched it slide slowly down the window glass and pool, oh so softly, on the sill. Outside, there unfolded a spread of purest white that rippled down the hill and to the lake. There were light shapes on my father's table. I hugged thoughts of snow sculptures and hill-sledding to myself: I might creep out, to the village, when it stopped and tell my mother I went holly-picking.

'He has asked for you and we have answered joyfully in your place, for though you are young...' (he looked upon me with something quite like fondness) '... your mother thinks your strong will and melancholic temper well suited for the disciplines a wifehood will require, and he has sworn to be patient and to take over our teachings. You will learn to be a helpmeet, wife, and, in good time, and if the Lord wishes it, mother.'

The snowflakes were settling in thick triangles against the leaded glass. We might be snowed in again. Had we enough food to last us out? Last winter we were heartsick of potage by January.

'He will raise you up, my child, and, we hope, bring you great happiness. And we will be happy too, for Tyringham will have you well provided for – and you are to have a very handsome jointure.'

He asked then that we kneel together. Afterwards, he dropped a kiss upon my brow and bade me run off and tell Mary and Goodsoule and my brother and sister that I would soon be wed.

'Wed?' I said, half into my chest.

There was a blister on my finger that fascinated me. I would ask Goodsoule for a tincture.

'At the end of summer,' he said. 'And first Tyringham will come to court you and dine with us as often as he can – he will not be a stranger, by then. It is our dearest wish, my Ursula, that your love for him will grow and when the time is come for you to go to the church door, you will do so with a great and godly joy.'

'Does Mother know?' I said, and my voice had begun to tremble.

'Why of course, child,' he said. 'Did I not say she thought marriage would be suited to your temper? It is she who has encouraged it in faith, though at first I confess I thought you too young. But as she has said, you are wise beyond your years. And I think you will like Tyringham; for what I know of him, he seems a good sort of man and will likely make a strong husband, and will love you, I think, as I have loved your mother.'

He kissed my head and, with a press of my hand, sent me off out of the room. I walked slowly, dragging my feet across the hall, to the parlour, a sick feeling pulling at my insides. My mother was not there. She was not upstairs.

'Mother!' I called. She did not come.

I leant against the oaken panels of the wall, breathing slowly in and out, in and out. Marriage, I said inside my head, I was to be married, and have a husband, and it was not to be my long-lost sweetheart Samuel, or any other young man neither, but an old man, I thought, as old as my father. I felt in my pocket for my little wooden bear, for I was hot all over and could not cool, and against my will my hands and my arms were shaking and would not stop. I gripped the little bear and tried to slow my breathing, though my thoughts were all in a whirl. I had not thought to marry yet, at fifteen years, and had thought even my betrothal a good way off, if I had thought of it at all. Mother was sixteen when she was contracted, but one-and-twenty when she married, my Aunt Phyllis three-and-twenty or more, I knew. Kitty Goodsoule was seventeen and betrothed but that was altogether a different thing, for the village folk were lusty and married young to save themselves from sin.

I had not thought of Lord Tyringham at all in truth, for I had met him but once, and then we had exchanged barely two words together. I could not think why he had asked for me – it seemed a famous liberty, or at the very least, strange. I tried my very hardest to recall him, but had only an indistinct impression floating in my mind, of a dark man with a deep voice, and could not, for the life of me, remember his face.

The thought of Samuel's face came at once then into my mind: his merry brown eyes and his twisted smile, the feel of his soft lips against my own, the brush of his fingers against my skin... I held up my little bear and, crossing my fingers, silently wished upon her that Samuel might somehow come back to me, and rescue me from matrimony with a stranger. I kissed the bear to seal the wish and slipped it back into my pocket.

My brother and sister were in the nursery playing tipcats, chanting 'Jack Be Nimble' and giggling all the while, but Goodsoule was not there, and Mary neither. I ran back downstairs, climbing the stone stairs down to the kitchen and called for them, but there was just Eliza's old dog, scratching its shoulders by the fire, and the red-knuckled woman who swept the scullery, snoring gently in a chair.

I breathed in and out, in and out, wiping the tears from my face.

I ran outside.

The snow burned my feet.

# XIV

# PUNISHMENT

*In which I am disobedient and must suffer for it*

Try as I might I could not and would not adjust to the idea that I was to be married. I had attempted to reason with my mother, but she said only that I must be obedient, and she knew I would be a happier wife than I was a daughter. I spent many sad hours in my chamber weeping on Mary's shoulder at the injustice of it all, and the fact that despite my wish, Samuel had not come to save me, for I still thought of him tenderly in my secret heart and had hoped that we should one day come together again. The fear that I must be parted from Mary and her mother and Catherine and my father loomed up and frightened me, and at this I sobbed too, until at last my companion grew bored with me, and said she must go home when I knew she must not. I begged Goodsoule to speak to my mother on my behalf, but she only said it was not her place, and marriage was a thing that all women must bear and I would soon come round to the thing and look forward to it.

The week immediately following the interview with my father was a hard one. On Monday I relapsed into a fit of sulks and would not speak nor eat nor pass a dish at table and was sullen and drooping the whole day long. On Tuesday I had sworn I would not marry Lord Tyringham, or marry ever, if I had to die to stop it, by jumping from the clock tower of St Ninian's. On Wednesday I did not rise from my bed, and instead lay in it from morning 'til dark, sweating in the sheets, and moaning a little now and then, and was only saved from starving by Mary bringing up a bowl of pigeon broth when Mother had gone out. On Thursday I screamed long and loud that my mother and my father both could go to the Devil, and be hanged, and be hanged by the Devil, and stayed the whole day in my room; and on Friday I had whipped myself into such a frenzy of misery and anger and fear I had a great paroxysm at dinner. At Mother's sharp request that I help Catherine with cutting her pie, I threw my cup onto the floor and ran around the room, slapping myself about the face and pulling at my hair, howling all the curse words I knew until my voice was raw in my throat and my face burning hot and the children frightened and crying themselves.

My mother, who had borne the week's calamities with strange blank looks and scowls at my father, began to get red about the face herself, and rose up from her seat, her meat half uneaten.

'Enough,' was all she said.

My father got up, too.

'What, husband,' she said. 'Will you bid me sit another day, while our child dishonours us in such a way?'

'She has been very naughty,' said my father. His voice was low and he did not look at me, though I tried to catch his eye.

Mother called for Mary and, in a calm voice which belied the trembling of her hands, bade her take me to the nursery. I went up dragging my feet, Mary fretting that she did not want to do it, but must. I slapped her away. She took it as she always did, with one of her looks and the sucking-in sound that came from her cheeks, a trick she had learnt from Eliza when we were children. But still she held me firm, her old familiar smell that was cotton and straw and her own sweet-ish sweat making my limbs go slack, even as I turned my face away from her. I was a half-mad, wild thing. Flux was running down my chin and my hair had come down at the back from my rages. I did not care. I twisted out of her grasp and stood there, wet and furious, and ready to strike. Mother came in and shut the door, in her hand a birch rod.

'Stop!' I cried, seeing the plan. Mother came towards me. I ran for the door, but she and Mary caught me by the arms and between them took me to the flogging frame and put me onto it, Mother taking my shoulder and pushing against my back. I struggled against her grasp, but she struck my face, and I stopped still and lay against the frame, panting.

'You can go, Mary, for all the help you are,' said Mother.

'Mistress,' said Mary.

I heard the door close.

It was quiet and cold up in the nursery: Mother did not believe children needed fires – they would get warm with their jumping and games. There was the hobby horse that had once been mine, carved out of wood, his lips curled back and his teeth bared, as if in the midst of a great and noisy whicker. I had called him Peterkin. He likely had another name now: Catherine was very careful about the naming of toys.

I stared at the wavy lines of his wooden mane and the small points of his ears. His painted red and yellow saddle was flaking where shoes had scuffed at it, one of the stirrup-pegs was snapped off at the end, and his reins, which were of leather, had gone slack and crumbly with handling. We had ridden far and wide on his back. Sometimes I was a comely, low-born maid who helped look after animals, and rode about a farm, tending to poorly lambs and ducklings with bad legs. Sometimes I was a dashing adventuress who rode alone, apart from her companion dog, who would trot alongside (if we could make Muff stay and play the part and she never would).

The air whistled as the rod came down and stung the soft skin of my leg backs.

Thwick! Thwick! Thwick!

Twelve times Mother got it right above the top of my stockings, where it hurt most and would leave a mark. Peterkin would not stop smiling.

Afterwards I lay face down on my bed and beat my fists and cried with shame and anger until my voice was cracked and my eyes puffed up and spongy to the touch. I quietened down when no one came, not even Father, to ask me to sing with him in a harmony before supper. I knew then that they were serious. I was to marry Tyringham, if I must be flogged daily and dragged to the church by my hair.

I sat up, then, to think. I should run away, to a place where no one knew me. Mary might help me if I asked it, for we had sworn with our crooked fingers over the lucky stone to be one another's friend for all eternity, on pain of horrible, lingering death.

But Mary could not give me the silver coins that I would need, nor stop the men that would surely be sent after me. I could saddle up Blue Boy, and make off in the middle of the night... but I did not know the way to Norwich, or to London, or to York. A lone girl on a hunter would be set upon by highwaymen and cutpurses before she could say 'Cock Robin'. I could ask Mary to come with me. A young country wife and her lady's maid. Perhaps we might somehow get word to Samuel to come and meet us. Then there might be a chance.

When it was time for the household to retire, Mary was waiting in my chamber.

'There, there, dearest,' she said, and crooned a lullaby as she helped me out of my gown.

'Oh Mary, I cannot marry him – I cannot!' I said, throwing my arms about her and pressing her to me. 'He is old and a filthy brute, no doubt. And I do not want to marry yet – unless it is a handsome boy of my age. I cannot leave you or your mother or Catherine. I have not finished my lessons. I was to learn Dutch in the spring. Oh, I cannot do it,' I moaned. 'You must help me, as my bosom friend, for if you do not I am undone.'

I laid my plan before her. Over the next few days – it might take as long as a week, I had to check the almanac for the next full moon – I would take provisions from the kitchen and store them in the stable, with my cloak and boots, and her outdoor things. After a secret signal, given at dinner, we would both rise at midnight, meet at the stable, and make for the nearest coaching inn, on Blue Boy, I posing as a young widow (I would wear a vizard, or if I could not get one, a veil), she, my lady. From there we would get to London, where we would possibly find Samuel, but if not, surely, our fortune, and be happy all our days.

Mary was very quiet at this. Presently she said she did not think it a very good plan, and besides, she said, she did not want to leave her mother, or her brothers and sisters, who would miss her. Eliza was sure to notice the missing provisions from the kitchen, she said; and the next full moon was three weeks hence; we would be found and brought back before we could get to a coaching inn – the nearest one was at Templeton, which was surely fifteen miles away, if it was one.

How, she asked, would we pay for our board when we got there?

I would take money from Father's purse.

How would we get to London, without a protector, two women on our own?

I did not know.

How would we live and feed and clothe ourselves when we got there?

I did not know.

How would we make our fortune?

I did not know.

'It is hopeless. I see now,' I said.

Back inside my chamber, I laid my heavy head down and she stroked my brow.

'Hush now, my dear one,' she said. 'There is another fate for you. All will seem better when a new sun has risen in the sky.'

# XV

✤

# BETROTHAL

*In which I meet the man who is to be my husband*

❧

The morning of the day Lord Tyringham was to visit us, I crept out into the garden before any of the house was awake. The snow had stopped falling now, but the air was raw and stung my face. Grey strands of mist hung about the garden and made it look quite strange – I could not make out the maze. The plants about the gate were without their flowers; dew coated every darkened, drooping leaf.

Down by the pond, the pave-stones were greenish and slimy with moss. I stepped slowly in my usual walk around it, all the while trying to unpick the tangles of troubles that swelled in my head: Lord Tyringham; the dinner; the strangeness of my life to come.

At the thought of seeing my soon-to-be-betrothed, and acting as I knew I must (I raged inwardly at the prospect of flirtation), my belly tipped up and down; I stopped a while and sucked in sharp little mouthfuls of cold, wet air. My throat was tight and sore, and my eyes still ached from many hot, frustrated tears: I had raged at my parents for the past seven days or more, as the prospect of my betrothal loomed closer, and became a vivid, corporeal thing.

I gazed at the still surface of the pond and thought about my marriage. My teeth chattered; my skin was pricked with goose-flesh. I walked around and around, until the sun was full in the sky and Reginald was at the back door, calling me in.

Though inwardly I boiled, I had resolved immediately I was recovered from the thrashing that I would not let my mother better me. Instead I would affect the appearance of reluctant obedience, until I had found another way out of my marriage. To this end, and because I had reached the age where I had a secret yearning to be thought pretty, even if it was by a husband I did not want, that morning I gave great care to my dress.

My hair was curled in an extravagant style we had copied from a drawing in a book sent from France. I cleaned my mouth out most thoroughly and, because my face was pale and shadowed-looking, pinched my cheeks until they ached. Mother came in and out of the room at intervals, a tight look upon her face.

'I hope you will look your best,' she said. 'I hope you will behave as you ought.'

I said I would.

While Mother stood and lectured me on what to say and do, Mary came in and laced me into my newest, finest gown, while she chattered and wept a little – gentle soul that she was, I saw she felt the pain of my punishment keenly. I made our secret sign that we should talk later in our meeting place and she wiped her face and went away, saying that my eyes were too shiny and I looked prone to fits and she would brew me a tisane, to which my mother grunted.

My reflection in the glass was pleasing, and despite myself, I felt my spirits rising. The gown was quite the most grown-up thing I'd ever known, with a bodice that came down low in front. I pushed it off my shoulders and hoped Mother wouldn't see (she did as soon as she came back into the room and it went straight back up again). Ignoring her chiding, I hummed a ditty, imagining myself at Court and dancing with handsome gentlemen as I stepped into my shoes, the consolation for the day – they were of green satin, with a little heel I found most satis-fyingly elegant, and long laces made of ribbons.

I was afraid of looking too young, and a country fool, so when everyone went away to primp themselves, I went up and down the corridor, swinging my skirts as I thought a lady might, and practising the way I said 'How d'ye do,' until my voice sounded odd to my own ears and the words themselves lost meaning.

❀

Time dragged; the hour drew near. Mother and I sat ourselves in the parlour with our sewing. I was arranged to best advantage on a chair in the window and in my lap had the jewel-box I was decorating, laboriously, with oak leaves. My mother, a little way off, almost out of sight (but not quite out of earshot), was picking at a screen.

Muff came and lay down on the rug near my feet, and snuffled a little, laying her scruffy brown head onto her paws: I knew she had come to comfort me and I talked to her in a crooning voice until Mother sharply bade me shush. The clock on the mantel click-clacked the minutes, while we waited; Mother stiff and staring at the doorway, I tight chested, with shallow, hopeless breaths.

At two o' clock, he came, stooping into the room behind my father and bowing to my mother, both my parents pink-cheeked and gibbering witlessly like lunatics.

'Lo, such fog!' I heard my father cry, and my mother add, in a too-bright voice that came out like a cry: 'Why will it not lift?'

Tyringham, I knew, was not handsome, but I hoped he might be kind. I looked over his face for signs of an even temper, or a twinkle in his eye that might foretell a romantic or lusty nature. His face, pouchy and pale, gave nothing away. He did not wear a periwig that day; his black hair a foamy thing over one side of his face, and on the other receding back into his head; his brow a white sloping curve beneath it. His moustache twitched when he spoke, and he had a skinny neck under his chin, which, too was small and indistinct.

Presently he came over to me and bade me 'Good day' and at my mother's encouragement – she trotted around him, I loathed to see it – sat himself down in the chair near mine. I saw now his eyes were washed-out blue, and bulbous, with dark lashes. He stretched his hand out to pat Muff on the head; the dog cringed and he laughed, and pulled at her ear; she got up and ran away. There was fine black hair lying flat across his knuckles, and sprouting at angles from his ears.

I sat stiffly in my chair, wishing Mary could be there to see him and we could laugh at him together. She had said she would try to slip in with some excuse if she could, for she was as curious to lay eyes on him as I was, but the door remained steadfastly shut, and I could not think of a reason to ring for her.

'Well now,' said Tyringham, fastening his eyes upon me. 'How do you do today? May I be permitted to address you as Ursula?' He had a hopeful look on his face, though he did not smile.

I glanced up at my mother, who was making her eyes wide.

'I suppose you ought,' I said. I tried to look at him but his nearness made me shy. I found myself gazing at the floor. My tongue felt strange in my mouth and there was a hot feeling creeping up the sides of my throat.

'It gives me such joy,' he said, 'to contemplate our union and the joining of our families.' Here he looked backwards at my parents, who were nodding and had simpering looks on their faces that I had not seen before.

'Yes indeed,' said my father. 'We are all most contented.'

''Tis a good match,' said my mother, too loudly, misjudging the distance from the back of the room. 'And I pray that you will be happy together. Though Ursula is young, she is a good, clever girl and is ready to be a true and obedient wife.'

I felt something start to work its way about my stomach. The tea I had drunk earlier was swirling about and felt too high in my body.

Tyringham was watching me again. 'I think to tell you a little about myself and my family. For I must seem to you little more than a stranger.'

'That would be very good of you, Tyringham,' said my father.

Tyringham nodded, and bent his body forward and leant towards me with his elbow on his knee. 'Well then. My father, who is dead these fifteen years, was a silk merchant, and my mother a gentlewoman of a good Dorset family. My father bought us our country seat, Turvey Hall, in the county of Wiltshire.'

'My sister Phyllis has been there,' put in my mother. 'For her husband grew up at Bath. She says it is a godly sort of place, with many farms.'

'Oh it is a very pretty county,' agreed Tyringham. 'My mother lives there, at the Hall, still, as it is a great house of ten bedrooms and as many acres, and its own chapel. You shall have a fine chamber, Ursula. And your own garden too if you wish it – I know how women like flowers and such pretty ornaments as a garden may provide. My sister, alas, is delicate' – here he cast his eyes down – 'and cannot tend to a garden of her own. I have a house in London too, at Covent Garden, though you shall not have much need of going there.'

'But faith, I would like to see London,' I said quickly, swallowing down the tea. 'For it has long been my ambition to visit the playhouse. I would greatly like to see a play. A real one, that is, with actors and actresses. For my brother and sister and friends may do their best, but they have not learnt the craft, and so it is not quite the same. But I have had it from Grisella that the playhouse is where all the ladies of quality go and is famously diverting withal.'

'I did not think you would... be interested in such entertainments,' he said, surprise on his face.

'Oh aye, I would,' I said.

'All this with the playhouse!' said my mother.

'Ursula has a great many interests,' said my father.

'What else would you know?' said Tyringham.

'Will we go to Court often?' I said, leaning forward despite myself.

'I must go, for I must oft visit the King and tell him of the plans I have made for the navy. But there will not be much occasion for you to go. 'Tis a strange place to those not used to it – for country maids such as you are!' He slapped his thigh a little back and forth as if this was some great jest. My mother made a tinkling sort of laugh.

'Oh but I would wish it!' I said passionately. 'For I have a great mind to see the King and my Lady Castlemaine and Nelly and all his other mistresses! And the fashions – and the jewels too. I have been practising my dance steps with Mother for just an occasion such as that and so... I would like it,' I finished lamely, for I could see his face had taken on a displeased look, and was pinched about the mouth.

'Well, we shall see,' he said, nodding. 'But what do you say, then? Have you heard enough? Will you have me?'

I was startled at this direct sort of questioning and my mouth gaped open a little to hear it. My mother bustled over then.

'Why yes, yes, let us have the betrothal words and then we shall know what we are about!' she said, beckoning to my father. 'I remember when I said them myself, and the gown I wore, and now my daughter is...' She trailed off, for her voice had gone a little weak.

'Aye,' said my father, stepping forward. 'I was a handsome fellow then and in a very good coat, though I could not fit into it now.'

'Not handsome,' coughed my mother, her face now in her kerchief.

'There, there, dearheart,' said my father, patting her back, to which she twitched but did not move away from his touch.

Tyringham took up my hot hand then and held it in his moist one. I could do little but let him have it and sit there with my arm out, most stupidly.

'I do here seriously swear, in the presence of God, before these two witnesses,' he intoned loudly, 'that I do contract matrimony with thee, Ursula Flight, and shall take you for my wife.'

I stared.

'Ursula?' prompted my mother. 'Do you remember?'

'Oh,' I said. 'Aye. Then, I do contract matrimony with thee and I shall take you for my husband,' I said quickly, and then my mother and my father were kissing me and Tyringham had got something out of his pocket and was holding it to me: a gold ring set with garnets and pearls. The first bit of real jewellery I had owned. I stared at it.

'Then this is my token,' he said, placing it on my palm, and I took it and tried to put it on my finger, but I was clumsy and it slipped from my hands and bounced on the floor carpet, and then rolled away under the chaise.

'Oh dear,' I said. 'Oh dear.'

I put my hand in my pocket and turned my carved little bear over and over, but for once, it could not comfort me.

✤

# FAVOURITES & WISHES LIST
## TWELFTH NIGHT 1679/80 A.D.

*THIS PAPER TO BE BURNT WHEN ALL THINGS
HAVE BEEN ACQUIRED*

1. Sweet animals of all sorts. I would like pets of dogs & pigs especially (how nice the sows are at the Merrimans' farm, when I step over the stile they come running and press their snouts into my shoes). I do not much like goats, which have gleaming eyes and try to eat my sleeves.

2. Pale blue dresses with great sweeping skirts. (This looks well, I believe, in the dancing.) Fastened with yellow lover's knots all over. Mother says bows are *lavish* and pale blue dresses are not to be had – I know they are.

3. Street ballads. Mother will not hear them sung; Grisella knows all the words. We sang 'Cuckolds All Awry' this very morning to each other in the barn. Fie!

4. Hair primped into little curls on the brow and glued fast to the cheeks at the side.

5. Catherine. My sweet little sister.

6. Corn-roses, bluebells, feverfew, hearts-ease. All tied up in a pretty pink ribbon and given to a sweetheart. NB: I do not have one and all flowers are dead and under snow.

7. Plays. Above ALL things. I have not been to any, but if they are like the mummers' show, I think I will like them. They involve, I know, the wearing of fine clothes and the eating of nuts and oranges (which I do very well). I must see one soon or I know I will DIE from the lack.

8. Amethyst rings on every finger.

9. Orange ribbons for my velvet shoes!

10. People who do *not* try to touch your hand. Or speak to you, or whisper things into your ear at table. Even if you are to marry them.

⚜

# XVI

# SLIDING

*In which I am sociable with my sweetheart*

I had been nervous all the morning at the thought of seeing Lord Tyringham again, for I was still adjusting myself to the fact of our engagement, and I did not know what I would say to him. Mary and I had had many talks about the betrothal and how sweethearts were supposed to act, and she had pointed out that there might be kissing, as that was what Kitty and Jack Browning were about, and more besides, for they were permitted to bundle – and so he would go into her chamber, and talk there all through the night, and I hoped that would not be the thing in my case, for I did not know what I would speak of for such an amount of time – and as for the kissing, with this man, the prospect of it did not seem attractive, and so I fervently wished that it would not come about.

I was seated in my usual place in the window when my mother came through the door with Tyringham behind her, he in a brown suit of velvet and a cassock coat, his courting clothes: I had seen them before. The colour in his cheeks made me think him in good spirits – he was not so sombre and stiff as before. I smiled at him. Perhaps today I would like him a little more. He took off his hat and, while Mother dithered by the Chinese cabinet, came forward to perch, hunch-backed, on the chaise next to me. His eyes roamed down the front of my dress. Looking downwards to avoid his burning gaze, I saw he had a bag in his hands, laced shut with a thong.

'I have brought you something, Ursula.' He gestured at the bag. 'A gift.'

How my spirits rose at this! I murmured he was too kind, and prayed fervently for emerald silk or a rope of pearls. But he made no move to open it and, while I shifted in my seat, merely mumbled questions about my health and sewing.

'It looks a strange shape indeed,' I said, at last. 'That bag.'

'It does, indeed,' said he.

My cheeks burned.

He chuckled then and, with a flourish, unlaced it and brought out two thin, curved pieces of wood, with iron parts hewn onto them, and brown leather straps all over.

He looked at me expectantly.

'Why – why, *thank you*,' I faltered, turning to my mother, who frowned and flapped her hands.

'They are called skates,' he said, setting them down by my feet. 'For sliding on the ice.' And then, when my fingers stretched out to touch the gleaming metal, 'The blades are sharp.'

My mother had called my father in to see what their would-be son had brought their first-born daughter.

'I have heard of these,' said my father. 'They look dangerous, sir!'

Tyringham made a bow. 'I thought to take Ursula sliding on the lake.' He turned his eyes towards mine. I looked at my mother.

'You are too generous, my Lord,' she said.

I got up and curtseyed, still wondering at the discovery that my betrothed could be kind.

'Truly, sir, I thank you,' I said. 'I have dreamed of ice-sliding for… why, ever since I heard about them doing it at Court. I shall run and tell Reginald – how green he will be!'

❧

We stepped out of doors. The snow rose up to my calves; the wind whipped my hair across my face. I wore my old woollen cloak, Mother's mangy rabbit-fur muff (I hid the bad part) and I had taken one of Father's hats and set it over my curls at an angle, as I had seen in a sketch. Tyringham eyed it.

''Tis the latest mode,' I said, and then felt immediately silly, for his reaction showed that he disdained my nervous prattle.

By the frozen lake, jagged trees pocked with crows were black against the pearl-grey sky. Bulrushes fringed the edges of the bank, their fronds bent double with frost.

Tyringham bade me come to him and set the skates down, holding them upright for my feet. I laced them on, leaning on his shoulder – he had a sour smell; of wet leather and old wine. His face came up from his own skate-lacing splotched all over with the effort and I felt a burst of shyness in my stomach for our first time alone together. He, too, seemed lost for words. We talked in pleasantries, our words strangely stilted.

# 'TIS PITY
# HE'S
# A BORE

*a* Tragedy

---

*Acted by*

## THE KING'S MAJESTY'S SERVANTS

*at*

## THE PHOENIX IN DRURY LANE

---

*WRITTEN BY*

## MRS. U. FLIGHT

> *A* MAN *and a* MAID *stand by a frozen lake.*
> *The* MAN *has strange eyes that fix on the*
> MAID *when she turns her head; she can feel*
> *them burning into her arms, her chest, her neck.*
> *The English countryside, mantled white with*
> *snow, rolls away into the distance around them.*

MAN: [*Wobbling tentatively onto the ice*] I will make a check to see that it is thick enough.

MAID: I am not that heavy, my Lord! Though I did eat a famous lot of dumplings at dinner.

> *The* MAN *clambers onto the ice. His feet slide out*
> *in all directions. He bends his body forward, then*
> *back, then forward again, and touches the ice.*

MAN: Confound it!

> *The* MAID *hides her smile behind her muff.*

MAID: It looks mighty difficult, my Lord!

MAN: It is a little strange. I must get my balance. I have seen it done, I must... right myself.

> *The* MAN *is moving in a jerking motion across*
> *the surface of the lake. His skates make strange*
> *patterns. The* MAID *watches him.*

MAID: How is the ice? May I come onto it?

MAN: There is a patch here we shall have to avoid but you may try it now – if you are not afraid.

MAID: No, I am not afraid. [*She steps onto the ice*] Oh! I almost fell... ah. Ha! I see now...

> *The* MAN *tries to move closer to the* MAID.
> *His arms windmill about him.*

[*Skating*] I have wanted to try ice-sliding ever since I heard about it from Grisella – Grisella Shadforth, who is my bosom friend. She lives but two miles from here and she has lots of older brothers, and one of them is at Court, and brings back all the tattle. He has been to the Frost Fair...

MAN: [*With flailing arms*] It is not becoming in a man to gossip. [*Suddenly still*] Ah. Take my hand now, and we shall skate together.

> *The* MAID *stretches her arm out, but the* MAN *unsteadies her. She slips once, twice, thrice; scissors her feet, then topples backwards, landing flat-backed on the ice.*

MAID: Fiddlesticks and God's teeth!

MAN: Are you hurt?

MAID: Not much, I think.

MAN: You went down very hard. Lean on my arm. I have got your hat.

MAID: I've cracked my head hard enough to coddle my brains!

> *She brushes the frost from her skirts*

Now I have a fancy to try one circle around the lake.

MAN: I do not think that is wise.

> *She pushes off. He watches her moving across the ice.*

MAN: Do not go too quickly, Ursula! You shall fall.

> *She is moving swiftly now, the wind throws her hair back behind her.*

[*Louder*] Ursula!

MAID: [*Putting her hand to her ear*] I cannot hear you! 'Tis like dancing – or flying! Watch, I am Pegasus on the way to Mount Olympus! I shall carry Bellerophon to slay the Chimera!

> *The* MAID *is whipping across the lake now, in a steady rhythm, her arms stretched out. She flaps them up and down, like wings. She sticks out her tongue to feel the frigid air rushing across it. The snicker of the blade as it cuts across the ice.*

See how fast I gooooooo!

MAN: Stop now, I say. It is enough…

> *The* MAN's *feet come out from under him and in one quick movement he falls heavily onto the ice.*

MAID: Oh!

> *The* MAN *does not move. The* MAID *stands stock still, hesitating. In the trees, the crows begin to caw.*
>
> *Curtain*

# XVII

# ACCEPTANCE

*In which I see my bosom friend and bare my soul*

Mother was ill again after trouble in childbed (it died). I was sent to stay with Grisella so that I did not make noise around the house, the little ones having gone, with Goodsoule, to my Aunt Phyllis. I had begun to feel the difference between our ages, for at seventeen, and two years my elder, Grisella had grown into a pretty young woman with a curving figure and coffee-coloured hair that she wore primped at the sides and in a long coil snaking onto her bosom, which she already powdered, along with her arms which were smooth and white and as rounded as any Court beauty. Being the youngest girl child, with two elder sisters and five elder brothers, who were all grown up and gone, Grisella was very spoiled, but nevertheless I loved her, for we had been playmates so long, and unlike Mary, she was of the gentry, and therefore my equal, and so could understand things that my Mary, however much she loved me, could not.

'My dear Ursula, hearty congratulations to you!' cried Lady Shadforth, no sooner had I crossed the threshold of Billingbear Park. 'For I have had your happy news from Grisella, and we have talked of nothing else – for what else *is* there to talk of? No doubt it is an excellent match and Tyringham I believe to be quite prosperous.' Here she came to me and patted my cheek. 'I have had it from Lady Downshire that he is well known at Court, has a great house at Wiltshire and is above five-and-thirty, though why that should matter, I know not. Shadforth is thirteen years my elder and we have been quite contented these one-and-twenty years – though he was impatient with me at first and given to admonishments, in time we got used to one another, and are now really quite amicable.'

I was trying not to giggle, and she saw my face moving and took it, I think, as symptomatic of a soon-to-be-blushing bride.

'But who cares if he is old, if he is rich, as I say to my girls. For then you may live in the country, and he in the town and you may form your own amusements, and do as you please.'

'Or may it not be him in the country and me in the town, Lady Shadforth?' I said, which provoked Grisella to sniggering behind her hand. 'For of late I have set my heart upon the stage and I cannot rest until I am an actress as much admired as Mrs Barry or Mrs Gwynn.'

'Oh you girls!' cried Lady Shadforth, with darting eyes. 'You know you must not speak of such things to me.'

'It is true, Mumsy,' said Grisella. 'Ursula and I have been practising at our recitals. We speak Shakespeare and Fletcher and strike poses like this – and like this.'

Here she made some dramatic postures.

'And we are quite good enough to be seen at Drury Lane,' I added. 'If only we could be got up in the fashions.'

'In the fashions!' screamed Lady Shadforth, feeling about for the staircase behind her, and stepping on the cat, which yowled and pelted up the stairs with its ears pressed backwards on its head.

'What we really need, Mumsy, is for you to take us to the playhouse. Frederick could do it, if he could get away from the Temple for a moment.'

'He will do no such thing,' said Lady Shadforth, groping for her handkerchief. 'He is a good boy and must not be distracted from the law.'

'Why, Mumsy, he is at the playhouse every afternoon, I'll warrant,' said Grisella, whirling about and careening into me, which made me titter. Grisella's silliness was always catching.

'Of course he is not at the playhouse!' scolded Lady Shadforth. 'It is not the place for young men of the quality – nor young ladies either. Let us have no more talk about it. Or I will have to go to your father and tell him about it – and I know he will not be pleased.'

We were quiet then, for Lord Shadforth's short and blustery temper was well known to us. We had often been subject to his bellowings and chidings when we were romping about the house. I did not like to be shouted at, for I was not used to it at home.

The afternoon was fine and cloudless so my friend and I spent it out of doors, first teasing the cat, by putting it in a baby's bonnet, then making leaf garlands when it ran away and crowning ourselves with them, and then following the trail of the stream known as The Cut up to Peasey Hill, which was often our habit when there was nothing in particular to do. When the sun went in and the air became chill, and having left our mantles behind, we went and sat in the little barn of the neighbouring farm which was kept stacked with hay bales, and so was convenient for lounging.

'Oh how will I bear it, Griss,' I said. 'I have put my plot to run away entirely aside, and must resign myself to my coming state of marriage... but how?' I cast my limbs out in an attitude of despair. 'Oh if you could have seen him at the sliding! He came round from his concussion most groggily and was very ill-tempered afterwards. I had to support him back to the house like he was my grandfather, for he would moan and carry on about the wrench in his neck and the soreness in his head...' Here I imitated him.

Grisella tittered. She had been so far unsympathetic to my anxieties about Tyringham, being certain of a marriage to a young and handsome duke, for her mother would have it no other way and scolded her father about it almost daily.

I sighed. 'He is not handsome and he is old. I'll warrant we'll spend all of our evenings from now until Domesday stock still in the parlour, he droning on about the war – there is always a war somewhere, it seems – you have not heard his voice, it rattles like a drum – and me docilely picking at a linnet until my fingers bleed.'

Grisella laughed.

'You must promise to come to me and visit with us and then we can make messes in the kitchen, and practise our dancing, and I might be able to bear it.'

'I'd give all my gowns to get a husband and be safe away from this dreary place,' said she, getting an elm twig out of her pocket, and chewing at it. 'Mumsy is really quite unbearable since she got an ague, and then another, and then a third, and believes this latest one will not ever leave her. She is forever getting tinctures made up by the apothecary at Oakingham, which are horrid and do not work. Poor Aunt Tilda tried the potion made of bat droppings and nettles, and turned quite grey, and was sick in her lap. She had a cake in it at the time, and was most put out to lose it.'

'That apothecary is quite famously bad; I believe he has no talent, and gets all his remedies from Lilly's book, which you or I would do much better at following, for we at least can read. You must go to my Mrs Goodsoule for she is Wise and has given our family many remedies for things, when we are ill. Why, Mother was looking a great deal better when I left, for she has been drinking a posset daily, and Mrs Goodsoule chanting over her, when she may. Mother's eyes were so much brighter for it, I almost asked if I mayn't stay home after all.'

'Why, I believe you spend all your time with that family, drinking nasty potions and incanting things. And your accent has turned quite countrified you know; you have quite a burr coming along and sound just like Mary these days. Don't scold me now, for I know it to be the truth. Egad, wouldn't I laugh my head off if were me who had to sit in their dreary little cottage, with straw on the floor, no doubt, and a pig in the kitchen. I'm sure you come away quite reeking of it. Come now, do admit it isn't quite nice, spending all that time with the servants. It's quite strange, Ursula, really it is.'

'Mrs Goodsoule is a kind woman and has been very good to me, though some haven't,' I said stiffly.

'Oh yes, I daresay,' said Grisella, yawning, which meant she was becoming bored. 'You needn't get cross. Only Mumsy wouldn't let me go near any of the villagers in case it harmed my prospects, or somesuch, you know. We aren't children any more, Ursula.'

'No indeed.'

'Does His Worshipful Tyringham know about your romps? I'll fancy it would make his eyes boggle to learn of them.' Here she began to pretend to passionately kiss the back of her hand. 'Oh Samuel,' she said, in a silly high voice. 'Thank you for the love token, though I would have much preferred a sapphire necklace.'

'I would not have preferred a necklace,' I said crossly. 'And you know very well Tyringham does not know anything, and if you dare to breathe a word, I'll tell all of your bundling with Septimus Harrington round the back of the shepherd's hut, and then you'll be sorry.'

'Such petulance!' She watched my face. 'But I don't suppose it matters much now you are betrothed. I must say it makes me quite green-eyed, Ursula, despite your husband's decrepit age. Mumsy says you shall have so many fine dresses – made of lace and silk – think of that! And fine jewels, I'll warrant, if you can wrench them off his mother. I've heard Polly say that the mothers are the worst part of it, hanging onto the family heirlooms for dear life, and their sons too, if they can. Have you yet had an audience with the elder Lady T?'

'Nay, but Tyringham says she's a godly sort of woman, who will take me on quite as a daughter. She lives in the east wing up at the house and has her own apartments and servants, so it will be quite all right. But,' I added, seeing Grisella's eyes widening with what looked like glee, 'I believe we will dine together five evenings out of seven.'

'Aye,' said Grisella, digging at a hay bale with her stick. 'After she has given the order for dinner and told you to wash your hands and behind your ears.'

'I'm looking forward to meeting her,' I said feebly. 'And the other parts of the family, though I believe it is not large.'

'It wouldn't be – that's where you come in. But I am looking forward to meeting your trousseau, which I expect will be very fine indeed and much better than you're used to. You must say now what you will have and then you will be ready for it when the time comes for him to ask about it.'

'A great hat with peacock feathers!' I cried.

We talked of clothes and fripperies of love, and who we should like as our sweethearts, until the sun was dropping in the sky and we came in to supper with reddened cheeks and shining eyes.

'Oh to be young again!' cried Lady Shadforth.

That night I could not sleep and when I finally drifted off, my dreams were all of running, and never being able to get back home.

# XVIII

# DINNER

*In which we dine en famille and I am perturbed*

I had been betrothed for a whole two months long, when Mother announced that Lord Tyringham would be joining us for dinner, to which Reginald let out a great 'Wooooooo!' and made me blush, and my father told him to get on with his conjugating, for he had not taken to languages as I had, and did it very ill indeed.

I had a pair of new gowns, for we had had the dressmaker make up dresses for my courting, and I had new stockings and slippers too, and Mother bade Mary help me quickly put them on, and tidy my hair, for Tyringham had sent word he was arriving at noon.

My sweetheart had a pinched look about his face when he came into the parlour and wished us all how we did: he was chilled from the ride, he said; the wind was bitter and had whipped about his neck. My mother and father murmured their platitudes, and I dropped my curtsey, to which he came and took my hand and kissed it at the wrist, leaving a small wet mark that I wiped on my skirts.

In honour of our guest, a great fire blazed in the hall, and soon Tyringham's cheeks were as rosy as our own. He did not seem to favour the heat: as we sat at table, passing dishes and being served by Lisbet (who had washed her apron for the occasion and was much given to bobbing), Tyringham set about a great series of scratchings, at his periwig and his face, and twitching in his clothes, which I thought to be his finery, for they were different to what I had seen him in before.

He had wide petticoat breeches and a long waistcoat, but it was plain dark cloth, and without gilt threading, I thought it very drab, and his boots had great buckles, though they were not jewelled, but of a fine wrought silver. Father, confessing that being above five-and-thirty he did not follow modes in the slightest, said he looked very well today, and asked after his tailor. I think Tyringham saw me smiling into my sleeve then, so I coughed to cover it and sipped at my cup of mum, which I had in place of wine, for I had discovered it from Grisella's brother, who drank it at home like it was ale.

Our meal seemed to go on for many hours, for Eliza had been up all night cooking every dish she had a recipe for and had filled the larder with sugared concoctions and hot spiced pies. We had fried oysters, boiled carp, chine of veal and buttered apple tart, but Eliza mistrusted French cooking, and so there was not a kickshaw or fricassee to be seen. I thought all of it very bland and some of it cold, and I blushed to taste it all, for what Lord Tyringham might think of us. I exchanged glances with Mother, who whispered for Lisbet, and she hurried out of the room with a red face, and everything else came up hot.

As Mother had instructed me, I sat at table very meekly, speaking only when I was spoken to, for Father and Tyringham's conversation was mostly very dull and of war and of the King and of men that I did not know. I stole glances at Tyringham as he spoke and saw that he often had a frown creased across his forehead, and that he shook his cuffs out before cutting into the mutton, ate with his mouth open on one side, and made a liquid noise as he chewed. My betrothed, too, had a habit of wiping his moustaches between courses and I saw that his chin quickly became shiny with gravy. When the calf's-head pie came out, my Lord looked at it disdainfully and scattered anchovies all over his cheese curd-cake.

I was spooning potatoes into my mouth in a scornful way when I felt Tyringham's eyes upon me. Pale and toadish they were, swivelling about from me to my parents' chatter, and I thought them very bulbous and yellow-looking in the candlelight. He had hair creeping out of his collar and up his thin white neck and there were little pearls of sweat clustered at his temples. His periwig was coming uncurled. I looked at my plate.

Midway through the feast, Father excused himself from the table. I thought he had gone to piss in his pot, but he came back with a little bow and a proud look upon his face, bearing a jug of tea, a dish of which was served to Tyringham with a flourish, while Father told his favourite tale of how he got it and how much it cost.

'You will like this, Ursula, for I have heard it at Court,' Tyringham said, making a small bow at me over his cup. 'Queen Catherine takes her tea with cream and sugar lumps as sure remedy against the sweating sickness.'

This set Mother's jaw hanging open and her ringing all the bells on the table to get some cream brought up from the kitchen, but there was only milk.

Tyringham set about asking me many polite questions, in his rumbling voice, about who were my friends and what I did, my mother prompting me with sharp little pinches to talk of my embroidery and my singing, as we had practised. I said I liked to read and to write, and my mother frowned at this, saying:

'Ursula reads the Bible and *Foxe's Martyrs* very well.'

'And my almanac, every day – and I have been reading plays – and writing them too,' I added.

Mother's face twitched.

'Do you watch the stars, Tyringham?' said my father, sloshing hock into his glass. He was becoming merry, as he only did with guests, for he didn't usually take much wine, believing it bad for the constitution.

'Ursula was born at the time of the great comet. But happily, she has turned out quite auspicious and is a very good girl indeed.' He chuckled at this, raising his glass to me.

'The comet brought the plague – and the fire, 'tis well known,' said my mother. And then seeing my father's face, she added: 'But we were blessed that our eldest girl came to us with it besides.'

I felt Lord Tyringham's eyes upon me for a moment, then he laid his spoon down and said: 'It is my belief we would all do well to better heed the teachings of the bishops over the astrologers and apothecaries who make much mischief with their charms and chantings.'

'Aye,' said my father evenly. 'Aye.'

The quaking pudding was brought in at last (it was runny and had not enough rosewater) and I felt him watching me again as I dipped into it with my sugar-biscuit. I lowered my lashes and shifted in my seat.

'Do you like pudding, sir?' I tried, in a jovial tone.

'As well as I might,' he said, flicking his eyes away.

As we all made to leave the room, Tyringham came close to me and, giving his thanks for my company, touched my hand. Then, with both Mother and Father's backs turned to the doorway, he slipped his fingers up my arm, and, so gently it made me shiver, tickled at my wrist, and then my forearm, and caressed me all the way to my elbow, where he found my sleeve, and tried to force himself into it, but he found he could go no further, and let me go.

I, who had been frozen to the floor, stared at him with a thudding heart and shook my arm away but he only chuckled and made some riposte to Father, and went with him to the library, for they had been talking of the New World, and needed the atlas.

I said to Mother: 'Did you see him touch my arm? He stroked it most strangely and tugged at my dress.'

Mother raised her eyebrows. She looked at the ground. She coughed. Then she said:

'There is not time for acting the dolt, Ursula. Go into the parlour now, we will have some music.'

'I don't feel like singing,' I said.

She pushed me out of the room, but she did it very gently.

# XIX

✤

# DIFFICULTIES

*In which I am faced with many troubles*

❧❦❧

## HERE BE THE

## MOSTE SECRETE

## DIARY

### OF

### U. FLIGHT

### 1680 A.D.

*Knowe Thyselfe*

## MAY

### 10<sup>th</sup>

'Tis now but three MONTHS – there I have written it down – 'til
I am wed. Some days my fingers quake to think of it, others I feel a
wriggling in my body. Grisella says it is heart fluttering and a lover's
complaint, but it is not a feathered, bird-like thing, but a squirming
sensation, more like a fish; like my innards have been twisted about.

### 13<sup>th</sup>

HE came to call again today and we walked out of doors although
it looked like rain. Mother did not send Mary to follow me this time
and he gave me a posy he had bound up from his garden and said he

could not wait for me to walk in it and pick the blooms with my fair fingers! He took my hand in his, and called me sweetheart, and told me, with a few little coughs, that he thought me very pretty and he was impatient to be husband and wife together. I was nervous at this, but he did not notice and told me about his mother who wants so very much to meet me, and his sister, Sibeliah, who says we will be bosom chums!

### 15*th*

I am having a daily posset of valerian and geranium and other pungent things from Goodsoule that I know not what they are, but it is for my nerves. Today Mary came in and told me not to get up for it was an inauspicious day and no good would come of anything and so we lay together talking of my wedding gown. Father has taken the ague and goes about coughing into his kerchief.

### 20*th*

Mother says I must put my almanac down and nothing will come of poring over it. I have been trying to ascertain what might happen in my first few weeks of marriage. The weather will be stormy, then fair, then wet. September is certain to be fine, and there are many godly days for romance then. We might walk about the grounds of the Hall, with his hand about my waist, as I have seen lovers do.

### 24*th*

Grisella and I have been talking of the marriage bed and how I may bear it. I do not want to be hurt, but Grisella says that is the point. She watches the animals on the farm and says none of them seem to mind it much. She says the male gets away as soon as possible after the act. I think I would like it if Tyringham went away – the idea of sleeping in a bed with him is too horrible. Father looking very ill at dinner and took little food: the ague will not leave him, though he has slept every night with the window shut fast. Goodsoule says it is the worst time of year for miasmas, which will come down the chimney if they cannot come in at the door. I hope I shall not catch it; for I do not like to be unwell.

### 30*th*

I told Goodsoule about the worsening of Father's cough and she has made him a remedy that will surely cure him. It has liquorice and willow bark and fennel, which, all things combined together, is a sure remedy for afflictions of the lungs. I went to his chamber (he has now taken to his bed) and showed him what I had brought – I had a little pot covered with a cloth. 'Oh my Ursula,' he said, reaching to stroke my head, and his hand felt hot and clammy as he did it. 'My nurse has come to cure me and I suppose I must do as she says.' He took the cup from me and threw it back with a brave sort of look, complaining after that it was most bitter (I did not tell him about the catgut or the weasel tongue, for I thought he would not have it if he knew). After, I began to read to him a little from *The Mistaken Husband*, doing all the parts, but he said his head was aching and he would sleep and so I went away.

## JUNE

### 5<sup>th</sup>

A dull day. Went out walking with Muff dancing at my skirts, but she would bark so, and so I sent her home again.

### 7<sup>th</sup>

Since Father took ill, Reginald has become very naughty; he has been shouting about the house, when Mother has asked us to be quiet for Father's sake; he will not stop teasing Percival and he was caught by Mary pulling at the stable cat's tail and he got a scratch for his efforts which serves him right. I took him by the hand and tried to scold him, but he twisted it away from mine and went off singing a rude ditty about doing a po' in the pot.

### 12<sup>th</sup>

Found Mother crying by the backstairs. She pressed me to her. 'My daughter,' was all she said. I find myself most given to weeping.

### 15<sup>th</sup>

I have a strange feeling that will not leave me – as if something heavy is pressing on my back. It is hard to breathe deeply, and instead of dozing until the sun is up, I wake before the dawn most mornings, straining my ears for Father's wheezing.

### 19<sup>th</sup>

Father is took much worse and is feverish and so Mother sent for Mr Meek, who has the apothecary shop at Oakingham. He trotted in, a stout fellow in a tricorn hat, and set about emptying a great case of vials and philtres. After feeling my father's feet and looking at his ears, he declared him bound up with choler and, the moon being safely in Pisces, an advantageous phase for the letting of blood, purged him a little, for it seems he is hot with humours and that is the only remedy. My father's skin was deathly pale as the instrument was inserted into the soft flesh of his inside-arm, and he grunted a little as the blood began to flow and pour into the flagon Mr Meek had brought for the purpose. Mother had to look out of the window and was breathing very heavy, but I was curious to see the insides of my father, which were red and sharp-smelling, though I was sorry that it pained him. Afterwards, Mr Meek said Father had bled very well and would be cured within the week, but though he smiled at me weakly and said he felt brighter, he looked to me very much worse, and he has been drowsing ever since, while Mother paces about the hall, wondering aloud if the man was not a quack.

## 21$^{st}$

With my father in his bed there is a void in the house. I cannot run to him with my questions: why does Muffy turn before she sits? What should I read next? What bird is that? – as once I did. I go often to the Goodsoules', for it comforts me, and they do not mind my sulks.

## 24$^{th}$

A message from Tyringham, who has heard of Father's sickness, and an offer to send his own physician, who cured his mother of the small-pox. Mother said he might as well come. I sent back to Tyringham and went in to tell Father of the doctor's coming, and held his hand, but it was burning hot, and he seemed not to know me, his breathing very laboured, with a sort of whistle that I did not like. A strange tangy smell hung in the air, and so I sprinkled some lavender water on the bedsheets, but he did not rouse. I write this with my candle burning as I cannot sleep and lie awake praying to God in heaven that my father get better soon.

## 29$^{th}$

It took four days for the doctor to come, by which time Father was very yellowish-looking and with flickering eyelids, and much quieter than before. Mother and Joan and I take turns to mop his brow, as he is very hot, and the scars of his blood-letting bright and burning to the touch, the bad odour much stronger and sharper now. Doctor

Pinknaye is a grave sort of man with a long white beard and an eye-glass. He sent all of us away while he examined my father and then called for Mother who went in and closed the door. The little ones and I waited outside, Percival clamouring to go in and give Papa a kiss, Catherine very quiet. After a little while I heard Mother give a great cry, and I took them away to the nursery, despite Reginald kicking at my shins and screaming that he would not, all the while feeling sick and shaky in the limbs myself, for I knew in my heart that the news was not good and afraid to hear it from my mother.

### 30<sup>th</sup>

I find that I fall to weeping at the slightest provocation. This I do in secret so that Mother will not hear and be more distressed, for her eyes are always red, and the hollows beneath them so deep and grey that I am greatly afeard she will take ill herself.

## JULY

### 2<sup>nd</sup>

My father will not live. The doctor says he is too weak, and has something on his lungs. His poor lungs, which whistle so. They are infected with bile. I do not want him to die. I do not want him to die. Oh God in heaven, save my blessed father. Oh Jesu, I will do anything. I will be good all my days and say my prayers every night if he live. I will be a wholly obedient wife to Tyringham and agree with his prating and simper and curtsey and let him touch my arm. Oh please God. Oh please God.

### 3<sup>rd</sup>

My mother told me yesterday the doctor said had we got him sooner he might have effected a cure. I could have wrung his fat neck with my hands, but he had already gone off on horseback, fortified by our bread and ale, so I made do with pounding my pillows and screaming into them so that no one might hear me.

### 5<sup>th</sup>

My father labours. Mother is took to her bed, she has sat up with him all the night long, and only went away when Joan came in at cock-crow. I sat by his bed watching his chest rise and fall and took his hand and petted it, and told him of the goings on of the house and how we all wished him well and he had the prayers of the Blacklocks and the Shadforths and Rector Thistlethwaite besides, who has written to the Bishop to get the monks at the case. I asked him to get up soon so we could finish my lesson on Pythagoras, for I was getting on very ill without his instruction. Catherine came in then and we sang him a lullaby, but though his eyelids flickered, he did not open them. It is very hot today: there were bright little blue-tits on the branches of the sycamore tree outside his chamber window, twittering a gay sort of song, as if all were well and good in the world, but it is not.

### 7th

This is what it is to have a heavy heart. I feel that I cannot bear the pain of what must come, and pray every night to Jesu that he will take my cup of suffering away from me and bring about a miracle. I shall pray every hour on the hour, for it cannot do harm, and there is nothing I would not do, if it would bring my father back to health.

### 9th

The Reverend Whale came and gave my father the last rites, we children all on our knees at his side and Joan and Goodsoule and Mary too. The good priest says we must sing him on his blessed journey but I cannot give him up to God. O my poor father!

### 13th

I do not want my father to go, but I do not want him to suffer, as I know he does. Last night I crept into his chamber to sit with him – Mother drowsing in the chair, and I held his hand, so thin and cool it is now, the veins purple-blue. It is like the hand of a much older man. 'You must not stay for us, Father,' I whispered in his ear. 'You must go to God now for he calls you back to Him.' My voice broke with the effort of this; the tears rolled down my face. But he did not stir, and Goodsoule came in, and sent me to my bed.

### 14th

~~My fa~~
~~He has~~
My father has gone to God. My mother was with him and he did not rouse, but went away to Glory before the sun came up. I woke up to a great wailing, and found his chamber door flung open, and all the servants in the hall, and he lying quite still, the little dancing

dapples of sunlight on his hand and pillow being strange with the set of his face; the sombre feeling in the room, as if the very air was heavy. He did not look much like my father any more – I think his soul had taken flight and gone to heaven, to live with the angels. I crushed his hand to my heart and bent over him and put my arm around his body and wept my heart out on his still and silent chest.

## XX

# MARRIAGE

*In which I go to church*

The morning of my wedding dawned chill and bright and the sun made rippled diamond shapes on the floor. Tonight I would be in Tyringham's house, in his chamber and he my master in all things, for all my days hence... I lay abed, shivering beneath the coverlet. I would not get up; not yet. I often liked to stay in bed these days, for now Father had gone from us, the feeling in our household had changed – and there was little to get up for without my lessons. Mother had receded into herself and become even quieter than she was before, and even the children, it seemed, played less rambunctiously than they had done, and the house felt sombre and strange for it.

Goodsoule and Mary came in and kissed me awake and put me in my gown of blue and gold: a heavy, brocaded thing that chafed me at the neck and wrists. I had blue silk stockings and my mother's old lace garters against the Evil Eye and my high-heeled shoes were very fine, embroidered with silver and gold thread, and with a buckle set with pearls. I sat on the stool as Goodsoule uncurled the rags from my hair. When I looked into her face there were tears shining in her eyes.

'Oh my Ursula,' said she. 'You have been a daughter to me. And you to wed so young! I thought to have you for some years yet.'

She wiped her eyes with her hands. Red, rough hands I knew so well. They had taken me by the nose when I was naughty and stroked my poor, hot head in fever.

'And it has pleased God to take your father, but though he cannot walk you to the church door, he will watch you from above, my sweet, and give you his blessing from up on high.'

I could not answer her. Something had risen in my throat and lodged there, and would not go down. We three of us pressed our heads together and wept.

I was primped and preened most fully, when Lisbet ran up to say that it was time, and Mother waiting in the hallway for me, and growing ever-more impatient for our departure to the church.

'Thank ye, Lisbet,' I said, getting up, 'but if I cannot dally on my wedding day of all days, then I do not know when I might.'

I went quickly past them onto the landing and slipped down the backstairs and along the servants' corridor to my father's study. I turned the handle and pushed open the old oak door, as I had so many times before. The frightening silence; the chill of the unused room on my skin. There were only a few ashes now, in the grate, and the books and papers on my father's desk were all neatly stacked in piles, as they had never been when he was alive. I went over to them, drew up my old low stool and leant on the arm of his chair, now cool to the touch, and covered in a film of dust. I laid my head down and wept there for the loss of him, and for the loss, too, of my whole childhood, for I knew now I must go and be a grown-up, and I did not know how I would do it.

By the time we set off for the church the sun had gone in and the sky was grey and heavy-looking, the birds flittering about in the branches of the trees and chirping as loud as I had ever heard them. Blue Boy was led to the mounting block and I smiled to see him in my gloom, for Mary and Catherine had decked him with flowers as a wedding gift and he had cornflowers and daisies and lavender wound about his reins and threaded in his mane. He seemed to think himself very fine indeed, picking up his feet and tossing his head up high at every passer-by as we made our way in procession down the path to the church. I found that I had become insensible to my surroundings, even as all the villagers came out of their cottages to smile at me and wish me much joy –

I could do little but lift my hand up towards them. There was a distracting thought, too, that swirled about my mind: should I still have to marry if Father had lived? For the idea had descended that I might have changed his mind – he was a reasonable man, in the face of reasoned argument. Mother had seemed immovable though, as she was in all things now, insisting that everything must continue exactly as it had before. There was safety in that for her, I felt – a refuge from the painful novelty of widowed life. But if Father had lived, it might not have come to this.

My hands had grown shaky and the palms quite damp with sweat before we had reached the church gate, and as Reginald helped me dismount (he did it very ill), I caught my foot in the stirrup and fell against Blue Boy's flank, dragging my gown in the mud in the process, and twisting my foot right out of my shoe. Then they all went before me, and left me alone before the dim portal to the church, save for Reginald, for he was walking me in, in my father's place, though he did not much want to do it, and had whined at my mother until she threatened him with the whip.

Though I knew this was the first time I should lay eyes on my new relations, my mind was a swirling fog as I made my way up the aisle: the rustle of my heavy gown; the click of my heels on the tiles of the floor echoing loudly in my ears. I could not take in who was in the congregation, and afterwards had only a faint impression of a woman with a sharp little face beneath a great Puritan coif that was the fashion of more than five-and-twenty years before, and the reedy girl beside her, who wore a cloud of flaxen hair so far forward on her face, she was little more than a nose.

At the altar, Tyringham was waiting, grim-faced and stiff in his wedding clothes, and when I got to him, he first gripped my arm, then took my cold hand in his, and I felt that his palm too was moist with sweat.

When we knelt together, I found he smelt of clove powder and ale. He did not let go of my arm, as the priest began the marriage service, but stroked the fabric of my sleeve, his breath smelling very sour as it puffed onto my face. I tried to smile at him, for my own heart was thumping wildly in my chest, but he seemed not to notice, and I took it to be piety, for he kept his head bowed very low during the prayers and murmured his 'amens' in a fervent voice. Before I knew what I was about, I was plighting my troth, and the priest had pronounced us wed.

There was a long sermon then, about women submitting themselves unto their husbands and having chaste conversation and a mild and quiet spirit – I looked all this up later in *The Book of Common Prayer*, it having little impression at the time, for I was growing mightily bored at the length of the speech and there were pains in my legs from the kneeling, as well as a prickling of my skin at my being the object of so many pairs of eyes, at the thought of which my armpits grew ever wetter, while sweat beadlets ran freely down my back.

What a strange and heady thing it was to hear the organ strike up for me, and the congregation singing as I drifted out of the church doors a married woman on the arm of my new husband. My wedding ring felt strange and tight upon my finger, but it looked very well there I thought, and I turned my hand in front of my face to admire it, as we went up the path.

'Take it off a while, and look inside it, wife,' said my new husband, who was holding me very close.

I twisted the gold band off with a little difficulty, for my fingers had swollen in the dark, dead air of the church. But I held it upon my palm and saw he had had it engraved, like a poesy ring. On the inside of the band it said in sharp, bold letters:

NO JOYE IN LYFE LIKE A VERTUOUS WYFE

'I composed it myself,' he said, watching me push the ring back on my finger. 'And you shall never take that off again. And so we will have great joy, with God's help, sweet wife.'

And with that he gathered me up and kissed me on the mouth, while his hot hands roved about my waist. I held my arms stiffly at my sides, not knowing what else to do. His lips were thin and wet against my own, and the taste of his mouth was bitter and strange, and I thought of Samuel then, and had a little pang that it was not he I was kissing. I felt my husband's tongue flick around my teeth, and wondered what he was about, but waited patiently, with my mouth opened for him to complete his investigations.

Just then came a great crack of thunder, and the heavens opened, which made him withdraw and pull me to the trees, but not before great sheets of summer rain plastered my wedding hairstyle over my ears and drenched my gown right through to the skin, where it would chafe me for the rest of the day.

❀

How strange it was to see my dear Bynfield Hall decorated for our wedding breakfast! We were to spend the night here, and ride on to my new home in the morning, and I gazed with brimming eyes at the long table laid to dine, the silverware all polished for the occasion, and the pretty garlands of twisted ivy that hung from the rafters, for the hours with my family were dwindling and I knew I must savour every sweet moment. I supped cockscombs with pansy, and picked at my oysters, in a silver dish. I had sweetbreads with oranges, I chewed at boiled pike and pineapple. I swallowed all with a tight smile, tasting none of it, for I could not feel joy while the white face of my husband flickered before me in the candlelight.

'You make a very pretty bride, wife,' said he, at length. I did not answer. He forked the mutton into his mouth. 'I am lucky to have such a sweet young maid as you,' he said. 'And though I am some twenty years your elder, I hope you can learn to look upon me with some semblance of love.' He peered at my face to see how I took it. 'I will try to be a good husband.'

'And I a good wife,' said I.

The musicians had struck up, and when the dancing began he took my hand and led us in a courtly passepied, at which everyone cheered, and when it ended, he steered me into the shadows of the hall, his hand around my waist.

'And now I think we will slip away,' he said in low tones. 'I will send for a flagon of sack, and we will have it in my chamber.'

'But the dancing is not yet done, sir,' I said, pretending to laugh.

I shook my curls and tried to lean out of his embrace. He pulled me closer, tightening his grip. His breath was on my neck, then his wet mouth. His cheek was whiskery and rough. The tendrils of his periwig fell against my face. I looked for my mother over his shoulder.

'You will have ribbons and trinkets and songbirds in cages,' he murmured. 'You will have fine clothes sent from Paris and jewels set in Venice.'

'You are kind,' I said, but my voice shook a little, and he heard it, for he loosened me, and was panting.

'But you are afraid of me?'

'I – I would not leave the dancing.'

'Hush, now. We will go up, but you may return to the dancing, later, if you wish.'

He had me by the arm and walked me out the door and up the stairs. There was silence now between us, just the whir of my gown and the groan of the stairs as we went up, up, up to begin our married life.

# PART

## *The Second*

# I

# LOVING

*In which I enjoy my honeymoon*

The
# RELUCTANT
# BRIDE

---

## *A COMEDY*

*O mihi praeteritos referat si Jupiter annos – Virgil*

---

Acted by *the* DUKE'S MEN *at*

THE HAYMARKET THEATRE

---

*WRITTEN BY*

LADY URSULA ~~FLIGHT~~ TYRINGHAM

*Dawn. A grand chamber with a canopied bed. The sun is a slanted orange square on the claret-coloured bed curtains. The curtains twitch, and a small white hand is thrust out. The hand wrenches back the curtains — it belongs to a* GIRL, *who is pale in her creamy shift. She wears a nightcap tied over her curl-papers. The* MAN's *head on the pillow beside her is dark. He snores, his mouth a slack, dark hole below his courtier's moustache. There is spittle on his cheek. The girl looks at him; sighs; then suddenly and violently sneezes.*

GIRL: Ah-shoooo!

MAN: [*Starting up from the bed mid-snore*] Whuh?

GIRL: Forgive me!

MAN: Mmm. Wife.

*He stretches out his arm and drags her to him.*

There now. My girl.

*She grimaces in his embrace. He strokes her hair. She twitches.*

Good morrow, wife. How did you sleep in my great bed?

GIRL: Well, not too badly. It was odd being in bed with a man. I have not tried that before, for as you know, Mother does not believe in bundling. I had a queer dream...

MAN: Hmm, let me see. Was it about... a handsome prince and a pretty young maid?

GIRL: Nay, sir. It was that I was a famous actress 'pon the stage and was taking my curtseys while all the handsome gallants in the stalls threw yellow roses at my feet. And in the dream I had writ the play as well as acted in it and even the King stood up in his box to shout 'Brava' for the finest lady playwright in England.

MAN: It must be all of that curd-cake you took at dinner. For I fancy whenever I eat it, I have a cauchemar.

GIRL: Aye.

MAN: Well now, Lady Tyringham, my sweet new bride, I drifted off last night being so fatigued from the extravagances of our wedding day. But I find myself quite awake now.

*He twists his body, pressing it to hers.*

GIRL: Husband?

MAN: Aye?

GIRL: I thought yesterday I heard you say to your mama that fornication was a sin. Did you not say that?

MAN: Eh? Aye, aye, but 'tis not if it be done in matrimony.

GIRL: Have you not fornicated before now then? I am trepidatious then, for I hoped you'd know what you were doing.

MAN: Why I – of course I have. 'Tis different for men.

GIRL: I have heard that it is so, in all things. But faith, husband, I do not remember the part which says fornication is a sin only to women. I will have to look at my Bible again and apply myself more rigorously to the commandments.

MAN: [*Annoyed*] 'Tis not said expressly in the Bible – but 'tis known widely that it be so. I cannot explain it beyond saying 'tis the way of the world. But you are a child still, and would not know it.

GIRL: Aye, I am but fifteen years old.

MAN: You have a woman's wit and way of twisting things about that belies your years.

GIRL: Thank you, sir.

MAN: 'Twas not a compliment! Now. [*Resuming his nuzzling*] Oh, my lambikin. Oh my pretty, silken rabbit.

GIRL: I must have had it wrong from Mother.

MAN: [*Breaking off*] What?

GIRL: She said that I must allow no man to conquer me that has not first conquered my heart. For 'tis not godly, without love, Mother says. And Jesu will look down and punish they who do not commune together in the spirit of true affection – with an empty womb and a useless, shrivelled seed...

MAN: Why, but I have! Have I not wooed thee with the softest tongue? Have I not given thee trinkets – and billets-doux – and jewels? Gad – have I not married thee and vowed to cleave by thy side?

GIRL: Aye, but it has not worked.

MAN: It has not *worked*?

GIRL: Gad, I do look upon you with a kind eye, but I do not yet feel that a spark has been lit... or a fire started in my belly, such as might engulf me in a torrent of molten-hot flames – my mother told me there should be such a fire before I, young girl as I am, consent to submit to ardour. [*Aside*] 'Tis all a lie, I have read all this in plays!

MAN: Why, I have never heard the like. Away with this silly modesty, and let us do our duty as husband and wife. The marriage is not legal without it.

GIRL: With all the guests who came in with us last night and threw the stocking and caroused and bore witness to our bedding?

MAN: 'Tis not enough.

*He begins to kiss her neck.*

GIRL: I have heard it said that flattery often helps in these matters.

MAN: [*Breaking off again*] Flattery?

GIRL: Aye, and perhaps you should attempt it, for who knows, it may work to soften me, as tallow does a rough and inflexible hide.

MAN: The Devil!

GIRL: I will lie here like this, husband, until you have thought of it.

*She serenely closes her eyes, folds her hands.*

MAN: [*Muttering*] I do not see why – uh – why...

*She does not move.*

MAN: Fine then, have it your way... Oh... your beauty. Gad, I am – struck quite dumb with it.

GIRL: [*Nodding with closed eyes*] 'Tis plain.

MAN: But it also – it fires my soul.

GIRL: [*Opening one eye*] Go on.

MAN: Your face – it – it is so very pretty. And it – your face I mean – would launch a...

GIRL: Mmm?

MAN: ... hundred... barges.

GIRL: That cannot be it.

MAN: Well then, I am a – a slave to your wondrous charms... I am wretched with love. A poor, poor wretch.

GIRL: [*Wriggling*] How so?

MAN: I've got it! Uh, would – would I were a sailor charting the blue seas of your limpid eyes...

GIRL: Yes... it may be working.

MAN: ... and your voice is... music. And so sweet. Like the singing of a choir of angels!

GIRL: [*Burping*] I beg your pardon. I had a great slab of pie at dinner and it seems it has come back to haunt me. Do continue – I am feeling much more malleable already.

MAN: I worship at the heavenly altar of your celestial body! I will let my burning kisses fall down onto your lips like hot rain!

GIRL: [*Aside*] Everything I have been taught suggests that is impossible.

MAN: Let me be your dog, I will lie on you!

GIRL: Oh husband, I find my heart going pit-a-pat. But it may well be the talk of pie.

MAN: Wife!

> *He pulls her to him. Pushes her arm back above her head.*

GIRL: First, swear that you will have none other but me.

MAN: I did so on the Holy Book. Yesterday. Now let us get on with it.

> *His arms disappear beneath the bedclothes.*

GIRL: Wait! For I am afraid, now I think 'pon it, that I cannot now see the advantage to it.

MAN: Advantage! Advantage or not, it does not signify for I have the law behind me in this.

GIRL: The law was writ by men and so it does not surprise me that you have it behind you. What do I have behind me but this bolster – and an invisible army of a thousand angry women with gnashing teeth and hellfire in their eyes? [*Pause*] But, Gad, I suppose we must try it – for I have always wanted to see heaven.

MAN: [*In the midst of mounting her*] Heaven, child? I hope it will not be that bad.

GIRL: Nay, it has just come back to me now – for I have heard [*Aside*] or rather, read – that that is the advantage of the sport of love. That the couple may reach such a state of earth-shattering joy that they may – at climax of their sheet-shaking, at the peak of their princum-prancum, at the crescendo of their frenzied feverish fadoodling – actually *see* heaven. And in truth I am excited, for it must surely be a better sight than Wiltshire. And so let us begin. [*Murmuring*] Oh it will be so beautiful. I shall tell all my friends that I have seen it and exactly what it looked like.

MAN: I'm not sure that's a good idea.

*Curtain*

⚜

# II

# DOMESTICITY

*In which I spend a quiet afternoon with my husband*

To stand in a field on Tyringham land was to note the vastness, the emptiness of the landscape. It rolled away in all directions: dark green and pale green and brown; unrelieved by a pathway or a dwelling – save for a tumbledown shepherd's hut that the weather had reduced over time to squat heaps of stones. On the brow of a hill, a line of elms had submitted to autumn and become jagged black things in which rooks hopped about the branches, croaking to one another before wheeling about the sky on their endless mysterious errands.

To stand in such a field three months after my wedding day was to be in need of a tricorn and cloak, or get drenched to the skin, for a great storm had lashed the countryside, and though it was no longer thunderous, a deluge of rain carried about on the current had filled every furrow with murky water. Mist rose up from the dark slickened grass and through the haze the field-mud looked black. The hedgerows trembled and rippled in the wind, their leaves turned inside out. Some were torn off and floated, across the hills and far away, to freedom.

From the vantage point of the field, it was possible to perceive a large hole in the hedgerow, flanked by mud-patched grass. To clamber through this hole was to find oneself ankle-deep in the soft earth of a flowerbed, on the far side of which was the edge of a winding gravel path. This path, when followed eastwards, wound through a little copse of trees and past an ornamental fountain, before skirting the side of a great maze with vast, brick-like bushes. To hurry through the green tunnel of a bowered walkway, then, was to emerge breathless, wet, mud-flecked, at the back of a grand brick house, three storeys high, its parapets flanked by proud stone bustards perched on chequered shields: this was the seat of three Tyringham generations. This was Turvey Hall.

Gazing up at this noble edifice one might observe then – through rain-blurred vision – rows of windows with rippled, lead-crossed glass, one lighted amongst them with a figure seated at it, a green and gold smudge. Coming closer to the window would let you see what I see now: a pretty girl in a green gown, her light hair pinned up on both sides, a row of kiss curls on her furrowed forehead. She has a book in her hand. Her skin is pale. Every now and then as she turns the pages, she sighs. There is a downturned look about her little face, despite her gay clothes, and the lushness of the window drapes, and the bright flickering of the light behind her, which can only be the product of dozens of candles, in chandeliers, sconces, candelabras... the whole room is awash with light. She looks up from the book and stares out into the darkness. She frowns. Behind her someone is approaching. A man's voice, deep and low:

'Ursula! I said to myself you were like to be reading again – and here you are.'

My husband came over to me, and looked pointedly at my little book, which was bound in pigskin, and ugly-looking. I shut it with a clap, and gazed up at him. He petted my head and pulled at my curls. I found myself shy of his nearness, and the smell of him – the nutmeg of his wig powder and the leather of his boots. We had lain together last night and he had pressed his hot skin on mine and called me sweetheart, but now, here in the daylight, it seemed we were different people, and I could hardly look on his face. I felt myself blushing red at the thought of what we had done.

'How sweet you look here in the window, wife.'

I put the book down.

'Thank you, sir.'

I had not got used to his compliments and still did not know how to make my reply. I had discovered, too, that they often seemed to rouse his passions, and found the less I said in response, the less likely it was that the conversation would lead to lovemaking. I shifted in my seat.

'Will we converse a little, wife? Or shall you play at the harpsichord to amuse me?' he said. 'Mama writes from my brother's house that it will do you good to keep at your music practice and I concur, for the playing of melodies is improving for the female mind.'

'I could read aloud to you a little, husband, if it will please you?' I said, picking up the book. 'This was a wedding gift from my Aunt Phyllis, and very pretty verses they are too. Shall I speak one?'

He grunted at this, and went and sat himself in his favourite chair, a lumpen brocade thing that was ragged and patchy with moth. I shrank from it myself, for it had been his father's, who had died in agonies of the plague.

I smiled at my husband and began:

> A lonely maid sat on a hill
> And crowned herself with flowers.
> She waited for her lover there,
> And sang to pass the hours.
>
> The sky grew dark, the rain came down
> And still he came not to her.
> She tossed aside her sodden crown,
> And sheltered in the bower.
>
> She waited on, she called his name,
> She shivered and she moaned,
> At dusk she saw he would not come,
> And took herself off home.
>
> She woke at dawn with burning skin,
> At noon they started praying,
> She died alone as the sun went in,
> Still murmuring his name.

She's buried in the churchyard now,
Her grave grows thick with roses,
And hopeful maids with lovelorn eyes
Anoint it with their posies.

'What think you?' I said, closing the book quickly so he would not see my handwriting.

He scratched at one of his ears. 'Yes, yes... Tolerable stuff, I suppose. Though having no taste for poetry, I cannot rightly say.'

'Is it not pretty – and sad?' I pressed.

'Why yes,' he said. 'I suppose it is.'

'A love of verses is a thing that can be nurtured, as my father often said, when he taught me literature,' I said brightly. 'We shall read together and make a poet of you yet! You have a volume of Dryden in the library – I spied it hidden away on the highest shelf.'

'I do not much wish to study poetry,' said my husband, a little stiffly. 'Nor recite Greek verbs or Latin conjugations, nor watch the skies at night when everyone should be in their beds.'

He looked past me towards the window, and I saw his jaw was working a little.

'Oh,' I said. 'Well, I am sorry. But perhaps you might teach me of all the things *you* know. I should very much like to learn about the Court, and the King's ships, and more mathematics – my trigonometry is quite pitiful – for Father had not got onto that yet when he died.' I swallowed the great lump that had grown in my throat. I knew already that a woman weeping irked my husband like no other thing. I had found that out at our wedding.

'I know too,' I added, 'that counting is a most essential part of keeping the affairs of the house in order, and balancing the books and seeing that we have money to feed and clothe us.'

'In Jesu's name, will you not speak of *money*!' he cried, in a loud voice, which startled me, and I jumped a little in my seat. 'Or mathematics or ships! None of which are your concern.' He seemed to get control of himself then, and his voice was quiet and steady as he said: 'I should like to hear music, Ursula – if you will condescend to entertain me.'

'I would not anger you, husband,' I said, for I hated to quarrel, and was learning ways to pacify him. 'I will play for you, verily.' I got up and rustled over to the harpsichord, seating myself at the stool which had been re-upholstered just for me, in damson-coloured damask, and trimmed with tassels all around. I spread my skirts out.

❀

# MY *HIDING* PLACES

## *OR*

Where I stow my writing book since my husband began a-locking
the library last week so that it is safe from the eyes of the servants
and my husband & all who would think to stop me!

🌿

1. Betwixt the mattresses on my side of the bed, under my back, near the middle. 'Tis a comfort to feel it pressing into me, at night, like a friend. Oh, sweet book of mine, thou art my only friend here!

2. On the top of my cupboard, at the back, where no one can reach, even me, save when I stand on a stool. I must pick the stool up quietly, & not drag it, else the servants will appear & ask why I'm moving the furniture, for Gad, they are nosy creatures & watch me wherever I go.

3. At the back of the parlour under the cushion at the bottom of the chaise which no one sits upon for 'tis uncomfortable and rickety – like every stick of furniture in this gloomy old house.

4. In the under-stair cupboard, inside a sack. Fie!

5. Inside the grandfather clock in the hall, which does not work, so never gets wound. Fie!

6. At the bottom of the old linen press, underneath the bedsheets which are never got out, for they are full of holes and covered with yellow stains & smell of camphor. Pooh!

7. Behind the curtain in the guest room that no one comes to, for no one is mad enough to come here. I wish they would.

# III

# SERVANTS

*In which I become accustomed to my new position*

Imet the servants of the household the day I came to Turvey Hall, a new bride with a blue silk gown and a face that was given to blushing. I pulled at my earlobes, newly pierced and threaded through with pearl drops: they were sore and hot under my fingertips. It was a bright day in late August. My wedding band flashed yellow-gold in the low afternoon sunlight as I shielded my eyes to look into the blank faces of those who had lined up in rows either side of the driveway to greet the brand-new Lady Tyringham. That was me.

The servants did not look much affected by my arrival; they were a sullen-seeming bunch, standing in the strange-shaped shadows of the house, which glowered over all who stood beside its bright brick walls. The maids whispered amongst themselves and I saw no kindness in the eyes of the cook or the kitchen wenches, who stood with grim faces and stained aprons. Tyringham took my arm in his, and spoke their names to me as we passed by them one by one, chanting the litany of Jack, Joseph, Sarah, Jane, Clara, Tizzy, Tom that I would come to know off by heart, as I did the books of the Bible, in order of rank, from my mother-in-law's butler and my husband's man right down to the boy who ran the errands. There were many more servants than we had at Bynfield, above twenty of them who toiled inside the house and many more out of it, and there was nowhere to escape from so many pairs of eyes. While we dined, they slouched against the panelled walls with downturned faces, awaiting the call for a dish of cream, a salver of buttered eggs, a fork. They were in every room of the house, it seemed, for I could not stir from my chamber without one creeping around the corner and asking me: 'Help you, my Lady?'

One of the chief sadnesses of my new married life was that I had not been permitted to bring Mary with me. In the weeks before our wedding I had asked Tyringham if she might come to live at Turvey, and be my lady there, but the answers that he gave were of the 'we shall see' variety, and my mother chided me for making demands, for fear that he would not have me after all. When I got to my new home, Tyringham told me – as we crossed over the threshold and into the darkness of the portico – that he had especially engaged me a woman, with help from his mother, who had a sharp eye for slovenliness and could spot a lazy servant from a good twenty paces. I did not know how the girl who was to be my companion could have been looked over with such an eye, for at nineteen years old, Beck was as slovenly a wench as I had ever seen, with a broad country accent, brown teeth and a strong odour of onions. She had stringy twig-coloured hair under her starched cap, and a high complexion, and knobbly hands with short stout fingers, which I saw were as rough and red as could be – they did not look like the hands of a lady's maid.

The first morning in my new home, Beck came to me, after my husband had gone off for his morning exercise, to help me with my toilet. Though I greeted her with a cheery, 'Good morrow to ye,' she only muttered 'Mm,' in return, and her curtsey was a dip so quick and shallow I barely caught it. Beck then made it plain that she had nothing but contempt for the process of my dressing, and me besides, for she hardly looked me in the face, and unlaced my frilled wrapper with a very rough tugging, holding out my skirts for me to step into with a sigh and a whistle of her teeth, which she kept up as she put on my sleeves and tightened my bodice. I sat at my dressing table and watched in the looking glass as she caught up my tortoiseshell comb and began dragging at my hair with all the grace and attention reserved for currying a mule.

'How many hairstyles do ye know?' I asked her, examining what she had done in the glass, which felt loose on my neck where it was pinned up at the back. I pushed at the curls on my forehead. 'Ought we to set these with sugar-water, for they seem likely to drop?'

She did not answer my questions, but gave a sort of shrug, and went to get the water, and took such a long time, that I had almost given her up. I was starting to feel cross by the time she came back, and took the bowl from her, and began to pat it onto my curls.

'Cook says ye cannot be having the master's sugar for your tresses,' she said, with a gust of onion, 'for he will not like it,' and she pursed her lips in an insolent way.

I was amazed at this, and said: 'Why, it's none of the cook's business what I do with my hair,' but she only shrugged again, and kicked at my chair leg with her foot.

'Would you fetch my orange-flower water,' I said, to cover my irritation, for no one had taken the trouble to unpack my trunk, and my things were still bound in their parcels. She grunted at this, and set about tearing at the bindings, and dropping things onto the floor, and I found that tears came very suddenly into my eyes, for Mary had packed for me, and lovingly bound each bundle with a ribbon, and a lavender sprig. Seizing the phial at last, Beck came over to me and banged it carelessly onto my dressing table. She stood there insolently, her mouth agape, a string of her greasy hair across her face, while I dabbed at my throat and wrists and bosom.

'Unpack my things, now, Beck,' I said, as boldly as I could, though my eyes were still brimming and my voice came out too high. She seemed to smirk to hear it, and did not make to move. I stared at her, and added: 'My husband would have things tidy and so we must respect his wishes.' This mention of her master seemed to stir her, for she began grabbing at the things in the trunk, and lifting them out, and laying them in the dresser, though she did it in a harum-scarum sort of way, and hummed a tuneless ditty all the while.

I did not get my husband alone until the evening, when we had been put to bed and the servants gone away, and our prayers all done, and then I said to him as he was rolling back the feather quilt:

'Husband, you said to come to you should there be anything I need... and there is, for I am not sure Beck will do.'

'Why, what is wrong with the wench?' he said, in the midst of pummelling the bolster. I had already observed he spent a good deal of time shifting about before laying himself down to sleep.

'Well, she does not seem... willing,' I said. 'She is not neat in her habits. And she does not know any hairstyles.' I looked to see how he was taking this, but he was still slapping at the pillow. 'I do not think she has washed beyond her elbows for above a twelvemonth.'

'Then you must point out her errors and chide her for them,' said he, 'for 'tis one of the duties of the mistress of any great house – servants must be taught to be good: they cannot know it on their own. Beck came to me with the promise of a good singing voice, and it was on that basis I engaged her, for I thought it would amuse you to hear her when the winter evenings draw in.'

'Mary could sing too, and play the tabor,' I said. 'And she was always clean and tidy besides – and she was a faithful companion to me as well as an obedient servant.'

'And?' he said, and the tone of his voice had become hard.

'Well, sir, I – I would not be lonely.'

'You shall not be,' he said, laying his head down, and pulling up the covers. 'For Mama and my sister will soon be here. And 'tis well you learn now the difference between a lady and her servants. I did not like to chastise you for it in your father's house, but now you are here 'tis best you learn. Your kind and Mary's are not meant to fraternise together, for no good can come of it. She will pull you down, or you will pull her up, and neither is right, for every creature in this world must know their place before the King – and God.'

I said nothing, though I longed to stick out my tongue at him.

'Beck has come to us with the assurance that she is a godly girl, and you must take the trouble to show her how things should be done. I am sure, with your instruction, she can learn to be just as good a lady's maid as your Mary was.'

'I suppose so,' I said.

'I am tired,' he said, and snuffed out his candle.

'Goodnight, husband,' I said, stealing my hand under the pillow to feel the reassuring presence of my little wooden bear, for she had travelled with me to my new home, a talisman of my old life to comfort me in the new one.

The very next evening I bade Beck to come to the parlour and entertain us after supper. She stood there with her red hands clasped behind her back and sang 'The Merry Rover' in a bland country voice which could carry a tune but nothing more. My husband watched her with his eyebrows furrowed and then bade her stop before she had finished.

'Get away now, Beck,' he said. 'And learn some other songs, for the Dowager does not like a street ballad and I find that I do not either.'

She slunk away with her face twisted up at the sides; whether she was apt to cry or laugh, I could not quite make out.

❧

The next morning was a fair one, and Tyringham had said after he had finished with his man of business that he might show me the grounds of the estate, and so I had put on my new bonnet. A trousseau gift from Grisella, it was trimmed with ribbons and bunches of cherries. I thought I looked very well in it, and my husband might be pleased to see me looking pretty, but he made no mention of the hat, and only nodded when he came to find me in the parlour, where I had sat myself on a low chair by the window, and was leafing through a book I had found in the library: *A Treatise Concerning Enthusiasme*. I liked the author's foreign name, but nothing more about the tome: a very dry and dull thing it was.

I shut it.

Tyringham looked down at the book in my hands. 'I see you have discovered my unlocking of the library. Did it please you?'

'Yes,' I coughed, to hide my embarrassment. 'For all books do.'

He smiled at this and sat down beside me. 'You will find nothing in there that is not suitable for the eyes of women and servants – if only they could read it.' (Here he gave a chuckle and patted my hand.) 'Mama oversaw the stocking of it and so the Tyringham library has every book a gentleman could possibly require.'

'Aye,' said I, for I did not think it politick to point out his lack of Catullus and Sophocles and Seneca and Sidney, so I simply said, 'Did your father not have a taste for ancient poets? Or Latin – or Greek?'

'Nay,' he said, with a flick of his hand. 'The barons of Tyringham have no need to shut ourselves away with the meanderings of other tongues, for our place is by the King, to advance our name, and the King is a merry man, and we do not need to chant Latin at him.'

'Tell me more of His Majesty,' I said, twisting my body towards his. 'Is he as tall and proud as they say? And what of the Queen? And of her ladies? Are they very clever and gay?'

He pressed his face into its thin-lipped smile, and told me of the King, and how he liked to play at tennis, and to hunt, and how he had a pack of little dogs with silken ears that barked around his ankles. The Queen, he said, was a quiet lady with foreign but noble ways, and he did not think much of some of her women, but he would not be drawn on why that was so.

''Tis not Her Majesty's fault,' he would only say. 'For the King overruled her.'

'And what do they like for entertainments?' said I.

'Ah,' said my husband, wagging his finger. 'Naughty child. For I know where this is leading. I shall say the King is known at the Theatre Royal in Drury Lane and the Duke's in Dorset Gardens, and there are many masques at Court, and other entertainments besides, for Rex has a good many friends, and they are all as merry as he.'

'If only I could see it,' I said, clasping my hands to my bosom. 'For I know I should like it, and I should like to see Mrs Nelly, for 'tis said she is a wise and witty woman.'

'But you never shall,' said my husband evenly, 'for a Tyringham woman's place is not in the playhouse – there are such goings on there as would discompose any God-fearing wife. And so we shall hear no more of it, but take our exercise as planned.'

Not noticing my disappointment, he took my elbow then, and led me out into the sunshine. Swallowing his chastisement of me, I smiled to see the garden, which had many fine bushes and flowers in bloom. My husband began talking of the design, which had been done by his mother when she was newly wed, and he had not liked to change, though it was outmoded he supposed. Around the path we stepped, me with my hand on my husband's arm, and he with his hand on mine, past the rows of sweet-smelling plants. I began to feel my spirits lift and a sort of happiness creep into the space under my ribs: that though my husband was a rigid man, I at least had a library, and a linnet in a cage that sang in the mornings, and these pretty gardens that I might walk in whenever I wished.

We came past a trio of great twisted yews, and stopped at an ornamental fountain with a great stone god as its centrepiece. Magnificent and terrible with his trident, the statue was dappled with green spores and flanked by cascades of flapping stone fish, from whose gaping mouths water trickled into the jade-coloured pool below.

'Why, 'tis Poseidon,' I said, dropping onto the curving stone seat, and dipping my fingers into the cool, green water. ''Twas he who drove his chariot through the waves and struck Acropolis with his spear – I'll warrant that smarted! He often took the form of a horse, which must have been very merry, for who would not love to canter now and then?' I gazed up at the statue. 'I am happy to see him here, for he reminds me of my father and the tales he told me when I was a child.' I swirled my fingers around.

'Did you not hear me?' said my husband.

'Husband?' I said.

'Do not put your hands in the water, you fool – for 'tis brackish and like to cause chills.'

I took out my fingers and wiped them on my skirts, at which he frowned.

'I was speaking of the return of Mama and Sibeliah,' he said, 'but you did not heed me with all your babbling.'

'Ah, it will give me great joy to meet them properly at last,' I said quickly, taking his arm again to placate him. 'Our interview at the wedding was too fleeting. I miss my sweet Catherine greatly, and am overjoyed that I shall have a sister again – and a mother, besides,' I added, searching his face to see if I had mollified him.

He shook me off, but his voice had softened when he said: 'And in her you shall have the best of women. So godly and so sweet is she – in her I see every good quality a lady should have. I hope you may learn what it is to be a Tyringham woman from her, and that Sibeliah may be of good influence too, and your dearest bosom friend. Mama has taken great pains with her and she is the model of good womanhood.'

'Oh aye,' I said, though I crossed my fingers behind my back. Talk of devoutness was always like to bore me, but if there was one thing I had learnt thus far of marriage, it was to always seem pliable, though inside I might rail against my condition.

Tyringham crooked his finger towards the chapel.

'Wife, it seems to be a fitting time to give thanks for our happy marriage. Let us go there together now.'

We knelt in the front pew of the empty church and Tyringham prayed aloud with his eyes fast shut that the Lord Jesu would keep us from sin and help us in our duties as a husband and wife before God. And as his voice echoed around the darkness of the room, my eyes lighted on a slant of sunshine that fell through the high mullioned window onto the altar, like a miracle from heaven, and in my head I heard myself saying over and over again, like a prayer, 'Where there is light, there is hope. Amen.'

❧

# IV

❧

# HUSBAND

*In which I note down the essentials of the man I married*

⚜

## NINETEEN FACTS ABOUT

## *MY HUSBAND,*

### LORD OSWOLD JAMES TYRINGHAM

*Fact the first:*
He has a habit when speaking of swallowing the end of sentences,
and so people that do not know him are always having to say, 'I beg
your pardon, my Lord?' 'Can you repeat that, Tyringham?' and so on.

*Fact the second:*
His skin is pale as milk, but his hair is starling-black. There is not
much of it on the top of his head, but the stuff around his shoulders
is as light and fluffy as spun sugar and lifts up in the gentlest
breeze. His periwig is extravagantly curled all over, with a row of fat
little curls on the crown which make me laugh. It lives on a block in
his dressing room, and is combed out for nits on the first Tuesday of
every month by Brignall. It came from a wigmakers called MESSRS.
TALLENTYNE & TRUNDALL, DISTAFF LA., LONDON, which I
know for 'tis printed on the box in gold lettering. The box, and the
wig, both smell of tobacco and ale and the tang of men's sweat.

*Fact the third:*
He is not often merry.

## Fact the fourth:

His father was in service to the first King Charles, and then was a gentleman to Cromwell. The family, like many, got very Puritan then, and I think have not quite shaken it off. Tyringham has been in the King's service since he was Restored and all the streets ran with wine, and my husband went and paid homage and got round the part about his papa and Cromwell, I do not know how. His official position is Master-General of the Ordnance, which means he gets supplies for the navy and army, and so he may award contracts, and has many people petitioning at him from morning 'til night.

## Fact the fifth:

He is reasonably tall, I suppose, but not so much as Father, and he is a solid-built man with a paunch, whereas Father was slim, and so am I, despite all my efforts to be fat and fashionable.

## Fact the sixth:

He does not like to bill and coo as I have seen some couples do (my aunt and uncle!), but occasionally takes my hand and bids me 'And how do you do today, madame?'

## Fact the seventh:

He is not always lusty, but I often feel his eyes roaming up and down my person. Strangely for a husband (I *think*) he has bought me articles of dress: coarse knitted hose, the ugliest pair of low-heeled shoes. The day, at his insistence, I tried these on, he became much inflamed, and had me against the wall of my chamber, rubbing at the stockings and feeling for the shoes all the while. I was blushing all afternoon, and hid away all my plain clothes, though he asks frequently where they are and I pretend I have forgotten until I can put it off no longer. I wonder if this is usual for old husbands?

## Fact the eighth:

He calls me dearheart and bunnykin, when we are in bed together, and before he is spent, but at no other time.

## Fact the ninth:

He is not fond of dogs, and refuses me a spaniel.

## Fact the tenth:

His body is carpeted all over with dark hair, with tufts rising up on his back near the shoulders, and a great drugget of it running down his front from his throat to his toes (which are squat-looking and yellow). When we lie together, I feel his bristly skin damp under my hands and recoil to touch it, though I try not to show it on my face.

## Fact the eleventh:
He will not hear of childbearing or midwives, but is keen on the getting of heirs.

## Fact the twelfth:
His favourite food is egg pie, followed by artichoke pie, followed by potage, and so he is oft complaining of stomach miasmas and a twisted gut. He spends a good while on the pot. He believes French kickshaws unsubstantial and a sweet tooth dissolute and ungodly! Despite this I cannot taper my passion for Naples biscuit, orange pudding and all kinds of fool. Fie!

## Fact the thirteenth:
He has broken two bones in his life: his forefinger, which set strangely and is now half twisted round (I do not like to look at it, especially when he crooks it at things), and his nose, on a fall from his horse. The horse escaped without a scratch and is now retired and living with a widow at Bromley.

## Fact the fourteenth:
He exercises his horse in the mornings for the King plays at sports whether fair or foul, and his courtiers have taken up the habit to please him. Some of them have taken up the King's other fancies too, my husband says, which are poesie and the playhouse and wenching, but Tyringham does not follow him in those.

## Fact the fifteenth:
He was surprised, when we met, at how grown-up I seemed in some ways but how like a child I was in others. I have pressed him to expound on this but he refuses. I told him when I met him I was afraid of him for I thought him much older than Father. He did not laugh along with me at this.

## Fact the sixteenth:
He makes his ablutions (his words) every half year in the hip bath kept in the scullery. Between that he has a curdy kind of smell and a tang to his skin, especially his hinder parts.

### Fact the seventeenth:

His father died of the last plague, in 1665. He caught it in London, after eating a dish of oysters at a tavern, and never came home again, but got locked up in the inn, and a cross put upon the door (this according to Sibeliah, who delights in the tale). Being riddled with the pestilence, his body was never brought home, but lies in a filthy pit near Bedlam.

### Fact the eighteenth:

His closest friend is a man called Master Jeremiah Malloborne who lives in London, at Cheapside, but he does not often see him, save when he goes to Court, for Malloborne has nine children and is therefore asleep by eight of the clock most evenings because of the exhaustion.

### Fact the nineteenth:

He does not love me. I am as sure of that now, as I am of anything.

# V

# RELATIONS

*In which I get acquainted with my husband's family*

My husband's mother and sister surprised us all by coming home some ten days earlier than expected. They had gone away the very same day of the wedding to visit relatives in the Black Country, leaving my husband and I most awfully alone together in the echoing corridors of the Hall. It seemed they had decided our honeymoon had ended.

A cry went up around the house within moments of the sound of the coach wheels rolling up the end of the drive, and once the news of their return had spread as far as the servants' quarters, there began the tap-tap sound of running feet, which echoed around the corridors and made me open the door of my chamber to see if there might be a fire or the Dutch had come to murder us all in our beds. A girl I recognized as the laundry wench, a slight girl with a drooping gait and bright eyes, rushed past me then, her arms full of linens. I called to her.

'Tell me, girl – what on earth is the matter?'

She paused, and turned to me, dropping open her mouth to see me, for she was one of the lowly servants who was always hidden away backstairs and unused to being spoken to by the quality. She blushed and dropped a wobbly curtsey.

'Please, my Lady,' she panted, "tis my Lady Ty – nay – the *Dowager* and my Lady Sibeliah who have returned before they was expected, and we backstairs all in a great pet to set the house to rights, for the grand sweeping is not until Friday.' She looked at me, to see if I had comprehended her. "'Tis Wednesday,' she added.

'Ah I see,' I said. 'Thank ye kindly.'

'My Lady,' said she, and scuttled away.

After pinching my cheeks to rouse my complexion, I went down the stairs to make ready to welcome my new relations, while all about me the servants scurried to and fro to light the fires, polish the tables, and dust the ornaments, for, as I had already heard, my new mother-in-law was in the habit of running the tips of her fingers along surfaces, and woe betide if they came up with even a modicum of dust. I dawdled awkwardly in the hall, sniffing at the cleaning smells of linseed oil and soot, and then the door crashed open and a reedy girl with a frizz of light hair stepped over the threshold, her blue eyes wide.

'Where is Master Brignall?' she said to me, in an urgent voice with traces of a lisp. 'Mama will not get down from the coach without help, and the coachman is a hired gentleman, and does not know how to hand her down the way she would have it.'

'I will ring for him,' I said, picking up the silver hand bell from the hall table. I jangled it.

The girl pushed the velvet hood of her cloak back and leant against the wall panels, steadying her breath. We looked at one another.

'Forgive me,' she said in a slow voice, 'I am in such a quandary that I have not said "how do". Hello again, Ursula.'

I went to her and kissed her cheek. There was a strange scent that clung to her that was half-rotten, half-sweet. 'Sister,' I said. 'I am pleased that you have come home, for I have been lonely here without a playmate, and Tyringham away.'

'Oh is he away?' she said carelessly, her eyes widening. 'He's always doing that. I expect you'll have to get used to it.' I felt that she was watching me.

'Oh aye,' I agreed heartily lest she think me a weakling, but then Master Brignall had come into the hall, and was out the door, without a glance at either of us.

'He's famous devoted to her,' said Sibeliah. 'He has been her butler these fifteen years, and knows her ways better than anyone.'

Snatches of a woman's brittle voice floated through the open door to where my new sister and I stood.

'... no one here to greet me, for shame...'

Then the rumbling of Brignall's voice, but I could not hear what it said, and the Dowager came slowly through the door, leaning on his arm, with a great rustling of skirts, for she wore them very long and black; she looked shrunken inside her clothes, as if she played at dressing up in her mother's things, but still she peered down at me.

'What's this? Is this Ursula?' she said, her eyes darting from me to her daughter. She released Brignall, who gave me a sour look, and disappeared down the corridor.

'Yes, Mama,' Sibeliah said, before I could open my mouth to speak. 'My brother is away and I believe she is in search of occupation.'

The Dowager swivelled her eyes towards me. 'How diverting,' she said.

There were three black patches on her cheek, and one, in a diamond shape, on the tip of her nose. Her hair was chalk-white, and swept away from her forehead, which was riven all over with deep, downward furrows, that looked to be the product of scolding. Her face was moonish pale, and seemed to rest, neckless, on her high lace collar. I would come to know she was never without these collars: prickly-looking things that made her throat red, for she was always scratching at them, and scraping her skin, but she would not leave them off, for she thought them fine, sewn as they were in a convent, in France.

She came towards me then and grasped my shoulders. 'But you're such a teeny thing out of your bridal gown,' she said, catching me about the waist and squeezing me in a way that I did not like. Her hands felt strong and bony. 'Such a little girl. Like a bird.' She touched my cheek.

'How do ye do, my Lady,' I said, staring her in the face, for I did not know how I should conduct myself, and then, remembering my manners, dropped into a curtsey. 'I am mighty pleased you have come home again.'

'And bold too,' she said, stepping back, and sweeping her eyes up and down my person. 'My son told me so. Hmm, but you are young yet... A little wan – but that is to be expected in a new bride. I expect you have not been sleeping overmuch.' Her eyes seemed to pierce into me. I began to feel a hotness seeping inwards from my ears.

'We shall retire now,' the Dowager said, holding her arm out for Sibeliah, 'for it has been a long journey. But we shall converse a little more at supper, for I would like to know all about my new daughter. My son has told me you are a scholar.'

She seemed to be expecting an answer to this so I half-mumbled an 'Aye'.

'How peculiar,' she said, her black eyes still pointed at me. 'Fare thee well.'

Sibeliah tittered.

'Fare thee well,' I said.

# VI

❖

# CORRESPONDENCE

*In which I write my letters home*

◈

Dearest Mother,

Did you get my last letter? I sent it with the coachman, but I wonder if he mislaid it, for I have had no word from you and it has been twelve days since.

How is your health? (I wrote this in the letter that I now believe mislaid, so I shall do so again.) I do so hope you are keeping well, and are not too lonely there without me – and Father. I think of him often: whenever there is a clear night, I open the windows wide and search for the Great Bear, the constellation that he named me for, and now reminds me of him. I know he watches over us.

It is strange to be here without you and Muffy and the little ones. I ache to see you all – it tears at my heart that I cannot talk with you and hold you close to me! I would tell you about my new life as a married woman – it is not quite as I expected it – and I have some things to ask you, so do write, sweet Mother, I beg you.

The Dowager likes me to talk to her in her room, though she does not often agree with what I say (imagine!). She is a commanding sort of person and seems to manage the house and all the servants – I often wonder if my husband (and I!) are in charge at all, or if 'tis she, in fact, who rules all.

I do not know what to make of Sibeliah yet. But it is nice to have a sister – though she cannot replace my Catherine – tell me, has she grown? Is she reading her Bible? And how is Percy? Do you speak of me often? When I am sitting here in the parlour, watching the low flames flicker in the hearth, I often think I would walk a mile in the rain, just to feel one of Reggie's sharp pinches.

Will you come and visit me, with Mary? Not now, for Tyringham says it is too soon for friends to come a-visiting. But perhaps in the spring, when it will be warm for your journey. I could send a coach for you – it should not take above two days, and you can stay at The Swan, as I did on my way here – the innkeeper is a good fellow, and there is a chamber for the quality.

Kiss the children for me. And Mary. And Muff. Kiss them all and tell them I am always their affectionate

*Ursula*

❀

TURVEY HALL
Wiltshire
The 7th day of December in the Year of our Lord 1680

My dearest merry Mary,

I know Grisella will be reading this to you – I salute you both, dear friends!

Oh, it has been such a time since I saw you. I think of you often and long to see your face. Do write how you and your mother and your father and the children do. Do you go to Bear Wood often? How I long to be back in its shade, and have all of you about me, and clamouring for a new play. I fear they are not so keen on playing here...

You will want to know about the Hall, I think (and you, Grisella: listen well). 'Tis a great, grand house, of ten chambers, and a dozen or more downstairs rooms, and servants' quarters, and stables, oh there are so many rooms that I have not yet been into them all. There is a large hallway, and a carved wooden staircase which sweeps upwards in two directions, hung about with portraits of my husband's relations, all of them sour-faced with the same thin lips and beak-nose as the Dowager.

The whole place is crammed full with decorations and furniture and objects: my eyes are ever darting about to take in the painted card tables, the carved chess set, the china puzzle jugs. The walls are mostly decorated with scenes from the Bible (for they are famous devout here – do not snigger, Grisella!). My chamber is prettier though, for Tyringham had it painted as the Garden of Eden as a marriage gift to me, and the walls are green and wild and beautiful – daubed with wild grasses and climbing plants which snake about its corners, with painted flowers of every hue blooming about the windows (how strange then that the Tyringhams would have me rot away indoors all day – fie!). In this painted paradise, Tyringham is Adam and I, dear friends, am Eve. The Adam-him is rendered tall and proud (Grisella, pray do not let your mind wander! I speak of his face, which is haughty). The Eve-me has flowers in her fair hair which falls to her waist in pretty curls, and a gown of acanthus leaves and ivy. (How I wish for such a costume as that in real life, for I would look well, I think, with flowers in my hair – think you not? I am reminded of the May dancers – shall you be one of them this year, Mary?) The screens that hide the pissing pots are painted too, but these are black and brought from China, and so they are covered over with strange Chinese houses on sticks, and flying storks and nightingales and ladies with puffed hairstyles and great blocked pattens.

But I must tell you of the lights – oh the lights! There are more candles here than I have seen in any abode, and there are polished chandeliers in all the downstairs rooms, burning merrily away all evening long, for there is no need to scrimp on wax. Every room is so bright that at first I would blink as I walked about – it is strange to be lit up so (I am certain your mother, Griss, would find it 'vulgar' – I can just hear her saying so and sniffing in the way she does). In this light, everything glitters – and there is so much silver all about me: the candelabras, and the spoons, and the spittoons, one in every room; all are shining and glinting in the light. The looking glasses are carved and gilted, and I have never seen so many of them – Grisella, when you come to stay you shall go from room to room and revel in them. 'Tis a strange sensation to be walking about and ever catching a glimpse of yourself. At first I thought it was another girl with golden hair following me about, but it was not, 'twas only your

*Ursula*

*Burn after Reading!*

**TURVEY HALL**
Wiltshire
The 17th day of December in the Year of our Lord 1680

My dearest Grisella,

I am now sixteen years old and I bless our Lord Jesu for delivering me from the pox for another year (for I have heard it has come in on a ship and rages at Bristol)!

I gobbled your sweet letter down all in one delicious read, tucked away in a dark and dusty room draped all about with bedsheets – Lor' knows what they use it for. I am glad your mother is well and that you have a new gown: it sounds famous fine and I yearn to see it.

You ask what it is like to be wed — well, it is still so new I don't know what to tell you, in faith. It *is* good to have the pretty things I have, and to walk about the Hall and know that I am the Lady of it, though I am learning slowly to command the servants – especially my own woman, who is a slovenly wench such as I have never seen – you would pinch her.

My husband's mother (and now mine, for as you foretold she has taken charge of me most thoroughly!) is, as you foretold, a TYRANT. The lady has her own suite of rooms in the east wing of the house, and 'tis well she is not near mine, for she is always in her chamber, crouched on her chaise, or hunched in her bed, sucking on her strange little pipe (I have never seen a lady smoke tobacco before, you would die laughing to see her blowing out clouds of lilac smoke, scrabbling at the coverlet and calling for her lady in her screeching voice).

*You* would think her very plain in the face, for she has a Puritan hatred of beautifying, and so she does not primp, and she cannot abide the use of rouge, and scolds me for hair-dressing! But (these bruits I got from Sibeliah) after a rare visit to Court, in which she laid her eyes on the Duchess of Disbury, whose visage, I am told, was fashionably decorated with black velvet patches, she took to wearing them herself, but her eyesight is failing, so there are tiny crinkled spots which move freely about her face and land in peculiar places: her earlobe; her nose; her waxen, wrinkled brow.

There is always the pipe-smoke floating in the air; the rasp-rasp of her dry, scratching fingers; and the high whine of her voice calling for people to come to her, come, come and see me, for I need you, and I cannot be alone. But I can be alone, for I am your own true

*Ursula*

❧

**TURVEY HALL**
Wiltshire
The 17th day of December in the Year of our Lord 1680

Dear Mother,

Did you get my letters? I am much afeard that you are took ill or one of the little ones has and I beg and implore you to send some word of how you do to your loving daughter,

*Ursula*

❧

My dear Griss,

I am honoured at the quickness of your reply – the man must have galloped all night through to deliver it, poor beast, for there was a famous bad storm.

Aye, your mother is a canny woman to guess that the servants here are inert, or if they are not that, insolent, compared to ours or yours. But I have been practising, at your suggestion, 'queenly, commanding' phrases in the looking glass, though I feel mighty foolish to do it, and am always afeard I might be disturbed. These I have tried:

'I'll thank ye to hold your tongue.'

'Do not cross me!'

'Do as I say, Beck.'

'I shall not repeat myself.'

Say you are proud of me?

A curious thing – I have found that I can 'command' all the better if I imagine myself to be somebody else – a haughty duchess, or the Dowager (Ho!), or the blessed Queen herself, and say the words in character, as if I were speaking a part. (I can hear you cry, 'Aye, the part of a woman who can properly manage her servants.') But I cannot be she, I can only be your

*Ursula*

❀

My darling Father,

Last night I dreamt again that you had come to take me home.
In the dream, your dying was all a mistake made by that scurvy
physician, and you had been living secretly in the under-stair
cupboard, nibbling the cheese from the mousetraps, and chuckling
that you had tricked us in your clever way.

When I broke through the dream and awoke – oh, the terrible lurch
in my belly; the knife-twist in my heart as it dawned that I had
dreamt it all... I wish I could learn how to linger a little longer with
you in that hazy place betwixt sleep and waking, for the dream-
you is always smiling, and reaching out to press me to your side; to
stroke my cheek...

I know in my right mind you are gone and silent still, and under the
earth in the churchyard, where bright green moss grows over you,
and there are no books to read or children to scold...

Oh my Father, how I rue all the cruel things I said to you and Mother.
If only you knew how I sob my heart out over it when my husband is
asleep.

I open the window every night and look up at the stars – for I know
you are floating up there with the angels. I send you kisses up to
heaven until my husband scolds me, but I pay no mind for I am not
his, but instead forever your loving

*Ursula*

⚜

# VII

✤

# REGIMEN

*In which I describe our daily life, such as it is*

⸙

## A DAY IN THE LIFE OF
## MY HUSBAND & I
## by Lady Ursula Tyringham,

### 17th April Anno Domini 1681

### ❧ DAWN
At the first chirping of the birds on the tree outside our chamber window, with a loud yawning my husband rises. He yanks the bed curtains open, which wakes me, but I drift back off to sleep with the sun slanting on my face. He dresses, and goes out on his rounds of the estate, and visits with his manager, or the groom, or exercises his horse.

### ❧ SEVEN OF THE CLOCK OR THERE ABOUTS
I open my eyes. I close them. I groan. I push my head under the pillow.

### ❧ A SHORT WHILE LATER
I am awakened by Beck with a pinching. I slap her away and shout 'No NO NO.' The click of her wooden shoes on the floor.

### ❧ A LITTLE AFTER THAT
My linnet has begun his morning trill and flits about his cage. Beck swipes at the bedclothes, and I open my eyes to see her greasy face

below her bonnet and the gown which does not fit her plump figure. The waft of onions. She says: 'Good morrow, my Lady,' with the leer she has. 'The Dowager was wondering if you were breakfasting this morning or nay.'

## ❧ COMING ON FOR EIGHT OF THE CLOCK
I am tugged into my gown and have my hair wrenched out by insolent Beck. At first, while she laced me into my buskin or helped me tie up my garters, I tried to speak of gay things – the fashion for plumed hats in Paris, or the new-born foal that had come out unexpectedly skewbald, but she made such short answers, or grunts, that I gave it all up for lost. Now we go through my dressing in a silence that is not quite comfortable.

## ❧ EIGHT OF THE CLOCK
I break my fast alone at the long table in the dining room, served by Tizzy. Most likely 'tis kippers, and bread and ale and a cheese or a capon, and a pickle, or a fruit. The servants clear the table while I am still eating – 'tis plain they disapprove of the quality breaking bread any time after dawn, but I care not, and go on chewing as slow as I may with a smile upon my face, and a firepit of mirth bubbling up in my belly.

## ❧ BROAD MORNING
I walk out of doors if 'tis fine, breathing in the rosemary and sage of the kitchen garden or else I try to get myself lost in the maze, but 'tis always too easy and I end up back at the bench. There is a pretty part of the walled garden that is concealed from view, and there I whip out my book from the secret pocket in my skirts I have sewn for the purpose. I pace briskly up and down the gallery if it rains, thumbing my nose at each one of the Tyringham portraits in turn.

## ❧ PAST ELEVEN OF THE CLOCK
The sound of footsteps. Someone is calling my name. I stow my book and get out a bit of lacework. Fie!

## ❧ MID-MORNING
I am summoned to sit with the Dowager to assist her in some dreary task such as winding her thread, or finding her thimble. She will engage me in prattle and, with a slyness that I took for vagueness at the first, attempts to pry into my thoughts with trickery. 'Brignall is blunt in his manners, think ye not?' she will say,

with her eyes wide and innocent as a new-born babe. Or
'Do ye not find having a husband a trifle… toilsome?' And then
if I say something mild such as 'I suppose so,' she will seize it and
say: 'Indeed – and why do ye think that, how astonishing,' with
a hungry look on her face and I will have to fashion a reply that
comes out all a-babbling. I do not know why she teases me so.
P'raps she is as bored here as I.

## ❧ MIDDAY
Dinner. My husband kisses his mama, then me. We all sit at table.
The servants stare while we chew, and I know they are hanging on
every word we say. On Thursdays we have company, which means
the rector, or the Widow Rampshaw, who lives in a spindly house on
the village green and is afflicted with a goitre.

## ❧ EARLY AFTERNOON
My husband returns to his business. The Dowager and Sibeliah go to
rest on couches, for they stuff themselves so full of food, 'tis all they
can do to digest it. I read and write my letters now, knowing I will
not be disturbed for above an hour. 'Tis my habit to stow my letters
in my bosom and I take them out often, to comfort me.

## ❧ LATE AFTERNOON
My husband comes in. Often he will hold forth about some topic –
godliness, or his observations on the depravity of human nature.
He seems content if I nod a little and offer the occasional 'Egad,
how enthralling!' though this can be a trial. He once talked of
the Royal Society and I asked why they did not admit women,
to which he laughed and patted my hand and said I was a sweet
little maid.

## ❧ FIVE OF THE CLOCK
After supper, we all convene in the parlour, the women at
instruments or tapestry screens. My husband strides about the
room, or pokes the fire, or snores fitfully in a chair, or prates
with his mama about relations I do not know. I tried once to lead
a conversation on the discovery of a new moon in Saturn that I
had had from a pamphlet, but the Dowager eyed me as if I were a
Bedlamite, and Sibeliah giggled behind her plump white hands and
so I gave the business up.

## ❧ DUSK

Lamp-lighting. Jack comes round with a taper and talks jovially with my husband. Tyringham enjoys their badinage; his shoulders drop, and he throws his head back and laughs heartily. We do not laugh together, my husband and I. I wonder if any married couples do? I miss the merry times I had with Mary and Grisella, rolling around the floor, weak with mirth, tears springing out of our eyes, stuffing our petticoats into our mouths to stifle our howling. I have not laughed like that for a long time, though there is plenty to find risible here.

## ❧ A LITTLE AFTER EIGHT

We all retire. The candles are snuffed out behind us as we tap up the stairs in a troupe and part on the landing. If he is in good temper, my husband sends the servants away and unlaces my buskin himself. Oftentimes he barely speaks, or makes idle chatter with Beck as she undresses me. I turn my face to the window and think of other things.

## ❧ PAST NINE OF THE CLOCK

We lay abed. The hall clock ticks. The wind around the gables. My husband's sigh. A while ago, I asked him to comfort me, for I had a homesick ache and missed my mother. I brushed my fingers along the sheet, feeling for his hand. A cold, clammy thing it was, and I tried to pull it towards me, but he only sighed, and turned himself over, and snored.

## ❧ TEN OF THE CLOCK OR THEREABOUTS

My husband drifts into sleep. If he has had me, I creep into my closet, and do what I must behind the screen. Oftentimes I creep in front of the curtains to sit in the window, lean my head against the glass and gaze up at the night sky. I have stopped weeping at night for the most part, but if I cannot contain myself, I tiptoe into my closet and stuff my shift into my mouth. And then, God willing, I may sleep.

# BEDDING

*In which I muse on the duties of wifehood*

Though the first few times it had pained me and made me bleed, after several months of matrimony, I was growing used to lovemaking. I had learnt that the redness of my husband's neck and the bulging of his eyes were signs that his ardour was inflamed. I discovered, too, that I could hasten our joining by being pliable in his grasp and answering his kissing with a soft and moving mouth. When he bade me lie down, I did so quickly, throwing my legs apart with abandon, turning my head while he lapped at my neck, and sighing only when he rooted under my shift.

I became accustomed to the strange way he laid himself on top of me, and poked at me with his part, and clutched at my bosom, his dog breath clouding onto my face, the prickle of his whiskers against my skin. He liked to snake his tongue into my mouth and both this and the tang of his spittle disgusted me, though I told myself it was all my duty to bear, and so did not complain. Once he got himself inside me and started at his thrusting, I could be calm, for I knew I could pass the time pleasantly enough conjugating Latin verbs in my head. I learnt to let my limbs go slack and heavy, and lay there gazing at the canopy of the bed, which was a sky wrought in soft silk. On one side bloomed a great orange circle: the sunrise, embroidered, its curling flames rippling outwards. At the other end of the awning, an expanse of violet with pale purple planets and sharp yellow stars: the night sky.

I stared at it often, while he moved above me, and let my mind float upwards, the loamy smell of him all around. Later I would sleep, and dream that I had a young and gallant lover of the sort that was writ in verses, who would try to win my hand with love tokens, pretty words and ardent declarations.

'Soon you will bear our children and they shall have my dark hair and your light eyes,' he told me one morning, as the sun rose up and made the room glow pink. I gripped my hands into fists and did not answer him, though he tipped my chin towards him.

He bought me a new night-shift, with a high old-fashioned collar. Such a strange thing for a man to buy his wife, my eyes said when I unwrapped it, but he only said, in a voice that was deep and low, 'I hope you will wear it.'

The first time I put it on, he bit at me and clawed at the strings and had no sooner got under it and pushed himself into me, than he ended his labours with a great convulsing. I held him to me and, over his shoulder, suppressed my mirth.

My mother had told me of the getting of babbies, and what I must do with his seed inside my womb, so at first I would lay abed, not daring to move, for fear it would spill out of me. It seemed that it always oozed onto my thighs, and onto the sheets, which were marked with it in the mornings, and I knew the servants must titter over this, as they did the bloodstains from my courses. I was a child in those early days, and did not know what the getting of children might mean. I knew only what I had been told, and did not think beyond my duty as a wife. Later, I learnt. And then I did not stay still.

❧

It was a crisp, grey day in early spring when the Dowager bade me visit her chamber. Sibeliah was gone from her usual place at her mother's side, and there was only old Sarah, sitting on a stool, untangling the knots of crewel work gone wrong. I never liked to stay in her chamber over-long, for it was a dark, sombre place, oppressively hung all about with tapestries, which were woven depictions of ancient hunting scenes. There were purple grapes and brown dogs; green trees and golden goblets; flaxen-haired youths and galloping deer. Despite the heavy beatings administered to these hangings by the servants, the air was always thick with their dust.

'Ignore Sarah,' said the Dowager, fluttering her hands about in the way she had. 'For she pays what I say no mind, and knows I'll have her tongue cut out if she speaks a word of it backstairs.'

At this Sarah grunted.

The Dowager looked at me with her dark eyes half closed. 'I have bidden you here to ask you how goes the getting of my husband's babby, for we must have an heir, and you do not look as fat as you ought.'

'Well, madame,' I said, feeling my cheeks growing instantly hot at her directness. 'I am not yet with child, though I pray for it every night.' (This was an untruth; I prayed every night that God might send Catherine and Mary to live with me and keep beside me, as once they had.)

'What are you doing for the getting of it?' she said roughly, scratching at her collar. 'Come now and don't be bashful, for the goings on of my son are my business, as well as yours.'

'Well,' I said. 'I do not know how to answer you.' I clasped my fingers behind my back.

'Is he having you, child?' she said, and now her eyes were wide and staring into me. 'You know what I mean, I think, for I cannot speak plainer.'

'Why yes, my Lady,' was all I could say in reply. 'I think so.'

She leaned forward in her seat. 'And do you let him do his duty?'

'I – I do not know. I... Yes.'

'For 'tis well known – though mayhap your mother did not speak of it to you, which was remiss of her, for she should have instructed you in every wifely thing – that a woman shall get with child much quicker if she let her husband do what he will, and not be slapping him off, and pinching his nose, and crying rape.'

'I have not cried rape,' said I. 'I have not slapped him.'

'Well then,' she said. 'But mind you never do, and you let him go about the thing when he will.' She smoothed the inky fabric of her dress. ''Tis harmful for men if they do not have the release, for it blocks up the humours and can cause all manner of complaints, and kill a man besides. You would not want to murder your husband, would you, child?'

'No, my Lady,' I said slowly.

'Well then,' she said. 'See that he has you often and with the grace of Christ Jesu we may soon have an heir for Turvey, and the title assured besides.'

I went away then, and began to muse on the possibility of my having a child, for I had pushed it to the back of my mind, with all the strangeness of my new life to distract me. My mother had not said overmuch on the subject beyond her commands that I try to lie still, for I knew how babbies came, having seen her at her lyings in. Mother had assured me that I would not have need of instruction in the subject at the first, for, as she had said: 'Your husband will not bother you much for it yet, you being a child still.' But in this she had been wrong. Should I write and tell my mother and ask for her to bring me home?

I thought of Mother, groaning in her unlaced gown, and the little white bundles, and my father's face. Childbed was a thing fraught with danger, for my mother was always saying what luck she had with Mistress Knagg, when so many midwives were filthy sluts who tore at you with sharpened fingernails, thrust a strap between your teeth to bite on and left you to your fate. Mistress Knagg was too far away to be sent for if I had a babby, and I did not think Beck or Sibeliah much help in the matter. My mother might come, or Mary, if my husband allowed it, but I did not know if he would.

The fear of getting with child began to bloom in me, growing stronger with every day that passed at Turvey. What good would getting a babby do me? If it did not kill me in the birthing of it, the Dowager was like to send it off for nursing, and I would hardly see it until it was grown. I said nothing to my husband of this, but grew restless after his lovemaking. Instead of lying docilely down to sleep, while he snored, I began to creep into my closet, where I went behind the chamber pot screen. Here I tried to scrape his seed out of me with a cloth I had hidden there, and, as quietly as I could, I danced and jumped and rocked and shook my body about like a mad thing, and my luck held, for I did not get with child.

***

## MY MOTHER-IN-LAW AND I, A CONVERSATION

### May 1681, night, the parlour.

DOWAGER: Are you quite well, child? You look pale, but not pretty.

URSULA: [*Shyly*] I do not know, Mama. I have been feeling a little strange these past few weeks, mostly...

DOWAGER: [*A greedy look on her face*] Yes?

URSULA: ... mostly in the mornings.

DOWAGER: [*Seizing hold of her about the wrist*] You have been sick in the mornings?

URSULA: Aye. I have brought up the flux...

DOWAGER: [*Eagerly*] Aye?

URSULA: And I feel... that I do not have the appetite that I did.

DOWAGER: The food, perhaps, tastes more strongly than afore? A bitter sort of taste to it, perhaps?

URSULA: Aye, 'tis so. The only thing I can stomach – oh but it seems so foolish. And we do not have it much. Perhaps 'tis better that I go hungry...

DOWAGER:    Out with it, girl.

URSULA:     Sugar pies and hazey pudding. And iced cream. And
            honey wine.

DOWAGER:    'Tis the way of these things. I shall tell Mrs Jickell
            to make you some, for 'tis important you eat and get
            the nourishment from it.

URSULA:     [*Eyes downwards*] I suppose so. Thank ye kindly,
            Mama.

DOWAGER:    Are you tired child, as you are sick?

URSULA:     [*Pause*] Gad, I do not like to complain, but I suppose
            I do have a weariness that runs through my limbs.
            I do not much walk about, for my body feels so
            swollen – and full – somehow. I know Sibeliah means
            to be kind, but praying can be fatiguing and...

DOWAGER:    Well now, today you shall not pray but shall lie
            abed the whole afternoon. 'Tis blowing a gale
            outside, and there you will be warm and in no
            danger of taking a chill.

URSULA:     But oh – Sibeliah's embroidery of blessed St John
            the Baptist! I had promised to help her with it, for
            she struggles greatly over the blood drips which
            issue from the severed head.

DOWAGER:    She will well understand when I explain it to her.
            'Tis not your fault you are not well.

URSULA:     You know best, Mama. But will Tyringham not be
            angry with me? He cannot abide the sin of idleness,
            for 'tis against the blessed Bible, amen.

DOWAGER:    Do not disturb yourself, for I will talk with him
            also. 'Tis not sinful when there is good reason.

URSULA:     If you say so, dear Mama.

DOWAGER:     I do.


*Ending: A glorious afternoon feasting on puddings and laying cosily abed*
*with no one to trouble me, reading play scripts and working on my scribbles.*

&#x2766;

# OBSERVATIONS
## ON
### *a*
# MOTHER-IN-LAW

———❦———

*being*

# A
# BOOK
## of
# DIRECTIONS

*ON LIVING WITH THIS
DEADLY AGUE*

———❦———

Printed for URSULA TYRINGHAM
at *the Sign of the Cat* in Giltspur Street LONDON

PRICE: 2s BOUND

## HOW TO RECOGNIZE WHEN the CANKER HAS SET IN

MAKE no mistake, thou shalt know when thou have a mother-in-law who thinks to rule thee for she shall seem mild mannered but as soon as thy husband's back be turned she shall open her jaws and snap with all the evil of SATAN. If thou will not have her rule thee, throw thy head back proud and high and perceive her with a fiery look and say 'I am mistress here, for I am Lady Whatsit'. If that does not sate her, throw scorn upon her suggestions that thou do not go out of doors, or read edifying books, or romp about the house, and if that does not work, then ignore her and do as thou please. Remember: 'tis not a sin to make merry, nor to continue as thy father hath taught you when thou were in thy own house, which was a better house than her one in many ways, in character, if not in size.

## THE SYMPTOMS of this TERRIFYING CURSE

THE first sign that thou hast a dreadful and fearsome mother-in-law is that she will not let thee be, no matter if thou try to creep about the house and hide from her; whether thou be shut up in a closet, or crouched on thy bed with the curtains drawn, she will sniff thee out with her animal sense, and ask why thou be not darning the stockings of her lambikin, her first-born son, with his feet so wet and stinking that the fug of them burns through the cloth and would have thee at thy needle mending the holes from morning 'til night. And if thou pay her no heed, she will have thee by the elbow and pinch at thee until thou submit. And so I warn thee, wives, conceal thyself with as much art as thou may, for then she will not find thee, and there will be no strife.

## WHAT ye MUST do to BEAR THIS ABOMINABLE AGUE

THERE is no cure for this cursed ague, the malevolent germ that is the mother-in-law, for once thou art wed, none may break thee asunder, save for those who may divorce and give thee thy freedom, but only after heartache, for be sure that a mother-in-law will not yield her fortune, but hang onto it with a gnashing of her sharpened DEVIL'S teeth. So I say to ye unwedded maids: do not enter into matrimony until thou hast first earnestly discovered the nature of thy husband's mother, and if she be mean, or cunning, or sharp in her habits, think thee carefully before thou contracteth thyself, for 'tis the mother thou wilt be wedding as much as the husband, and unlike him, thou cannot pacify her with love-kisses on the nose and a tweak of the hindermost part. HEED YE WELL.

## YE CAN OUTWIT THE CREATURE if THOU CANNOT RULE HER

IF thou wouldst fox the mother-in-law thou must plaster a look of such sweet innocence upon thy phyzzog and go about the house with a look of the utmost devotion to her nutmeg-pie, her son, and if she discover thee at something she liketh not, put on a look of the most enduring sorrow, and say in the saddest voice that anyone ever heard: 'I shall try to do better, canst thou forgive me mine errors?' And then fall down on her person and weep and beat thy fists against thy chest, and if thou can bear it,

tear out thy hair and chew at it, and believe me she will leave off her scoldings for fear thou hast lost thy mind and be shut up in a madhouse, which will look bad upon the family name.

## ON the COMING of THY CHILDREN

ONCE thou hast borne children it may be worse or better with thy mother-in-law, I know not, but if you do not have them, thou shalt suffer, for there is nothing this wrathful HELL creature wanteth more than the spread of her own withered fruit about in the world. And so thou mayest submit to her proddings and pokings and interferings with the maids as to whether thou hast gotteth the curse or nay, and what hast been on the sheets or nay, and to this I say: let her do it, for while thou dost not have a babby, thou will not be trapped like a slave in a cage, and so there is reason to be merry, for even while she is rooting through thine underthings, thou shalt go to thy chamber and dance and sing a merry ditty on the freedom and lightness of thy body which shall not enslave thee, nay, not for a good while yet.

# IX

# SISTERHOOD

*In which I spend time with Sibeliah*

My husband's sister was a curious girl, such as I had never come across before. At two-and-twenty Sibeliah was six years my elder but as yet unmarried (though I suspected this was not for want of trying). You would not think her a full-grown woman to speak to her, for she had little conversation, and was as winsome and vague as her mother was snappish. She had a soft way of walking about with her arms floating out at the elbows, and she would always appear when you least expected it, from an unexpected direction, like a wraith.

Sibeliah had rooms near her mother's at the east side of the Hall, for it was their regular habit to bundle up together under the bedclothes and whisper, a thing I overheard the servants talking of when I was reading out of sight, hidden behind the painted screen in the withdrawing room, where there was a squat little chair that was low and comfortable.

'Twas the fashion amongst ladies to keep a cabinet of curiosities, and being otherwise devoid of occupation save for her religious embroideries, Sibeliah was one of these ladies. In the withdrawing room her collection stood, arranged on shelves in a large ebonised-wood Chinese cabinet, which teetered on scaly dragon-legs. Inside were ornaments got from all over the world: a little hopping monkey from Paris juggling gold-leaf oranges; a Dutch girl from the Low-Lands with a high white coif and sabots painted with tiny yellow tulips; a fuddling cup in the form of a black cat with pointed ears and an upheld paw from which water could be poured, which had come from Venice, on a packet ship.

Though cosseted by her mama as an invalid, Sibeliah was gorgeously plump, and seemed to enjoy good health as much as any person, save for her teeth, for she was a martyr to toothache. She went about with a mustard plaster pressed to her jaw, carrying a phial of oil of cloves in her hand, which she dabbed on her gums each time she passed a looking glass, perfuming the air with spice even as she grumbled at the pain. Though her teeth seemed to be rotting in her head, Sibeliah was mortally afraid of the barber-surgeon, the apothecary and the physician too and would not have the teeth out, though her mama and Sarah cajoled her daily to submit to any one of these medical ministrations, and my husband went after her with a set of pliers, which had her screaming and running about the house. It was the rotten teeth which made her breath foul, and against this she had taken to sucking sugared almonds, which she kept in a little velvet pouch strung with ribbon at her waist. The sweet-rotten scent of her breath told you when Sibeliah had been in a room, for the smell was wont to linger there, long after she had left it.

At Tyringham's encouragement, rather than her own, I attempted a friendship.

'Will you not walk with me, Sibeliah?' I said to her one fine day after a week of rain in which I had felt restless and trapped in the house. 'I thought to take a turn about the fountain – and we may walk under the bower if you wish for shelter.'

Clank, clank, the sound of the sugared almonds against her teeth as she sucked on them and thought of her answer.

'Mama says my constitution is too weak for exposure to the air,' she lisped, pulling at the velvet pouch and popping another nut into her mouth. 'For I am bound to get a rheum after all this rain, and the last one I had laid me up for above a month, and Mama was afeard it might carry me off and kept vigil by my bedside every night, praying on her knees for Jesu to deliver me from the snapping jaws of the Devil.'

They were a great family for praying in general, and I suffered to attend regular devotions in the chapel, which were led by the Reverend Bainbigge, who I suspected had a stipend which was increased by the Dowager the more fire and brimstone he could bring into his sermon. We slouched there, docile and sleepy in our seats, until the time for the 'Te Deum', when we would lift up our voices, Sibeliah's reedy tones wavering high above the rest and sliding around the notes, inventing new ones that were never there to begin with.

'Oh Lord, in thee I have trusted. Let me never be confounded.'

❦

Early one morning Sibeliah came into my chamber. I did not hear her tap and she found me humped underneath the bedclothes, and poked at me until I started up in fright.

'What is it?' I said, turning over and scowling at her. The stench of her breath filled the room and I scrunched up my nose at it.

'I am sorry to wake you, Sister,' she said, swallowing the grit of a sugared almond, and sliding a new one into her mouth. 'But I have come to keep company with you. I rose at dawn, and have been praying with Mama since then, and so it feels famous late to me.'

I sat up and peered at the lantern clock which stood on the dressing table. It was just after eight o'clock. 'Oh,' I yawned, stretching my arms up. 'I am weary. What is it? I thought to doze a while yet. For I have had horrid cauchemars all the night through and woke up sweating every hour.'

'How dreary the mornings are now it is coming on for autumn,' she prattled, sitting herself down at the foot of the bed. 'But as the good book says, "Through sloth the roof sinks in, and through indolence the house leaks." That's rather lovely, isn't it? For who wants a fallen-down roof and a leaky house? Not I!' She thumped at my legs under the bedclothes. 'I do love to read the Bible, with Mama – well she reads it for me, for I cannot. It's Ecclesiastes, I think. A strange sort of name, but then many of them are – Deuteronomy!' She made one of her high-pitched giggles, pressing her fingers to her mouth. 'Leviticus!' She let out a hiccough of laughter.

'It's a Latin translation of the Greek translation of the Hebrew,' I said.

'What is?' she said.

'Ecclesiastes.' I was waking up. 'It means "teacher". And not a name, but a *nom de plume*. The others aren't names either, though my friend Grisella's brother has a horse named Deuteronomy, a dappled grey with a habit of bucking him off at the first sight of a puddle.'

She leant back and squinted at me, with the thin lips of her mother pressed together.

'Yeeees,' she said slowly. 'Mama told me you had book-learning.'

'I was taught by my father,' I said, pushing at the bedclothes. 'To read, and to speak languages, and of history – and other things.'

'Pray, what does it feel like to be a woman with such things in your head? Mother will not have me learn anything beyond my needle and my harpsichord, which I play very well,' she said. 'And I can sport at cards too. But not chess. For that is a man's game with all its knights and kings.'

'Why, I do not know,' I said. 'For I have been learning since I was eight years old and I know no other way of being, in truth.'

She did not look satisfied with this answer.

'One thing I do know,' I said, 'is that there is no pleasure on this earth better than reading. I have been transported,' I said, 'to realms beyond my wildest imagining, to places I shall never see, for they are on the other side of the world, or do not exist at all. And I have been made to cry – and to laugh and to think and to be peaceful, and all of this I have got from books.'

She stared at me, taking this in, and then said, 'It sounds quite frightening.'

'Why no,' I cried. 'For what is frightening about the discovery of bright new worlds? There are plays I have read which are droll enough to lift any temper. You would howl, I think, to see *The Mulberry Garden* or *The Merry Wives*. I shall read them to you, if you wish, after supper one evening.' My voice was rising at this suggestion, for I had been yearning to do plays again.

She looked shocked at this. 'Oh no, Ursula,' she said, in a low voice, as if someone might hear us. 'You must not speak of such things. Mama would not like it. The playhouse I know is an ungodly lascivious place and not for gentlewomen such as you and I.'

'But it is not,' I said, 'it is—'

'Now, Sister,' she said, putting her fingers to her lips. 'Hush.'

# X

# TOGETHERNESS

*In which I enjoy a grand family dinner*

## AND
## SO
## TO *DINE*

---

*Acted by*

the KING'S MEN

*at*

THE VERE STREET THEATRE

---

*written by the* noble

*LADY* 'X'

*An oak-panelled room lit with sconces. Flames send darts of flickering light upwards. A long table spread with a white cloth is set for dinner. There is a sheep's head on a pewter dish, and a round pie with a shiny, frilled crust with a cross pricked out on its top. There are tureens of stewed gurnet and dishes of apple cream; crystal goblets of sack and steaming jugs of hot spiced rum, the scent of which drifts in the air and mingles with the roasted meat and the burning wax.*

*MAMA sits at the head of the table in a severe black gown, against the fashion. Her mouth is set into a line; she watches all that goes on and strokes the prongs of her fork. TYRINGHAM breaks a piece of bread and tears at it with his teeth. The crumbs fall all over the table. Beside him, URSULA watches him sideways. Her hand is on her goblet. She picks it up and sips it, but her hand is shaking, and as she sets it down, it spills; a black-red bead runs down the stem and falls onto the white cloth. She grimaces. Opposite her, SIBELIAH opens her mouth and titters.*

SIBELIAH: [*Pointing*] Ursula, you dolt, you have upset your wine again!

*URSULA looks down at the stain, which blooms outwards. It is the size of a pea, then a penny, then a shilling. She covers it with her hand.*

TYRINGHAM: Careless wench! [*He taps at her hand*] What shall we do with her?

SIBELIAH:     [*Eagerly*] Tweak her nose until she squeals and then
              lock her in the closet until she whimpers!

TYRINGHAM:    Ho, Sister! Remember when that was our
              punishment, Mama?

MAMA:         Aye, for you wailed fit to wake the dead the first
              time you went in.

SIBELIAH:     And our brother Joseph scratching at the door all
              the while to frighten Ossy it was rats come to gnaw
              him to death – or the Devil, with his long sharp
              fingernails!

MAMA:         I should have had all three of you whipped soundly,
              for all the good it did.

TYRINGHAM:    It did me good, I'll warrant – why, look at me now.

MAMA:         A married man.

SIBELIAH:     It took you long enough.

TYRINGHAM:    Aye, but I had to find the right woman! A true lady.
              For I could not make do with any wench, now could
              I, Mama? You know your son.

MAMA:         You will be a father soon too, if it please our Lord
              Jesu...

SIBELIAH:     Amen.

MAMA:         ... and then our family name is secured and I may
              stop turning about in my bed at night, for fear you
              shall be carried off of an ague and all our fortune
              with it.

TYRINGHAM:    Oh, Mama. You must not derange yourself. We shall
              get a babby soon, I am sure, for we pray for it every
              night, do we not, wifelet?

URSULA: Oh, aye. Most thoroughly. We pray for it so often I am quite fatigued, in truth.

SIBELIAH: Christ Jesu watches us always, and knows what we do.

MAMA: That he does. [*Her eyes linger on* URSULA, *who is spooning stew onto her plate. Some of the juice slips from the ladle and runs down her arm*] Tell me, Ursula, how does your mother do, in her widowhood? I dearly sympathize with her, for I have been alone myself so many years.

URSULA: [*Looking up from her mopping*] Oh very well, I think. She writes that Reginald is to go away to school, for she cannot spank him any more times. [*She guffaws*] He does not turn a hair from it, so it is quite a waste of time. She is not too lonely, I think, for she has my sister Catherine, who is a sweet and good girl, and Mary, who is now her companion, as she once was mine, and so I know they must go on well together. How I miss my Mary!

MAMA: 'Tis fortunate that you have Beck in her place.

URSULA: I couldn't be luckier if I had a gown made of four-leaf clovers and a rabbit foot for a head.

MAMA: [*Rapping on the table*] It is time, children!

SIBELIAH: Oh goody.

URSULA: For what?

SIBELIAH: To say what we did today.

URSULA: Oh. Splendid.

TYRINGHAM: I shall go first. *On this gracious day of our Lord I...* rode as far as the Bristol ten-mile stone. Clopper has got over her worm and is now running well, though she is still a little shy of jumping, so we practised putting her at the fallen oak at Windmill Corner. Then we rode about the village while the tenants doffed their caps to us.

SIBELIAH: I do adore it when they doff! So *sweet*.

TYRINGHAM: Then I went over the Fines Book.

SIBELIAH: Hazzah!

URSULA: What is the Fines Book?

TYRINGHAM: Have I not told you of it yet? I am remiss! 'Tis a wondrous thing to control the servants that my father began called the Fining System, and we have stuck to it, for nothing keeps common folk honest like the threat of losing money.

SIBELIAH: 'Tis one penny for a door left open. And one penny for idleness. And one penny for a dirty shirt or smock or hands.

TYRINGHAM: 'Tis one penny for an oath. And if a servant strikes another. And so on. It all goes down in the book.

SIBELIAH: [*Excitedly*] But 'tis one *shilling* for being late to morning prayers. The rule is, they must be in their pews before the bells have stopped ringing. Oh how funny it is to see them running, red in the face and fit to burst into tears! Ursula, you will roll with laughter when you see it.

URSULA: But what if they do not have the shilling?

SIBELIAH: Then they are whipped soundly until they squeak!

URSULA: But truly, they cannot have much, and what if they need it for bread?

MAMA:          [*Deliberately*] And so we go on. Sibeliah?

SIBELIAH:      *On this gracious day of our Lord I*... read from the
               book of Numbers with you, Mama, and tried to
               commit its passages to memory, though my brain
               is very weak and I am sure I will not remember
               it tomorrow. But never mind, for I am certain its
               goodness will soak into me. Ooh – and I worked on
               my Bible cover – I am embroidering it, brother, as
               a Saint's Day gift for Sarah. I found I had a glut of
               red and orange and yellow, and I could not think
               what to do with them. And then it came to me,
               while I was gazing into the fire: I shall cover it all
               over with hell flames! And there will be the Devil,
               capering with his long spoon and shining hooves,
               and Lucifer too, but I shall need jet beads for him
               for his great black wings – for I am certain they
               turned dark as soot when he fell down from the
               heavens and went to live in the fiery chasm of hell.
               They would have been singed. The smell must have
               been awful, for there is no scent worse than burnt
               feathers.

URSULA:        [*Aside*] I can think of one.

MAMA:          *On this gracious day of our Lord I*... prayed to Christ
               Jesu and asked him to watch over our family. And I
               had Sarah distribute alms to the poor in the village,
               for I had heard that the Brownlow woman was
               begging again...

SIBELIAH:      Pooh! I have seen the old hag screeching for coins
               in the marketplace. Horrid-smelling thing! I dare
               not go near her, for fear she should bite me or cast a
               spell that turns me into a mouse.

| | |
|---|---|
| URSULA: | [*Aside*] Or a shrew. |
| MAMA: | And I spoke to Mrs Jickell about us having more rabbit at table, for they are all hopping about the fields and I cannot fathom why they are not in the pot. I have got a book of French receipts coming from Cousin Agnes, and I am sure that will set her right, for it is said the French are very fond of cunny. |
| URSULA: | I have heard that. |
| SIBELIAH: | What did you do today, Ursula? |
| URSULA: | Why, I walked in the gardens and climbed up a hill, and then it rained, and my bonnet got wet, and so I came down again, which was providential for I just missed that great storm. Then when I had dried myself off, I went to the library and read a very interesting little book about the history of the Romans, who conquered the world and did a great many wondrous things, and 'tis strange that we should have forgot them all and become as stupid as we are, but that we did. And then I trotted up and down the gallery practising my Italian conversation with an imaginary friend who I have named Faustina Caterina Luchia di Piazza San Marco. [*Gesticulating*] *Faustina Caterina, sono infelice qui. Voglio scappare!* And then I sat down and worked at... my writing – by which I mean, my letters – to Mother and Grisella, for I am anxious to hear of them and how they do and to tell them about... you all. |
| SIBELIAH: | Faith, how do you think of such things? I know I should get a head pain if I moved my body as much as you do. Do you not feel weak from it, Sister? I |

fear you shall take a head-cold and be killed.

MAMA: Did your mama allow you to romp all over the countryside at Bynfield? I hardly think it can be decent. At any rate, now you are a Tyringham, and a Lady, 'tis not.

TYRINGHAM: You must be more sober, Ursula. And I would see you play the lute and work at your screen a little more. I like to see my wife making herself useful – and making the house beautiful besides.

URSULA: But I am not—

MAMA: That is your duty.

URSULA: I do not know if—

MAMA: With Jesu's help you will find the strength to grow into goodness.

SIBELIAH: Amen.

URSULA: [*Aside*] Well this does not bode well!

*Curtain*

# XI

# ALLY

*In which I am comforted by a friendly face*

Grisella had come at last. She arrived on a wet morning, her cloak stained with rainwater, her nut-brown curls frizzing in the damp. She had scarce come into the hallway, when I ran to her and squeezed her tight to my body. She smelt of lavender and oranges and road-dust.

'Oh Grisella, my dear friend!' I cried, kissing her face, and stepping back from her to admire how grown-up and pretty she looked. 'You cannot think how pleased I am to see you at last.'

'You said so in your letters,' she said, pushing back her hood with hands that I saw were now adorned with gemstones, 'all of them.'

'You're a rotten correspondent,' I said, taking her arm and leading her through to the parlour.

'Aye,' she said. 'But it takes me so long to write, and then I must have Frederick do it for me, and he tells me not to be a gossip and suggests very dull things I should put in, such as "The weather is very mixed." And "I do hope you are enjoying excellent health."'

'Mayhap I should write to Frederick, instead?' I said. 'For your brother sounds a very pleasant young man on paper.'

'Oh no, he is very dull these days,' she said, throwing her arms out. 'For he has a sweetheart called Philippa and goes about all day with a simple look on his face, and I do not know why, for she is quite plain and has a limp.'

'Poor Philippa,' I said.

'Poor Frederick,' Grisella corrected me.

Grisella wandered about the room looking at all the objects on the mantelpiece with an appraising air. 'I shall take you on a tour of the house presently,' I said. 'But let us sit and drink a dish of tea.' I sat myself down on the chaise and patted the vacant space beside me. 'You must be weary from your journey. And I cannot wait a minute longer to hear news of home.' She sat down and took my arm and we bent our heads together and whispered.

'And what of little Catherine?' I said eagerly. 'I think of her most of all, for she cannot write and Mother does not tell me everything as you do.'

'She is coming on very well, I think,' she said. 'From what I have seen of her at church, but I do not always go, for it means getting up in the morning and I do like to laze in bed – which I expect you have been doing a lot of, with your *husband*,' she said meaningfully, pinching my thigh. 'Tell me, have things improved, or do you still have to lie like a statue with your eyes shut, as you wrote in your last letter – do not stir yourself, for I have burned them all, and Mumsy shall not see them. I'm sure that isn't how it's usually done, for I was walking into the village and I heard the most diverting talk betwixt Mistress Deerhorn and Mistress Bland, you know, the lawyer's wife. And Deerhorn says (looking very flushed in the face, so I think it was God's Honest Truth): "Gad, I am all undone this morning, for Roderick has had me every which way last night, and I am sauntering like a sailor." And Mrs Bland goggles her eyes a bit and then says—'

Somebody coughed. I started, and Grisella gripped my knee so hard I flinched. I swept my eyes around the room and saw that it was Beck, who had been stood by the window all the while, but we had not seen her, for the morning light was streaming in and had made her little more than a dark shape against the folds of the great baize curtain.

'Oh,' said Grisella.

'Why, Beck,' I said, angrily. 'What, pray, are you doing there?'

'Eavesdropping,' said Grisella archly.

'Yes, eavesdropping,' I said. 'And it will not do.'

'My Lady,' said Beck. 'I was awaiting my orders. For Brignall said to stay myself here and wait on ye and your guest in place of Clara, my Lady, who is took ill, but then I had a cough.' She licked her lips in her saucy way, and I felt my body clench with anger. How many other times had the crafty girl watched me without my knowing?

'Go and fetch us the tea tray, for we shall try the new blend,' I said, in what I hoped was a sharp, commanding voice. 'And mind you are quick about it, for Lady Grisella is thirsty. Bring her some of Mrs Jickell's ginger cake. And a flagon of raspberry wine, while you are about it. And if there are any of the roasted eels left, bring them too and we will have them cold with the quince jelly.'

Beck nodded and rubbed at her eyes. She did not look chastised in the slightest.

'And I will have words with the master about this when he is home.'

'If it please ye, my Lady,' she said blandly. 'I will take my leave now, my Lady,' she said, and stepped quickly into the shadows of the doorway and was gone.

''Pon my soul,' said Grisella. 'I have never seen the like! Why, you ought to have got her by the nose and pinched her roundly, for I know I would have done the same in your place. Mumsy has been plagued all her life with wayward wenches and she swears 'tis the only way a slut will take notice, and even then they likely will not, and will only be tamed with a whipping.'

'Tyringham does not like to beat the servants overmuch,' I said. 'For we have the Fines Book, as I told you – I can see you sniggering behind your hand – and he believes it is God's duty to give us our punishments, on the whole. "Slaves, in all things obey those who are your masters on earth,"' I intoned.

'God's teeth, I swear I do not know you at all!' she said, staring at me. 'For you, married less than a year, are quoting the Bible at me where it used to be Margaret Cavendish, and drifting about this dark house all pale and drab...' She touched my shoulder. 'And where did you get that shawl? It looks like something my grandmother would have worn on her deathbed. And those collars went out with Cromwell, may he burn in hell for ever.'

'The Dowager gave me the shawl and Sibeliah sewed me the collar, for I had admired hers...' I saw her face. 'I was being polite.'

'That is not like you either!' she cried. 'For where are your books and your plays? And where are the ink stains on your hands?' She grabbed my hand and turned it over. 'White and fair and not a mark on them,' she said.

'I have not written anything for a while,' I said, twisting my hands and looking down at them, for I did not want to look into her eyes. 'Tyringham does not like to see me scribbling and I am confined to snatched moments, and when he is away at Court, as now. But my lute is coming on quite well. After supper, you shall hear it, and Sibeliah shall accompany me on the harpsichord...' I trailed off. 'It is lamentable, I know,' I said, my voice beginning to wobble. 'For I cannot—' I could not finish the sentence.

Grisella looked at me a long while, and then took up my arm again and patted it. 'Well now, we cannot have this. But 'tis easily remedied. After we have taken our tea – if that lackadaisical slut ever brings it, no doubt she is ladling some of it into her pockets to sell at market – we shall go and act a script together. You must have something we can play at? For I cannot believe you have written nothing all these months.'

'I have a few fragments,' I said, knuckling my eyes. 'But faith, they are not ready...'

'It does not signify,' she said, waving her hands. 'For we shall act it out together, and be merry all the while. And you shall not weep.'

# THE MAID'S FROLICK

a
*cautionary tale*

---

*Acted by*

URSE & GRISS

*at*

THE THEATRE

IN LITTLE LINCELUS–INN FIELDS

---

*From the Quill of*

THE

EVER ARTFUL *'Lady T'*

DRAMATIS PERSONAE

MAID/LORD – Lady Ursula Tyringham

LADY – Lady Grisella Shadforth


ACT II, SCENE II

> *Morning. A lady's chamber, in disarray. The*
> *drawers of the dressing table stand open.*
> *Fripperies spill out – green ribbons, ropes of*
> *pearls, white handkerchiefs, bits of lace. On the bed*
> *a hump of lilac and sky-blue and saffron yellow.*
> *The hump begins to move. A head and shoulders*
> *emerge. It is a* MAID, *dressed in her lady's*
> *finery. She spins in a circle. The striped petticoat*
> *she is wearing flares out. She rights herself;*
> *pulls something from the pile – a fur – and*
> *drapes it around her neck. She backs away from*
> *the pile and takes three steps to the looking glass.*
> *She is singing.*

MAID: A brisk young man, dilly dilly/Met with a maid/And laid
her down, dilly dilly/Under the shade/There they did play,
dilly dilly/And kiss and court/All the fine day, dilly dilly/
Making good sport!

> *She holds out her arms. Dances a couple of steps.*

MAID: Lavender's green, dilly dilly/Lavender's blue/You must love
me, dilly dilly/Because I love—

LADY: [*Crashing the door open and striding into the room*] Beck! You
did not come so I – oh!

> *She slowly comes towards the girl. Stops. Looks at*
> *the bed. Looks back at the girl.*

LADY: Came to find you. What – *what* – are you doing?

> *She stands in front of her maid. Slowly looks her up and down.*

LADY: My things! All my clothes – that is my... you are wearing my new petticoat! And that – that is the ermine pelisse my mother gave to me as an Advent gift. And my best silk chemise! This – is a – a scandal!

MAID: My Lady—

LADY: And you stand there so bold, looking me in the eye and you say 'My Lady'. My Lady what? What excuse can you have now, Beck? I think you will have none, for there can be none.

> *The* MAID *says nothing, but gazes ahead, clicking her tongue.*

Kick off my slippers – now! They do not even fit you – you will stretch them with your great feet. Take everything off immediately. I will have to have it all cleaned for the stench of you will be all over it.

> *The* MAID *obeys, silently. She takes off the stole, drops it on the floor. Shakes her feet out of the slippers. She bends down and pushes herself out of the skirt, leaving it in a messy puddle.*

Pack up your box and make ready to leave this house. Brignall will give you your wages, with your fines deducted, and that is more than you deserve. You shall not have a reference, for you have been nothing but trouble to me, and I would not wish you on another, and so you must shift for yourself.

MAID: My Lady.

LADY: My Lady, what?

MAID: We'll see what the master says about it.

LADY: The master? What he says does not signify for you are my maid and I am Lady here.

> *The* MAID *smirks.*

LADY: You dare to meddle with me?

> *She slaps the maid smartly around the face. The* MAID *takes the blow doggedly; she is used to it. Her smirk grows wider.*

LADY: There! That hurt my hand.

> *The* MAID *presses her hand to her cheek.*

LADY: Do not tarry here, else I'll fetch the constable to see you off.

MAID: If you say so, my Lady.

LADY: Be gone from my sight!

> *Exit* MAID.


ACT II, SCENE III

> *The same chamber, later that day. The room is turned yellow with afternoon light. The clothes and fripperies have been tidied away. The* LADY *sits in a chair by the window with a book in her hand. She is scribbling in it furiously. She looks up as the door creaks open and stuffs the book hastily behind a cushion. The* LORD *comes into the room, and frowns when he sees her in the chair. She gets up quickly. Turns around to check the cushion is still in its place.*

LADY: Ah, husband!

LORD: I came up to find my gloves. There's a nip in the air – you wouldn't think it from in here.

LADY: Nay. [*Pause*] How does Sir Bernard do today?

LORD: Oh, much the same, eyeing me mournfully, and seems rather low in spirits. Hanging his head and so on. But he took a good meal last night, and we hope he shall recover yet.

LADY: How I pity that horse, for there is nothing worse than a belly ache – we women know that more than anyone.

LORD: You are still troubled by the... pains then? I thought I had not noticed the signs of your cursing.

LADY: I have been craving pineapple since Tuesday last, and that may be a sign.

LORD: It may be a sign that you are craving pineapple.

LADY: 'Tis true. But I can do nothing but hope. And pray, of course. Lots of praying.

LORD: Hmm. Have you seen my gloves?

LADY: Are they in your closet?

*He goes through a door. Sounds of rummaging.*

LADY: Husband, I am glad you are come, for there is a matter I would speak with you about.

LORD: [*Enters, holding the gloves*] Inside one of my boots! Who would do such a thing?

LADY: This vexing matter...

LORD: I am very vexed – by the gloves in my boots.

LADY: I have pondered long and hard on the subject...

LORD: You do prattle, child. What shoes are you wearing today? Are they the ones I bought you?

LADY: [*Sliding her foot out from below her skirts*] No, they are the rose-pink slippers.

> *The* LORD *sighs.*

LADY: I thought about it, and I realized that I, a woman, should not attempt to tussle with my quandary for my brain was not made for it and it is too hard.

LORD: You talk too much of brains. [*Putting on the gloves*] I believe you're trying to get round me.

LADY: Indeed not, husband. I only, as your loving wife, wish for your help and guidance in this difficulty.

LORD: Well out with it, for I have business to attend to and cannot shilly-shally all day.

LADY: 'Tis Beck.

LORD: Not this again.

LADY: This morning I found her in a compromising position.

LORD: Is that so – indeed I... where were you? I mean, what position was it? Forgive me, a position! My, my, how dreadful.

LADY: Here in this very chamber, I found her – and this you will not believe – dressed head-to-toe in my garments and wearing all of my jewels.

LORD: Oh.

LADY: And she was singing!

LORD: I see.

LADY: I told her that such abominable insolence could not be tolerated, and she must leave us at once.

> *She watches his face. He is smoothing out each*
> *of his gloves in turn. He considers his hand.*
> *Wiggles his fingers.*

LORD: Nay, nay, we cannot do that.

LADY: What, husband? Why?

LORD: 'Twould not be wise.

LADY: But she has been disobedient! She has worn my clothes – she with her stench and her... greasy bosom.

LORD: Aye. I shall ask Mama to scold her roundly. And she shall be fined. One shilling. That should do it.

LADY: But I have told her – I have given her notice. It will look... it will look... as if I am not mistress here.

LORD: You are young, child. But you will learn that it does not do to speak to the servants when your passions are roused.

LADY: I am sixteen now, and will be seventeen three months hence!

LORD: Now, now, lambikin. Beck has committed a... misjudgement. But no harm is done, really. The clothes are not torn... the jewels are not tarnished – are they?

LADY: Nay, but they shall all have to be washed, for they stink of her!

LORD: We will have her clean them all, then, and that will be her punishment.

LADY: But I do not like her, Tyringham. I do not want her here.

> *The* LORD *fumbles with his gloves. He does not meet her eye.*

I am Lady Tyringham. I am your wife! I—

LORD: Aye. You are my wife. Do not forget it.

> *He turns on his heel, banging the door behind him.*
>
> *Exit* LORD.
>
> *A pause.*

LADY: God's gizzards, did this really happen, Urse? But this is monstrous.

LORD: Aye, 'tis the truth.

LADY: I fear marriage is not the piece of currant cake I thought it.

LORD: Nay, Grisella, 'tis not that at all.

*Curtain*

❦

After our playing Grisella enjoyed herself immensely, rifling through my trunks and boxes and making suggestions such as 'You ought to have pearls sewn at the top of these sleeve slashes.' And 'A brooch would look very well on this hat.' 'Frederick says all the London ladies go about in famous high pattens to wade through the filth they have on the streets there; you ought to get some made, for you could do with a few inches.' I managed to distract her from this with a tour of the house, during which she said uncharacteristically little, but instead made a collection of polite noises like 'Ohmm' and 'Ah'.

I ended the tour where I had begun it, in the entrance hall. 'And that... is Turvey.'

'Oh Urse,' she said, sweeping her eyes up from the marble statues to my face. 'Isn't it spooky! How do you walk around it at night?'

'Why, I don't come down here after lights out,' I said, laughing at her rounded eyes. 'And if there are spectres walking here, I haven't heard them.'

'Yet,' she said. 'Let's go outside, out of the gloom.'

The sun was high in the sky, and the weather fine for September, and it felt good to walk about with my arm tucked in Grisella's, she chattering all the while. The walled garden (which had got rather wild) and the maze she liked better than Poseidon ('Ostentatious – but not in the right way') or the Dowager's ornamental flower garden ('Tis plain colours are not her forte. She should apply to look around Hoyden

Park, for Mumsy has been and even the kitchen garden looks the better for it').

That evening we assembled in the parlour. The fire belched out coal smoke in thick grey plumes, for we were experimenting with this new kind of fuel; though the Dowager predicted no good would come of it, my husband said it was what the King had at Whitehall. Grisella, coughing a little, settled herself on the settee beside me in an attitude of exhaustion and kicked her feet onto the little stool, all the better to show off the shoes her papa had got for her in Italy, which had buckles studded with seed-pearls and a high wooden heel.

'God's giddy gizzards,' she sighed. 'I am quite done up with all our larks today, Ursula.'

'Why, we only walked around the house and gardens,' I said, watching the Dowager.

'Aye, but 'tis all the fresh air out here in the country. I swear I could drop dead in my chair as I sit.' She yawned extravagantly behind her hand.

'Bynfield is hardly the town,' I began, but Grisella had already revived herself.

''Tis wonderful to be here, Countess,' said Grisella when we were all settled in our places. 'Turvey Hall is... just as Ursula described it to me.'

The Dowager nodded graciously and had a thin sort of smile on her lips.

'Do you not sew?' said Sibeliah from behind her screen, a needle trailing scarlet thread in her hand. She had been eyeing my friend very closely indeed ever since she had laid eyes on her at supper and seemed to find her baffling, or entrancing – I could not quite make out which.

Grisella laughed very gaily and shook out her curls, which she had re-primped before we came down to supper. She was wearing a butter-cup-coloured gown I had not seen before, and she looked peachy and beautiful in the firelight.

'Ho, no, none of that for me, though Mumsy will scold me about it almost every evening. I sometimes strum a lute, for I have lovely plump hands and arms,' here she extended them for the company to view, 'and it shows them to their best advantage – I have heard,' she added, an earnest look on her face. 'I would not say so myself.' She folded her hands artfully in her lap and leaned back in her chair.

'We are not idle in the evenings here,' said the Dowager, picking up her sewing. 'Ursula will fetch a lute for you if you wish it, and you shall accompany her on the harpsichord, which we are all keen for her to practise more.'

'I can play the first bit of Lully's *Miserere* almost all of the way through without looking,' I said.

'Oh, no one modish listens to Lully any more,' said Grisella scornfully. 'It's too depressing. You have to wonder what goes on at Versailles, really you do. But that is those frog-eaters all over, in faith.'

The Dowager was heard to cough.

'I think it's beautiful,' I said. 'It makes me weep.'

'And why would you want to weep, indeed?' said Grisella in a way that sounded exactly like her mother. 'But I expect it's hard to keep up with things out here in the country – why, the nearest village must be ten miles hence. But I knew it was so, and I have brought reams of sheet music with me, got by Frederick in London especially for you, Ursula, which includes...' here she moved her lips about teasingly '... and Urse will know what I am about – one Master Henry Purcell, who I have heard has a very fine calf on him, and not a bad face – and there is an etching of him on the frontispiece.' She winked at me. 'You will like him, Sibeliah, for he has written much of it praising the Lord.'

The Dowager opened her mouth and closed it again.

'Why, I do enjoy a godly refrain,' said Sibeliah, pausing in her embroidery.

'Grisella, you are kind,' I said, squeezing her arm.

'Not at all,' said Grisella, turning her head to me. 'It is wrapped in my trunk, if we may send someone to fetch it.'

'I will ring,' said the Dowager, picking up the silver bell which she kept by her side. 'But we do not oft send the servants running about for trifles.'

'Oh, this isn't a trifle, Countess Tyringham. 'Tis a necessity,' said Grisella, and laughed.

# XII

✤

# FRUSTRATION

*In which I consider my position, and am unhappy*

⟡⟡⟡

The mantel clock ticked on and on. I was lying on the couch in my chamber one October afternoon, my head on a silk cushion, my skirts thrown over the seat back. It had been raining, but the sun had come out and now the windows were dappled with minuscule raindrops, each one lit up and shimmering in the light. My linnet had stopped singing a week ago, and a musty smell floated around his cage. He no longer hopped onto my finger when I opened the little door, nor fluttered from perch to perch in a flurry of feathers. Neither did he flick his head into the little thimble of water I had placed there for him, and filled up every day, as Beck – who despite all my protestations had not been put out – could not be trusted to remember and I did not want him to go thirsty. I tipped my head back to look at him. He stood, silently, on the floor of the cage.

'Are you bored, my little one?'

It was four hundred and fourteen days since my marriage: I had marked my almanac, crossing off each day as it passed: the pleasing slice of the pen as it struck through a sunset, a sunrise. Four hundred and fourteen days at Turvey Hall, with the dust and the wind and the slitted eyes of servants and the taste of strange food on my tongue, and the rustle of my stiff new clothes. Four hundred and thirteen nights, with my husband wheezing his sour breath into my face, the press of his limbs on mine, the wet kisses he laid on my forehead, the way he took my star-shaped body, while my mind floated far away, up to the bright night sky.

I still did not feel like the lady of my own house. I could not do the things my mother had told me would be expected of a wife, and all my practising with her at ordering dinners from the kitchen, and keeping stock of the housework, and overseeing the servants, had come to naught, for the Dowager did it all, and shushed my every complaint. So I walked about the corridors of Turvey Hall in a frilled silk wrap, and supped my potage with a silver spoon embossed with my initials, and dreamed of another, more useful sort of life.

I let my arm fall down from the pillow and trailed my fingers along the surface of the carpet, which was thick and red and brought from Persia. I looked up again at my linnet. Such a pretty cage he had: with slender bars stretching upwards in a dome shape surmounted by a little golden figure, a nightingale, its beak pointing proudly to the sky, clawed feet resting on a scroll which had my new name – not so new any more – picked out in cursive script: *Tyringham.* The cage, and the linnet, were a gift from my husband, who had had it sent all the way from Paris, where it was the fashion for ladies to keep songbirds, which were pretty pets, so much prettier than dogs. That's what my husband said, as he whisked away the cloth that covered it on my first day at Turvey Hall, and said he hoped I would be amused and comforted, for he wished me to be happy and content.

'Oh my pretty boy,' I said, to the bird. 'Perhaps you are lonely, and that is why you do not sing. Mayhap I shall get you a sweetheart, and then you may sing together as happy as the day is long.'

His head disappeared into his breast and twitched there a while.

'But mayhap you don't want a wife at all.'

I sighed. The clock chimed the hour. I was weary; my thoughts moved slowly around my head as if in a mire. I had not read a book for twelve days. I had not put my pen to paper for seventeen. I suffered from head-pains. I did not know myself. I did not know this Lady Tyringham, a dull, insipid girl who sat and meekly worked at a tapestry.

I did not have the energy to write many letters, and I did not get many, now.

Feeling very warm about the neck, I cast off my wrapper. There was an ache in my ears that had started up and my throat was tight and dry, and when I touched my forehead it was warm underneath my fingertips. Heaving myself off the chaise, I made sure my door was tight fastened and then got out the little box I had stowed under my petticoats, which contained my writing book and my almanac and my little wooden bear, for she was becoming dirty with frequent handling, and so I had stowed her here all the better to preserve her. Here too were my secret pouches of dried herbs – and I rooted through them, for I had decided to doctor myself with a posset – I was greatly afeard of taking ill, for now I knew where that led.

I tipped a few good glugs of sack into a flask and dropped in pinches of each ingredient, as Goodsoule had taught me, remembering to chant over the mixture as I stirred them together.

> Remember wormwood, angelica, nutmeg, nettle,
> And you, scurvy grass, horseradish and juniper.
> Against the fever, against the ague,
> Against the dropsy, against the plague.
> Seven herbs picked in a waxing moon,
> Seven days apart,
> I speak this charm but seven times
> To cast the poison out!

I drank off a cupful of the potion with a flourish, which went down mighty bitter, but comforted me withal, for it seemed to draw me back to the happiness of my childhood, with Goodsoule and Mary. I had made a flagon of the stuff and saw that I had better finish the whole, or else be discovered in the ways of a wise woman, which I knew would anger my husband, for all cunning ways did. So I drank the whole thing down in great gulps, hiccoughing several times after it.

'I beg your pardon,' I said to my linnet.

Feeling somewhat revived, but still a trifle warm, I resolved to go out of doors to cool myself and set off downstairs. I stepped out in my slippers, feeling the damp of the rain-sluiced grass soak into my stockings as I hastened quickly across the lawn, fearing that someone might see me and call me back. The breeze lifted up, and I sighed to feel its coolness blowing across my burning cheeks.

Swinging my arms, I followed the way past the maze to the orchard. Here I had a favourite low-boughed apple tree, which when surmounted had a pleasant view of the surrounding county. Not feeling vigorous in my spirits, I instead leant against its familiar knobbled trunk and, after gazing about at the rolling hills before me, felt in my skirts for my long-neglected book, drew it out and kissed it.

'I am sorry for forsaking you, book,' I said, laying it against the branch as my writing desk, and took out my pencil.

# *A* DISCOURSE *on* MATRIMONY *&* WIVING *for* NEW BRIDES

BY

A MARRIED WOMAN
*who* KNOWETH

'Tis arduous to be a new bride and married to your husband, & if you are young, you may rue your union. But I say listen to me who is a wife & I shall tell you how to go about the thing with these four rules for happiness in wiving:

*Article the first:* Submit unto your husband and master in all things even if he be not learned and is strange and cold in his ways, for the fault lieth with ye, and ye must strive to correct thyself!

*Article the second:* Be quiet and meek in your discourse, confining yourself to idle chatter on the following suitable topics for women:

> The weather
> The King's health
> The Queen's health
> The fashions (to other women)
> Music – excepting street ballads
> Health – excepting childbearing
> Weddings – excepting marriage portions

*Article the third:* Your husband's happiness is above all things, so put ye aside your wants and needs, be tender and coo to him in the gentle voice of a dove, though he scold you and beat you and be rough with you in his wooing, and you shall not see heaven, however many times you say you crave to look upon it and beg him in the name of Jesu to love you kindly!

*Article the fourth:* If all other courses fail you, and you are brought down by worries or woe or other encumbrances suffered by the dutiful wife and feel fit to burst with ill-feeling and frustration and love-lack, steal yourself out of doors away from prying eyes and running as fast and as furious as you can, scream every oath you know in English, and other languages, or if this be not possible, and you are an educated woman, set down your strongest feelings in a secret book, and hide it, and think upon it, and get much private satisfaction from it withal!

I put down my pencil, and, feeling now quite bold from all the wine that I had taken, I thought I would take my own advice.

'Ahhh,' I tried. Two blackbirds lighted on the grass, quite unperturbed. 'Arrrrrgggggghhhh!' I cried, and rushed at the blackbirds, who rose up in a great flapping of wings. I turned and ran into the wind, and back again, capering like a fiend. 'The Devil rot those addle-pates who would lock me up!' I cried, my mouth now feeling as loose as my limbs. 'I... I curse their blood and I spit in their eyes!' I staggered a little, for my head was light. 'I am bored witless! God damn me body and soul!' I called out to the sky above.

I stopped, panting at my efforts, and looked around me, slightly fearful that someone was near. The cursing had brought my colour up even higher. I could feel the wine churning in my belly. Perhaps I had taken too much on an empty stomach. I bent forward, and took a few steady breaths, noticing that my slippers were now wet through entirely. This made me laugh, which in turn revived me, and I set off around the side of the house to the stables, for it had come into my mind that I would go there and see about a horse.

I leaned against the doorway of the stable, breathing in the old familiar smell of horse and hay and leather. It was a bigger stable than we had had at Bynfield, and had a tack room, and a hay store, and a great many stalls of polished wood. Stepping into it, my feet creaking on the floor, I called out a greeting, but perceiving the stable hand was not there, I lifted a bridle from a hook, and went from stall to stall, peering into each one. The fifth one along had a pretty nutmeg-coloured mare, who tossed her head up at me as I unlatched the door.

'Good day, madame,' I said. 'I would put this on you.'

I held my palm beneath the horse's muzzle and she snorted into it, all velvet and whiskers, but made no protest as I pushed my thumb and then the bit into her mouth, slid the bridle over her head and led her out to the mounting block. I had heaved myself halfway onto her back when I perceived I had forgot the saddle, and chuckled a little to myself at this.

'Forgive me, friend,' I said to the horse. 'I have had too much of my posset and am somewhat dishcombobulated.'

Swinging my legs over, I sat myself astride the mare with a man's seat, as I had many times at home when my mother was out, my skirts bunched up above my knees. I took up the reins and bade the horse walk on, gripping her sides with my thighs, and feeling the familiar rolling motion of her body under mine.

'Huzzah!' I cried as we began moving off down the drive. 'I am liberated!'

I had not been much into the village and thought to look upon the old ducking pond, and so I twitched the reins towards the green sunken lane that led there. How wondrous it felt to be moving, and out in the air! The sun had come out and now toasted my face and the scent of wildflowers drifted up to where I sat.

'Ah!' I breathed in. 'Ah!'

There were birds chittering in the great holly bushes that sprang up from the roadside in black-green tangles – I held my hands out to feel their prickles under my palm and picked off a blossom, and put it in my hair. Presently, we passed a brown-skinned farmhand crunching on an apple, and he touched his cap in reply to my 'Good morrow,' and some time after that a gentleman on horseback in hunting dress came by, who gave me an appraising look as he trotted past.

We had nearly come upon the green, for I could see it in the distance, when I heard the call of a deep voice behind me. I pressed my heels into the horse's belly, once, twice, thrice. She sped up to a trot, but then, flicking her ears back to the voice she recognized, slowed again to a plodding walk.

'Ho!' I called. 'Let us move off now, I beg you.'

But my husband (for it was he) was upon us (a little out of breath) and had caught up the reins and halted the mare, who consented to this with a great snorting.

'Ursula, what in Jesu's name do you do... whoa there!' (This to the horse.)

'Good morrow, husband,' I said, blinking at him. 'I thought to take a ride.'

'I see that,' he said, his voice a low tight thing that frightened me. 'And so do all the servants who were gathered at the windows to watch their mistress go down the drive on a pony with her legs and petticoats on display like a bawdy-show.' He led the horse around and jerked me off it roughly, twisting my arm and pressing his fingers so hard into my flesh that I yelped, against my will, for I hated him to know that he had hurt me.

'Have you coddled your wits?' he said loudly, straightening me up and shaking me, for I had fallen against him and twisted my ankle in the dismount. 'Your face is scarlet and your shoes are in tatters.'

'Mayhap,' I said.

Taking my arm then, he marched me back to the house in such a pet I had to skip to keep up with him, and then he said I must go to bed while he thought what he must do with me. For once I did not argue, for a weariness had slid back over my limbs and I dozed all the afternoon through, waking a little after dusk with the gong calling me to dinner.

At table I chewed mournfully at my bread and stirred my pudding round and round in a whirlpool. My husband would not meet my eyes. I picked up my spoon, and put it back down again, for everything tasted sharp on my tongue.

'Why,' said Sibeliah, forking her way through a great hash of hare. 'What ails thee, Sister? I have never seen you forfeit your pudding, even if you have shunned the potatoes. I had thought your adventure would give you an appetite.'

I waved my spoon at this, ignoring her barb. 'I am a little fatigued,' I said. My voice sounded strange in my ears. I shook my head.

Tyringham frowned and picked up my hand and put it next to his cheek.

'You're hot as an oven,' he said, looking at his mother with something in his face that I could not decipher. 'Feel her, Mama.'

The Dowager rose creakily from her chair and rustled over to where I sat. Her thin hand on my damp forehead was cool and dry and she pressed it there. I lolled back against her. She smelt of pipe-smoke and camphor and wine.

''Tis a fever,' she said, and then, bending over me, in a louder voice, said: 'You must lie down again now, child, for you are took ill.'

Was that concern in her eyes? I scrabbled about for her hand, but could only find her wrist, and squeezed it anyway, the lace of her cuffs crackling under my palms. I felt her moving away from me.

'Aye, I am come over famous bad,' I said to the ceiling. 'For I cannot see the stars, and ye know what that means.'

I laid my heavy head down on the table, feeling the sweat pricking my top lip.

'I hope I do not die,' I said.

# XIII

# AGUE

## *In which I am unwell*

I woke in the night. The coverlet was stuck to my skin; at my neck my hair was wet. A dull ache crept up my throat and there were two pincers of pain at my temples. I heaved myself about, twisting my face into the bolster. I slackened my limbs, willing sleep, but the room was light; it would not come. My blood boiled in my ears and my head throbbed and I knew the yellow bile was rising from my belly and coursing around my body and all of its humours. I pushed off the covers.

There was moonlight in my eyes. A sliver of white had slanted through the curtains and fallen across the bed, the wall. I stretched my fingers out, the line of my arm blurred in the darkness, and touched the bright shape that crossed the bed post. I wiggled my fingertips, all aglow with silver.

'Oh Mother moon, oh bright star, oh heaven-light which I hold in my hand,' I chanted, a vision of Mary swimming before me.

'Mary!' I called, raising my body up towards the door. 'I have a sickness.'

There was silence in the house, not even the creak of servants on the stair, just the whisper of leaves, in the branches outside.

I sank back on my pillows, a rhythmic wah, wah, wah sounding in my head. Perhaps it was the groan of a branch in the garden, or the lute playing of my mother at dinner. Wah wah wah: her fingers strummed the strings and the tangle in my head pulsed in time with her hands. The strings, her hands, the strings. Wah. Wah. Wah. But that was not today but long ago, for I was now married, and my husband was gone, and Mary was gone, and nobody would come.

What day was it? It was Wednesday. I had been here three days. Or was it five? Yesterday, my husband went to London, to see the King about a grant to supply the ships to fight the Dutch and I had dined alone in my chamber, the rattle of my cup and bowl in the empty room, Clara slouching against the wooden wall. They brought me only cold soup, hard bread and a jug of warm ale, for I was a girl and would not scold them. I was a haughty duchess but I could not command my servants. I had tried to swallow to keep up my strength, the whisper of the ague dragging at the back of my head, the gloss of a fever on my brow, but I knocked my wine onto the floor with a careless arm; Clara watched from her dark corner as it spread in a puddle by my feet, but did not move.

'The rats will drink it later,' I had said, before taking myself back to bed.

Sleep, where was sleep? My eyes watered. They would not close. I needed pennies to weight them. I closed my eyes. I drifted.

The night before my wedding we had dined on pickled samphire and a nutmeg hash and ginger-bread (I did not have ginger-bread now; Mrs Jickell did not like biscuits) and I had felt so full and contented as I leafed through *Foxe's Martyrs* by the fire, and Reginald had teased me and said I might go into a convent, and I pinched him 'til he squeaked I could go there now, to that memory. I was warm and full and sleepy. I was hot and Reggie was pinching me. I was by the fire and falling in, I was in the eye of the flames, calling and crying, but no one came.

I sat up, feeling the world move about me. How long had I slept? Out of bed, the floor cold under my feet, puppeting my legs, standing. I dragged on the coverlet as a cloak and walked the few steps to the window, and, leaning against the wall, pressed my fiery cheek against the stone. 'Ahhhhh.' My breath misted on the window. I rubbed it away with my sleeve.

The garden was shrouded in night: black leaves, dark trunks, pale lawn. I was aching, my bones were creaking and the bile and blood swirled within me, getting hotter, always hotter. The wind was up; the clouds scudded across the moon.

A noise from outside: a whine, a cry, something high that flew on the wind. I looked down at the garden. Standing there, on the grass, was a goat. The curve of horns, white body, legs lost in shadow. It turned its head and listened, bent its neck, tugged up a few blades of grass and chewed them slowly. The moon was in Capricorn and the ram had come to save me. The creature flicked its ears up and down and opened its mouth and called out to me with its goat-song.

My head began to swim and so I stepped back to the bed, flopped onto my back. The ceiling was dancing with shadows. I watched them, spellbound; a child with a bobbin. I coughed and turned over, the nightgown stuck to my skin. I would never get it off.

In the garden, the goat kicked its heels.

❧

## *A LIST, HIDDEN UNDER THE FLOORBOARDS:*

### THESE ARE THE THINGS HE HAS CUFFED ME FOR:

Speaking a charm against warts (the one on his thumb).

Talking too much of the playhouse, and of literature.

Overuse of my almanac. (Sibeliah must have been spying again.)

Crying too much and too long and in hearing of the servants.

Saying I hated him and would run off as soon as I could and take a horse and live as a wandering woman, or failing that a harlot, and would die in the streets, bedraggled and pitiful and covered with rotten cabbage soon as be his meek and dutiful wife.

❧

'My Lady! What do you do on the lawn in your night-shift? My Lady, you will catch a chill. You must come to bed. Can you hear me, my Lady?'

'Do you see the goat, Sarah? He is dancing with joy. He has come to carry me off and I will ride on his back to the stars and beyond to the heavens, where my father waits in his library.'

'I can't see no goat, my Lady, but you are dreaming in your fever, and have wandered outdoors. Come with me now and I shall lay ye down.'

'I want to go home.'

'That ye shall do, my Lady.'

'Look, the goat comes with us. He trots along beside us like my faithful dog, my Muffy.'

'Yes, my Lady.'

'Mary – where are we? I am took ill, I think.'

'We are in your chamber now, my Lady, where ye must lay down and be quiet. The doctor is coming tomorrow and will make ye all better.'

'No! He killed my father with his bleeding! I will not be cut! I will keep my blood boiling in my own veins, I thank ye.'

'I will tell him, my Lady. Goodnight and bless ye.'

'Mother? Hold my hand, Mother.'

'Here you are, my Lady.'

'Oh Mother, how I love you.'

'Rest now, my Lady.'

# XIV

# CONVALESCENCE

## *In which I am much surprised*

Someone was dabbing my forehead. I opened my eyes. The room was all aglow; the sun was streaming through the mullioned panes. A figure, in a grey gown, red hair spilling out of her bonnet. Red hair. Red hair. I knew red hair.

'Mary!' I croaked. 'Is it really you? Am I dreaming still?'

'Nay, 'tis I, in the flesh, here and coarse and common as ever. Feel.' She pinched my arm, but she did it very gently. 'I have come to nurse you, for you was took so bad they didn't know what to do and you would not have the doctor and screamed the house down when he came, and fought against him, and blackened his eye.' She chuckled.

'I did not!' I said. 'I do not remember it.'

'You did, and he has gone away again in a pet and says he will not come back, even if 'tis French pox.'

'How long have I been ill?'

'Why, three weeks or more, I think. They were worried when you kept on breaking out of doors in your shift and mumbling all the while of goats and stars and wishing you could fly.'

'Oh Mary, I am so glad you are here. I've had such terrible dreams.'

I pulled her to me, and wept a little, and she did too, though she turned her face from me to do it.

'And you have made me better and nursed me with your mother's remedies?'

'Aye and she has been here too, though she has gone away now, and your mother too, for they thought you would not live.'

'Mother came!' I said, struggling to sit up, though it was hard to do it and my limbs felt weak. 'Oh, but I do not remember it!'

'She came, and sat with you and whispered things into your ear, I know not what, but you smiled at them, and mumbled and seemed to sleep the better for it.'

'Ah,' I said.

'Now,' she said, going over to the dresser and getting a pot of something from it, 'you must have some medicine now you are astir, for it has been difficult to get you to drink it, and I have resorted to pinching your nose and pouring it down your throat.'

'You did not!'

'I did, Mrs. Drink.'

I took a sip. 'Jesu, what's in it?' I sputtered. 'It tastes worse than that toadskin concoction you had me drink for womb-pain.'

'Catgut, and feverfew and tansy... boiled with the tail of a drowned lamb... and honey and chamomile to sweeten it.'

'It's hardly sweet,' I said, but I pinched my nose and drank it off.

'Chew on this to take away the taste,' she said, pushing a little posy of parsley and mint in my hand. I chewed it.

'Mary,' I said, after I had swallowed. 'Why am I rustling?'

'You are bound in brown paper, against a chest-rheum, for you was coughing enough to wake the Devil, and so much choler came up, in lumps as big as my fist. That was when your husband went away and left us to our work, and you much the better for it, for we had not liked to chant over you while he was here.'

'Oh yes, my husband.' In my weakened state I had forgot that I was married. 'Where is he?'

'Gone to Court at the command of Old Rowley,' she said, straightening the row of bottles and jars which now stood on my side table, a pharmacopeia in miniature. 'And weren't the servants prating on it, thinking him gone off to find a new wife, with you being likely carried off with the next shower.'

'Huh,' I said.

'I do not like your Beck,' said she, her voice a whisper. 'She stamped on my foot on purpose and looks at me with evil in her eye.'

I sighed. 'I do not like her either.'

'Hmm,' she said, taking hold of my bedcoverings and smoothing them down, and tucking them tightly under me.

'Do not fuss!' I said, but I did not mean it, and fatigue began to seize hold of me again, and I drifted, slowly, lightly, happily, this time, to sleep.

❦

Such a joyous time we had in the weeks that followed, my Mary and I. The snow was too deep for her to be sent home, and for my husband to return neither, and so we had the house to ourselves, with only the Dowager and Sibeliah to spoil it, and they would not come near me, for fear of catching what I had. Mary and I spent the mornings closeted in my chamber, talking and dreaming and combing our hair. She told me of Malcolm Longfoot, who was no longer her sweetheart, and Jep Collins, who was courting her, and played the pipe under her window. She told me of Catherine, who could not read still, but was a hale and hearty child, and as happy as she could be, without me there. We thumbed through pamphlets and memorized ballads and said verses to one another aloud. We made up a new hairstyle that was ribbon bows tied all over the head, and went about like two peas in a pod, she trimmed with pansy-pink and me with sea-green.

'Oh, I have never been so happy as this,' said I, one bright morning, as I sat hunched on the window-seat and gazed out at the soft white garden below me. 'I hope the snow will never melt, for I would have my bosom friend beside me always. You shall stay, I hope, if my mother will let you.'

'I hope so,' she said.

A tap at the door; the rustling of skirts. A sickly fug I knew well.

''Tis I, Sister,' said Sibeliah, sliding into the room with her hands before her. 'I have come – or rather I am sent to tell you that it is coming on for dinner-time. Mama worries that you are up here chattering again, and shall be late down.'

'O thank ye, Sibeliah,' I said, while behind her Mary rolled her eyes about in her head and made me giggle. 'We will come down very soon, I should think.'

She hesitated in the doorway. Clank, clank. She felt for her sweet-pouch.

'Would you like a marzipanned nut, Mary?' she said, holding it out. 'They are good for the teeth and sweeten the breath withal.'

'No thank ye, my Lady,' said Mary primly. 'For it will ruin my dinner.'

'Oh aye,' said Sibeliah. 'I suppose it will.'

As she drifted away we exploded into a fit of giggles almost before her back was out the door.

'They must never find out,' I said, with a heaving back, 'that we have a sugar-cake inside the wardrobe!'

We wept.

# XV

# DISCOVERY

*In which I find something out*

# MISFORTUNE, DISCOVER'D,

a

*TRAGEDY*

BY MRS. TYRINGHAM.

LONDON

*Printed for* THO. DRING *at The Harrow at the corner of Chancery Lane in Fleet Street.*

*1682 A.D.*

## ACT III, SCENE IV

*Early evening. A darkened house. Outside the sky is streaked with pink.*

*URSULA, a girl in a cornflower-blue gown, walks briskly down a dim gallery. Her skirts swing from side to side. Her hair is primped with curls and tied all over with bright ribbons. In her hand, a book.*

URSULA:      Maryyyyyy! Maaaaaaaa-ry!

*Silence.*

Mary! I give up! You win! You are Queen of the Castle and I'm the Dirty Rascal!

*She pauses by an overstuffed chair. Behind her, the soft sound of slippered feet. She sniffs the air. She whirls around.*

URSULA:      Got you!

SIBELIAH:      Good evening to ye, Sister.

URSULA:      Oh, Sibeliah, where did you spring from? I am looking for Mary, for we are playing hide-and-seek, but I fear she has bested me and won again.

SIBELIAH:      I — nowhere. I am hurrying back to Mama, for 'tis getting on for nightfall and she does not like me to be alone about the house after the sun has gone down. [*Dropping her voice to a whisper*] When *ghosts walk.*

URSULA:      But they do not... ah yes, of course. The ghosts. [*Waggling her fingers*] Wooooooh! I'm famous frightened of 'em.

SIBELIAH:      You do not sound it.

| | |
|---|---|
| URSULA: | [*In mock fright*] WHAT WAS THAT! |
| SIBELIAH: | [*Clutching at her*] What? |
| URSULA: | Oh nothing, I thought I heard... |

> *They both strain their ears.*

> [*Swinging around*] WHAT WAS *THAT*!

| | |
|---|---|
| SIBELIAH: | [*Crying*] Oh Lord Jesu in heav'n, save us! |
| URSULA: | No, no. On second thoughts it was probably just rats. |
| SIBELIAH: | Rats! |
| URSULA: | [*Lolling against the window-sill*] Or the ghosts of rats, which are much, much worse, for they cannot be trapped, or poisoned, or *seen*. And when all the candles are snuffed out, then ye will hear them: prowling about the corridors and scrabbling against the wainscot with their wispy, ghostly claws. I believe they like to feast on human flesh at suppertime, for 'tis like nectar, to a ghost rat. |
| SIBELIAH: | Holy Mother, I shall have the vapours on the spot! |
| URSULA: | No you shall not, for they do not exist. Forget your fears of spirits and look out of the window now, for Gad, 'tis a glorious sunset, which means the snow-storm is over and perhaps we may go out of doors, presently. |
| SIBELIAH: | I cannot look at the sunset! |
| URSULA: | Plainly you must open your eyes first, or you will not see it. [*She takes the girl gently by the elbow and pulls her to the window*] Come, Sibeliah, there are no spectres here. Just I, your wayward sister, who teases you. |

SIBELIAH:      You're a sprite and a pixie, Mama said, and are not
               quite as you should be.

URSULA:        And how should I be, pray?

SIBELIAH:      Good and not wicked and always hidden away,
               keeping secrets.

URSULA:        Do you not have any secrets, Sibeliah?

SIBELIAH:      Nay, for Christ Jesu watches and knows everything
               we do, even when we are in our beds and private
               with ourselves – which we must never be for he sees
               it. Do not look at me with your eyes boring into me,
               for I do not have a secret. None that are mine. Not
               mine.

URSULA:        Then whose secrets, Sibeliah? Your mother's? Faith,
               I do not want to know hers.

SIBELIAH:      No. I must – I must find Mama.

                         *She runs off in a flurry of skirts. Turns over her
                         shoulder.*

SIBELIAH:      She-goblin!

                         URSULA *stands at the window a while,
                         watching the sky turn to violet, then to purple.
                         At last she turns away and continues down the
                         length of the room.*

URSULA:        Mary!

                         *She passes down a staircase. Turns back on
                         herself to the corridor below. The lamps have been
                         lit – it is comforting. She smiles. Stops. Another
                         sound in the empty corridor. Not feet this time.*

               [*Whispering*] Mary?

*She moves towards a room. The door is half open. Light blazes from the gap. A tapping sound. A cry. The mumble of voices. Another cry. The knocking of furniture. URSULA steps towards the door. Puts her palm to it. It creaks open, though she has barely touched it. The room is shadowy; a fire hisses in the grate. Against the wall, a woman's head, her hair tied all over with sea-green ribbons. A man's back, a man's legs, his breeches half down. The man's body pumps and thrusts. The woman moans. Lifts her head up. Opens her eyes.*

BECK:          Oh!

*BECK clutches at the man's shoulders. He swivels his head, slowly, ever so slightly. He turns it back again. He is still.*

URSULA:          Husband! I am... for once, quite lost for words.

*She turns on her heels and flees, her hand pressed to her mouth. She disappears into the darkness of the house.*

*Curtain*

⚜

# XVI

# CONSEQUENCES

*In which I am consoled*

O ver my husband's betrayal, I was at first most astonished, so that I could not take it in, and after I had fled back to my chamber, I began to walk to and fro about the room, not knowing what to think or what to do. Should I go back to them and scream? Slap Beck about the face and box her ears? Rail at my husband for breaking his marriage vows with this wench, of all of them? Though I knew that there was little sweetheart-love in my marriage so far, I had not thought it would come to this – I had not thought of this at all.

The sorrow of my lonely situation washed over me and, against my will, tears began to form in my eyes, for now I knew the very slender hope I had harboured that my married life would improve, perhaps, in time, was all ground to dust. I stamped my feet and gnashed my teeth and then dived face-forward onto the bed. I screamed into the pillow so that no one might hear, and kicked my legs, and screamed some more, whereupon I sat up, quite out of breath. Mary came to me then, and I told her the whole, and she pressed me to her.

'I'd thought as much by the way she'd acted so superior,' she said, stroking my hair, 'but I did not like to trouble you with it in case I was mistaken, though I am sorry for it now. 'Pon my soul, I should like to pound the slut, and murder him; I am ready to swing for the pair of 'em.'

I patted her and said it was not worth that. She talked to me of old times to console me, and that night we slept contentedly in each other's arms.

I did not have to face my husband, and I could not chastise him, for, perhaps in expectation of hot words between us, he went back to London at first light, waking me at dawn with the crunch of his horse's hooves on the drive, the cry of Jack wishing him 'Godspeed' on the treacherous roads, for the weather was still icy, though the snow had all but thawed. Beck, too, did not come to dress me, and so Mary did it, and we laughed to feel like children again.

Later I discovered Beck had been put out, and in her absence too, I found the things that had gone with her, for it could only have been she who had lifted my fine filigree necklace from its red velvet case, and torn my mauve silk gown from its hanger, and whisked, from under my pillow, the fine linen night-shift that I had worn on my wedding night. And it can only have been she, too, who wrenched my box of secrets out from its hiding place, and scattered its contents all over the floor, including my little wooden bear, who had fallen hard on the flagstones (or, as I suspected, been ground under an angry heel) and her tail quite broken off.

'Oh my poor little bear,' I said to it in a wobbly voice, as I wrapped it carefully in a stocking and tucked it away amongst my underthings. 'We are both not what we once were. But we shall be avenged, and that is my vow.'

To my sorrow, Mary was called back by my mother by letter the very next day, and went away from me but three days later, with wet cheeks and a watery smile, saying she would come back soon. I promised that I would send for her as soon as I could, and kissed her face, not daring to think of my life without her. We swore our old friendship oath as she climbed into the carriage, and I waved her down the drive with my kerchief, and watched her 'til she was but a dark speck, and then had disappeared from sight.

Now I knew that my husband did not care to make our marriage a happy one, I felt released from my charade as the dutiful daughter-in-law, and so, ignoring the calls of the Dowager and Sibeliah to sit with them and sew, I went out of doors every day it was fine, though the frost bit at my face. I climbed over stiles and tramped through fields, sometimes breaking into little runs for warmth, holding my face up to the watery winter sunshine, chanting my troubles aloud to Faustina Caterina Luchia di Piazza San Marco, and stopping to scribble feverishly in my book, for now I needed the comfort of writing more than ever. I sat in my chamber, and wrote long into the night as the moon blazed in at the windows, before falling asleep over my papers, waking late with a stiff back and clenched hand.

❧

Two weeks passed. My anger and my confusion had faded, for I had soothed myself by writing, always writing, and it had brought me a serenity of spirit. I wrote at last to Grisella, confessing the whole. Her reply came but two days later and I stole away from the parlour to read it in the privacy of my closet.

> I believe it is quite usual for men to take lovers, though Mumsy says good husbands do it discreetly. A servant, however, is considered terribly ungallant and a deed not befitting a gentleman. But Frederick says there's something about servant girls that he can't describe, and men get amours for them in boyhood, them being the only young females about in some cases. They are tempting bits of petticoat he says – and some of them quite pretty and not low-looking in the slightest. Oh and Mumsy also says one way of looking at it is if he's up to no good, he isn't bothering you, but I'm not sure that's a comfort (a new way of looking at Papa has crept into my mind; how I shudder!).

I was digesting this information when my husband came back.

To my wonder he came straight away to find me in my sitting-room, and bade me hello. He kissed my hand with the delicacy of a man a-courting and had a fine new shirt with long lace cuffs that fell out of his jacket sleeve to his hairy knuckles.

'Good day, madame,' he said, drawing up a stool, and perching on it, and I saw that he had decided to pretend that all was as it should be between us, though he was very stiff in his manners, as if it was I who, if anyone, was at fault.

I turned my head away from him.

'I have been with the King all this while,' he said, to the back of my head. 'For the French are growing evermore treacherous, and the navy must have their vittles. I am much fatigued, for Rex still likes to sport at piquet and carouse into the night. He has naughty friends who encourage him in it, and will not see that he tires.'

I did not answer him. I clenched my fists.

'And so I must stay up, and be as merry as the day is long.'

I could not imagine my husband making merry, or carousing, though I had begun to suspect that his time at Whitehall might not be entirely devoted to business, and so I did not answer this, but held my fan up to cover the curling of my mouth at the side.

The wind moaned around the turrets.

'But,' he began suddenly, 'the King has asked to meet my wife, for he grows tired of seeing the same faces of his friends, and would be entertained by a fair young lady.' He paused. 'Such as you are. I said that you would come, for I know that you have long yearned to see London and be at Court and lay eyes on His Majesty.'

I inclined my head slightly towards him.

'Will you then?'

'You would show me kindness now, sir, though it has been your recent habit to dishonour me most foully and show such little care of me, though I have been ill and almost carried off with it?' I said in a loud voice, never caring if the servants heard it.

He opened his mouth, making an 'O' shape, like a pike-fish.

'You would have me go before the King and play the part of the dutiful wife while you are casting your eyes about the place for courtesans, for I have no doubt now that it has been your long habit to cuckold me, and that greasy jade just another in your cast of strumpets.'

He sighed and pushed at his periwig. 'Well, what do you want me to do?' he said at last, in a sharp voice. 'For I am a man and must get what I need – though, faith, I do beg your pardon that you caught me at it, but it is done now, and we must get over it.'

'Get over it!' I cried. 'Ha! Aye, for you got over it enough – many times – I'll warrant. Now I shall get over it too. I shall cast my eye about and find a likely personage. No doubt there are many that would have me get over them.'

At this he scowled. 'Enough with your silliness, Ursula. I have begged your pardon and could do no more. Will you come with me to Court as the King commands it?'

'I do not know,' I said haughtily, quite amazed at his lack of chagrin or shame. 'I will think on it a while.'

He paid little heed to this and said he would attend to business, and went out with a black look upon his face.

Though I held my chin up to show his behaviour had not affected me, against my will my mind quickly began to crowd with images: me riding on Rotten Row in a great plumed hat, being admired by gallants. Me at Court, bedecked all over in jewels, with a dozen gentlemen clamouring for the next dance. Me carrying my writing to a printer, and publishing a pamphlet, and becoming famous as a wit. I would go to London, I decided. For I saw now that harmony in marriage, like London, had a price. I got out my notebook and began to write.

❦

# XVII

✦

# EXPEDITION

*In which I set off for the capital*

⟊⟊⟊⟊⟊

I had never travelled so far in a coach before – London was above three days' journey, and the roads famous bad. The carriage thumped over tree roots and potholes, throwing us about in our seats. A bitter wind blew in at the windows and all around our ears, and the window covers flapped, and the carriage shook and squeaked enough to make us both sick. Whenever I spoke, the rocking made my very voice tremor in my head, while the slightest impediment in the road shook the vehicle from the wheels to the roof and made it judder so violently that our conversations went like this:

ME:        'Tis beautiful c-o-u-n-t-r-y-s-i-i-i-i-i-i-i-d-e h-e-r-e i-s it not?

TYRINGHAM:  I had m-y-y-y-y-y-y-y e-y-e-e-e-e-s closed.

My husband drifted off to sleep and stayed that way for a good long while, for he said there was something about the motion and the clop of horses' hooves which sent him off to dreamland. I risked stealing my hands to my pocket and getting out my book and starting a few verses, but that too was useless for my pen would not keep still and so I

C      O

U    l

d

n  ooo t

*WRIHHtt*

write at any length. I gave it up and stared out of the window, letting happy thoughts of London and the people and the Court and His Majesty run riot through my head.

The crow of the coachman, the slapping sound of the whip on horse flesh, the skid of the wheels on earth, and we pulled up halt at The Halfway Inn, a large house of yellow Bath-stone with a great many chimneys spooling smoke into the sky, and people bustling all around — grooms leading horses, low-looking men with tankards, rosy-faced wives with travel-stained caps and baskets of provisions.

'What place is this?' I asked, craning my neck out of the window, for the newness of it all had begun to infect me.

''Tis New Bury,' said my husband. 'Here we will change horses and put up for the night.'

The next day, being not much rested – the bed at the inn was lumpy and squeaked every time my husband turned over, while the roasted veal we'd had for supper lay heavily on my belly – I drowsed in the coach, waking up with a start every time we hit a pothole. I jerked awake again as we rounded a bend at speed, and branches crashed across the roof of the carriage.

'Huh!'

'We are soon to enter the Maidenhead Thicket,' said Tyringham, 'and must be on our guard for highwaymen who lurk in the trees, for the woods grow close and dark in these parts and so are overrun with vagabonds.'

'Gad!' I said, sitting up, and forming the wild hope that we might be set upon and I kidnapped by a handsome rogue. 'I have heard that highwaymen are very gallant gentlemen,' I said. 'For my Aunt Phyllis was once waylaid by one, and she said he had his way with her heart, as well as her jewel-box.'

'They are scoundrels and beggars, all,' said he. 'But ye need not be afeard, for I have armed the coachman with a blunderbuss.'

As we entered the forest, a dank loamy smell rose up and I thought of Bear Wood. Leaning as far out of the window as I dared, I strained to make out shadowy figures in every thicket, and pricked my ears for the forest sounds above the rattle of the wheels. I pushed my hair back into place, lest I should catch the attention of a handsome scoundrel.

'I think that was a nightjar,' I said, twisting my head. 'Did you hear it?'

'Stay back, madame,' said Tyringham, and I thought there was something like fear in his face, though his jaw was set and his moustache an immovable black stripe across his upper lip.

The snap of the whip, and I felt the horses pick up their pace. One of them neighed in fright, for the branches were thickly woven overhead and the path had steadily been narrowing.

'Woah,' called the coachman, and our carriage began to keen from side to side so that I had to put my hands on the sides of it or else be hurled forward onto the floor. I knocked against my husband's shoulder and he caught hold of my arm and slid his hand down to my wrist, then moved it towards his lips, though with the lurching motion of the coach it flew up towards his face and against my will I boxed him on the nose.

'Gah!' he exclaimed, shaking his head like a dog. 'Hoo,' he said, feeling around his face. ''Tis not broken.'

A few moments later, his hand slid out again, and crept along my lap.

'Your travelling dress is very plain,' he said, and I saw that a steeple was forming in his breeches. 'And your cloak very sober. Your outdoor boots too,' his eyes slid down my body, 'are very sturdy looking. It is well you are wearing them, for it might get – ha – muddy.'

He pushed his hand down the shin of my leg to my boot tops and pushed my skirts away so that he might look at them more closely. 'Ah,' he said, 'sturdy.' The word came out like a groan.

'God's bones, is that a highwayman behind that tree?' I cried, but he paid me no mind; he crouched down on the floor of the carriage and began pushing his hands upwards to my garters. He slid my skirts up. I tried to hold them down.

'Pray, husband, the coachman can see us surely – or anyone outside,' I said.

'Nay,' he said, smoothing his hands over my calves, so that I felt like a horse that was being appraised for sale. 'Woollen hose... yes... very plain, yes... almost like the stockings of a... servant.'

With that he shook about the shoulders, and I felt his body shudder against mine. He collapsed forward into my lap, spent.

'I beg your pardon,' he said.

# XVIII

❦

# METROPOLIS

*In which I set down my first impressions of the city*

☙✿❧

*APRIL*

*12ᵗʰ*

*London*
*London*
*LONDON!!!!!!*

I shall write in this book every day, for I must remember every single thing that happens now I am here in the glorious capital! We arrived last night, and the house, which is very tall and made of brick with beams all across it, was in darkness. An old woman came to the door with a lamp and lighted us up to our chambers, mine with red bedcurtains and a damp, dusty smell. I could scarce get a wink for the excitement of it!

*13ᵗʰ*

Awakened by the trundling of wheels across the cobbles in the street below, and then the sing-song cries of 'Who will have milk? Sweet asses' milk for babbies!' and 'Quills, sharp and light for a penny!' I ran to the window and threw back the shutter, my heart thudding at the sight below: so many citizens toing and froing, a maid leading a cow on a rope, and beggars on crutches, and children playing hoops in the gutter, and two fine young gallants in tricorns, all of this in the few moments I stood, my forehead pressed against the glass in thrall to the sights and sounds of London, such a sweet cacophony after a lifetime in the country!

## 14<sup>th</sup>

This house stands on Bedford Street, in Covent Garden, which is convenient for Whitehall Palace, and so my husband goes there every day. I have not stepp'd out of doors overmuch, for I do not like to ask the servant Jessamy to go with me. But from my window I see 'tis the habit of fine ladies to walk the streets with one another and I am impatient to explore.

## 16<sup>th</sup>

As soon as T was gone to Court I had my chance to survey the house. It rises four floors high, with a chamber for me and a closet a-piece, and the servants are in the attics. There is a knot garden behind, which looks very pretty from the back chamber. I clicked downstairs in my slippers to the entrance hall, and, making sure there were no servants lurking in the shadows, skipped across the smooth floor of black and white tiles. Jessamy appeared and said, 'I hope you will find it as you wish it to be,' and I'll warrant she seems kinder than any Turvey servant, but still I only made my reply 'Hmm,' in the hope that she would go away, for I was seeking out a hiding place for all my writings, which I have brought away with me, for fear they should be discovered in my absence. I knew Tyringham would not think to search my trunk, and so I sewed them all into a bundle of cloth and waited until Tizzy and Darah had gone away, and stuffed it at the bottom betwixt all my linens, and hoped that the servants here would not make much of it, and they did not. And now I have taken it out and slipped it under a loose board in my closet onto which I have slid a box and so I do not think it will be disturbed.

## 19<sup>th</sup>

I am beading a needle case with peacocks that I shall send as a gift to Mary. 'Tis dull work when I can feel the whole of London about me, and the playhouses and bookbinders so close by! I have asked Tyringham when I might go to the Court, and he always says tomorrow, but it never comes, and I am most vexed with him, for if I thought he would be different in London, he is not.

## 20th

Jeremiah Malloborne came to supper; he was got up in a yellow waistcoat and told a long story at table, of how he was made an orphan, after his parents, having eaten oranges that had come off the cart of a wandering fruit-seller who afterwards was rumoured to be Spanish, and a gypsy, both took ill of the plague and died, hunched and swollen purple with buboes, in the very same week.

## 21st

Tyringham did not go to Court today and so I asked him to take me on a turn about the town, and we walked around the piazza, which is edged with grand white houses and pavements all about. There is a great house with many scented plants tumbling down its garden wall, and I later found it was the Duke of Bedford's, and St Paul's – a modern church with great columns rising up like a temple, and a huge stucco portico, and a garden behind it. There are columns all about Covent Garden, like the etchings of the Parthenon shown to me by Father. I would have walked further, but as we reached Drury Lane, Tyringham said we must go back, and though I was curious to see all the people that thronged about – for surely they came for the playhouse nearby – he marched me home, whereupon he disappeared again.

## 30th

I have been further about the city, for I could not tarry indoors any longer, and Jessamy is a kind servant after all, and said she would go with me so I might see some of the town. I believe she pities me my husband – she does not say it, but looks at me very long. The streets are narrow, and dark, for the dwellings lean forward at the top until they are touching – Jessamy has seen rats jumping from one straw roof to another, in search of better quarters! 'Tis famous easy to get stepped on, for all the people jostling for the wall, whether there be a cry of 'Gardy Loo' or nay, for these city dwellers are ever throwing stuff out of windows.

# MAY

### 5th

There is a hay market at Piquadillo which throngs with farmers,
and piles of bricks and carts of stones all about, for they are still
rebuilding after the Fire, which was worse than I had thought
it. Maypoles are very popular here, and there is a great striped
one near Somerset House, erected by the Duke of York for the
merriment of the people. Everywhere I look there are coffeehouses
and taverns and shops with swinging signs – faith, my head is in a
whirl at the number of 'em.

### 8th

Out with Jessamy again and we saw two gallants Jessamy says are
quack doctors called Rock & Bossy and they have already killed seven
people with their quackery. Jessamy reminds me of my Mary a little,
for she has red-gold hair, though hers does not curl, and her eyes are
not green, but hazel. She laughs a little at me, too.

### 14th

London has its own smell, especially on a hot day, such as today –
soot mixed with the damp stench of the Thames and the manure-
stink of burden-beasts, which lies on the streets in steaming heaps,
but no one heeds it: for they all go about with pomanders press'd to
their noses. The almanac says we are in for a long hot June, which is
godly for the harvest, but I do not think it must be so for the citizens
here, for there is so much filth everywhere, 'tis a wonder they do not
take ill of it.

### 21st

Jeremiah came again to dinner and the men were talking in low
tones that they hoped I could not hear, but I made out snatches
which enthralled me, though I kept my face unmoved.

WHAT I HEARD:
"Tis true that Buckhurst and Sedley spent a night locked up in
Newgate, for they were both in their cups...'

'... robbed at a Newmarket cathouse and Rex only got out of the scrape when he showed them his privy seal... rumour put about by Nelly for she cannot hold her tongue and thinks everything a great jest.'

'Castlemaine... and Frances will still not let him have her, though he has put her on the coin... gave Mrs Newbridge a locket and a bracelet set with seed-pearls big as plover's eggs. He is a fool in love.'

Oh, I do so *long* to go to Court!

# XIX

# PALACE

*In which I first lay my eyes on Whitehall*

Leaning on my husband's arm, I stepped into the ballroom, my heart pulsing in my chest. Outside the sky was as grey as the river that lapped at the mud-banks, but here everything glittered, even more than at Turvey: the great mirrors in their twisted golden frames, the bright eyes of the ladies, and the jewels they wore about their throats, wrists, fingers. Along the walls, dripping candles in their golden sconces made pools of amber light and sent sharp little shadows up, up towards the painted ceiling.

The room was a-hum with chatter and a few curious heads turned our way, painted and curled and tied all over with ribbons. The ladies shook out their fans with plump, white wrists; the men struck gallant poses with stout calves and buckled shoes. The crowd parted to let us through; the smell of sweat and lavender and wine; the hush-hush of silken slippers.

'She is with child, but Rex says he did not get it,' someone said, to much tittering, as we passed by, and I felt my husband stiffen at this slur upon his prince. He guided me to the room's side, where hung great wall tapestries embroidered with acanthus leaves and fanciful birds. At his suggestion I sat on a tall chair wrought with wooden figs and oranges which my fingers found and caressed.

I surveyed the scene, my mind fizzing with the thrill of it. At first I watched my husband as he crossed the room to get me my cup of punch, bowing here and there as he went. Then I spied on the gallant young blades in their frizzed and flowing periwigs, and the ladies who sat on tassel-trimmed settees in shimmering gowns of saffron and azure. The sight of their brilliance made my spirits sink: my own gown of the palest blue I knew now to be most provincial in hue. I coloured a little, thinking how fine I had thought myself as I stepped into our carriage that evening and with how much care I had dressed myself for this, my first visit to the Court. I shook my head to feel the pearl drops at my ears and the garnets on my fingers, both of these giving me great satisfaction, but, alas, the sum of all my jewels: my husband said that at my tender age I did not need many. I consoled myself that I, at least, like many of the ladies here, had great slashed French sleeves, whipped into folds. My hair, too, I knew looked well, twirled into fat ringlets at the front and around my ears and at the back caught up with the tortoise-shell combs that had once been my mother's. My mother had never been to Court.

My eye caught on a man with a grass-green coat, and I watched him move about the ballroom, his body held up, erect and soldierly. His clothes were vivid in colour, but compared to the other courtiers bedecked in adornments, he had little lace and few bows save for the violet rosettes on his boots. His periwig was long and brown and curled: he looked well in it, and handsome.

I flicked my eyes to my husband, stooping by the punch bowl, with his paunch before him. The ratty, black thing that sat lopsidedly on his head did little to conceal the pox scars on his brow. The other man was tall, and though he was broad and sturdy-looking about the shoulders, his cheek was as smooth as my own; I thought he could not be above one-and-twenty. He came upon a knot of women and stopped their conversation. I watched them all lean towards him, their fingers fluttering at their patches, their laughter very bright and high as he made mock bows to them all. Suddenly, he threw his head up and looked in my direction. I dipped my face downwards, for my cheeks were hot, but when I looked up again, I saw that he still looked my way, and then, as I gazed back at him, he mouthed something that I could not make out. I looked about me, to see if he spoke to some other lady he knew, but there was none.

He laughed, then opened his mouth again and made a deliberate O shape of it, with a tilt of his head. 'You,' he seemed to be saying. He made a gesture with his hand. He mouthed something again. I did not know what to do.

'That is my Lord Hanbury,' said a young blade in a froth of lace who had moulded himself to my side, his mouth full of the Court tattle, which was all of the King's many amours, and the playhouse, to which he went daily. He told me how the day before he had seen a play about a shepherdess who had suffered the afflictions of losing first her flock, and then her clothes, and had ended the night going home with a strumpet. I laughed at this, and asked the youth what Lord Hanbury did, as lightly as I could muster.

'My Lord is greatly thought of by the King and has been given many favours,' he said. 'Why, he—'

But then my husband came back and, seeing his scowl, the youth slunk off and I could not ask any more.

My husband scratched at his nose and complained of a head pain, before telling me at length of the men he had met and the gratifying courtesies they had made to him. I heard his voice, and made quick replies to his speech, but my eyes were on the handsome young man, who now moved to and fro about the room, with a proud, quick step, I saw him go between groups of people, and at each he seemed to provoke laughter. I thought he must be a very merry man indeed and wondered what he said. My husband droned on. As I watched, the young man seemed to catch my glimpse, and then I felt my whole body go stiff, for he had quickly changed his direction, and began to walk towards us, his eyes fastened on me all the while, sweeping from the top of my head to the hem of my gown and back again. By the time he had reached us, I was blazing red.

Lord Hanbury made a bow and Tyringham did the same – I saw that they knew each other, and that my husband was greatly pleased at his joining us, for he immediately started a conversation about the Dutch, who must be upon us at any minute, and what the King must do about the ships, which were assembled now at Portsmouth. I saw that Lord Hanbury seemed to become fatigued by the conversation, for my husband seemed much excited by the other man's presence, and could not stop gibbering at him.

'My Lord does me a great honour...' I heard my husband say, and then later make a strange sort of laugh, which was too loud and too long. Lord Hanbury slid his eyes towards me and then back again, and stopped my husband in mid-flow, and quickly began to talk of painting and of music and the witty verses of Mrs Behn, and I knew my husband must be quite tongue-tied beside him. I found I liked to listen to this stranger's voice; it was deep and strong, its timbre reverberated in my chest, and something about it pleased me, though I did not know why.

'I do so love a great play, for there is nothing I admire so much as writers,' Hanbury was saying, and my husband all in a fluster at how to answer him. It amused me to hear of the things I loved and I liked, too, to see him speak: he had a broad chin and above it a mouth much given to smiling and his eyes were brown and gleaming and flashed when he made merry. Twice as he spoke, he looked at me and caught my eye. Twice I stared back at him.

At length the chatter ended and he turned his body towards me and swept a bow. 'Your servant, madame,' he said, his eyes gleaming all the while.

'Lord Hanbury,' I said, holding out my hand in a queenly fashion, as I had seen the other ladies do.

'And how does the new Lady Tyringham find her first visit to Whitehall?' he said. 'Is it not full of much prating and foppery? Or p'raps my Lady only thinks to catch a glimpse of the King?'

My husband tipped his chin, which I knew was his sign I was permitted to answer.

I said: 'But I have already seen him, sir; the toe of his boot is most visible if you look to that cluster of people at the end of the room.'

He laughed at that and said I was as witty as Mrs Gwynn and must come down from the country as often as I may, to which my husband muttered something I could not hear.

'Where is *your* wife, sir?' I said, and he bowed and said she was in the country and there she would remain. Here he held my gaze. I blinked. My husband coughed.

''Pon my soul, I have a famous thirst,' said Hanbury, and I could feel him watching my face. ''Tis a shame I do not have my flagon of *cordial* about my person.'

'A flagon of cordial?' cried my husband, slapping at his shoulder. 'Nay, let us send for some Rhenish and we shall toast this great night, indeed!' He motioned for a servant.

I thought Hanbury would go off then, but as he moved, he turned his body quickly and held out his elbow, most pointedly. 'If you will allow it, sir, I will present Lady Tyringham to the King and she may look upon his whole, rather than his part.'

My husband could do nothing but give his pleasure and so I took Lord Hanbury's arm and felt it firm and strong beneath my own.

'I have got you away at last,' he whispered into my ear, and I felt a little shiver as his face brushed my neck. 'I am not sure I shall give you back.'

I made a strange sound – for I did not know what to say – that came out like a titter, and made me feel foolish. I looked at my feet, and nearly tripped on my skirts.

He stopped then and said: '*Lady Cassandra, is that you? I cannot make out your pretty visage in the dark.*'

'Pardon?' I croaked.

'*The moonlight plays such artful games. Is that my fairest love or else is it a mirage from my dreams...* something something. I cannot remember the rest.'

He reached for my hand. I found that my arms had gone weak.

'Ursula, can it really be that you do not know me?' he said, pressing my arm to his body. We passed through a little knot of courtiers and he stopped me behind a great marble statue, on a plinth, of the King, and hidden thus he turned his body towards me and took my hand. "Tis I, Samuel Sherewin,' he said, staring into my face and grinning all the while. 'Your old sweetheart, though it has been some years. Do you know me now?'

'Why,' I said, my mouth hanging open. "Tis – my eye! Confound it – I would not have known you. You are – a man,' I stuttered in astonishment, and Samuel threw back his head and laughed.

'Aye, and gone are my girlish limbs, my soft cheek, my curls too. I was short then, and a little pipkin of a boy. But,' he added, eyeing me, 'I do not think you minded it, when we were there, against the tree.'

'Shush!' I said, with a curve of my brow. 'For I am Lady Tyringham now, and you, sir, are saucy.'

'The Devil!' he said, taking my arm again. 'You're rather a pert sort of wench yourself, if memory serves me right. Did you not write a whole play just so you could kiss me?'

'I did not!' I cried. I saw that a knot of fops and ladies had turned their heads and were watching us with half-smiles twisted on their faces. I flicked up my fan. 'But I cannot take it in,' I said. 'For I did not recognize you as the boy I knew. But now I look at you closely, there is something familiar. Let me see...'

'My lips?' he said, pursing them. I rolled down my fan and tapped him smartly on the shoulder. 'Impertinence!'

'Well, I knew you almost immediately, there with your grey-blue eyes, watching all, but saying nothing, memorizing it all I expect – you probably have a paper in your bosom to whip out at the first sign of a pithy phrase. Yes, you are Ursula Flight still, despite your pattens and pearls. You have been deep – very deep – in the country, that I can plainly see, for your gown is cut high as a nun's and there's not a speck of rouge or a mouche to be found on your face.'

'Listen to you with your talk of the modes – what would your father say to hear you – and to see you besides? What on earth have *you* got on?'

'You would not know, country wife, but 'tis the height of fashion and just come from Paris, where 'tis the only thing worn at Versailles.'

We had passed through a gold door, into an ante-chamber with bright tapestries all about the walls.

'This is not the King,' I said. 'Where are you taking me, pray?'

'Oh there's plenty of time to meet him, for we will all be here 'til cock-crow, making merry, that's what we do most nights,' he said, with a flourish of his hand. 'I thought we might sit in here and you can tell me all about your beetle-head husband, for he is doltish, is he not? And old – how old is he? He is known here at Whitehall as The Bore, for he prates on and cannot be stopped, though the King seems to find it amusing.'

'Oh,' I said, a little stiffly, for I felt almost ashamed to hear that my husband really was as dull as I had thought he might be.

'You do not think he deserves it?' said Samuel.

'Oh aye,' I said. ''Tis fitting,' I smiled. 'And that is not all that is wrong with him.'

'Tell me all about it,' he said. 'Start at the very beginning. When were you married?'

❧

## MY HUSBAND AND I, A CONVERSATION
### June 1682, Henry House, London

HE:    You conversed very long with Hanbury last night; what did you speak of, pray?

I:    Why, I told you, he is my childhood playmate from Bynfield, and so we talked of old times and the places we once knew.

HE:    I came to find you and you were nowhere to be spied.

I:    P'raps you did not see me, husband, for I was in a little room next to Banqueting House, and 'twas heaving with people, but I was sitting on a chaise by the window, and could see the Privy Garden from it, which has a fine sun-dial.

HE: With Lord Hanbury?

I: Aye.

HE: And he too was in a chair?

I: Aye, husband.

HE: Which room was it?

I: I do not know the name of it, only that it was very fine, and had red baize on the walls, and a great chandelier, and tapestries all about.

HE: Why, that could describe any room in the palace!

I: 'Twas near a place called the Stone Gallery.

HE: Towards the Bowling Green? I think that is the Red Room.

I: I am sure you are right. It was very red.

HE: And my Lord Hanbury?

I: Quite a normal colour.

HE: How does he *do*?

I: Why, very well, as you saw when you talked with him. Since I saw him last he has married my Lady Hanbury – the title is her father's and 'twas a condition of their joining that he took their name, and they have two babbies, both girls, and live at Langley, though he has rooms here, and so is not often in the country.

HE: I was told by my Lords Dackson and Eaprick that Hanbury has a reputation at Court as a wit.

I: Indeed, sir? He did not make me laugh overmuch, though I suppose I did chuckle once or twice more than is usual with me.

HE: You know my meaning – it will not do to start whispers.

I: Whispers, husband?

HE: Of an intrigue. Dackson and Eaprick were intimating as much when they saw I could not find you, for everyone had seen you go off with him. I will *not* be the laughing stock of Whitehall.

I: If you are, it can hardly be because of one conversation had by your wife, in a very public place.

HE: Do not trifle with me, madame, for I can make things very hard for you.

I: [*Aside*] Yes, I believe you can. – Peace, husband. Peace.

# XX

# FLIRTATION

*In which I enjoy some witty repartee*

HONOUR
&
VIRTUE,

a

*COMEDY*

---

BY MRS. TYRINGHAM
LONDON

---

*Printed for* JACOB BELL *at* The Judge's Head
*near the Inner Temple-Gate in* Fleet Street.
1682 A.D.

## ACT II, SCENE I

*Morning. A London town house. A window has been thrown open and the sounds from the street below float up to the room: the clicking of hooves; the shouts of shopkeepers; the bright peals of a church bell.*

*A fair young* LADY *sits in a finely furnished parlour, a little leather book in her hand. She sits up straight, listening, then looks around furtively. Finally, she opens her book and reads. The sound of knocking. Enter* JESSAMY, *a servant.*

JESSAMY: Please, my Lady, there is a gentleman come to call on you, but the master is out, and said not to receive visitors, but he asks to see you. What shall I tell him, my Lady?

LADY: Oh! Did he give his name?

JESSAMY: His card, my Lady. [*She gives it to her*]

LADY: Ah, I see. Lord Hanbury is a friend of my husband's. Show him in, Jessamy.

*Exit* JESSAMY. *The* LADY *smoothes her hair and rearranges her skirts. Pats her cheeks. Picks up her fan. Fans herself. Puts the fan down. Enter* HANBURY, *a tall young man with conker-brown eyes. He is dressed in the habit of a courtier: there are feathers on his hat, jewelled buckles on his shoes, and his waistcoat is embroidered all over with golden oak leaves. He steps into the room and bows with a flourish of his arm.*

HANBURY: Lady Tyringham.

LADY: Lord Hanbury. 'Tis strange to call you that, I find.

HANBURY: It is strange to hear it, still. I fear I shall never accustom myself to it.

LADY: 'Tis the same for me, with Tyringham, I fear.

HANBURY: You shall always be Ursula Flight to me.

*Pause.*

LADY: Will you sit down, my Lord?

HANBURY: Thank you, I will.

*They sit staring at each other for a moment. An awkward silence.*

HANBURY: If I may say so, you look famous pretty today, Ursula Flight.

LADY: I... [*She laughs*] Well, you are very bold, sir, to lead off the conversation so. But I thank you.

HANBURY: Well it's the first thing that came into my head. Apart from 'How do ye do' and that seemed a trifle dull.

LADY: I thought it was your courtier's habits – flattery and [*She looks him up and down*] – frippery.

HANBURY: How dare you!

LADY: I dare.

*A pause.*

HANBURY: Why, it's so good to lay eyes on you again, Ursula. The Court can be a hard place, and it feels good to see a friendly face.

LADY: Aye, it seems very hard to be feasting and dancing and playing at cards all day long. And keeping company with the King and the Queen. And living in a palace. How do you bear it?

HANBURY: Well...

LADY: And the beautiful ladies-in-waiting, all white and bosomy and dripping in jewels...

HANBURY: There are many lovely women, 'tis true. But as I tell them, every one, I'm a married man, and besides that, I'm not rich enough for bastards.

LADY: I don't believe you for an instant!

HANBURY: Well, perhaps 'tis not all bad. But nevertheless, I mean it when I say it does me good to look upon you. Whitehall is not a kind place, though 'tis merry.

LADY: It all seems so strange to me, coming from the country, as you have said. An odd world, is this London, with the Court and the taverns and the coffeehouses...

HANBURY: And the playhouses.

LADY: [*Eagerly*] Oh, aye, the playhouses! Do you go often?

HANBURY: Every other day or so – 'tis one of the King's favourite entertainments, and we courtiers must do as he commands. Also, I like the orange-girls.

LADY: Oh! I so long to see a play, Samuel. The actors! And the playwright! And the ladies and gentleman of the audience, all a-rapt to see the wonder unfolding before their very eyes...

HANBURY: Hmm.

LADY: There is a playhouse very near here, on Drury Lane; do you know it? I have often traced its name on the flyleaf of playbooks: *Theatre Royal*, is it not a magical-sounding place? My husband says theatres are not a suitable place for godly women, but I have walked by it often (I confess, by my own design, for I am so curious to see what goes on within), and seen many ladies, and gentlemen too, going thither, and all of them the quality. I thought of going when he was at the palace, but the servants are always watching, and would tattle, I fear.

HANBURY: You have never been to the playhouse then? Not ever?

*The* LADY *shakes her head.*

You who have been writing plays since you were old enough to read? Why 'tis monstrous cruel, Ursula. 'Tis... inhuman.

LADY: He is... old-fashioned.

HANBURY: And a prig and a bully besides, I'll warrant. And he has made you unhappy. I can see it in your face. It's true, isn't it? Gad, what do you do all day? I suppose you are allowed music, at least.

LADY: Yes, most of it.

HANBURY: You poor child.

LADY: I – I don't think any marriage is *easy.*

HANBURY: Poppycock! Not all husbands are dreary. Some of 'em are merry. Some of 'em are too merry.

LADY: Well.

HANBURY: We must correct this wrong. I shall accompany you to watch a play. That will put the light back in your pretty grey eyes.

LADY: Oh, Samuel, there's truly nothing I'd love more... But I cannot. For one, I do not know how I would get out.

HANBURY: There is always a way. Why, the Court is rippling with intrigues and plots and we shall take our inspiration there. Tell me, how often does The Bore absent himself?

LADY: He goes to Court at first light, for he is working on a vexatious military problem for the King, and often does not return until lamp-lighting.

HANBURY: Well, we shall have you back long afore then and he'll never know the difference. The plays usually start at three.

LADY: Why, now I think you are serious.

HANBURY: Of course I'm serious, Urse, have never been more so. I will write to you... no that won't do, he might intercept it. Sit in the parlour window at ten of the clock tomorrow and I will get a message to you, with the whole plot therein. I have a friend – a lady, who shall aid us in this.

LADY: Of course 'tis a lady...

HANBURY: 'Tis better that way, if The Bore is not to discover us.

LADY: Oh, I see. Well then, if you mean it, I will.

HANBURY: I mean it, Ursula.

> *They look at one another. He takes her hand. Kisses it... for just a fraction longer than is usual. She does not move. He traces his mouth slowly around her wrist and touches his lips to the palm of her hand. She spreads her fingers out for him. Another pause.*

I am your servant, madame. Always was, always will be.

LADY: I... thank you.

HANBURY: *'Tis I, my lady love.*

LADY:       Ha, I... wait... *We do not have much time, my Lord. I am come to tell you that my father will have me wed to the evil Count Bonbon!*

HANBURY:    The scoundrel! The, er...

LADY:       Knave.

HANBURY:    Exactly, the knave! *I'll kidnap you and carry you off!* [*Pause*] I wish I had.

LADY:       You don't.

HANBURY:    I do. But now I must away, alas, for there is a tennis tournament at noon and woe betide the man who misses his chance to bat at the King. I will have to lose of course, for I do not want my head spiked on London Bridge.

LADY:       He would never!

HANBURY:    He might. He's a bad loser.

LADY:       Until tomorrow then, old friend.

HANBURY:    Until then. Wait by the window.

> *Exit* HANBURY. *The* LADY *watches him go. She sighs. She smiles.*
>
> *Curtain*

❧

# XXI

# ADORATION

*In which I achieve an ambition*

The noise was the first thing I noticed – the rise and fall of a hundred voices: the din of chatter, the calls of the orange-sellers and the birdsong of women's laughter; the drumming of feet as people filed into their seats or jostled for spots in the pit; the lilting strains struck up by the musicians who lolled against the boxes and dawdled at the front of the stage, a-playing all the while. I breathed in burning tallow and pomanders and perfumes and wine, and the mingling smells of bodies – so many bodies: I had never seen so many people in one place before – nor so many of the low sort, in truth – there were ordinary citizens as well as the 'prentices and plain-looking maids, and very proud and painted women too, with powdered faces and jewel-coloured gowns. My eyes were drawn upwards above the mêlée to the great swags of blue velvet in front of the stage, at the top of which glittered Prince James's coat of arms, in gilt, which were flanked by maidens – the muses, gowned in white; hands and feet stretched out to one another in an endless, graceful ballet.

'This way, Urse,' said Samuel, leading me up the stairs, for he had paid a shilling each for our seats and a good view besides. It was hard to see my way, for I was not accustomed to my vizard, or my high wooden pattens, which I had worn only once before, and were tricky to walk in, for they would catch beneath my skirts.

''Tis a dark day today,' said Lady Vyne, who had accompanied me out of Henry House, and all the way to the playhouse in her carriage, at Samuel's request. ''Tis well they lit all the candles, for I confess my eyes are not good in the gloom.' She flicked her white hands at the chandeliers that hung all about us.

''Tis your age, madame,' said a young gallant from the row in front of us, who had red cheeks and a suit of yellow brocade.

'Hold your tongue, buffoon,' said Lady Vyne from behind her vizard.

'Ah, Lady Arabelle,' said the fop. 'Always the wit. How the devil do you fare? I would not have known you behind that mask, save for your bosom, which cannot be missed. 'Tis not like you to hide your face. Too late for that, I fear, for everyone has seen it.'

She made a noise with her teeth. 'That is Mr Ruggle,' she said, twirling a strand of her long black hair around her fingers. 'Who cannot keep away from the actresses and so is a fly of the 'Tiring Room, always buzzing about, looking for young flesh to feast on.'

'I heard that!' cried he.

'Ah ha,' she said, turning her face this way and that. 'There in the box is Lord Wintleton, with the tricorn. And the Marquess of Disbury is beside him.' She unlaced her mask and dropped it into her lap, revealing a long, elegant face which was set off with white powder, and a sprinkling of heart-shaped patches. She tapped her fan against her nose and inclined her head. 'And there – Samuel, do you see that? 'Tis Madame de K and the Duke of Buckingham. They are mighty bold to be seen together when 'tis known Charles has threatened hanging to any who sully his women. But I do like madame's hat: there is something French about it, to my eye.'

'Louise is in thrall to no man,' said Samuel.

'Is that so?' said Lady Vyne, with a sidelong look at me. 'And what think ye, Lady Tyringham,' she said, 'of your first visit to the playhouse. It is not like this in... Wiltshire, perhaps?' She said 'Wiltshire' with a curling of her lips.

I smiled. 'No indeed,' I said, fiddling with my sleeves, which I had looped up with taffeta ribbons for the occasion, after seeing a lady pass by my window with the same, and sending Jessamy down to the ribbon-seller. 'I do not know yet, I am in such a pet to see the play – and the players – and the actresses. *The Country Wife*! A very good title, is it not? Do you think Mr Wycherley will make an appearance? For I would dearly like to see a real writer in the flesh.'

'Calm yourself, child, for you won't think that when you've seen him,' said Lady Vyne. 'But mayhap he will show himself, for there is nothing he likes better than applause.'

'Do not mind my friend Arabelle,' said Samuel, taking my arm. 'For she only comes to the theatre for the gossip, and could not tell a Molière from a Maundy masque.'

'I cannot deny it,' said that lady. 'And so you will excuse me if I leave you now, for my friend the Earl of Netherwick is signalling to me, and he has a box.' She got up.

'I want to thank you, my Lady,' said I, 'for your assistance today. My husband is greatly reassured that I have made the acquaintance of a respectable married lady such as yourself, who may accompany me to church, and on other seemly outings, while he is on the King's business.' I looked her plain in the face to see that she had understood.

''Tis no trouble,' she said, gazing down at me. 'For Hanbury put it to me in such a way that I could not refuse. Besides, who am I to stand in the way of true love?' She whisked her skirts away and made to leave our row. 'You are a slyer thing than you look,' she said. 'Good luck, Lady Tyringham.'

'Do not mind her,' said Samuel quickly. 'For 'tis only her way. She loves to tease.'

'Egad!' I said, clutching at him. 'That was a trumpet. And the curtain is rising! I have never been so happy in all my days. I feel as if I might burst or cry and fall into an attack of the vapours. I hope people will stop their prating, for I am keen to hear every word.'

'Oh they will never do that,' said Samuel. 'Not when there are so many things to talk about. And you must not get the vapours, for you will miss the play.'

The musicians then, who had all the while been playing as they strolled about the pit, came together in a knot and struck up a merry tune, and the players came onto the stage, and began a stately dance. I held my breath, my eyes fixed on the wonder before me: the first actors I had ever seen. Despite the faint murmur of the crowd, there was a pitch of fever in the air, like the vibrations of a just-struck tuning fork that could be felt in the body, rather than heard.

I turned my head about me. Though it was broad day outside, in here it was night. The sconce candles made soft light flare on the faces of those in the gallery, who hung their heads and arms over the balustrade. Circles of orange pooled onto the stage from the footlights, towards which the dancers moved, like moths, and lingered there. The light, and the shadows around it, made the painted scenery seem almost real, for the stage floor swept into a pretty country landscape that stretched back into the distance to hills and the lilac peaks of mountains, above which clouds drifted across a pale blue sky. I marvelled at the painter's art, for I felt I could walk into the backdrop and disappear, and be carried off to fairyland, as I had wanted to as a child.

The hubbub of the crowd quelled a little as the ballet ended and the first actor began to speak the prologue, and I soon forgot where I was entirely, abject in my seat to the sound of his voice. I found myself ooohing and ahhhing and clutching myself with mirth as the dashing Harry Horner, in a bright pink hose and all bedecked in lace, cuckolded husbands by the dozen, and Margery Pinchwife, played by a handsome actress with a white skin that I later knew as Mrs Boutell, was disguised in breeches as a youth (this causing a great uproar from the gallants in the audience, for she had a very pretty leg). I began to see that despite my childhood games, I had never known the true spellbinding power that was the craft of acting, until now. These men and women who spoke and moved and struck poses before me had me entranced; suspended in time. It was only they and I that mattered now, and all of life's troubles seemed faint and unreal.

Being part of an audience was a new thing to me too, this laughing and weeping and sighing in a body. A kinship with those around me began to build in me, that we were all come together in this wish to see a spectacle, and were part of it, for I saw it would be a different thing for those that saw it tomorrow, or the day after. I felt inextricably bound up with Samuel too, that he was here beside me, and seeing what I saw, and in bringing me here had given me the thing I wanted most in my entire life. I had a sudden rush of affection for him, and turned my face towards his smiling one.

'I have never been so happy in all my days,' I said into his ear, at which he felt for my hand and squeezed it, and we two sat like that for the whole first act; though my palm became moist and hot, he did not let go.

A new feeling began to wash over me: that now I had been here and had this new world open up before me, somehow things would be utterly changed. I did not know quite how this would be, only that within myself, I knew that I should no longer be so lonely, or so dull. Not when I had the playhouse to hug to me, and to escape to in my mind – if not in life, perhaps, with the help of my new friends. This place was not my mother's or the Dowager's or my husband's. This place was mine.

❧

Afterwards, it being still light, we went to dine at a tavern, and I thought Lady Vyne would join us, but she did not appear, and so Samuel said we had best be away, so that he may have me back before my husband came home at dusk. The spell of the theatre still hung about me and worked away at my insides as we stepped along the street and through the doors of The Seven Stars, where we had a private room, and Samuel ordered a barrel of oysters and a bottle of hock.

'My!' I said, throwing back my hood and snatching off my mask. 'I am still half there, for I was quite caught up with the magic of it and do not know quite what I am about.'

'It happens like that, sometimes,' said Samuel, his eyes dancing.

'I judge Mr Wycherley's story to be a very fine tale indeed, for it had as many knots and twists as anyone could want, and a great many witty words besides. Ooh, the part where the whole company danced in a great parade of cuckolds!' I said, my voice rising up in my excitement. 'How I clapped. And roared! 'Pon my soul, I am quite worn out with all the emotions I have felt.' I lolled against the wooden back of the seat. 'And, Samuel, wasn't Mrs Boutell triumphant? The way she laughed and threw her head back at the audience's applause... And how they adored her! I wanted to be her, and I think every woman there did, for all their faces were rapt in wonder... oh to be an actress!' I made a tragic face. '*For my own sake fain I would all believe. Cuckolds, like loves, should themselves deceive.*' I bowed my head.

'Brava!' said Samuel, draining an oyster and flicking the shell onto the floor with a practised movement. 'But I think your scripts just as merry. And you would not really like to be an actress, I think.'

'But it was marvellous!' I said. 'Everyone there thought so... Why, and so many different people go to the playhouse. I saw all types of person together, from apprentices to—'

'Strumpets!' said Samuel.

'I did not know what they were, but I thought it might be so, the way they were painted.'

'What gave it away, the abundance of rouge or the fact they had their bubbies out?' said Samuel, prodding me with his finger.

I blushed. 'I have not seen one before.'

'No indeed,' he said. 'Not many strumpets at Turvey Hall.'

'Nay,' I said, sipping my hock, the flushed, greasy face of Beck floating into my mind.

We sat there in companionable silence a little while, and then something sprang into my mind.

'Samuel, I was too much in a daze to remember it when you called on me before, but I have brought something to show you.'

Here I got out a little pouch, and plucked from it my little wooden bear, its tail tied on with a string.

'She is quite dirty now,' I said, brushing lovingly at the bear. 'For I have kept her with me all these years.' I held the creature up for Samuel to see. 'And she has been a great comfort to me in the lonely first days of my marriage.'

He seemed a trifle bashful then.

'Ah yes,' he said. 'What a gallant boy I was. Always with the sweetheart trinkets.'

'Oh,' I said. 'You had many sweethearts then. I did not think—'

'Nay, nay,' he said. 'None but you. I only meant it as a turn of phrase. And I bought that little bear from a table at a fair; how well I remember my father teasing me about it, for I had to borrow the coin from him to buy it. And how I yearned for you when I was sent away to school and could not get you a message.'

'For a long time I wondered why you did not come,' I said.

'It is so fortuitous then, that fate has brought us back together.'

'Oh aye,' I said. 'It truly is.'

The excitement that had carried me out of the house and into Lady Vyne's carriage and to the playhouse was subsiding now, and it had occurred to me that I was dining alone with a man, and did not quite know where I was or how I would get home. It was growing dark. I felt a little fizz dart up in my belly.

'I'm afraid I must be getting home now, Samuel,' I said, 'for I would not want Tyringham to come after me and discover me here with you.'

'Then I will carry you there,' he said, 'for 'tis just a step around the corner. I shall call for a linkboy to light us, and you may dart in through your front door and say that you came with Lady Vyne, but the horse had lost a shoe, or some such.'

'Thank you, Samuel. It has been joyous, and beautiful, beyond measure.'

'You need not thank me,' he said, 'but you might...'

He leaned his head towards mine and, with a deliberate movement, tipped his head to the side, and cupped my chin in his and opened his beautiful mouth, his eyes on mine all the while, a smile crinkling lines at their corners. I could do nothing but watch his face coming close, and then I shivered as he pressed his lips on mine, and his hand was in my hair, and on my neck, and he was kissing me... Oh, such a kiss, I felt my mind take flight and float away over the rooftops, and we were nothing but two bodies, and lips and tongues, as we had been before, but now it was different, stronger, knowing. His hand caressed my back, the bare flesh of my shoulder, it slid down the front of my bodice. I felt a shiver creeping up my back, and a heat on my chest and in my face. He laid kisses on my cheeks and my chin and my neck. I tipped my head back, but kept my eyes closed fast all the while.

'I must stop now,' he said into my neck. 'For if I do not I do not know what will happen.'

'I do not know either,' I murmured, for in truth I did not.

# XXII

# ADAPTATION

*In which I become accustomed to fashionable life*

My playhouse visit and renewed acquaintance with Samuel had enlivened me, for I began to see that life in London could be very fine indeed, with regular plays (viewed in utmost secrecy), and visits to Court, with all the grand balls, and fine banquets that the courtiers had there to entertain them. I wondered when my husband would take me back to Whitehall. I wondered, too, how long it would be until I made a few more acquaintances – for having had so many people all about me of late, I began to be conscious that I was as in need of companions in London as I had been at Turvey. I had Jessamy, but she was only a servant, and could not know my secrets. I supposed with Samuel to introduce me, it could surely not be long before I began to fall in with some other young ladies and gentlemen, and at this my heart began to lift.

Of Samuel, I thought often, for my mind was all in tumult after his sweet kiss; too sweet it was, for I felt it on my lips for days after he had given it, and felt I must be marked with it for all to see. I wondered if my husband might notice the merry mood that had come over me, and to this end I worked to keep my face as sober as it ever was. I ran over in my mind all that Samuel had said, and pondered what he meant by it, and what I should do.

Lady Vyne came to my aid in this, for true to her word – and, I hoped, at Samuel's encouragement – she began to pay calls on me, and sit with me in the parlour, and my husband too if he was home, though I could see by the narrowing of her eyes when she spoke to him that she took little joy in his company. It was Lady Vyne too, who had seen my thin stockings and country shoes, and insisted, in front of my husband, that she help me with the ordering of a new wardrobe. With her guidance, I had two fine new gowns made up, one of lutestring, the other moiré, and a smart taffeta jacket and a great cockade hat with feathers, like a man's, for 'twas the fashion for ladies to go about in them. In anticipation of the winter, I ordered too a new velvet surtout trimmed with sable, and mittens to match. Whispering that the gentlemen liked them, Lady Vyne had coaxed me into a new corset which was stiffer than I was used to – I had been admiring the effect on my bosom. All of this my husband had sniffed at, but he seemed in thrall to Lady Vyne, and while she prated on about my beauty in my new finery, he could hardly disagree.

These slight changes in my life had an improving effect upon my confidence. With Lady Vyne's friendship, I began to feel a little more grown-up, and with the roaming eye of the Dowager seeming ever further away, that I now lived in a house that was mine. I accidentally pleased my husband by asking if I might see about the moving of furniture, for he took it as an interest in the things that were his – I did not tell him that I sought to expunge the traces of my mother-in-law I saw in the dark fabrics and plain furniture, both of which Lady Vyne had tutted at.

'I think the card table will look well here, close to the cane chairs,' I said one idle afternoon after dinner while my husband read his Bible, his lips moving all the while. 'And we might have the chaise re-upholstered, for 'tis riddled with moth and needs re-stuffing. Arabelle says that orange damask is quite à la mode.'

My husband grunted a little at this, but let me have my way. I sent for fabrics and consulted colour charts, and after a visit by a short little man with puffed-out cheeks who danced about with a measure-tape and was much given to sighing, the chaise was transformed into a bright swollen thing that no one but Lady Vyne cared to sit upon.

Then I began a great effort of furniture arranging, consigning the plain blue and white jugs on the mantel to a cupboard and replacing them with a fine silver clock wrought all about with silver leaves, and two great Chinese vases that I filled with armfuls of roses from the garden.

'Does it not look well?' I said, when my husband came in that evening. 'For now we are ready for any more visitors who may think to call upon us.'

'Who are you expecting?' he said, frowning.

'I like to have flowers about me,' I said quickly, to divert him, 'for 'twas a habit of my mother's that I could not have at Turvey.'

'You could have had it there,' he said, sniffing the blooms and wrinkling his nose. 'I am certain that Mama would welcome your interest.'

'Oh yes,' I said. 'I must see about that then. Sometime.'

❀

## A PACKET OF LETTERS, FOUND IN PAIRS, ONE TUCKED INSIDE THE OTHER

*Ursula, dear,*

*I enclose this note from our mutual friend, for I did not have a chance to slip it to you earlier, with your husband prating on, so now I do my duty.*

*Should you like to step out to the 'Change tomorrow? I have a fancy for brooches. I shall send my carriage at nine of the clock.*

*A.V.*

Dearest Urse,

Forgive me the time it has taken to write to you, for I was away in the North Country on some business of C's that he would have no other man do, and did not have a moment to reach for paper or pen, as I hasten to now

I find you are ever in my thoughts of late, though I try to push you out, there you are, as I fall asleep, and first thing when I wake, your little face all in rapture at Mrs B, crying, 'I am changed forever!'

Might I call upon you soon? I should like us to be friendly, now we are come together again.

HANBURY

*Dear Arabelle,*

*I thank you again for your assistance in all my matters. A visit to the 'Change sounds very fine indeed. I enclose a reply to our mutual acquaintance,*

*Yrs,*
*Ursula*

*Sam,*

*I was quite astonished to get your note, and then pleased by it, and then I heard footsteps, and so had to quickly drop it in the fire before I could dwell on it any more.*

*I do not think it wise that you call on me here again, for Mrs Gourd has made some sharp comments which I fear she may one day do in the hearing of my husband, who by the by goes less to Court just now, and so I am not as alone here as I once was.*

*I thank you for keeping me in your thoughts, and you are in mine.*

    *U*

*Urse,*

*Since our little spree last week Lord Vyne threatens to cut me off and put it around the city that he'll no longer settle my debts! He is always jesting thus, and that is why I married the man, for I cannot abide ill humour.*

*I enclose this from our friend,*

                                       *A.V.*

Dear Ursula,

It seems an age since I saw you (a fortnight) and so strange that you are close to me, though I cannot see you and talk to you as I would wish.

Arabelle kindly agrees to call upon you, and carry you to a tavern, where if you say 'aye' I shall join you, and we shall make merry together, like the good friends we are.

I enclose a nosegay of violets, which reminds me of the sweet flowers that grew in Bear Wood, and I keep close to my heart now, for they remind me of you.

    S

*Arabelle,*

*Your husband loves you far too much.*

*The enclosed is for our merry friend,*

> *U*

*Darling Samuel,*

*I know 'tis madness, for if I am caught he may carry me back to Turvey and then I am undone – but I am so dull here, for there is nothing in the house left to improve, and I cannot write, for Tyringham watches me, when he is here.*

*I will come to meet you, but on the condition that you carry me again to the playhouse, for now that I have been I cannot abide the thought of risking all just for supper. I would see Shakespeare and Jonson and Dryden and Behn – or whatever is on, for 'tis all beautiful, to me!*

*Your,*
> *Urse*

Dear Mrs T,

I am cheered to hear that I will have the pleasure of your company next Tuesday at one of the clock and I will send my carriage to call on you.

A.v.

Ursula,

Your wish is my command. How I long to see you. My
sweet playmate.

Your own,

    Samuel.

# XXIII

❧

# ADULTERATION

*In which I attempt to conceal my feelings*

❧

I could not stop smiling – that was the first thing I think my husband noticed – I moved about Henry House with my mouth twisting up at the edges and a ready laugh, for everything seemed to be amusing to me, now. Tyringham found me in the parlour, gazing into the distance, and I did not hear him when he asked me what was I about, and if I would converse with him, until the second time he said it. He caught me singing at the window of my chamber and, since my voice was incapable of carrying a tune, moaned at me to stop, to which I only tittered, for nothing he said or did could hurt me any more. I carried my love for Samuel around with me as my shield, and no man, not even my wedded husband, could pierce it. How easy it was to bear his gruff ways and the very boredom of our evenings together when I had Samuel in my head to protect me.

✦

## WHAT I DID

## WHAT I THOUGHT ABOUT

Sitting by the fire in the parlour while the rain clinked on the window glass, my husband telling me a very dull tale about the history of the Tyringham family, and whence they originally came – from the depths of Northumbria – or was it Norfolk?

Meeting Samuel at the corner of Long Acre and Drury Lane, and upon greeting me, he taking my hand, and forcefully plucking off my glove, and then slowly and deliberately laying kisses on me from fingertips to elbow, all the while people rushing to and fro, any one of which could have discovered us! (But they did not.)

Dining with my husband, and he so concentrated on the food he barely spoke (the only word he uttered was 'Splendid!' and that was addressed to the turnips), but chewing at his mutton with his mouth open, and getting his cuffs in the gravy.

Samuel asking to read my latest scribblings, and then, when I met him in the shadow of the Charing cross, asking me to walk with him along The Strand and thence to the river where we took a barge, and he telling me everything he liked about my writing – somehow it has begun to form itself into a play, I know not how! He told me all he thought could be improved upon, for he has seen many plays and knows all the things that need to happen in them. He swearing to take me to the playhouse as often as he can, all the better to improve my writing!

My husband having Jeremiah to dine with us and they both of them conversing for above an hour about the problem of the succession, but in half-murmured tones, so that I could not properly hear it, but nor could I do anything else, for politeness' sake.

Being at the Duke's Theatre again watching *The Forc'd Marriage* by Mrs Astrea Behn (I have not until now been able to lay eyes on one of her plays – how wonderful it was!), me in my vizard and cloak, and Samuel very gently touching the back of my neck and behind my ear, and then, while the whole house was in uproar at one of the actors walking off, kissing the self-same spot with such a hot wet mouth I could feel it burning into my skin for hours afterwards.

---

My husband grunting while pulling on his boots.

Samuel telling me he loves me and only me.

---

My husband listing aloud the types of foods he would like to see on the dinner table including boiled tripe and calf's-tongue jelly.

Samuel coming to call on me disguised in a lorgnette and a different wig to his usual one and he pulling me into my closet, and without uttering a word doing everything short of having me on the chair which has been in my husband's family for four generations and was upholstered, in dull brown damask, by the Dowager.

---

My husband accompanying me to church and falling asleep during the sermon about fornication so that spittle ran down his cheek and dripped onto the sleeve of my gown.

In St James's Park at dusk with Samuel, where lots of masked ladies and gentlemen went to and fro amongst the bushes, and he leading me into a shadowy thicket and to a broad plane tree and kissing me most thoroughly and murmuring that he adored me, and me murmuring that I loved him – oh so much – and he falling to his knees and climbing right under my petticoats and kissing my knees, and then the top part of my legs most thoroughly and then letting his mouth drift upwards – oh so gently – across my thighs (which was most ticklish), and then suddenly kissing me at the part of me I did not know could be kissed!!! But him staying there, and going on with the kissing, and lapping, and working at it with his tongue, and something beginning to well up at the heart of me and me clawing at his head under my skirts and then the welling growing and building so that my whole body was tremoring and my mind humming and then – suddenly – an explosion behind my eyes; a shower of stars; and then me falling to the ground, and he falling too, and we laughing together until tears sprang at the corners of my eyes.

My husband recounting a story about the time he was sent as an envoy by the King to Paris but it being a story I have heard at least three times before so that I could almost recount it word for word. (The punchline is *Je n'aime pas manger les poissons.*)

Samuel hiring a sedan chair to convey me in the utmost privacy to his rooms and he taking me in his arms and rolling me onto his bed and us luxuriating there in each other's arms for above two hours, doing all but lie together fully (for we dare not lest I get with child), and we talking of our hearts' desires, and all the things in the world we loved, and how we must be together no matter what the cost.

# XXIV

✣

# ANTICIPATION

*In which I am entirely transformed*

꧁ᐠᐠ꧂

THIS BEING THE LAST
*WILL & TESTAMENT* of

# *Ursula,*

*Lady Tyringham,* FLIGHT AS WAS,

OF *Turvey Hall,*
LATTERLY HENRY HOUSE, BEDFORD STREET, LONDON

*On this day of our Lord, the 28th of August, 1682*

Being of sound mind (sort of), I set down my final wishes for I am
about to do something I am afeard my husband will kill me for
should he discover it...

Oh, such a handsome and witty man Samuel has grown to be!
I have had such joy these few months with him – after these
past few years at Turvey, I had forgotten what it was to make
sparkling conversation and see in another person's eyes the flash of
understanding. He does not begrudge me my writing, but admires
it, for he thinks playwrights very clever people, even if they be
women...

'Tis true he has got very foppish in his time at the Court, but such
is the age we live in, and I would rather have a man scented with
sandalwood than stinking of mutton gone bad...

This love Samuel and I have cannot be wrong, really it cannot, for though 'tis against the marriage vows, I was not the first to put them asunder and surely 'tis only just that I seek out my happiness too, for I have been so very unhappy...

Samuel has a wife, true, but 'twas not a love match and they are cordial with one another but no more, and he goes to his seat but twice a year, and will cleave to me all the rest of the time, for we are both married and in the same condition.

Oh, how I love S, beyond anything – I cannot stop up my heart! I did not know there could be such happiness as I feel when I am with him... I cannot think of aught but his face, and his eyes, and his arms around me... Yesterday I missed my step on the stair and fell down it, and paid no heed to what I ate (though 'twas a very good cream cake)...

Samuel Sherewin has my heart and my soul – and shall now, fully, have my body, if I can but get the courage to go to him at the Black Bear, as he has asked me to, tomorrow.

I have written all night... the sun is coming up.


Here is my will:        **ALL TO CATHERINE.**

God give me courage!

❦

A scrap of paper, inscribed with bright green ink, found inside an old linen press:

We are Truly

Lovers!

Lovers!

Lovers!

I am his and He is mine!

## THESE ARE THE POSITIONS WE HAVE DONE:

The Over and Under

The How Do You Do

The Topsy Turvey

The Merry-Go-Round

The Howling Hound

The Whoopsy-Me-Pardon

The Pestle and Mortar

The Milking Maid

The Sailor's Knot

The Ride-a-Cock-Slowly

The Whitehall One-Ball

The Cat-in-the-Pantry

The 'Tiring Room Tickle

The Good Wife's Encumbrance

The Gallant's Cockade

The Riddle-Me-This

The Bless-Me-Father

The Curdled Cream

The Bubby Blaster

The Prithee Master

The Row-Your-Boat-Slowly

The Maid's Genuflection

The Marry-Me-Later

The God-Give-Me-Mercy

The Wimple Wetter

The Bastard Begetter

The Roundhead

The Egg Coddler

The Haystack Splitter

The-Devil-Take-The-Hinderparts

The Chamber-Shamer

The Dutch Invasion

The Begging-Your-Pardon

The Old Rowley Poke-a-Holey

The Blink-And-You'll-Miss-It –
and that was in a confession box,
at church.

FIE!

# XXV

# DETERMINATION

*In which I reach a cross-roads*

It was dusk on a wet November day; outside the sky was leaden, and the cobbles on the street below slick and shiny with rain. The house was strangely silent – no hawkers' cries rose up to my window, and the weather kept away those who would to and fro about the piazza. We had been in London half a year, and I was a little brought down, for I had not heard from Samuel for the last five days. In recent weeks, carrying my love for him about with me had somehow changed from a thing that lit me up inside, to a burden that was physical and painful to me, and I was now verily sick with love.

I crept away from the servants to my chamber, and sat hunched on my bed, a volume of Rochester in my hands, a gift from Samuel – he had pressed it on me with a glittering in his eyes which now I had read it, I well understood. 'Twas not the first book he had given me – I had plays by Behn and Etherege and Killigrew bound especially for me in pale and pretty calfskin, and as delicate and beautiful to look at as they were to read. I hugged these treasures to myself – as material proofs of his affection, they were now the most precious things I owned.

I felt a burn of frustration that my current freedom from my husband was wasted – for Tyringham had gone away to Essex a few days before, and I was rejoicing in the peace of my solitude. How I had tried to suppress the look of happiness on my face as he left! He had bade me be good as he mounted his horse and pressed his long nose to the handkerchief of mine he had asked for and tucked into his sleeve, then trotted off with a jaunty wave of his gloved hand, his sword swinging at his bouncing hip. I skipped into the house and did a little jig of joy.

I lit the bed-sconces, and drew the heavy bed curtains about me, as was my habit, so that no one might come upon me unawares and see what I was reading. Outside, a gale began to graze the window-panes and rattle them, while I felt the thrill of holding a book in my hands and being, for this rare moment, completely hidden. I let my fingers drift dreamily across the paper and trace the lines of the text. I caressed the lovely leather of the binding: the calfskin was warm in my palms. My mind swirling with dreamy thoughts of Rochester and Samuel – and masked highwaymen in jaunty tricorns besides (for I had not forgot the thrill of the Maidenhead Thicket!) – I slid my hands up my skirts and, holding the book in my left hand, let my right hand wander slowly upwards, and then I began, with a sigh, to caress myself, for I found now I had been awakened that my veins were ever bubbling with lusty impulse and I needed a stopgap when Samuel was not near, and it was handy that my new hobby could be easily combined with reading.

'Mmm,' I murmured. 'Ahhh.'

Lightning snapped through the air and startled me: I laid down my book and waited for the knocking of thunder I knew must come. A loud clap came from somewhere in my chamber. Thinking something had fallen, I hurriedly pulled down my skirts and parted the curtains and peered through a slit of shadow into the gloom. The flames of the fire had grown low and my eyes laboured in the darkness. I pricked my ears for other noises but no sound, no knock, no movement came; there was only the fluttering of my breath. The wind groaned down the chimney, and I began to think the other noise a figment of my fancy, perhaps a far-off roll of thunder, or the misheard crash of a lightning-broken tree. I picked up my book and tried to find my place.

The squeak of a floorboard, the tip-tap of a stealthy foot...

I held my breath.

The curtain was wrenched aside, and my husband was bending his body to peer into the bed.

'Why, good evening, wife,' he said, sitting himself down somewhat stiffly on the bed. 'I am returned.'

'As I see,' I said, as brightly as I could. 'I did not expect you so soon.' Behind my back, I pushed my book underneath the bolster to conceal it.

'Aye,' he said. 'My business with Lord Knox was completed more quickly than I had foreseen.'

His face was pouchy and pale and I could see the shadow of his neck, smeared with road-grime. I sniffed at his sooty scent which was fire and leather and the tang of low taverns. He twisted his body towards me, and there was something like softness in his face.

'What do you do here, pray?' he said, looking around at the bed curtains. ''Tis dark downstairs for none of the lamps are lit... you are a little rosy about the face... and there – there is a rash on your chest. Are you took ill? I have been thinking that I should call for a physician, for you have not been yourself of late, and Mama writes that you may have been afflicted with a melancholy, and need a dosing.'

'I am not ill again, thank Jesu,' I began, a little astonished at the friendly tone in his voice, 'or melancholic – just a little... spent. London is so diverting. So I am... resting.' I trailed off for fear that I was babbling and making my deceit all too plain. I was uncomfortable at our sheer proximity too, for ever since I had given myself to Samuel, being near to my husband gave me disquiet. I had avoided his caresses as much as I could, feigning sleep when he knocked on the door of my chamber at night, and a cough when he sat by me in the parlour. Now there was a strange knot under my ribs that made it hard to breathe and I wished that he would leave me, and go downstairs.

'I fear I have not shown you enough of the city as much as you would wish,' he said, smoothing the coverlet.

'I – I am finding much to love about London,' I said carefully. 'But it does not signify who shows me it – I have Arabelle to accompany me to the 'Change for fripperies – and we have been to dine, and to walk in the park with some other young ladies – and a great many other things. She has been very kind to me,' I finished, watching his face for signs of incredulity – but there were none.

My husband nodded. 'I thought perhaps...' he watched my face, 'we might take a barge down the river – to Greenwich, perhaps, which is a mighty pretty place. Travelling by water is a thing most commonly done here, and you might like to try it for yourself, before we return to Turvey.'

'Aye,' I began, thinking of how Samuel and I had done the self-same thing but two weeks before, and kissed and whispered lovers' things while the oars of the boatman swished against the water. Then I stopped, realizing what my husband had said.

'Return to Turvey?' I stammered. 'But when – surely not soon?'

'Rex is to remove the Court to Windsor, for his physician thinks the London air too full of dark miasmas. And so your husband shall not be needed here.' This he said in a jovial sort of voice. 'We will leave on Thursday, I think – or Friday if the weather is inclement.'

'Oh!' I said. 'I did not think to leave so soon.' My voice sounded shrill in my own head and my throat had begun to stop up. 'Thursday is – a week hence – six days! I will have to say my goodbyes and pack, and...' I swallowed. 'There are many things to do. I think – could we not stay a little longer? A month, I think, would give me time to prepare myself.' I realized that I had bunched the coverlet in my fist while I spoke.

'A week is plenty of time to make ready,' my husband said, standing up and brushing at his breeches. 'And you can always write. I am sure Lady Vyne would forgive you that.'

'Aye,' I said, feeling for the book behind me. 'I can always write.'

⚜

# XXVI

# VACATION

*In which I come to a decision*

I awoke on the morning of the 10th day of December, 1682 with the sensation that I was hovering on the lip of a precipice, and whether I would trip at the edge of it and fall down to my death or run and take flight and soar over the mountain tops, I did not know.

Upon learning of my imminent departure, I had dashed off a note to Samuel, and sent it out with Jessamy, caring little even that I should be discovered, for I was so cast down in misery at the thought of being shut up again with the Dowager, away from the playhouse, and being without my love. His answer came but a short while later, as I lay with wet eyes upon my bed, having moaned into my bolster for the past hour or more.

It read in a bold, black hand,

MY OWN TRUE LOVE,

We knew this time would come. You must now come into keeping with me, and let me look after you and love you as only I can.

Be my Ursula Flight, always.

SAMUEL.

And I had answered, with tears on my face, that I would, oh I would!

*God forgive me,* I wrote in my little book. *But there is no other way.*

Though Samuel had consoled me by saying that at Court cuckolding a husband was as commonplace as catgut, I still fretted over the magnitude of what I was about to do, for I knew breaking my marriage would surely bring great shame on all that were tied to me by blood. I knew, too, that my life would never be the same, but precisely how, I did not know, for I had never heard of a wife who had left her husband; I had not thought it were possible, until now. When these thoughts gnawed at me, I told myself that I had little choice in the matter before me, for if I did not go to be with Samuel, I would surely die of unhappiness.

Thoughts of a new life with Samuel were the thing that kept me afloat in the mire of my anxiety – a life in which I could read and write and visit the playhouse as much as I could wish and perhaps have a tutor besides, for I believed Samuel was rich enough, and he said he would have me continue my instruction in languages and history and the science of all things.

Blessedly, my husband was out when a note came by messenger in which Samuel laid his plan for my escape before me. I turned it over and over in my mind, murmuring it to myself like a litany, in my closet, before putting it on the fire.

Over the next few days, I laid plans to smuggle out the things that I would need – a bundle of my favourite clothes were to leave the house in the guise of being sent out for mending, and Jessamy – whom I had bribed with a crown not to ask what I was about – would carry the books and papers I could not do without in a sack to a nearby tavern. The Flight family jewels I sewed into the skirts of the gown I would wear for my escape, leaving behind the ugly Tyringham heirlooms that sat heavily around my neck and wrists. I did not intend to take much with me, for I was certain Samuel would shower me with finery – besides, as the servants were packing our trunks for our removal to Turvey, the lack of too many of my possessions would be sure to arouse suspicion.

Waiting a propitious evening for my departure dragged agonizingly, for my husband, once so distant where I was concerned, had lately suffered a change of temperament. He seemed now curiously solicitous of my health and state of mind, and inclined to ask me how I did and what I was about, as well as hanging about the house in the evenings, watching me while I ate, sewed, or strummed my lute. Though inside I burned with exasperation, I had done all of these things as calmly as I could, concentrating my mind evermore steadfastly on the quitting of my dull old husband for good.

'You're too late,' I thought, every time he spoke to me, or patted my arm, or smiled. 'Far too late now, for I am no longer yours and belong to another.'

❧

*Henry House, London*
*The 14th day of December, 1682 A.D.*

TYRINGHAM,

I must set this down. I cannot say it to you in person, for you will try to stop me and that I cannot have.

Here It is:

I have been so full of woe being married to you I have been wracked with it.

I blamed myself at the first; I was a girl when you took me for your wife three years ago – what did I know of love? I thought our union was as it should be, and I would learn in time, to repress my instincts and desires, but, oh, how I have suffered for it!

I have wept in my closet, while you slept. I have gritted my teeth while you have laboured in your lovemaking ('tis the wrong word for what has passed between us, for there was no love in it). And all the while I thought: we are learning to love each other. One day, I shall look into his face and see that he delights in me and thinks me the best of women. One day, I shall be his true love.

But then I caught you with that stinking jade, and I began to see that our union was not as I thought it. And though I made every effort to love your sister and mother as my own, they had hardened their hearts towards me and could not like me for myself, for in wanting to learn things and improve my knowledge of the world, I showed that I am not like them and never shall be.

I have thought on all these things. And I am truly certain now that the day will never come when our hearts and souls cry out for one another. Therefore I can no longer be your wife.

Oh, what is the point of writing more, for you shall not take any of it in – I do not think you have ever listened – truly heard a word that I have said. You do not know me. You never shall.

Hear this, Tyringham: I release you from our contract and all duties and portions due unto me. I ask that you divorce me – I do believe that this would be the best thing for both of us. I pray that you will be happy with some other woman who is meant for you, for I am not.

I have taken only my own jewels and clothes, so pray do not cry thief at me, for what I have now is far less than you got from my father when we married. 'Tis the last thing I shall ever take from you. This I solemnly swear.

Do *NOT* try to seek me out – for you shall not find me, I am gone away to France and shall set up as a nun. By the time you read this I shall have one foot on the Continent, and thence I shall disappear into peace, and be happy at last as I cannot be with you. Do NOT seek me out – I pray that you will grant this one thing I ask, though you have denied me every other thing I wanted.

From she that is no longer your,

URSULA FLIGHT

❧

It was deep night when I stole out of the scullery door of Henry House, letting it close gently behind me, wrapping my cloak more tightly around me against the bitter air that seeped down my throat and made me catch my breath.

I stepped into the knot garden and across it as quietly as I could, my hands out before me in the blackness, avoiding the gravel path that crunched underfoot. In no time at all, I was at the back wall. I felt light and strangely unburdened – I had only the clothes I stood up in, and my winter cloak atop the whole. I climbed onto the upturned box that I had positioned under cover of darkness the night before and, bending my body, jumped and caught at the wall, before heaving myself upwards and throwing first one leg, then the other over it. Sitting atop the wall, I craned my neck backwards to have a last look at the place where I had changed from a sad little wife to a man's merry mistress, but I could only make out a long black shadow, for the moon was waning and the night was dark. The sharp turrets of Turvey Hall floated into my mind, a place I dearly hoped never to lay eyes on again. I smiled at this.

I twisted my body, and, caring not that I snagged my thin gloves on the rough brick, slid down the other side of the wall as lightly as I could, landing with a squelch, and a half twist of my ankle, into the pitch-black pathway that ran between the dwellings there.

I stood there, panting in the dark.

'You took your time, Cassandra,' came the sweetest voice I ever heard, and my Samuel was at my side, his woody smell mingling with the brick dust and mud and river-fog that was London. He took up my hand and pointed to the sky.

'See, Urse,' he said. 'The stars have come out for us, and will light us home.'

I found I could not speak.

He kissed me, and took my arm in his, and held it close to his body, and that is how we stepped together; down, down the little pathway, and out into the street, to freedom.

✤

PART

*The*
*Third*

# I

# JOY

*In which my new life brings me great happiness*

I was free of him. I was free. Oh, what it was to be free – I felt light with it, giddy with freedom, as if I were no longer attached to the earth and might float away at any moment. My body, too, felt like a live and glowing thing I did not recognise, for the first thing Samuel had done when he got me away to our new lodgings was press his hard man's body to mine, and, pushing his tongue into my mouth and caressing my secret until I sighed, had me against the wall, with a vigour I had not afore experienced, and then he had me again bent over the bed, and then I sat astride him on the only chair, which was then the only other stick of furniture in the room, and was not very sound, for as I began to reach my zenith and rode him evermore violently, the chair began somehow to collapse, and we both fell pell mell onto the floor, and that was how we christened the place, amen.

The lodgings Samuel had taken were quite comfortable, I thought, a set of rooms in a house outside the city wall, in the pretty village of Clerkenwell, which being an unfashionable part of the city, home to but a few watchmakers and merchants, was the perfect refuge from the Court gossips, and the ideal place for us to live as man and wife, without fear of discovery by my husband. Samuel had given out – once the bruits concerning my disappearance had begun to seep into all corners of the Great Hall and the Stone Gallery – that he was as shocked as any person to hear the news, and made certain to spend every night in his Court lodgings then, until the tongues had ceased to wag on my mysterious disappearance, and Tyringham removed again to Turvey. I shivered to hear this, thinking of how he must face the Dowager and her obloquy, and hugged to myself the thought that I would never again have to feel her dark eyes upon me and roaming hungrily over my belly.

I had money from Samuel for the hiring of servants, and I engaged a sweet-looking, plump-armed girl called Tara who went about her work with a cheerful vigour that reminded me so much of Mary, and a woman for the rough work – a widow with a surly eye and a bristly chin who sniffed at my instructions, fastening her eyes on my wedding ring, which I had not left off, for Samuel said we should only have to replace it with a tin one.

I set about establishing our little nest with an energy that I had not had when setting up house with Tyringham, and wondered at the difference that love made. Though our rooms were somewhat threadbare and plain, there was beauty to me in every Spartan inch of it, from the rough woollen window curtains, to the tatty rush matting and the scrubbed oak table where we took our simple meals.

In my first few days of freedom, I was much afraid to go out of doors, for fear I should be discovered – despite my ruse that I had gone to be shut up in a convent, I greatly suspected the shame I had brought down on the Tyringham name would be reason enough for my husband to comb the streets of the city to find me. I shut myself up therefore, and put the time I had to scribbling, for with Samuel's encouragement, I had begun to feel that I might be a passable writer after all, and that it was quite as worthwhile a hobby as stitching Bible verses or strumming at a lute. Though I longed to write to my mother and Grisella to let them know that I was safe and well, and not as far away from them as they might suppose, Samuel had advised me that I should not, for fear they would give us away, and so I shut myself up with my books and my papers, and my love, to console me.

Samuel came to me whenever he could, excepting those occasions when he could not excuse his presence from Court – for even in his advancing years, it still pleased the King to be in a whirl of balls and banquets and masques. Otherwise we lived as a true married couple, but in an accord such as I had never known in my old life. Samuel liked to talk – and to hear me talk – on diverse subjects, and so we conversed on every topic from the conquering of the Americas to the movement of the planets and the discoveries made by the fellows of the Royal Society which, being a courtier, Samuel was well-placed to hear. One evening, fortified by a bottle of Rhenish and a roast joint sent up from a tavern, we talked together until the sky was pale with sunrise, and laughed the both of us to see it. We went for walks around the village green too, when it did not rain, for we could talk then too, and be free in our ways with one another, for who would look twice at a young man and his sweetheart-wife, he with his hand about her waist, she laughing at some merry thing he has said, and the two of them looking as gay and deep in love as it is possible to be?

As to fucking, it was plentiful, for I had not yet grown tired of the sport that seemed so new to me. It was so different from what I had endured with my husband, and gave me so much pleasure, I liked to have it every night I could, and Samuel, being young and lusty, was mostly happy to oblige. I went about with a bright complexion and a lovelight in my eyes that made my sweetheart laugh and call me beautiful, and though I knew myself very wanton, I pushed all thoughts of sinning from my mind, for all else to me was a joy of the very truest kind.

# II

# DOMESTICITY

*In which I enjoy a pleasant evening at home*

---

## AND SO *to* DINE

ACTED BY
**THE LADY'S PLAYERS**

*at*

**THE THEATRE *in* DORSET GARDENS**

WRITTEN BY
MRS. U. FLIGHT

## ACT III, SCENE IV

*A cold winter's day. A parlour. At one end, a table is half-laid for supper. TARA, a servant girl, bustles about, sweeping the floor with a besom; wiping plates with a cloth. Enter MRS SHEREWIN, a pretty young gentlewoman in a green gown. She has grey-blue eyes and dark golden hair formed into kiss curls across her forehead.*

MRS SHEREWIN: It looks very neat, Tara. I will light the candles if you would go down to the inn and fetch up our supper. [*Tossing her a purse*] Here is the money for it – take a penny for yourself.

TARA: Aye, mistress. Thank ye, mistress. A leg o' mutton and a dish of oysters and a sugared cheese, I will fetch it, mistress. I hope Mr Sherewin is hungry.

MRS SHEREWIN: Oh, he always has a great appetite – 'tis a wonder he is so slim still, yet however much he swallows, his waist remains almost as tiny as mine, for I have remarked on it on many occasions, though his shoulders are broad and his legs very strong and good in the calf...

TARA: I will get the vittles now, mistress.

*Exit TARA. MRS SHEREWIN lights a taper on the fire and goes about lighting all the sconces in the room, singing all the while. When the candelabra on the table is lit, she lingers a while, staring into the flames. Enter MR SHEREWIN, with a stealthy tread.*

MR SHEREWIN:     And what does my pretty playmate do, staring
                 into the candle-flames like a witch casting a
                 spell? Dreaming up some witty thing to set down
                 in her play?

MRS SHEREWIN:    Oh! You made me jump, you bad man.

                 *He moves to stand behind her; murmurs; wraps
                 his arms around her waist. She leans back
                 towards him. He tilts her head towards his and
                 kisses her deeply. They slowly break away.*

MRS SHEREWIN:    I have missed you.

MR SHEREWIN:     And I you.

                 *Enter TARA, bearing a tray.*

TARA:            Good evening to ye, master.

                 *She sets the dishes on the table. MR and
                 MRS SHEREWIN seat themselves at it
                 and sip at their wine.*

MRS SHEREWIN:    And how was your day today, dearling?

                 *A pause. They both turn their eyes to Tara,
                 who is lifting the lid on the steaming dishes,
                 cutting bread. She completes her tasks and
                 wipes her hands on her apron.*

TARA:            I'll be taking my leave now, mistress and master.

BOTH:            Goodnight!

                 *Exit TARA.*

MR SHEREWIN:     Remember that we must be careful what we say
                 in front of her, Urse.

MRS SHEREWIN:    Aye, I know. I did not mention the Court, or
                 anything that would give us away.

MR SHEREWIN:    Nay, you did not.

MRS SHEREWIN:   And I did not say anything to disabuse her notion
                of us as a newly married couple. Faith, Sam,
                that part is easy for me, for it has only been two
                weeks but I already feel so truly your wife that I
                forget it is not so in law.

MR SHEREWIN:    You are truly my wife, in my brain and my belly
                and my heart.

MRS SHEREWIN:   I know it.

                *Across the table, they join hands.*

MR SHEREWIN:    Now, let us eat, for I am famished! There is nothing
                like hunting in the rain to make an appetite.

MRS SHEREWIN:   How I wish I could see you on a horse.

MR SHEREWIN:    'Tis not much, though the King seems to like it.
                Today, as we were riding at the gate, he said—

                *Sounds of violent knocking.*

MRS SHEREWIN:   'Tis late – I wonder...

MR SHEREWIN:    I will answer it, if you will fill our glasses again,
                sweet wife of my heart.

                *He gets up from the table.*

MRS SHEREWIN:   With a very merry will, husband.

                *She blows a kiss. He catches it, and puts it in
                his pocket. She laughs.*

                *Exit* MR SHEREWIN.

                MRS SHEREWIN *fills the glasses from a jug.
                Sips from her glass. Pokes at her food with her
                fork. At the sound of footsteps, she raises her
                head, gets on her feet.*

*Enter* MR SHEREWIN, *with a man behind him.*

MR SHEREWIN: [*Urgently*] I could not stop him, for he forced the door.

*He steps aside to reveal* LORD TYRINGHAM.

MRS SHEREWIN: Oddsfish! Jesu save us... Hellfire!

TYRINGHAM: So! 'Tis as the Court gossips are saying after all – my wife is not a nun, but a brazen whore.

MR SHEREWIN: I will ask you again, sir, on your honour as a gentleman, to leave this house!

MRS SHEREWIN: What do you do, Oswold?

MR SHEREWIN: Right, that's it, I'm fetching my sword.

TYRINGHAM: I am come to find you.

MR SHEREWIN: [*Brandishing his blade*] I command you to leave us! [*Pause*] You never said his name was Oswold.

TYRINGHAM: I have been searching for you these weeks, since I came home and found you fled, and all the servants bribed and silent. Did you think I would let you cover the house of Tyringham in shame, and drag us all into the mud along with you?

MRS SHEREWIN: I asked you kindly for a divorce, for 'tis a very simple thing as I understand it...

MR SHEREWIN: It really is not difficult...

MRS SHEREWIN: And then you may marry again, to some woman who can love you, as I cannot.

TYRINGHAM: Divorce! How you speak so idly of such abhorrence in the eyes of our Lord Jesu. I am

|  |  |
|---|---|
| | certain that the mere mention of the word would kill Mama. |
| MRS SHEREWIN: | [*Aside*] Would it were so! |
| TYRINGHAM: | No doubt this young fop is the one who fed such poison into your mouth, for he is well known at Court for his scandals. |
| MR SHEREWIN: | How dare you, sir, for 'tis my devilish good looks I am known for! |
| MRS SHEREWIN: | Take your leave now, Oswold, and forget me. 'Tis better that we part, that must be plain to you, after these three years of bitterness. |
| TYRINGHAM: | I did not think it was that bad. Not bad enough for this. |
| MR SHEREWIN: | You thought wrong; she told me it was terrible. |
| TYRINGHAM: | I shall have to challenge you to a duel, sir, if you keep on with your prating, for I am trying to talk to my lawful wife. |
| MR SHEREWIN: | I would like nothing better, if you will name your place, your weapon, and your second. |
| MRS SHEREWIN: | Let us not talk of duels; you will be arrested or murdered both, and I would not have that, despite all. |
| TYRINGHAM: | What does this popinjay know of duels? Though I warrant 'tis not the first he has been challenged to, for there is none more likely to get his head taken off than a known Court cuckold who sports at love and makes a habit of flirtation. |
| MR SHEREWIN: | Slander! I shall have to kill you on the spot. |

MRS SHEREWIN:   Nay, Sam. For I would have Tyringham go in
                peace, if he will.

TYRINGHAM:      I will not.

MR SHEREWIN:    Then I will slit your nose presently.

MRS SHEREWIN:   Do you not see that I am happy, here, such as I
                have never been before when I was shut up and
                useless in your house? Tyringham, take your leave,
                now, I beg you.

TYRINGHAM:      I will not leave until I have fulfilled my
                purpose. You look amazed, wife, and so I shall
                lay it down before you, if only you can stop
                up the mouth of this whoreson waving a blade
                before my face.

MR SHEREWIN:    On behalf of my mother, bugger your eyes!

TYRINGHAM:      Though I am grievously pained at the
                wickedness of your actions, I do not believe that
                news of your adventures have travelled much
                beyond a few wicked whispers in the Court – no
                doubt originating with this fool, for 'tis known
                he cannot stop himself from boasting about his
                amours...

MR SHEREWIN:    Ursula, you know this clod-pate lies!

TYRINGHAM:      ... And so you shall come away with me now,
                and we shall go to Ghent, and when we return it
                shall seem that you did go off to a convent, to
                better cleanse your soul, and I gone to get you,
                and none shall be the wiser of your sin withal.

MRS SHEREWIN:   I – I cannot take it in. You would have me come
                back to you as your wife, despite the fact you
                find me here, as I am?

TYRINGHAM:       I am too generous. But I shall get my reward in
                 heaven, I think. Come now, and get your things.
                 We shall put up at Henry House for the night,
                 and be gone for the Continent on the morrow.

                                 *Pause.*

MRS SHEREWIN:    Nay, Oswold, I will not. For in my eyes I have
                 married another, and shall no longer submit to
                 your commands.

TYRINGHAM:       Oh, I am certain he will let me have you, for
                 surely he is grown tired of this charade, and
                 would not wish to tarry here any longer while
                 his wife is growing fat with another babby at
                 home.

MRS SHEREWIN:    You have gone too far, sir. I know of Lady
                 Hanbury, and her... condition – and she shall
                 have a divorce too, when the time comes for 't.

                 MR SHEREWIN *falls to coughing.*

TYRINGHAM:       Hurry, wife, for 'tis getting dark. If you do not
                 have a trunk, we can send on for your things.

MRS SHEREWIN:    I am not coming, Tyringham. I love this man
                 with a fervent passion such as I have never
                 known before.

TYRINGHAM:       I'm sure you will get over it.

MR SHEREWIN:     She already has, many times, on that very bed.

                 *With a roar,* TYRINGHAM *draws his sword
                 and rushes* MR SHEREWIN, *who leaps out of
                 the way, and laughs.*

MRS SHEREWIN:    Peace! Tyringham, I cannot speak plainer – I
                 will not come with you, or be your wife. Leave

my house now, and do not come back. Forget me as I forget you.

TYRINGHAM: Foolish jade! You will regret this more than you know. He will cast you off! Ask him about Lady Frances! And Mrs Elton. Ask him!

MR SHEREWIN: The past is the past, I always say.

TYRINGHAM: God damn you both.

*He spits on the floor. Exit* TYRINGHAM.

MRS SHEREWIN: I cannot believe... how did he find us? How I shake!

*They embrace.*

MRS SHEREWIN: There was no truth, I know, in any of the things he said?

MR SHEREWIN: About me? Nay, of course not. Pay them no mind.

MRS SHEREWIN: Of course not, my dearling.

MR SHEREWIN: My Ursula.

MRS SHEREWIN: My love.

*Curtain*

✤

# III

❦

# CONTENTMENT

*In which I go about my daily business*

⚜

## THESE ARE THE THINGS I DID WHEN I AWOKE ON THE MORNING OF 27TH JANUARY 1682/83

❧ Blinked my eyes and yawned very loudly.

❧ Stretched out, eyes still closed, feeling with my hands for Samuel, and then finding him gone, got *She Would If She Could* from under my pillow (concealed there through long force of habit) and lay abed awhile reading, and laughing aloud all the while, for Etherege is a witty fellow!

❧ Reluctantly got out of bed, and put on a wrapper over my shift. Went into the little cupboard we have as a pantry, and got out a hunk of bread and a little pot of ale and dipped one in the other, and gnawed on a wedge of cheese.

❧ Wrote for a while, at the table, with a rug around my knees, having to poke the fire a great many times, for 'twas a bitterly cold winter's day, with ice inside the window-panes and a drift of snow up against the door.

❧ Tara dressed me, and I uncurled my hair from its rags and gazed into the glass, thinking how pretty love had made me. (I know this is vanity, but 'tis true!)

After Tara had gone to market, I sat at the table again with my papers and quill before me, but the words would not come, and so I lounged on the chaise reading what I had written before, and making many additions and crossings out.

Fell to writing letters to my mother and Grisella and Mary – for now I was discovered I could tell them freely where I was and it would make no difference. To my mother, I set down my side of the tale, and the reasons that I had gone from my husband, begging her forgiveness for any worry I had caused her in my disappearance, and hoping that she would understand my actions as those of a truly miserable woman. To Grisella and Mary I wrote of Samuel, and how we had come together again, and fallen so deep in amour, smiling as I did so, for even to write of my sweetheart was to feel happy and light.

Wrapped myself in my sapphire-coloured cloak and sable hood and trudged into the snowy street. I then called for a messenger, and gave the boy a coin to carry my letters to where they might go.

Coming in and stamping my feet and brushing the snow off my skirts, I noticed for the first time a letter addressed to me in Samuel's hand, propped on the mantelpiece, supported by a little cluster of bright red berries on their twigs, that I had bought from a flower-seller and placed there the day before.

✾

*In haste*

My dearest Cassandra,

A message came from my wife at first light that she is took ill with the babby, and so I have gone to her, and mayhap will stay until the child is come.

I have left twenty pound for you in the usual place, and this should last you for some months, but I shall not be that long, God willing.

May the Lord bless you and keep you.

Your,

Samuel

By the second week in February, I had written to Samuel seven times or more, but to my vexation, and though I stayed indoors for as long as I could so I should not miss the messenger, no reply from him came. At first I thought it must be the fault of the terrible weather – for the whole of England had been wracked by swirling snowstorms, and the snow lay a foot thick on the ground. In London the Thames had frozen over into a curving plane of grey ice three feet thick, and so the Frost Fair came again and I knew it was no doubt much worse in the country. But as the ice melted, the thought began to creep into my mind that my love had been took of an illness and died and no one had thought to tell me the news and I spent many long nights weeping and watching the dawn streak across the sky.

The twenty pound that I had looked on with glee as a great fortune, and spent recklessly, I realized only now was running through my hands like sand. Never before having had many dealings with money, for Samuel had paid all of our bills, and gave me only what I needed for fripperies, I was astonished at how expensive everything was. I had the weekly bill for sending out for dinner every day, a demand for the sewing of my new winter wardrobe from the dressmakers, and Tara's wages besides (for to save my shame I did not tell her of my troubles, and instead talked merrily of my husband's return), not to mention the nightsoilman, and the victualler, and the baker and the chits that had come from the quill-maker, and book-binder, and paper-seller, too.

By the time the end of February drew on, I was down to my last three pound, and growing desperate, for my letters to my mother had also gone unanswered, while Grisella's replies were short and curt-sounding, regretting that she had no means to assist me. My messages to Lady Vyne had been returned unopened. I threw them on the fire, even as I wept.

On the chill afternoon when I had sent Tara out for my dinner, and she had returned with the news that no nearby tavern would feed me until I paid them all what I owed, and just a short while afterwards, a knock had come on the door from the dressmaker's man, threatening bailiffs and to have me arrested (I got rid of him with a sovereign), I made my decision. I would use the last of my money to hire a coach to Hanbury Court at Langley, to see what Samuel was about, and if I could not find him, I would repair to my mother's; she would surely take pity on me and save me from starvation. The coachman was all ready and Tara and I putting the finishing touches to my trunk when there came another rapping at the door.

'Lor', do not answer it,' I cried, 'for 'tis certain to be a guard with a warrant for my removal to Newgate.'

But it was only a messenger, for a letter was slid under the door and, pushing Tara out of the way, I ran to pick it up, hoping against hope that my love had written to me at last. Turning it over, I saw my name – my old name – in a looping hand I did not recognize.

*Hanbury Court*
*Langley*
*The last day of February, 1682/83 A.D.*

*Mrs Flight,*

*I am writing to tell you what my husband plainly cannot.*

*He has given you up and stays with me and my children. I had a boy, you see, and he is the apple of my husband's eye, he having longed all this while for an heir, and he cannot bear to be parted from him. My husband now makes plans to withdraw from Court, and the King has given his blessing for it, for he well loves my husband, and understands better than any man, the need to be amongst your children. Did you know I only had daughters 'til now? Two of them, both with my Sammy's soft brown hair.*

*He has left each one of your letters unopened, and I found them where he had hidden them, in a foolish place, and so I read them, every one in turn, and burned them all on the fire, so that my daughters should not chance upon your sinful words to the man they know only as their ever loving father.*

*I do not wish to pain you, madame, for I know from my friends at Court that your situation is not easy, but it may aid you to know that you are one in a long line of women with whom my husband has dallied, before returning again to me. Such is the age we live in – and the nature of men. I think he liked you a little more, perhaps, than they, for he was quiet the first few days he came back to me, but he has recovered himself now, as he always does, and is husband to me again as he always was.*

*I pray you do not trouble my family again.*

*May the Lord God have mercy upon you,*

*Dorcas, Lady Hanbury.*

Hiding the tremor in my hands, I bade Tara go and visit her mother for a holiday, and no sooner had I closed the door on her, I let out a great cry of anger, before setting out to smash everything breakable in the house I could lay my hands on, including the fine china tea-cups Samuel had got me as a house-warming gift, and the pretty blue jug on the mantel that had held his daily posies, which still had its flowers in, and water besides, which tipped onto the floor and splashed up the grate. I ground the blooms under my heel, feeling the mush of the petals on the floor.

I found the little carved wooden bear, and dashed it with all my might against the wall, then wrenched all the clothes he had given me from their chest: a grand picture hat with a cascade of ostrich plumes draped all over one side, a pearl-white pair of lacework gloves, a fine linen chemise trimmed with ribbons, and a pretty silk gown of soft burnt orange – for that colour was the fashion then, and Samuel had said I must have it. I set about tearing these as best I could, screaming like a banshee as I did it, and throwing the pieces about the room. The hat I could not rent with my teeth or hands, and so I crushed it and threw it on the floor, and stamped on it, and howled all the curses I knew while I did it. In my fury I slipped on it across the floor, and fell down, and then I wept: first, that I had hurt my knee in the falling, and then that I had been a fool, and then that I had lost my one true love, and should never see him, or hold him, or laugh with him again, and then that he had forsaken me when he had sworn to be my own sweet-heart for evermore, and then that I would be lost and lonely all my days without him by my side.

I lay on the floor and sobbed my heart out until first the fire went out, and then the sun went down, and I laid awhile on the tatters of my ruined things, swollen-faced and wet about the neck with crying. I thought that now I did not have him, nor nothing to remember him by neither, and I wept again onto my broken hat. Knowing I had not the strength to kindle the fire or to call for vittles neither, I dragged myself to my bed, and finding my broken bear had landed there, her back legs now snapped clean off, bundled myself in the coverings in my misery, whereupon I sniffed at his side of the bed, which smelt of his woody Samuel smell, and I beat my fists into the pillow. I lay wide awake, with aching eyes, running over in my head everything that I must have done wrong and how I could undo it, and only when the cocks began to crow and the light in the room change from pitch-black to smoke-grey did I sleep.

❧

# IV

# CHANGES

*In which I begin to learn to shift for myself*

March came upon England that year with a fit of freezing rains, and all the pamphlets talking of the unending Ice Age that was upon us, and what message it brought from God, for the young and old were dying in droves. This was the first winter of my life that I knew what it was to be cold – not the bright-cheeked kind of cold for romping about the countryside and coming in to sit by a warm hearth, but the kind of unrelenting cold that ran into your bones and stayed there, and left you feeling weary, desperate, sick.

With Tara's help, I had begun to ration my outgoings while I waited for the reply from my mother, for I had laid before her my now very desperate case, and asked that she save me from starvation, or worse, by sending me a pound or two. Through this bitter weather, Tara stayed, sleeping heaped up with blankets on her creaking truckle bed, going out for firewood in the morning, though it left her boots and skirts wet and her sweet face chalk-white with cold. Our credit all run out with the taverns, we were down to simple meals that could be made on the fire, and so our daily bread was potage, made with the vegetables Tara got at market. We had fallen into a sort of ritual with this potage – she bringing home the vegetables in her basket, and peeling and chopping them and throwing them into the pot, which hung over the fire with the glutinous remains of potage from the previous day, and the day before that, and me stirring it, and seeing when it was ready, while she went about the other work of the house.

'I do not think much to this turnip,' I said, peering into the pot as I stirred it, on our seventh day of potage. 'I had a taste just now and 'tis famous bitter. If only we had some butter, or some mutton to flavour it.'

Tara, looking up from her trimming of the candles, coughed politely. 'I'll add some pepper, mistress and the rest of that tansy-flower, and that may disguise the taste. Mayhap there'll be tripe tomorrow, for that is cheap and has the goodness of meat, if not the taste. My mother boils it up with potatoes and barley, and 'tis a godly belly-warming stew withal.'

'Oh yes, we may try that. I'll find the tansy – here it is. I remember its spiky leaves from my girlhood. It is good for the digestion and aching bones.'

'Oh aye.' She brushed her hands on her woollen skirts. ''Tis a shame that Master Sherewin does not come back, for he must surely have the coin for mutton.'

'Well, as I told you, he is very ill, Tara, and is laid up in the countryside in a boiling fever and so is not even well enough to send coin,' I said, quickly. 'But I pray he may be speedily recovered and return to me.'

Tara said nothing to this.

'All the herbs in the world will not help us, for we must have meat, Tara – we cannot work without it – I mean you cannot, for you will not let me help you, though I am ten days behind on your wages.'

''Tis not for a lady,' she said.

❦

I was down to my last pound when I knew for certain that my mother would not help me. I broke the news to Tara that I could not afford her any more, and was heartsick-sorry, but would send on the remainder of her wages, as soon as I had word from my husband. She took this with a simple nod, as if she had been expecting it all along, and bundled up her few belongings, and the bright shilling that I had pressed into the palm of her hand.

'Good luck to ye, mistress,' she said as she stepped out of the door, and I saw in the twist of her little face that she pitied me, and what I had come down to.

Then I was alone.

When I woke next morning the room was so strangely and deathly silent, and ice-cold, though it was broad morning and I remembered that I had sent Tara away and there was no one to light the fire. I breathed in and out, watching my breath mist before me. Food-lack clawed at my gurgling belly. My dream of the night before came to me then as I swung my feet into my slippers, that I was a child again, and at my lesson books, and my father pointing out the words in a bright book that was open before me, which were in a strange language that I did not know.

'Thank you, Father,' the dream-me had said, gazing up into the dream-him's light blue eyes, the self-same colour as my own. 'I see now what I must do.'

Wrapped up in the bedclothes, I sat at the table and made a list.

# HOW TO GET SOME *COIN*

1. Go back to Tyringham & fall on his neck – NEVER NEVER NEVER not if I be a beggar in the streets and starving to DEATH.

2. Hire a carriage & go to my mother & throw myself upon her mercy, though she has not replied to my letters & I think would turn me away.

3. Go to Grisella & beg *her* mercy, though she has not written me neither, and perhaps she shuns me too, for the great shame that I have brought upon myself. I do not blame her for it.

4. Sell my wedding ring. For 'tis solid gold, and the only thing I have not sacrificed, for I would have people believe that

I was a married woman, or a widow I shall keep it a while yet...

5.  Go to Court and jostle with the hordes in the presence chamber. I may catch sight of Lady Vyne then, & she might help me get a place there (perhaps the returned letters were a mistake?). If there is a place more accepting of cuckolding than the Court, I cannot think of it. Though, 'tis true that I have not heard of a woman who has put off her husband & kept her head held high – now I think on it, 'tis always the other way around. (The more I dwell on this matter, the more I think I should have done away with Tyringham by means of a secret poison, or push down the stairs, for a widow in my position would be respectable & could marry again. But I did not think of that, when Samuel's mouth was on me. I was in a dream then, & could not awake.)

6.  I could get myself up looking as pretty as could be, & primp myself such as I have not done in weeks, & go out onto the street – or better & safer, a tavern, & fall into conversation with some gentleman, who may want to pay me to... go with him, & love him as a wife. Could it be much worse than what I have endured with my wedded husband? I think it cannot be worse... but mayhap I would be thrown out of a tavern... but I could go to the playhouse! For I have seen painted women there roaming about & plying their trade, & there is safety in numbers – might I not go there and see what they are about & how I might go about the thing...

**ADDENDUM:** I am being foolish, for there is something I have not tried that has been staring me in the face all along!

⚜

# V

※

# TRIALS

*In which I attempt to improve my condition*

⁂

I got up and dressed myself in the finest things I had. Five silk dresses had gone to a clothes merchant who stroked the fine fabric and winked at me and said he would give me a pound a piece, and me lucky to have such a price, and I took it though I knew they must have cost above twenty pound just six months before. My silver brush and mirror had gone to a man on the same street. To a jeweller at Hatton Garden, near the Sign of the Mitre: three pairs of earrings, a pearl necklace, the cross-shaped pendant set with rubies that I always wore on a ribbon around my neck, and the garnet ring my husband had given me for our engagement (which I saw handled by the man's rough fingers without so much as a sigh).

My favourite emerald-coloured dress I still had, and my soft leather boots, and my mother's hair combs, and my pearl-drop earrings. All of these I put on, and put up my hair as best I could, teasing it into my usual topknot at the crown of my head; my side hair clustered in clouds of ringlets at my temples. For luck I pasted three black patches on my cheek (and one on my chin to cover my birthmark), the constellation of stars that had become my habit, at Samuel's encouragement. With a dab of the last of my orange-flower water at my neck, and a pinch of my cheeks, I tied on my vizard, put up the cloak of my hood, and went out, the vision of a fashionable woman.

The snow had not fallen for many weeks now, but the air was cold as it could be, and I made fists of my gloved hands, watching my breath mist before me. The streets were still covered over with slush, now turned grey and brown, and as I stepped slowly towards the city walls, I saw ladies slipping on their pattens, and two apprentices, clearly the worse for drink, clutching each other, and bellowing all the while, and finally slipping over and falling pell mell into the gutter with cries of 'Zounds!' and raucous laughter. I was glad to have my vizard, for the air bit at my face, and I bent my body downwards, and trudged slowly towards the city.

Inside the walls the going was easier, for the ice had been melted by many feet, and hooves of horses and cattle on their way to market, and I was soon on Drury Lane, with a tingling skin, and a splashed skirt. It was strange to be on the street where I had so often been with Samuel, and so close to Henry House, and I felt for my vizard, suddenly afeard that someone might see me here. The playhouse did not look open, and I balked suddenly, at the boldness of my plan. I wondered too if those inside might see through my finery to what I really was: a frightened girl without a friend in the world. But again the picture of my father came into my mind, and I stopped up my courage and pushed open the door.

# *THE* REHEARSAL

## A NEW WORK

*BY*

MRS SHEREWIN

---

DOWN BUT NOT OUT,

& STILL WITH THE FIGHTING
SPIRIT

*that we* KNOW & LOVE

---

## ACT III, SCENE II

> *A playhouse. Interior. Day. The light is dim, for only one of the two chandeliers is lit, making the painted wooden walls and posts look strange, and giving a dull orange glow to the faces of the two actresses on stage. Behind them, an old woman who pushes a besom around with a brush-brush-brush. In the pit stands a short, rosy-cheeked gentleman, with a very fine red suit, and white periwig. A young woman, with a wan look about her face, watches anxiously from the doorway.*

PARRYKIN: Come on then, lovey, we'll just hear your speech again, and then we can rehearse the chase scene, which is bound to be bad, seeing as Mrs Sop's called in sick again, and so one of you shall have to share her parts between you.

MRS THRUCKLE: There's a surprise. Since her dalliance with Lord R began, and she now with coin enough to drink, she's been so very unwell. Though it is strange that she has been seen at Newmarket and at the Duke's and seemed at both times to be in her cups.

MRS CAREBY: I'll warrant a barrel of brandy-wine is her manager now.

> *They give each other meaningful glances.*

PARRYKIN: Quick as you like, my dears, for 'tis past one of the clock already, and I'd dearly like to open on time just once this week, if I may.

MRS CAREBY: Oh hush, Parrykin, for 'tis your prating that stops us from starting when we might, and not the slowness of my speechifying!

MRS THRUCKLE:   'Tis true I have never heard an actress speak more slowly than you do, Letty, but Gad, 'tis a wonder you get a word out at all, the way you make eyes at the gallants. But perhaps that is a part of your playing... I am sure you would not wish to come across quite so lewd as you do.

MRS CAREBY:   You are so very kind to mention the great popularity I have with the audience, Sukey – faith, my name on the playbill has filled out this house for the last eight days straight! Though 'tis a wonder you have noticed what I am about at all, you being so inclined to distract everyone from the pleasures of your acting with all your extravagant gestures.

*She strikes a series of mock tragic poses.*

MRS THRUCKLE:   It is far too good of you to compliment me thus, Letty! For 'tis true I like to use my body to the fullest when I act, but Lor', would it not be strange if I did not use the thing that so many have told me is my prettiest asset – and the only reason they come to the playhouse at all?

MRS CAREBY:   If it was Lord Knopdale who told you this, I must confess it now – he wears an eye-glass.

MRS THRUCKLE:   It was Lord Marlham, my dear, who I think you will remember, for he turned you down three times at Christmas.

PARRYKIN:   Ladies, ladies, let us not waste time with extravagant compliments, for we have a play to rehearse, and it will not do itself.

MRS CAREBY:   Forgive me, Parry, but you must know that I am as keen to rehearse as you are. I want to make sure I have the character exactly right, and must take a while to prepare myself. 'Tis a trick I learnt from Mrs Cox when I was 'prentice to her at the King's. You would not know of such things, Sukey, having come to us without any formal schooling... at least, not in acting.

MRS THRUCKLE: I have learnt how to spot a surly wench, at any rate.

> *Enter* MRS SHEREWIN, *a comely young widow.*

MRS SHEREWIN: Forgive me, I – I did not mean to interrupt you, but the door was open...

PARRYKIN: Your timing is excellent. [*Taking in the richness of her costume*] How do you do... madame. I am Parrykin – the manager here. I beg to ask if you can wait – for I'm in the middle of a rehearsal, and, as usual, 'tis proving tricky.

MRS SHEREWIN: I am Lady – I mean – Mrs Sh... I mean, Mrs Bear – Mrs Bearwood, a genteel widow who has fallen on hard times and must earn my living.

MRS THRUCKLE: Why, 'tis just like the script!

PARRYKIN: I'm sorry to hear that, mistress.

MRS CAREBY: [*Aside*] If she's a widow then I'm a vestal virgin.

MRS SHEREWIN: I shall not waste your time with pleasantries, sir. I am a passionate lover of the theatre; I can read and I can write, and I have been declaiming speeches since I was eight years old. I am acquainted with your theatre, for I have been coming here, as your patron, for these six months with... with my friends, who are nobles of the Court. I – I would have you audition me.

|              | I want to be an actress, Mr Parrykin. |
| --- | --- |
| PARRYKIN: | I see. The Court, indeed? Will you take off your vizard, madame, for I cannot know you by a mask. |
| MRS SHEREWIN: | Why yes, if you wish it. |

*She removes it.* PARRYKIN *appraises her.*

| MRS THRUCKLE: | She's quite pretty, I suppose, with those light eyes. An innocence in the face... she cannot be much above eighteen. |
| --- | --- |
| MRS CAREBY: | Young, with a good bosom... Of decent, though not tall stature... |
| MRS THRUCKLE: | But that fair type of hair is a long way from fashion. |
| MRS CAREBY: | You would know, having dyed yours these ten years. |
| PARRYKIN: | I beg your pardon: I do not remember you, madame. Who are your friends, pray? |
| MRS SHEREWIN: | I – I do not like to use their names so lightly. |
| PARRYKIN: | I see. Well, you have caught me at an inconvenient time, Mrs Bearwood, as you can see. Come again, some time next week, or the one after, and mayhap I will see you then. |

*He turns back towards the stage.*

| PARRYKIN: | Now then, where were we? |
| --- | --- |
| MRS SHEREWIN: | Pray, sir, but what is the play? |
| PARRYKIN: | The play? |
| MRS CAREBY: | *The Forc'd Marriage*, and it's dreadful. |

MRS THRUCKLE: The way you act it.

MRS CAREBY: I blame the director.

PARRYKIN: They always do.

MRS SHEREWIN: Mr Parrykin! I know that play off by heart and could speak it for you here as we stand without need for a paper, nor prompter neither.

PARRYKIN: I am sorry, Mrs Bearwood—

MRS CAREBY: Have you not thought of Sop's absence, Parrykin? If this... widow can say the parts, mayhap Sukey and I will not have to kill ourselves rushing about and changing costumes. We haven't even learnt her lines yet, neither.

PARRYKIN: But I told you to do that this morning.

MRS THRUCKLE: I did not receive the message.

MRS CAREBY: She was otherwise engaged.

PARRYKIN: So then, I am to understand, ladies, that you do not know Mrs Sop's parts, for the play that we are about to put on in two – nay, an hour's time?

MRS THRUCKLE: For once, Parry, you have got it.

PARRYKIN: I do not know... she looks a bit scrawny. And her arms are not white as they might be... can she act?

MRS CAREBY: Since when was that relevant?

MRS THRUCKLE: I don't know if it ever was, to you.

MRS SHEREWIN: I beg you, Mr Parrykin. Do let me try it. I will not let you down – and if I do, why, you need not pay me.

PARRYKIN: Not pay you!

MRS THRUCKLE: [*Aside*] Now she has got him, I'll warrant.

PARRYKIN: Oh, yes, yes, then, you may do it, if it will stop these two harpies and their screeching. And if you muff it, you'll not get your shilling, and that's a promise.

MRS THRUCKLE: Darling Parry.

MRS CAREBY: You sweet little man.

PARRYKIN: I'm five foot eight!

SCENE II

> *The same playhouse; the undressing room.* MRS BUNTY, *a dressing woman, is bustling about a rack of costumes.* MRS SHEREWIN, *now in a wig and with a painted face, stands gazing at herself in a full-length mirror.*

MRS BUNTY: Ye will have to go in your own bodice tonight, for Mrs Sop's a plumper thing than ye and her things would hang off ye, however tight I lace 'em. Though even your own skirts are loose on ye, see. When did ye last have a meal, wench? And do not lie, for I see hunger writ in your face.

MRS SHEREWIN: Uh... yesterday... a little soup. 'Twas fine when I scraped the mould off.

MRS BUNTY: Twenty years in the playhouse and I will never understand actresses, not if I live to be a hundred years old. Now then, miss. I've bread and cheese I will share with you, if only to keep you upright and stop you shaming the whole company by fainting on the stage directly you walk on it.

*She assembles a meal.* URSULA *sits down and eats it hungrily. Enter* MRS THRUCKLE.

MRS THRUCKLE: Oh, it's you. Bunty, my second-best bodice has burst again – can you fix it?

MRS BUNTY: No wonder, if you stuff it as much as you do – and don't give me that face, for I've seen you pad yourself fit to bursting with my very own eyes, and your dumplin' shop jacked up so high you can rest your chin upon it.

MRS THRUCKLE: I'm only slightly improving on what nature herself intended.

MRS BUNTY *guffaws.*

MRS SHEREWIN: How do you do. Mrs Thruckle, isn't it? I am—

MRS THRUCKLE: [*Cutting her*] Don't speak to me, wench!

*She moves off to a dressing table and begins to paint her face at speed.*

MRS BUNTY: There, there. 'Tis not the thing, for the bit parts to speak to the feature actresses, my duck. Not until you're promoted to the company.

MRS SHEREWIN: Why I... I see.

MRS BUNTY: I'm glad you do, for the ones that don't never last too long.

*Enter a* BOY.

BOY: Call for Mrs Thruckle, Mr Manners and Mrs Sop, I mean – the new girl who's playing her parts whose name I don't know.

MRS SHEREWIN: Mrs Bearwood.

BOY: That's the one.

MRS SHEREWIN:   Does that mean we go on?

MRS THRUCKLE:   [*Calling from her table*] Lor', not the brightest star in the sky, is she? I fancy we're all done for. Prepare for a pelting, Mrs Bunty, for I can smell the cabbages from here.

> *Enter* MR MANNERS, *an actor, in dandyish dress.*

MANNERS:   Sweetikins! Honeypies!

> *He kisses* BUNTY *and* MRS THRUCKLE *effusively.*

MRS THRUCKLE:   Percy, you old rogue. You're cutting it monstrous fine today.

MANNERS:   I'll admit it, you tasty wench: I've been up to no good. Gad, it was almost as hard to tear myself away from that one, as it is from you.

MRS THRUCKLE:   Oh, you blackguard! You knave!

> *They lock bodies and begin passionately kissing.*

MANNERS:   [*Breaking away*] Half a mo' – who's the blonde?

MRS THRUCKLE:   Oh, some orange-girl in a stolen dress who larks at being a widow. She's taking Sop's parts until we can find a real actress. You remember Sop, Percy. She used to be your mistress until you chucked her for one of Davenant's new mopsies.

MANNERS:   I haven't the slightest notion what you mean.

> *They resume their passionate embraces. Enter* BOY.

BOY:               Last call for Mrs Thruckle, Mr Manners and the new girl who's playing Sop's parts whose name I don't know. Three of the clock. Places everyone.

> *Exit* BOY.

> *The voice of* PARRYKIN *heard offstage:*

Come on then, lovies. Hear that? We've a full house, and The Earl of Grantby in the box. Let's not keep them all waiting.

> *Exeunt* MANNERS *&* MRS THRUCKLE.

MRS SHEREWIN:  Is that it? Oh, I am all afright!

MRS BUNTY:    That's it, lovey, on you go now. Break a leg, my dear one. Lor', ain't ye shaking. Deep breaths now, duckling.

> *She pushes* MRS SHEREWIN *out of the door, who walks towards the stage slowly, as if in a dream. Offstage left, she stands, with her hand in her pocket.*

MRS SHEREWIN:  Oh Jesu, I cannot do it! Oh, sweet Father of mine, if you have ever looked down on me and helped me, let it be now! I have one shilling left in my pocket. Here it is, cold in my shaking hand. But if I do this right, I will have one more, and perhaps another. I must do it. I can do it.

> *She steps onto the stage. The sound of applause, whistles, hooting...*

> *Curtain*

❦

# VI

⚜

# ADVANCEMENT

*In which I reflect on the novelty of the playhouse*

## MARCH

### 1<sup>st</sup>

Last night I trod the boards as an

*Actress*

*Actress*

*Actress!!!!!!*

I think I spoke my part well, for I did not have too many lines,
and only almost forgot myself once, for the shock of being thrust
afore an audience set my blood a-churning round my body and
briefly coddled my thoughts. But the audience hooted as loudly as
they might and at the end I took my bows with the company, and
Parrykin said he was much obliged to me, and I had made a fair
job of it, but mainly, was fair enough to look on throughout, and so
he was well satisfied. I can scarce note down all that I am feeling,
for I could not get to sleep last night with the thrill of it all pulsing
through my veins, and now I am weary and quite wrung out, with a
slight sorrow that I have not a soul to tell of my triumph. But I shall
shake myself down and go to the playhouse again today to speak to
Mr Parrykin, for I am in hope that Mrs Sop is still unwell and they
would have me for another performance.

### 3ʳᵈ

Plucking up my courage, I tapped at the door of **Mr P's** room and, hearing a sound much like snoring issuing from within, tapped a little harder, and he opened the door with his wig all askew. Our interview was short, for after he bade me come in, I asked if he might need me again in **Mrs Sop's** part for tonight, and he said that she had not come again to work, and that if she did not come again the next day, he would give her her notice, for he suspected she had become a drunk, and the part would be mine.

### 6ᵗʰ

I have held my breath these three days, chary that Mrs Sop would return... but the third day has passed and she has not appeared. And so I am to have the part! Jubilations!

### 7ᵗʰ

Today I overheard Mrs Careby having a row with her paramour, she complaining that he did not visit her enough and that she was wont to throw her affections elsewhere, he growing angry and saying it was more trouble to keep an actress than it was worth. She was greatly irked to see that I had heard the whole, and went off in a great pet muttering about long-nosed wenches who did not know their place.

### 10ᵗʰ

It is all about the coffeehouses that the **King** is brought down very low with his latest rheum. When he walks, he uses a jewel-topped cane, and always wears a cloak lined with thickest sable, even though it is a mild spring, and he has not been seen at any playhouse these last few months.

### 13ᵗʰ

Though Parrykin is polite and tells me he is pleased enough with my work, I have had nothing but cool looks from Thruckle and Careby, for I expect they do not like a newcomer in their midst. I have heard snatches of conversation that some of the 'Tiring Room gallants are keen to look upon me, and p'raps this explains it, and so I avoid tarrying there, and go straight home again when the play is done, and set to perfecting my lines.

## 16<sup>th</sup>

Last night, betwixt scenes, **Mr Manners** sidled up to me and, slapping
at my rump, asked if I would dine with him that evening for he
'fancied some sport' and thought that as a widow I 'might well
know my way around a nine-inch knocker'. He said this in such a
brazen-faced way, I found that it made me fall to laughing and,
thanking him heartily, told him I was greatly flattered, but wanted
to concentrate on my part. He took this very well and, winking at
me, went off whistling.

## 17<sup>th</sup>

*The Forc'd Marriage* is to be taken off due to dwindling numbers!
With my heart in my throat I went again to **Mr Parrykin** and, in
my anxiety at what I would do for coin, gabbled at him a great deal
about my love of the playhouse and how I would work at whatever
he would have me do. He said he would think on it and send me
word.

## 18<sup>th</sup>

The new play is to be *Tyrannick Love* – I have seen the playbills
pasted all about. No word from Parrykin.

## 20<sup>th</sup>

It has been more than a week since I begged **Mr Parrykin** for
further employment. My meagre savings dwindling ever lower, and
feeling in need of some company, I took myself for a walk into the
city. Coming upon the square at Piquadillo, which was thronging
as ever with people going hither and thither, I smiled to see
little carts set up for fortune telling, painted all over with mystic
symbols. Wondering if my luck was due to turn or nay, I called out
'Ho!' and passed through the curtained opening of one such cart
to find an old crone within who, despite her wrinkled face, was
nevertheless very brightly rouged, crouched at a dirty card table.
At her beckoning, I crossed her filthy palm with a few pennies, and
she, scoffing at this, said she could only tell me one thing of my
luck. Taking out a worn tarot, she thumbed a few cards down onto
the table. The Wheel of Fortune. Death. The Empress. The Star.

The staleness of the air as I waited for her pronouncement.

'It will get worse for ye afore it gets better,' said she, surveying
the cards before her with a gleam in her eye. She tapped the

Empress card. 'Ye shalt never be famous – yet mayhap thee shalt be remembered.'

'Oh,' said I, a little deflated at this. 'I thought the Star, at least, might be fortuitous... I hoped to hear of a luck-change, perhaps something of money – or of love.'

She let out a strange sort of shriek that chilled me in its strangeness. 'Love!' she scoffed, gripping the table. 'I shall tell thee naught of amours for thrippence!'

And that was all she would say.

## 23<sup>RD</sup>

It rained heavily all day, and did not let up, and so I gave up thoughts of going to call at the King's and see if they are in want of an actress, but lay abed all day gorging myself on books and amusing myself mightily with my scribblings.

## 24<sup>th</sup>

Today I rose early and went back to the playhouse, for after my rest I was newly invigorated to show Parrykin how earnest I was, hoping he might take pity on my lot. The new play going once again not as well as he hoped, he was in a great pet and very red in the face, but still I set about with my pleading, laying before him all the reasons I would work for him, and why I would be the most faithful of women withal. At last, I think, being fatigued with my begging, he said he would employ me as an understudy, with perhaps an occasional part to walk on, if only I would stop haranguing him. In my great excitement, I caught him up by the face and laid a kiss upon his nose, whereupon he blushed to his roots and bade me go away.

Huzzah for gainful employment!

# VII

# TRAVAILS

*In which I begin to learn the craft of acting*

A GLOSSARY OF TERMS I HAVE LEARNT *as an* ACTRESS
*at* THE KING'S PLAYHOUSE, DRURY LANE, LONDON

INCLUDING

NOTES ON THE FINE & NOBLE ART of
*STAGECRAFT*

BALLET – The dance that I and the rest of the company may
perform to distract the house while the scenery is changed. Mr
Parrykin likes us to do this very gracefully and very French, but I
am always sent to the back of the stage, with Thruckle and Careby
waving their arms so vigorously before me that I am sure I cannot
be seen even by the gallery. On my first few days, I was wont to trip
over their ankles, and though I protested that I was not clumsy, I
saw their flashing looks, and kept my own counsel, and the trippings
seemed to stop, though at the back of the ballet I remained.

BREECHES PARTS – When the audience numbers dwindle, Parrykin
is like to send on one of the actresses dressed in the clothes of a boy
so the men can admire the turn of her ankle, shape of her leg and
curve of her haunches in the name of appreciating a drama. He
has not sent me, for he says that my posterior has not yet grown
shapely enough to warrant the expense of the tailor.

CERUSE – A paste whip't from the white of one egg and a few
drops of water that is applied to the actress's face before she steps

on the stage. Having a tendency to crack when the face is moved, an actress with such an application must be less than loquacious with her smiling. (This concoction on my phyzzog is so disguising and I am so little myself that I am quite unafraid I shall be recognized by Lady Vyne, or Samuel, or anyone else who may care to know me!)

CRAYONS – Another tool of painting. They may be red, for touching to the lips (so useful to draw the eye for a kissing scene), or blue, to draw in the blue veins on a white arm or bosom, which is the sign of gentility and so looks very well when playing at a Queen or noble lady.

GOING-A-KEEPING – The aim of all actresses is not to become famous, though many of 'em do and are the talk of the Court, but to attract the attention of some rich gentleman, who will put them into keeping and hire them rooms and a carriage and give them many more jewels than kisses.

LIGHT – The thing that an actress must always be standing in. I must draw all eyes to my person, even if 'tis not my line, by lingering in the brightest part of the stage. When saying an aside, I should stand near the chandelier, or the footlights, for the flickering light there is most flattering, though my gown has twice got caught in the flame and set a-smoking and Parrykin very cross withal.

NEEDLE CHEAT – If an actress needs tears and cannot feign them, she may conceal a pin up her sleeve and, when the sorrowful moment comes, prick herself very sharply until the weeping issues forth.

ORANGE-SELLERS – Not to be taken notice of, though they may call to the stage and try to bait you, but an actress must point her nose in the air and perhaps her toe withal.

OVERTALKING – The art of throwing one's voice over the noise of the rabble, for the audience do not hush themselves when we act, unless they be frightened by an explosion. I am practising every night in my chamber, though I am hoarse.

PROGRAMME – The dates of the plays. We are expected to be in the playhouse ready to perform every day excepting Sundays, Lent, Passion Week and Christmas Day. 'The theatre never closes!' says Mr Parrykin; it does, if someone important dies, but that has not happened for a while.

RIPOSTE – I have learnt 'tis best to have some witty replies committed to memory, for the habit of the audience is to interrupt all the speeches with calls, and compliments and taunts. Last Tuesday I heard a gallant cry, 'She's not as fine as the other one, I'll declare,' to which I shielded the glare of the lights from my eye and gazed into the audience a while and said: 'Grandfather, what do you there? You have not had your tincture,' which sent those around the man into great fits of laughter and whistling.

SAFFRON WASH – According to Parrykin, my hair is neither one thing nor t'other and so he has got Bunty to make me up dye in which to dip it and make it as flaxen as a Dutch girl's, which may attract the gentlemen, which will make Parry enough shillings to have the scenery re-painted, for the flagstones are peeling and the magical forest is turning yellow with age.

'TIRING ROOM – Where the company retires after their hard work. 'Tis festooned with curtains and gifts sent by gallants, from posies of lavender and gillyflower to jewel-cases and once, a great rounded cheese. In the day, 'tis where we eat and rest between scening, but in the evenings, 'tis where the gallants come a-calling and where amours may take place in its darkened corners. Bunty tells me that a while before I came they had a very low actress, who afore that was an orange-girl come up from a Drury Lane stew, and so she sold her favours behind the dressing screen for tuppence a time.

TRAPDOOR OR 'THE TRAP' – From whence the villain of the scene emerges, to great effect and hissing and calling of the pit. A similar effect is had with wires, live dogs, loud noises, or any sort of open flame.

WITS — The fashion of the Court for men and women to be bold and jocular has infected the playhouse and I have learnt that if you can make them rock in their seats and howl with laughter and cry 'Brava!' then you have them, even if you be a plain sort of wench with a very bad gait. 'Tis shown in the manner of the plays we perform here which are mostly comedy, that being more popular than tragedy, excepting with maids of a tender age, elderly uncles, and widows.

⚜

# VIII

# FELICITY

*In which I muse on my bright new career*

As I grew in my knowledge of what it was to be an actress 'pon the stage, I began to experience a strange sensation in myself that I had not felt in a very long time – and that was a thing called happiness. There was joy in the pleasing routine of my new life, which left me little time for dwelling on my heartbreak, and in the mornings I found myself leaping out of bed and trilling like a meadowlark, skipping about the chamber for the whole of my toilet.

Whereas time had dragged in the dark, frigid corners of Turvey in an agony of drifting about, sweet-eating and couch-laying – and had also passed slowly during my life with Samuel when I had been often confined to our rooms – my days were now full of activity and of conversation – oh, such endless exchanges the company had about the intentions of the playwright and the meaning of a line – and how delicious it was to spend all day in these artistic discussions. I was bodily occupied, as well as intellectually, for the acting life demanded that I stir myself for much of the day. Though, from my childhood games, I had known the work that went into the learning of an actor's lines, I had not considered the corporeal demands on a person that danced and sang and bellowed all day to earn their living. Despite my romps about the countryside, I had never moved myself as much as I now must do, and tumbled into bed every night like a dead thing, waking every morning with a dry mouth and aching limbs.

Despite these arduous beginnings, and though the other actresses complained about them hourly, our daily rehearsals were a great joy to me, for I found every minute I was in the playhouse a thrill, and could not call any of it work. Upon coming together in the morning, we would sit on the edge of the stage, or dawdle in the front row, or horse about with the props cupboard, until Parrykin appeared and admonished us all for being late and lazy, though he rarely showed his face afore nine of the clock, but said he had been up in the office on matters of business while Mrs Bunty, who was always a-lurking in the background, made disbelieving clucking noises with her tongue. Then, Parrykin gave us instructions on the day's rehearsal, which was usually notes from the previous day's performance and would always go the same way.

PARRYKIN:   Now, Manners, you are doing that thing again when you come on in the second act.

MANNERS:   [*Examining his nails*] I vehemently disagree.

PARRYKIN:   But I have not said what the thing is!

MANNERS:   Oh, I know what it is.

PARRYKIN:   So you admit that you are doing it?

MANNERS:   I do no such thing.

And so on.

That we were all thrown so closely together, and that I worked so tirelessly to remember my lines, besides all the other things that were expected of an actress, seemed to have a softening effect on Mrs Careby and Mrs Thruckle, for after two months or so had passed, Thruckle called out to me as I was putting on my outdoor shoes and pulling on my cloak at the end of the performance.

'Won't you step out with us, Mrs Bearwood?' she said. 'For 'tis a fine enough afternoon and Letty and I had thought to call upon the 'pothecary, and the ribbon-seller, and take a dish of something besides.'

'Oh!' I said, a little taken aback at her affability. 'But I do not have the coin for fripperies, alas, for I must shift for myself on an understudy's wage.'

'It does not signify,' she said, with an airy wave of her hand, which I saw was wearing a sky-blue glove. 'For you do not have to buy anything, and I expect we can stand you a dish.'

This I thought politic to accept, and found myself pressed between the two women as we came out of the stage door and passed along the street, they still in their stage make-up and patches, and drawing much attention from the passers-by, especially the gentlemen who all made bows, or pressed their hands to their hearts, and gave such sighs, at which we laughed and called out greetings to them good-naturedly.

'Always remember, it's them that pays your wages,' said Thruckle, solemnly. 'For we are nothing without them.'

We called at the apothecary first, whereupon Careby bought a box of Spanish Paper, which were tiny sheets tinged with cochineal that she said were necessary for the playing of blushing parts, namely 'country virgin', 'comely bride', and 'troublesome boy-child'.

Mrs Thruckle caught up a flagon of belladonna drops, to put in her eyes.

'For though ye may be acting in a tragedy, ye may not always be feeling one,' she said, shaking her parcel. 'These make a girl's eyes shine as wet and bright as a baby rabbit's and will have the whole house in a fit of weeping.'

We went to the ribbon-seller's, where we looked at lace and silk and satin, and bought none of them, and then on to the sweet shop, where Careby ordered a tray of French bonbons to be delivered to her rooms, for her sweetheart, who was at present a gallant called Sir Fringle, and seventy years of age, kept his energy up with an excess of sugar. At each shop we were greeted either with enthusiasm or disdain, depending on the shopkeeper, and I saw that while many of the gentlemen were happy to sell their wares to actresses, some of the women did not seem to like it, and gave us thin smiles even as they snatched up our coins and put them in their pockets, and I kept the thought to myself that if they knew I was a true lady of the quality, how they would fall over themselves to do my bidding; Careby caught me in the smirk and teased me that I had a lover.

It suddenly started to rain then, and though it was not heavy, Thruckle said we must come to her rooms, which were on the very next street, and take a dish of tea, and this we did. I was curious to see the living quarters of an actress, for I myself now lived very plainly, though in my old life I had grown accustomed to extravagance, and for sure, there were buttercup-coloured window silks, and a tall vase of peacock feathers and a screen painted all about with purple and crimson fruit, and a great gilt mirror, but the maid when she came up was small and slovenly, and the tea served in a pewter teapot, rather than a silver one.

'I do declare,' said Careby, throwing up her legs on the chaise, 'that *The Winsome Widows of Wickham* is the dullest play we've ever done.'

'Aye,' said Thruckle, who had gone behind her dressing screen and was exchanging her usual buskin and skirts for a pretty gown of pale lilac, for she was expecting her sweetheart to call.

'Were it not for Mr Manners and his amusing ways, I'm sure I'd go to the Duke's in an instant.'

'If they'd have you,' said Careby.

'Mr Manners seems a good fellow, though he is ever in an amorous mode,' I said, sipping at my tea, and finding it over-stewed. 'He has been very kind to me at any rate.'

'Ho, I'm sure he has,' said Careby, with a flash in her eye I understood. 'For he has a great way with ladies, and they all of them fall in love with him in an instant.'

'Not all of 'em do,' called Thruckle from behind the screen, and came out quite cross looking, with her skirts on backwards.

'Have no fear – I shall not fall in love with him!' I said. 'For I have had quite enough of that for the present.'

It did not take long before I felt I was getting accomplished at acting, and was as comfortable 'pon the stage as I had been a-raptured in the audience, and Parrykin said he thought of promoting me to the company by and by. Though I had picked it quite haphazardly to cover my identity, being the first thing that came into my head, my new name of Bearwood seemed to have done the trick of disguising me, for if Samuel heard it, and found it familiar he did not say, and if Tyringham found me out again, he did not claim me. Parrykin put about the story that I had given him, that I was a young widow newly come to London after the tragic decease of my husband, and if anyone questioned the veracity of my tale, they did not say so to my face.

Save for the disastrous *Forc'd Marriage*, my first few months of performances had enjoyed larger than usual audience numbers for that time of year, and all of the people very merry and bustling besides.

'It's always the way whenever we get a new girl,' said Parrykin, stirring through the takings box after curtain one day. 'All the gallants in town are in boxes pressing eye-glasses to their faces to get a squint at her – especially if she is rumoured to be a beauty. The jury's still out on you, but we had York in the other day, if you noticed the disturbance? He and his men had a bit of sport with a couple of the orange-girls and got pelted by rotten fruit, and all around them in uproar. If he says you are a beauty, then it may get to Rex himself. And then we've made it.' He squeaked the palms of his hands together.

But the Duke did not return, and the takings began to dwindle again to what they were before, which was still as good as any playhouse, for it was a merry age, and the theatre the haunt of every man and woman of mode.

'It's a shame you ain't raven-haired and milk-white and then they'd come a-running and you'd be taken into keeping afore ye could say "Jack Sprat",' said Bunty, combing out my curl-papers one day.

'It does not signify, Bunty,' I said. 'For I am happy enough just to be here, even if I am not the talk of the town. I take comfort that even if I be not pretty enough for the King to notice me, I am witty enough to make ordinary people chuckle, and that is plenty for me.'

# IX

# APPRECIATION

*In which I receive some messages*

My dearest Mrs Bearwood,

Forgive the impudence of addressing you so familiarly when you have never laid eyes on me, but I have laid eyes on you, every afternoon for the last fortnight.

You may recognize me as the broad young man with a fiery beard in the gallery (stage left). I always take the same seat in the hope that one day you will look up from your bows and notice me.

Until then I am your ardent admirer, madame,

JOHN NAZEBY of Scalding Alley

(Merchant, with £28 a year. Expectation of a family house.)

Dear Mrs Bearwood, aka the lady who has rent my heart in two for evermore!

Permit me to call on you after today's performance of *Love for Love*. I will wait outside the 'Tiring Room in the hope of admittance to your *inner sanctum*.

YOU WILL NOT REGRET IT,

LORD CYRIL LYGGE

To the Blonde One That Cannot Act But Looks Fairly Well,

I will give you 5s for a quick whoopsy (your choice of location) that need not trouble you for more than a moment or two.

Send word to the Sign of the Leg of Mutton if you will have me,

MR 'COPIOUS PIZZLE' (bathes above twice a year)

Dear Mrs B,

I find your light eyes dazzling, your small foot enticing, and your arm flesh entrancing and I would like nothing more than to shower your pretty shoulders with kisses.

I ask that during tomorrow's performance of *Cymbeline* you make a sign to me (I will be in the pit wearing a tricorn, if some nasty fellow does not snatch it off). I suggest inserting the word 'fiddlesticks' into a line of the play, if it be not there already, and twitching your head in my direction as you say it, and then I will visit you directly and we can be together as I know we must be.

MASTER WILLY BROWN

Sweetheart (may I call you that?),

Your skin was glowing in the footlights tonight. You did not look up to me, but the nosegay of violets that hit you in the face in the third act was mine: a symbol of my undying devotion.

I have told my mother all about you.

I shall wait on you again after the curtain and hope that this time you will condescend to see me,

JOHN NAZEBY

Mrs Bearwood,

If that is your real name – no doubt half of you stage whores have made one up.

Someone should tell you that you are a terrible actress and not fit to tread the boards. I could not hear half of what you said in yesterday's *Jew of Malta* and Ophelia is not meant to be funny.

A CONCERNED LADY

To the Blonde,

7s and that's my final offer.

'C. PIZZLE'

Dearest Ursula,

Permit me to address you thus? I found out your Christian name from your colleague Mrs Careby – Gad she is a toothsome jade (though not so much as you). She was most keen to hear all I had to say about you and found it endlessly amusing, I believe.

For the price of 2s, she allowed me to handle the costume you wore as 'third laundress' in *A Man of Simple Pleasures* and I am certain I could detect the clinging scent that can only be your own.

Let me lay my cards before you now, as I infer from the lack of responses to my notes that you do not believe me to be seriously a-courting: I would like to set you up into keeping. I can offer you a grand set of rooms, finely decorated (perhaps near me at Coleman of Throgmorton Street, 'twould be most convenient), all meals and board, and a new gown every three months and jewel-gifts such as I should deign to make them. All that I would ask in return is that you admit me to your bedchamber every Tuesday, Friday and second Saturday, and give up the playhouse. According to Mrs Careby you will not mind this, being only a minor actress and only in the company to attract the gallants.

I beg you, I am serious,

JOHN NAZEBY

A man of his word.

# X

# INSPIRATION

*In which I am privy to something interesting*

The stench of dung, newly dropped, was rising from the cobbles as I made my way down the hill to The Strand and the river behind it. It was a warm day for April, and the city lightly humming with odours, and I, having extricated myself from the rabble in the 'Tiring Room, felt very much inclined to clear my nostrils out with some river air. I stepped quickly along the street, enjoying the sensation of heads turning as I passed, for I wore a silk gown of saffron yellow, with a bodice of azure, and a pretty matching amethyst necklace and ear-drops that I knew no one would know were paste. As I came towards the little alley that would take me down to the river bank, I spied a tavern that I had been in before with the company, for Mr Manners had a wanderlust when it came to drinking spots, and was ever leading us all about the city, in search of new ales and new friends. Being quite thirsty, and wanting to use the chamber pot before I took myself on my walk, I stepped through the doorway and went quickly to the bar and asked for a mug of ale. This I took into a secluded little corner, so that I might not be disturbed by the type of man who bothered actresses, for I had learnt to keep my wits about me in this regard, having been chased several times by lusty gentlemen, who could not believe that acting and loving for money were not one and the same thing.

It was cool and dark in the tavern, and I leant my head against the wood of the seat behind me, letting the day wash over me. Being not much past six of the clock and the weather still very hot, the tavern had only a few lonely drinkers, though I could hear the rumbling sound of gentlemen's laughter coming from a part of the inn I could not see.

'Haw,' came the braying voice of one of the laughers. 'Everyone is at it these days, whether they have the gift of the pen or not. Why, I had it from the Duke of Monmouth himself – well, at least, gentleman in his company – that every man at Court thinks himself a playwright now, and they are at their papers from morning 'til night, and Rex does not like it, for there are none left to entertain him in his sickbed.'

More laughter at this. My ears were now well pricked, for I had heard the word 'playwright' and wondered who the gentlemen were.

'Small wonder we had so many cards this month, asking to gain membership,' said another, deeper voice. 'I am thinking of changing the rules so that only *established* playwrights will be allowed to our club.'

'Which I suppose,' said someone else, 'means they need to have written a poxy comedy that was put on in a Hounds-ditch playhouse, and then taken off after three days, for being completely unfunny – much like your play, Gregory.'

Laughter. The slapping of hands on a table.

'There was an outbreak of scarlet fever and nothing wrong with *She Was Better Than a Bawd*, for Etherege himself came to see it and said he was very impressed,' said the man who was presumably the feckless Gregory. 'And so I invited him to join the Playhouse Pizzles and he may come next week.'

Then the first gentleman called order.

'Mr Windlesham here would have it known to all the members,' he said, and I thought it sounded as if he were reading from a card, 'that Parrykin's is in dire need of new play scripts and will consider all kinds of genre, only he is weighed down with dull political stories, and would rather have a drama – or a nice little comedy.'

I had sloshed the ale out of my cup in a start at hearing Parrykin's name. In need of play scripts! I sat stock still all the better to listen.

'Send 'em to him at the usual address as soon as you've bloody written them, all right?' the speaker continued.

'I suppose I shall,' said someone. 'For I have a mind to get closer to that Mrs Careby, who I believe to be bewitching.'

'She'll never have you with all them plague scars, Harry,' said one of the men, and the rest of his sentence was drowned out with jeering. I got out of my seat and, pressing a coin onto the table for my ale, went out into the street in a daze, my mind turning over all the while with the meaning of what I had heard.

The very next day, I started work. A comedy, they had said – or a drama. A comedy would be best to do, I thought, for being constantly in the business of reading plays, and with a merry soul at heart, I had got rather good at landing jokes, and would sometimes add little asides to my scripted lines, for I dearly loved to hear the audience in fits. Some of these I had jotted down in my faithful notebook, and it only needed the usual plot – a feckless young man... a maid who would get to a nunnery... an aristocratic rake... a violent duel... a spot of lovering, and a chase around a thicket – and it would surely rise above anything the Playhouse Pizzles might be producing.

Licking the nib of my quill for luck, I dipped it in the ink pot.

❧

# A YOUNG WOMAN'S INNER VOICE UPON SITTING DOWN TO WRITE A PLAY

DEVIL: You can't do this.

ANGEL: Yes I can.

DEVIL: It will not be funny, and everyone will point at you.

ANGEL: I have been writing since I was eight years old. I have been working towards this all my life, though I did not know it.

DEVIL: What you are attempting is scandalous; it is most likely against God.

ANGEL: The God I worship is a merry one and would have me happy.

DEVIL: You cannot do it.

ANGEL: Yes I can.

DEVIL: You cannot do it.

ANGEL: YES I CAN.

❦

# AFFLICTIONS I HAVE SO FAR INCURRED DURING THE WRITING OF A PLAY
## 1683 A.D.

✿ A sharp cramping pain in the palm of my hand where it grips the quill, and makes it form, against my will, into a claw, and as the days of writing wear on has traversed up my arm right to the elbow.

✿ An ache in the lower part of my back and the midst of my shoulders from hours sitting at the table, that no stretching or bending or cushion can cure (in fact the only remedy I have found is a little dish of brandy-wine taken all at once, but after taking it my writing suffers).

✿ A great head pain that came on after working with only a few candles lit, which pinched at the soft place behind my eyes and at the back of my neck and lasted above three days, despite all the remedies I applied to it.

An inability to fall asleep after a long late night of scribbling, for my mind has been a-whirring with ideas, and me ever getting up to note them down before I forget, and so I am now in the habit of keeping my writing book beside my pillow!

I HAVE

*finally finished*

MY PLAY

*Play!*

*Play!*

I AM *an* AUTHOR
&
VERY PROBABLY
*a* GENIUS!

# XI

# LAPSE

*In which I begin to feel peculiar*

'Uuurrrrgh.' I let out a great belch and rushed again for my chamber pot, though when I got it I could only heave and spit out a little greenish water.

No sooner had I finished my first full grown-up play, than I had fallen sick with a stomach rheum, it giving me such twists and churnings in my belly that I sweated with the pain of them. Despite my lurching queasiness, I felt very pleased and proud of the thing I had written, on so many leaves of foolscap, though it had many ink blobs and several crossings out. After many changings of mind, I had finally named my play *The Sweetheart Charade* and, after thinking on how I could affect my scheme, disguised myself in a vizard, and sent a boy with it to the playhouse, telling him it was from my husband, for I had signed the manuscript in the name of MR GEO. J. FLAMSTEED, in as manly a hand as I could manage, noting that word could be sent to the author, newly come up from the country and not yet in lodgings, care of The Rose & Flag.

That I had seemingly begun to take ill of a sickness that laid me down very low at this important time, caused me much irritation and I prayed to Jesu in heaven that I would not get more seriously ill, and chanted a little to this effect. When I pondered upon it, it seemed that the malady had come upon me directly after I had finished the last line of my work (oh, such a joy it had been to scrawl CURTAIN with a flourish!). I wondered if perhaps I had over-exerted myself in the last few weeks, for I had worked late every night and sometimes risen before dawn to put pen to paper. I tried very hard to calm myself, thinking that perhaps the rheum was partly in my mind. It was true that I had many flurried feelings at the great liberty I was taking – for while I was writing it had crept into my mind that Parrykin might be very angry when he discovered my trick, and put me out, though even as I had fretted, the compulsion I had to try my hand at a playwright's life grew stronger, and I found I could do nothing but continue with the thing.

Arriving at the theatre for rehearsal a few days later, I immediately had to run backstage and vomit up a good quantity of bile into a bowl, while Bunty pushed at my back and muttered soothing words, wondering if I had eaten something disagreeable, or caught it from the audience, for in the hot months the playhouse was alive with contagions.

Parrykin seemed that day to be in a very mild temper, for he strolled onto the stage with a careless tilt of his head and came to stand with us performers, with his hand on his hip in a jaunty sort of way.

'Looks like Mrs Parrykin has finally allowed him his bi-annual billy-cocking,' whispered Manners, near my ear, which made me laugh, and Parrykin glare, so I straightened my face.

'Now then,' said Parrykin. 'I have a new play for us, by a promising young playwright, whose name is...' Here he consulted the papers in his hand. 'Geo. J. Flamsteed.'

'Well, that sounds made up or I'm a nun,' said Manners.

I found myself beginning to blush.

'It's a light sort of comedy – perhaps not as romantical as it could be – it seems to cast the hero in a rather foolish light... but, it is lucky in having parts that seem quite suitable for all of us and so we shall try it, though I will keep my pencil out, for it will need a few amendments here and there.'

The rehearsal began.

❦

We had been working on *The Sweetheart Charade* for almost a week, and it being now certain that it would be put on, I decided that it was time to speak to Parrykin and accept whatever fate had in store for me, for I could no longer contain my glee that he liked my play. I had been dosing myself with China tea and catmint and chamomile against the sickness, and it seemed to heal me, and I was feeling much better; roses now bloomed in my cheeks where there were none before and when I looked in the glass I saw that at last I was becoming plump and almost pretty, and I put this down to the happiness I had from knowing I had writ a play at last.

❦

## PARRYKIN AND I, A CONVERSATION
### *The Prop Room, April 1683*

ME:        Parry, I must have a word...

PARRYKIN:  Oh no. By the look on your face methinks you are going-a-keeping. Who is it? I'll warrant it's Mr Laughton. For he will lurk in the 'Tiring Room tweaking the arse of any wench that passes.

ME:        Nay, you have it all wrong. I am here about the play.

PARRYKIN:  Look, if you want a bigger part you'll have to earn it, lovey. Maybe next time. For as I told Thruckle—

ME:        Nay, Parry. 'Tis about the author of the play, Mr Flamsteed.

PARRYKIN:  What has he done? If he has made improper advances I can speak to him, though 'tis a shame, for Gad, his work is really not bad. Not bad at all.

ME:              Please do not be angry, Parry, but – [*Taking in a*
                 *great breath*] – it was I who wrote it, in truth. I am
                 Mr Geo. J. Flamsteed.

PARRYKIN:  [*Guffawing*] Good one!

ME:              The play came by the hand of a boy in a bright blue
                 jacket. It had a wax seal atop it in the shape of a star.
                 And it was tied with a sea-green ribbon. I know this,
                 for 'twas me who sent it to you.

PARRYKIN:  Nay, it cannot... why 'tis a play, and... I knew you were
                 pert but I did not...

ME:              Indeed it was I, Parry. For I do so love to write, and
                 thought to be like Mrs Behn, and everyone a-roar
                 at what I have to say. And hearing in a tavern that
                 you sought some fresh material, I set myself to write
                 something that you would like.

PARRYKIN:  [*Patting himself with his kerchief*] Why, I find I am
                 astounded. Why... [*He stares at her for a long while with
                 his mouth hanging open*]

ME:              Parry, are you quite well?

PARRYKIN:  'Tis the shock of it, forgive me... A lady playwright?
                 A lady playwright! How strange even those two words
                 sound together! [*Pause*] Ah, but who helped you in it?
                 Was it Manners? For he dearly loves to tease me.

ME:              'Twas all mine, every word.

PARRYKIN:  Ho. I see. [*A long pause*] Well, I find... I find I am quite
                 cross now I think upon it, Mrs Bearwood. For you have
                 made me look a fool to my company. I ought to have
                 spotted the work of an amateur – and a woman – and
                 now we have wasted a week rehearsing it. You have been
                 audacious, madame.

— 363 —

ME:          I know it and I dearly beg your pardon, sir. P'raps it
             was foolish. But I truly could not help myself. Forgive
             me. And pray let us keep the play on. I will not breathe
             a word of what has passed between us now, and we
             shall continue as we are. Why, I dearly like the changes
             you have made to Act Two, for the whole thing is so
             much improved, and I am ever anxious to see what you
             will do with it next.

PARRYKIN:    I do not know... It is not orthodox... I will think on it,
             Mrs Bearwood, that is all I can say. But know that I am
             greatly displeased!

   *Ending: me in a great pet that I will be put out, Mr Parrykin in a
           black mood the rest of the afternoon.*

❦

I could not stop singing. I trilled every saucy street ballad I had ever
heard as I sat before the great looking glass we had in the undressing
room, painting my face ready for the day's performance.

'Tra la la,' I sang. 'Tra laaaaaa!'

'Egad, will you stop up your mouth!' called Careby from the
wardrobe. 'For you cannot carry a tune and your squawking is enough
to carry me to Bedlam.'

I opened my mouth and closed it again.

'Oooh,' said Thruckle, beside me at the glass. 'Look at her phyzzog.
Methinks our friend Ursula had an intrigue last night.'

Manners had strolled in, with an apple in his hand.

'What are we talking about?' he said.

'Nothing,' said I, and closed my mouth, pretending to concentrate
on my rouging. In truth I was bursting with excitement and nervous
energy, for it was the first night of the very first play I had written under
the name of Geo. Flamsteed, and I in a great pet to see how it would
go. There seemed that day to be a magical sort of thrum to the air, for

it was one thing waiting to go on to speak someone else's words, and quite another to say the words you had written in the very scene you had conjured from your own imagination! I found that I felt light and giddy, such as I had not since Samuel's leaving.

'Mayhap it is first-night nerves,' said Manners, crunching his apple. 'For we are under-rehearsed and I do not know how it will go.'

'I hope Mr Flamsteed will make an appearance,' said Thruckle, in the midst of tying a ribbon around her throat, 'for I fancy he is a very witty fellow, though Parrykin acted strangely when I asked him and said he did not know if he would come.'

'Mayhap he is bashful,' said I, 'and cannot bear to come into society and have people point and whisper.'

'Then why write a play?' cried Careby. 'Most playwrights are vain and peacocking fellows, ever wanting to be praised, for most of 'em are both self-doubtful and swollen-headed all at once.'

'Hear hear!' said Manners.

A few hours later I was very much chagrined, and did not join in the first-night toasting in the 'Tiring Room, but instead disconsolately pulled off my costume and went quickly away to my lodgings. I had not at first been worried when I saw from the wings that the pit was only half full up and there were many empty seats besides, for 'twas often so with an unknown author, but as the play went on, my doubts in it had begun to grow. I had noticed parts that did not work as well as I thought they had on paper, and some of the lines sounded stilted and false in the actors' mouths. The audience's laughter was not as loud as it might have been, despite Manners's mugging, and the spatter of applause at the end sounded half-hearted, and no one cried for the author, and we did only one curtain call, for the audience had lost interest, and got up after the first.

How I fretted away that evening in my rooms, for I could not concentrate on writing, nor reading neither, and ran over the play again and again in my mind instead, wondering all the while what could be done to improve it, and whether I was fit to be a playwright after all.

To my surprise Parrykin was not much cross with me when I saw him the next morning at rehearsal, but only nodded at me, and aloud said that we would make some changes to the script we had, and see if we could improve things, but his ameliorations were not enough to save the thing, and the takings dwindled every day for two weeks, before we learnt that the play was to be taken off.

As for me, I was well chastened by the experience, for though I longed to re-live the thrill that I had had while writing the thing, and my excitement at its performance, I had learnt that the craft of playwriting was a much harder thing than I had thought, and resolved to practise at it in private so that one day I might write a true success.

❀

I had grown much vainer about my looks since I had become an actress, and was pleased to note that I was getting evermore peachy looking as the spring went on. I realized that the other actresses had noticed my recent blooming into beauty, for they once again grew callous in their behaviour towards me, and when I was taking my cloak off before rehearsal in the mornings, Careby had taken to whispering things to Thruckle behind her hand with a malicious light in her eye.

'What say you?' I would call, to which she would reply, with very wide-opened eyes:

'Oh nothing, Mrs Bearwood. I was just commenting on the coming of the April showers and how today's downpour had wetted Bunty's wig.'

Bunty had become something of a friend to me, for it was she who had told me all the things that I did not know the whole time I was learning my craft, as well as making sure that I was fed, by sending out for my dinner when she got hers, and combing my hair out like a mother does a child.

It was she who, tugging on the lacings of my bodice (I was to play

Clorinda) and puffing out her breath, said:

'It's no use, duckling. They won't go no tighter and that's a fact. Not if I put my foot to your back and yanked it with all my might.'

'Oh, do not tire yourself, Bunty, for I am sure I have got a little stouter since I first arrived. Lor', I was all eaten up with heartbreak then and could not bear the taste of bread!' I turned myself before the mirror and admired the body that was no longer all bone. 'The actor's life agrees with me, Bunty! And all those fine tavern dinners! I ate two pork pies and a lemon curd yesterday.' I reached around me and tickled her.

'Is that really it, my darling duck?'

'Pass me that comb would you, Bunty? Aye, I think that's it.' I set about teasing the tendrils on my forehead. 'For I swear I have never been so gay in all my life, not since my father was alive and me merry with my playmate.'

'Jesu bless him,' said Bunty, crossing herself. 'Have ye not stopped your courses, then, Ursey?'

'My courses? Nay, I had it... now let me see... the way Parrykin works us I have quite forgotten when it was...'

Bunty was burrowing in the wig chest.

'Well I cannot recall but...' I laughed, but even as I did my mind was whirring.

Bunty came out of the chest, a curled chestnut periwig in her hand.

'So you're not with child, then?' she said simply. 'You was greatly sick and spitting up the flux... and now ye are too broad for your gown. When did ye last lay with a man?'

Thoughts of Samuel rushed into my mind. I had done my jumping up and down when at first we were together, but there were times when he had said he would protect me. But in the heat of love, had he? I could not now remember. Fear began to rise in me. I opened my mouth and shut it, then opened it again.

'My, er, husband...' I stuttered, 'afore he – died was the last... time.'

'Well, perhaps the Lor' Jesu was lookin' down on ye that night and has given you a piece of his soul to remember him by. That is – if ye want to keep it.' She looked at me with narrowed eyes.

'I – God's gizzards. I feel quite strange, all of a sudden.'

'Of course, ye cannot stay at the playhouse with a belly full o' babe. Ye shall have to go away, until it has come, and then of course there's no guarantee ye can have your place on return – though I doubt you will be usurped by Mrs Sop; last I heard she was living at White Friars, and whoring herself for a penny, for the demon drink had taken her over and her gentleman cast her aside like a mouldy fruit.'

'I cannot. Nay, I cannot have a babby. 'Tis not possible...'

'Easily remedied,' said Bunty, with a shrug. 'Ye must go and see an apothecary I know, by name of Dandywine, and he shall give you a potion that will bring down your course and cure you withal. He does for all my girls, and none of 'em have died from it yet.'

'Oh,' I said, and turned it over in my mind. 'You are good to me, Bunty,' I said at last, kissing her on the forehead. 'I shall go to him directly tomorrow.'

❦

After the performance I stumbled into the street, my mind a tumble of strange thoughts, for it was a thing so momentous that here I was with child! I found myself peering at women as I went down the road, and wondering if they too might be in the childing way, and looking at wenches with children, or carrying babbies in shawls, in a way I never had afore; I could scarcely see myself as one of them.

Once at my lodgings, I verily ran up the stairs to unlace my gown and stand before the mirror, quaking all over to see what pregnancy looked like. Now that I viewed myself properly (for I was always in such a rush to get to the playhouse and had not done so for a while), I saw that my belly had become a soft round thing where it once was flat, and my bubbies, before not much to speak of, had a full, womanly look about them, the veins in them glowing pale mauve, the nipples large and dark and pink (which I confess I quite enjoyed, for 'til now I had never been plumptious of bosom). I turned around, regarding myself from all angles. There was a bright, fresh look about me that I had not had since I left my family for Turvey Hall and I looked soft and girlish, as I never had before. I patted my cheeks, and squinted at my bosom. Was getting a babby all it took to be beautiful?

But even as I enjoyed my appearance, there was a low feeling in my middle. I had spent all these years trying to not get with child, and with my life as an actress keeping me busy and merry besides, I now found that it was hard to set my mind towards the prospect of childing. I lay back on the bed (for I realized my legs had come over quite weak) and let my mind run over the ways I could manage it. I tried to entertain the idea of bringing up a child alone, and think upon a wet-nurse, and the costings thereupon. I found, though I searched my heart, that I did not feel how I knew a mother must – for whether it was the shock of my new condition, or my husband-lack, I could not find a part of me that yearned to hold a babby in my arms, or dandle it on my knee. Who would believe that it was my husband's child? And how would I clothe and feed it? All my shillings earnt at the playhouse went on paying off my debts, and keeping me fed, and I had nothing left over, even for ribbons – I had taken to borrowing from the wardrobe when I had need of something lavish. Now I was shifting for myself I had to think clearly. I shed a few tears at the hardness of my luck, but after a while, I dried my face, and got out my book, and went again at my writing, hardening my heart to what I knew that I must do, and wondering all the while if this was what the fortune teller had meant when she had said things would get worse for me, and when, oh when they would begin to get better.

# XII

# TONIC

*In which I visit the apothecary*

Having set my mind determinedly to the task ahead of me, I checked my almanac to see if the day was a fortuitous enough one, and finding that it was 'goodly for new enterprises', I put on my cloak and vizard and, taking a few deep breaths, for I found my hands shook a little, made my way down a narrow little street that wended its way towards the river, and had an aroma of mud and fishguts in the air.

I found the shop quite easily, it being marked by the usual swinging wooden sign of a mortar and pestle, and so I pushed open the door, which jangled dully as I stepped into the room. An old man stood behind the counter, with a velvet claret-coloured waistcoat and silvered hair that grew in three tufts from his head. He made a bow.

DANDYWINE:   Good morrow to ye, mistress. How may I be of service to ye?

ME:   Good morrow. I am come... I am come...

DANDYWINE:   Was you wanting the apothecary side or the astrology side? I do both, you see, mistress. Afore you, you see all my phials and bottles and cure-alls, and beyond that curtain are my charts and my tarot and other divers instruments to predict your future. I just laid the cards for a very happy lady who learnt that she will soon be meeting her fourth husband. The first two died of the plague and the last one of earache. And 'pon my soul 'tis true she had a booming voice such as I have never set ears at before.

ME:                    I thank you, but 'tis not my horoscope I seek. I am sent here by Mrs Bunty—

DANDYWINE:   Ah! Now I look at you more closely I see the mark of it upon you – 'tis the way you hold yourself – there, most plainly, a follower of Thespis! Tell me, when were you born?

ME:                    Why, on the night of the Great Comet.

DANDYWINE:   The comet! I remember it well, for I had been watching the skies, knowing it would soon burn overhead... I ran into the streets crying to all who would listen that pestilence would come upon us again, and then fire, and so they did. My old father died in the outbreak and my aunt, and my cat, and then my old shop burned down.

ME:                    I am greatly sorry to hear that, sir.

DANDYWINE:   Do not be sorry, for I had seen it written in the movement of the planets, and had removed all of my flammable goods to my sister's house. And I am certain that one of these days she will see sense and give them back.

ME:                    Sir, I dearly love to watch the skies, and would talk with you longer, but I am in haste—

DANDYWINE:   Forgive me, mistress! I am but an ignorant Gemini and apt to let my mouth run away with me, as those born under the twins are wont to do.

ME: Mrs Bunty said you would be able to help me with an... ailment.

DANDYWINE: Ah, yes. The vagaries and the vexations of Venus. I think it is the cure for the unblocking of the – ha – humours that you want? The type that make a lady – swell? Have I got it, mistress?

URSULA: Aye. Can you help me, sir?

DANDYWINE: I shall make up the remedy – Dandywine's Rule of Three! [*He bustles about the phials and bottles, taking a little from each*] First, a decoction of mugwort and the leaves and berries of the bay tree. You shall boil this in some cinnamon water, and then sit over it until it has cooled, mistress.

URSULA: Sit over it?

DANDYWINE: Aye, in a cauldron, or a pot or some such, so that the vapours may disperse up where they are needed. [*In a stage whisper*] TO YOUR DUCKING-POND. Next, some juice of myrrh mixed with sweet marjoram and some water pimpernel which you will need to fry in vinegar, and then – ha – put under as a – ha – pessary, do you understand me? [*In a stage whisper*] IN YOUR BUTTER BOX.

URSULA: Sir, I assure you, I understand you.

DANDYWINE: When 'tis warm, not hot or you will frazzle your – ha – quim. These two together should draw down the courses. But, if they do not, the main event, my wonder potion – pennyroyal, colewort, saxifrage, a bit of Devil's bit... Swallow the whole of it, and then take yourself on the bumpiest carriage ride ye can muster, and that will shake the – ha – humour free. There is a monstrous bad road out to the village of Hampstead that's full of potholes and rocks – that may do the trick.

❧

The very next day after my visit to the apothecary's shop, I set about his 'Rule of Three'. First the decoction, which I poured, steaming and pleasantly cinnamon-scented into my empty chamber pot, and, lifting up my skirts, sat myself over it. I did not notice any rumblings in my belly, though my cunny grew quite toasty in the rising heat, and my legs cramped in the squatting position. I went the whole next day in a pet that the potion would do its job at the playhouse, but I felt not so much as a stirring, and so I knew I must move to the second part of the physic. This was an altogether unpleasant thing, for the pessary was acrid and burned when (with burning cheeks – for it seemed an ungodly thing to do) I rubbed it on, and though I tried to bear it for as long as I could, and walked about humming, and chewed on my fist, and hopped on one leg, and conjugated verbs out loud all the better to bear the pain, I could not tolerate the sensation for as long as I knew I should, and was compelled to wash it all off before I set to screaming. I knew then that the third and final treatment was my only hope.

The almanac told me Wednesday would be an auspicious day, and I, telling Parrykin that I had to go and visit my mother who was gravely sick, went abroad at an early hour to see about the hiring of a carriage, swallowing the potion, which had a strong sharp stench and burned as it went down so that I had to fight to keep it there.

'Oh, sweet babe I will never know,' I said, patting my belly. 'Forgive me in this, for 'tis simply not your time.'

❧

The bitter taste of the potion was still on my lips as I twisted my body about and bent forward, and dragged my knees up to my chest and lay back against the dark cloth of the carriage, writhing in my seat, and biting at my hand, but I could get no relief from the pain, such a pain, such a fiery ache; like nothing I'd ever known.

The coach rumbled on, bumping over the cobblestones with its rhythmic thump-thump-knock thump-thump-knock; the scraping of iron on stone as the wheels ground onto the potholes and rubble of the road; the squeak as the carriage juddered on its thoroughbraces; the drifting tang of horse sweat; and all the while I trembled and burned, lit up from the inside with what I had drunk, which, with every shake and every sway, oozed further down into my belly, on its way to the germ of the child I carried, to free it from my body.

We had worked up to a breakneck pace, and the coach began rocking more violently – I was thrown against the sides, and against the seatback, and I fell forward – and still the poison squeezed at my womb as it blazed its way downwards, tugging the babby out of me in wave upon searing wave. I panted in and out, in and out, but the pain took hold of me in a white-hot burst, and I clawed at the carriage walls, my nails scraping lines down the leather. Against my will, for the sound rose up and keened out of my throat, though I pressed my fingers against my mouth and tried, oh I tried, to quell it, I began to cry out for the driver to halt, God save me, stop the coach, but my voice was lost in the whine of the wheels as they trundled over and over on their axes; the clanking of the wheel-shaft; the rattle of wood and metal and stone.

Throwing back my hood I leant my head against the window frame, feeling the damp air rush in and cool my cheeks, while the colours of the street outside streamed past my eyes at speed; a long blurred strip of green and brown and black and yellow, so bright against the darkness of the carriage.

The spasm swelled inside me then, and what was the searing stabbing of a blunted poker became the vicious thrusting of a sharpened blade, and the carriage quaked, and sweat broke out on my forehead, and the bile rose up in my chest. My hands grew cold and clammy and I gripped the window with my fingers and clashed my teeth together the better to bear it, chanting the refrain in my head that drummed in time with the thud of the horse's hooves: I cannot have this child. I cannot have this child. I cannot have this child.

Later, I awoke from a great sweat feeling weak and sicker than I'd ever known, and gingerly twitched the bedclothes from underneath me, squeezing my eyes open, though I feared to see the blood I knew must have pooled out of me while I dozed (the apothecary had warned me of this). But to my astonishment, and my fear, there was none, and when I pressed at my belly, I thought I felt another heartbeat pulsing there, as strong as ever it had been.

# XIII

# AMELIORATION

*In which I set about realizing my ambition*

A

## *LADY'S*

# ADVANCEMENT

*by*

URSULA
BEARWOOD

## ACT I, SCENE III

> *A noble playhouse in England. Morning. A small company of actors lurk about the stage, which is strewn with props: a table set with cup and bowl; a hobby horse with a yellow mane; a glinting metal crown set with green glass.*

> *URSULA enters, looking pale. Though she smiles when the other actors greet her, it does not reach her eyes, and she twists her hands together, her eyes staring and unfocused.*

PARRYKIN: Ah there you are, Mrs B. How was your mother? You are looking a trifle peaky. Does something ail you?

URSULA: Nay, I am only a little brought down, for I have had some bad news... but I will not let it affect my work, if I can help it... at least, I will try.

PARRYKIN: Come, Mr Manners, I see you behind Mrs Careby. Let us have no horseplay today, for we have much work to do.

THRUCKLE: Our Parry is in a pet because his new play will not come right.

PARRYKIN: Well, what of it?

MANNERS: He has spent above a month writing it, but he does not want anyone to know it is his play, in case it is no good, and so he writes under a pseudonym, in part because his wife told him to and he is henpecked more than any man I know.

THRUCKLE: Clifford Montgomery Clyffe.

URSULA: [*Looking up from the floor*] Not really?

MANNERS:     Truth, sister. And he is worse than Letty for
             superstitions – he will not have it open on a waning
             moon, he will not have three of anything in it, and
             yesterday he kicked Bunty's cat for crossing his path
             on a Wednesday.

PARRYKIN:    [*Striking a tragic pose*] Why, oh why, is it always
             actors' sport to make fun of a writer?

THRUCKLE:    We must be wrack'd with envy, Parry.

MANNERS:     Speak for yourself, jade!

PARRYKIN:    Enough and let us get on with it. Manners, you are
             Ponsonby, the rake. And Sukey, you his wife Nibbs,
             who is being cuckolded, and Ursula, you shall play
             Verily, the servant girl who he's doing the cuckolding
             with, but is also cuckolding him with the stable boy
             who is a prince in disguise but no one knows it.

MANNERS:     Fie, you have spoiled the ending, Parrykin! No point
             reading it now.

PARRYKIN:    Act one, scene one, I will read the stage directions.
             And – action!

                   *The company take their places.*

PONSONBY:    Good evening, wife.

NIBBS:       Is it?

PONSONBY:    There is a most beautiful sunset, with a blood-red sky,
             and the air is sweet and perfumed with jasmine.

NIBBS:       You seem most romantical for a man who has just got
             back from visiting his aged mother, and read to her,
             and spooned curds into her slack and toothless mouth.

PONSONBY:    I am a romantic man.

NIBBS:         [*Aside*] Don't I know it.

                    *Enter* VERILY, *a very pretty servant.*

VERILY:        Did you want anything, mistress? Oh, master, you are
               returned. I see by your manner that you had a very good
               day.

PONSONBY: What gave it away?

VERILY:        Your breeches are on backwards.

NIBBS:         He has been to see his mother again.

PONSONBY: Fetch me a flagon of sack, Verily. I want to toast this
               beautiful wife of mine.

VERILY:        [*Aside*] That's stretching it! – Gladly, sir.

NIBBS:         And I will have a dish of tea.

                         *Exit* VERILY.

NIBBS:         You look a trifle weary, husband. Methinks you have
               ridden too hard.

PONSONBY: [*Aside*] If only you knew. – You know how it is.

NIBBS:         Poor lady. I shall come with you next time.

                    *Enter* VERILY, *bearing a tray.*

VERILY:        Here is your wine, sir.

PONSONBY: I thank you, Verily.

NIBBS:         No need to overdo it.

                            *Pause.*

PARRYKIN:  And that's as far as I've got in that scene.

MANNERS:   I've just got the joke.

CAREBY:      That Parrykin sports at writing?

MANNERS: No, I thank you, *verily*. No need to *overdo it*.

PARRYKIN: Aye, it just came to me. But I do not know where to go now.

MANNERS: Back to the drawing board?

PARRYKIN: In the play, Manners.

URSULA: Perhaps, to the garden? Perhaps the rakish husband might be seen attempting to seduce the maid. If 'tis more comedy you were wanting, perhaps he might do it very ill and...

PARRYKIN: I beg your pardon, I thought I was the writer here.

THRUCKLE: Mistress Bearwood works at getting herself more lines.

URSULA: I do not! Forgive me, Parry, I simply thought it would be good for the play.

PARRYKIN: I shall read on... let me see, where is it? Ah! *Scene two. Aboard a grand sailing vessel. Her colours streaming behind her. A swashbuckling pirate by the name of Three Legs McManus...*

CAREBY: God save us!

MANNERS: I vote we try Ursula's way, for those seagoing adventures are no longer the mode. I fancy 'tis romancing in the parlour and cuckolding in the drawing room that captures the heart of a merry audience, such as our age demands.

PARRYKIN: [*Appearing to be considering Ursula thoughtfully*] Oh, well then, you have all convinced me. We must let her have her say, I suppose, for p'raps she is more experienced in playing than she looks. What would you have us do, Ursula?

URSULA: I would... if I may?

CAREBY: Let us have it, Urse, else we shall have our ears tweaked by Parry's prating when the house is empty.

PARRYKIN: Who doesn't like a pirate? Everyone likes a pirate!

URSULA: Well then... scene two. A pretty garden with roses all about. The sun is dipping down behind the apple trees casting pale shadows across the lawn.

THRUCKLE: Oh very poetic, I'm sure.

MANNERS: Hush!

URSULA: Butterflies still hop from bush to bush.

PARRYKIN: We can do that with papers on wires...

URSULA: Verily is walking in the garden, a letter in her hand... And then... I shall play it. 'Oh where is my true love, Jack the stable boy? I have received this note to meet him, but I cannot tarry, for any moment my mistress will find me gone. Hark, I hear footsteps!' And then – Enter the rakish husband!

MANNERS: Oh, me! [*He jumps up*]

URSULA: Say something about the scent of the garden, or the prettiness of the scene, for you are a foppish sort of man, I think.

PARRYKIN: I saw him as very handsome, and very brave.

URSULA: I think it will be merrier this way.

MANNERS: Ah, the fragrant scents of late summer! Soon the apples will be dropping from the trees, but now I shall walk in the garden and take the air!

URSULA: And then maybe something like, 'There is music in this breeze, I fancy,' and then...

MANNERS: Ah Verily, what do you do here...

A few weeks later, I stood in the wings. I was fizzing with excitement at the prospect of acting the second play that I had had a hand in, and felt much relieved that this time I would share the blame with Parrykin if the audience did not like it, feeling also that it was better than my attempts as Flamsteed, for I had been studying all my play volumes very hard, and had gone over and over my additions to Parry's script, re-polishing the lines until I felt sure they were as droll as they could be. My belly was a strange and liquid thing, and I pressed at it, listening to the hubbub of the pit. The babby I carried was now an immobile lump that had risen steadily in the night like a buboe, and though swollen, was mostly concealed beneath Bunty's artful dressmaking and could mostly be ignored. It chose this moment to turn a sudden somersault inside me.

'Oooh!' I cried, clutching at my middle. I had now let the cast into my secret, knowing that to delay this would only have served to continue their ill-disguised whispers. None of them had seemed very surprised. Actresses were ever getting with child and ruining their careers.

'What is it?' said Thruckle, taking her place beside me in costume as the dull wife. She had been padded out to look broader than she was, and had carmine smeared over her nose and cheeks.

'Here,' I cried, grabbing her hand and pressing it to the swell of my belly. 'I think I felt it move! A fluttering sensation, like the brushing of a bird's wing!'

'Aye,' she said, pulling her hand away. 'I am sorry, Ursula, but now it has quickened 'tis unlikely to come away without a struggle.'

'It does not signify,' I said, 'For I am resolved to give it up as soon as it is born.'

'Well, you may be cheered that those which are set out to wet-nurse are mostly carried off inside a year, and 'tis a blessing in faith, when a woman has her career to think of and must shift for herself.'

'Aye,' I said again, but quietly, as I realized that though I made secret plans to find the child a rich barren woman, who would adopt the child, and raise it as her own, I had begun to think of the babby as something much more than an encumbrance. I found that I did not know when the change in me had occurred, but there had been a sort of gradual melting, and as the child grew within me, and thumped its heart along with mine, I began to soften to it and think of it as mine. I did not have time to reflect further on it then, for the musicians were reaching their crescendo which was our cue for the opening ballet. I made myself ready.

Was it my imagination that the scenes that I had written earned the loudest guffaws of the whole play? As the epilogue was spoken and the applause rang out, we took our usual bows, all joined in a row, and then the audience got to their feet and a solitary cry of 'Author!' was heard. Out of the corner of my eye I saw Parrykin breaking from the wings in a fluster, and stepping quickly before us, he took his wig off with his hat as he swept his bow, which made the audience whistle more, some of them thinking it was by design or part of the playing.

'Well I never,' said he as we trooped off the stage to rub our faces with grease. 'To think I'd have a reaction like that... 'tis very pleasing, very pleasing indeed.'

'Mayhap you should have Ursula help with all your sceneing,' said Manners, tearing at the buttons of his waistcoat at high speed.

'Help me? Well...' said Parrykin, taking off his wig and rubbing at the waxy strands of hair underneath. 'I'm not sure that's why they like it.'

'I am,' said Manners, sending his breeches flying through the air. 'She's a wit and a poet and no mistake, Parrykin, or hadn't you noticed? Which is lucky, for in truth she's a middling actress at best.' He avoided my pinching fingers. 'There's a sweetheart pie,' he said, kissing my cheek. 'Get her to help you, Parry, if you want to take your bows like that every night, which I know that you do for you're a good deal vainer than me, and no mistake.'

❦

# XIV

# CONSTERNATION

*In which I begin to work at scripting in earnest*

URSULA'S NOTES *on*
*FOR THE LOVE OF A DEMNED GOOD WHORE*
*by* CLIFFORD MONTGOMERY CLYFFE
A.K.A. RODERICK PARRYKIN

Title – suggest we consider a few more options. Good Woman, perhaps, rather than Whore? For there is nothing in the script to suggest she is getting paid for her labours.

Millicent – I enjoyed her badinage with Master Tomfoolery, but I question whether he has to have all the best lines. Suggest she may come across as a real woman if she has a *tiny* bit of wit about her, for all the ladies I know do.

On that – I do not know any wife who does what her husband commands unthinkingly and believe it would be better for the joke to be upon the man – as it often is in life.

Query: do they have pease pudding in Africa?

Sir Ladle I think is meant to be greatly attractive to women with all his preening – but mayhap the audience should laugh AT him rather than with him. He needs other qualities besides, to make it believable that Lady Scandalous would leave her husband for him at the drop of a pin. Perhaps he be very witty and may make her laugh, and her husband a drudge, and that is what motivates her to go.

Query: do elephants come when called?

In the scene in the castle, would it not be more amusing if it was the maid who was rescuing the man from captivity, and not the other way around? You could have this as a breeches part and the whole pit in an uproar at it.

I have noted the audience are apt to get caught up in a tale if they are able to see a mirror of themselves in the hero. Might he be an ordinary sort of man trying to make his way in the world, as they themselves are, for the most part?

I'm afraid I do not feel, upon reading it twice, that there is enough tension in the first act, for we do not feel Mistress Lightly is in any real peril from the mad and lusty count, aside from his wandering hands. Could things move more quickly in scene three to quicken the drama?

Query: is it possible to get from London to Scotland in an afternoon?

Mr Tibb the barber disappears and reappears at will.

I pray you will not mind that I have made some adjustments to the speeches in order to show off the nature of the characters more plainly, for in many parts, every person sounds the same and has the same habits.

I hope you will like what I have done, Mr Parrykin, for I greatly enjoyed it, and believe with these minor adjustments it will be a very great play indeed.

*Ursula*

❦

'I must confess, though I did not think it would go well at first, that I am greatly enjoying our little writing partnership,' said Parrykin to me as we sat in the room he had as his office; he sprawled on the chaise he used for naps, me at his desk, my bulk propped up by cushions, scratching away at our latest script.

'Here is another note from Lord K saying he thinks *What's Wrong With Raking?* the best one yet, and an anonymous lady who thinks I am the finest playwright in England!'

'I suppose you will write back saying that you barely wrote a word of that one, and it was all the work of one Mrs Bearwood,' I said, from the corner of my mouth.

'She does not send her direction!' he protested, flapping the paper. 'And at any rate, Mrs Bearwood might think herself lucky to be in employ, despite being huge with child, and not fit to be seen in public.'

'Not so huge, please, sir,' I said, aiming a ball of paper at him. 'I do not think anyone noticed, save for those in the pit when my cloak fell off in the bedchamber scene.'

'Oh, they have seen it all before,' said Parrykin, waving his hand. 'And the takings will go up when you return, for it will be packed full of women with eye-glasses, looking to see if you have lost the weight, along with the babby.'

'I have been thinking on that, Parry,' I said, turning in my chair. 'I do not know if I will want to go back to acting, after the child comes. I love being here,' I said, gesturing about the room with my quill and helplessly watching the resulting spray of green ink fall onto my skirts. 'But I do not think I am so very great an actress.'

'I have seen worse,' said Parrykin, picking up another letter and tearing off the seal. 'You have improved immensely. And since you got plumpish, the admiring letters have greatly increased. There is one here praising the pretty fat pad under your chin.' He waved it before me.

'But I so much prefer to write the plays,' I said, ignoring this. 'The applause of the audience is nothing compared to the feeling of hearing an actor speaking the words that you wrote yourself! I have become quite used to it, and cannot bear the thought of leaving it off.'

'Well, see how you feel when the child is come,' said Parrykin absently, his nose still in a letter. 'For women are apt to change their minds in these situations. I have seen such weathercocking many a time.'

'I am having a babby, not a brain-fever,' I said. 'And I shall not change my mind on this, for I have never wanted anything more. P'raps,' I added musingly, 'I will go to the King's Men, and show them all I have written here, and see if they will not take me on.'

I saw that Parrykin had put down his letters at this.

'And,' I said, turning back to my papers, 'I'll warrant they'll give me more than ten shillings a week as I get playing company, for I have been asking around and many playwrights get seven pound per script at least.'

At this he started up and knocked some of the letters to the floor, where they made swirls in the dust.

'Do not be hasty, Ursula,' he said, his nose getting redder. 'For we love to have you and no mistake. And... *and* we shall not be prejudiced that you are a mother with a babby, and make it difficult for you, or enquire into the parentage of it – or of the whereabouts of your late husband's family. Nay, we shall not do that at all.'

'The babby is going out to nurse, as I told you, and so shall not be a burden or an impediment to my career in the slightest,' I said firmly. 'There is a goodly woman at Waltham Stow that Bunty has found me, who will let me visit it every week, or whenever I may, and I shall only bring it back when 'tis grown, and then I shall get a nurse for it, or some such.'

'You may marry again,' said Parrykin.

'I shall not marry again, sir,' I said, with a tilt of my chin. 'So do not think of that. And as for the babby's parentage, make what investigations you will, for you will find nothing to trouble any godly person on that account.'

He was quiet then.

I got up slowly from my chair. 'Well, Mr Parrykin. Thank you for all that I have learnt here...' I moved towards the door. 'I will not forget your kindness when I most needed it.'

'Now, now, madame,' he said, and I saw that there were little beads of sweat on his bald pate. 'Do not be so hasty. We can come to an arrangement that will satisfy us both. You shall have ten shillings a script, and for that you will go on as before, and help me write the plays...'

'And I too would write my own play, under my own name.' It had burst from my lips before I had even thought it through.

His jaw sprang open at this.

'Now you have astonished me,' he said. 'And I do not know the wisdom of that, for they know Mrs Bearwood as an actress, and may not take kindly to her wielding a quill, if they do any petticoat-writers...'

'Then I shall go by Ursula Flight, which is the name I was born with, and I was loath to leave in the first place.'

'Ah,' he said. 'Ah.'

'I have a play almost written, that I can have ready within the month,' I said. 'And it could not go on as a Clifford Montgomery Clyffe, for 'tis all about a woman's condition, and is plainly written by one – I have been writing it all my life, as you shall see. As for being a petticoat-writer, if it is good enough for Mrs Behn, then it is good enough for me.'

❧

The next morning when I came to the theatre, Parrykin was waiting for me.

'Fine, fine, have it your way, minx that you are,' he said, mopping his brow with a kerchief. 'I told Mrs Parrykin about it and she says if I do not let you put on your play I am more of a dolt than she thought I was. She for one would dearly like to see what you have written about the life of a female, and so I suppose she cannot be alone in it. She is not often wrong.'

I threw my arms about him and kissed his nose. 'And you shall pay me properly for it, and will not let my babby starve? For there's the midwife's fee to think of, and the price of its nursing, and...'

'I will pay you two pound a script, and five per cent of the takings for the run. Which will probably not be more than a week or so...'

'I will take five pound and twenty per cent of the takings, for I am certain this gamble will be worth my risk.'

And, though he sighed, on that we shook hands.

# XV

# EXERTION

*In which I labour*

## THE LORD GOD GIVE ME STRENGTH, IS THIS IT?

oh oh oh
oh oh oh oh
oh oh oh oh oh

I BREATHE, I BREATHE, I HISS THROUGH MY TEETH

(Hissing hissing hissing)

If I could go back and undo it, I would. It was not worth—

oh oh oh
oh oh oh

## *Oh. OW! OWWWWW!*

(*Grind, grind grind, grind, wrench*)

## LOR', I CANNOT TAKE THIS. I CANNOT BEAR IT. I CANNOT DO IT

I cannot I cannot I cannot

Forgive me, but I'm terribly sorry, I cannot

I AM TOO TIRED. I AM SO TIRED. IT HAS
BROKEN ME. DELIVER ME. PLEASE DELIVER
ME FROM THE *P-P-P-P-AIN*

# GET AWAY FROM ME, YOU DAMNED BITCH!

oh oh ohhhhhhhhhh
oh oh oh oh oh oh oh oh oh oh oh oh oh oh

NO.

# NO!

Will I die? I do not want to die. Hello? Will I die? Will I—

DAMN THAT KNAVE SAMUEL I WILL KILL
HIM I SWEAR IT I SHALL TEAR HIM LIMB
FROM LIMB THE WHORESON DECEIVER
DAMN HIS EYES THE DOG THE CURR, I
CURSE I EVER SET EYES ON HIS SCOUNDREL
PHYZZOG, IF I COULD I WOULD *BREAK IT*

I will break it. I will break his face. I will break his—

OH OH OH OH OH OH

# *THE BURNING!*
# *OH THE BURNING!*

HELP ME HELP ME HELP ME HELP ME
HELP ME

I beg

# GOD HAVE MERCYYY
## YYYYYYY
## YYYYYYY
## YYYYYYY
## YYYYYY

✻

It was but one hour past dawn when the midwife went away with the bloodied sheets, leaving me dazed and propped on my bolster in the grey morning light. Having laboured for the best part of a day, I was dappled all over with sweat; the babby she had bathed and rubbed and slapped into life beside me, a red little thing, with balled-up hands and fists. My head dipping with fatigue, hair plastered across my forehead, I gazed at her in wonder, watching her swivel her eyes and lay her arms across her face, moving all of her limbs in turn as if testing that they belonged to her. My babby worked her mouth and kicked her stiffened legs, and howled a little, at which I rubbed her belly until she blinked and quietened. The cries had made my breasts, bound up by the midwife in cabbage leaves and bandages, feel fit to bursting, and I twisted my body to ease the discomfort. Against the midwife's instructions, I picked my babby up, nudging her into the crook of my arm. She groped blindly for my breast and, when she could not find what she sought, stretched her mouth into a round gummy squawk.

'I am sorry,' I said, looking down at it tenderly, 'but I cannot feed you if my milk is to stop as it must. You are to go to another lady who will give you what you need.' The babby closed her mouth and goggled at me a while. 'You know me, do you not?' I whispered, touching her feather-soft face with my thumb. 'I am your mother. You are my daughter and you are the most beautiful thing I have ever known.'

I watched her for a while. Then I whispered: 'I will name you Cassiopeia, for I looked at the stars last night and saw that very constellation burning bright above me, and knew then that my father had sent you to me, to love me in his place.'

The babby closed her eyes, seemingly satisfied at her new name. So did I.

I woke at a knocking within and called out 'Enter.' It was the wet-nurse, cloaked against the rain, and she came in, trailing water, in a great bustle of skirts.

'Oh, what a dear thing. How did you do? Mistress Mould said you had a long time of it – 'tis always like that with the first.'

'I – I am tired,' I said.

'Let me see the precious babe,' she said, advancing. I reluctantly held out my arms.

''Tis best I take her now, madame, before either of you get too attached.'

The babby burst into a guttural cry.

'There, she is hungry. I will feed her now, if I may, madame, and that will right her for the journey.'

I nodded my assent, and she pulled out a chair and sat in it, before pulling at her clothing and putting the baby to her in one smooth motion.

'There, she has latched on most hungrily, madame. 'Tis a good sign.'

I found I did not like to watch my babby in the arms of another woman. I began to feel quite wretched and as if I might weep.

She was watching my face. "'Tis hard at first, madame, but it will grow easier, with time. And you will see her seven days hence – or sooner, if you may.'

'Oh yes, can I come sooner?' I said eagerly. 'Perhaps in a few days, when I have rested a while and am fit for the coach.'

'Aye, madame, that will be well.'

I watched them.

'Her name is Cassiopeia,' I said.

'Oh, aye,' said the nurse, 'very pretty. Is it foreign?'

'Greek,' I said. 'My father taught it to me when I was but a child myself.'

She did not seem to hear this, engrossed as she was in the feeding. She looked down at my child. 'She sleeps now. I will bind her to me, and carry her under my cloak, for we do not want you to catch a chill on your first day in the world, do we, Miss Cassy-oh-peeah?' This she said to my babby, carefully sounding the foreign vowels of her name.

'Nay, we do not!' I said, the fear rising in me that she would catch a fever and be dead before I could see her again.

'Be not afeard, madame,' said the nurse. 'All will be well.'

'Aye,' I said, but before the last footsteps of the nurse had died away and the cries of my daughter with it, I had burst into a fit of weeping, that lasted until I slept.

❧

## MY DEARLING DAUGHTER, I SWEAR TO YOU, ON YOUR BIRTH-DAY:

I shall give you everything I never had.

I shall never make you marry where you do not love.

I shall be a friend to you, and always keep your secrets.

I shall teach you everything I know & I shall never punish you for wanting to know more than you should.

I shall furnish you with books and papers and you shall write to your heart's content (if it be your wish).

I shall never send you away or push you from me, but I shall love you and cherish you all the days of my life.

This I do swear 'pon the soul of my blessed Father. AMEN

# XVI

❧

# RECUPERATION

*In which I return to the playhouse*

⚜

My stomach was a loose spongy thing beneath my corsets and my bubbies still bound and given to leaking when, conscious that I must not lose my place, I was back at the playhouse but nine days later. I stamped through the doors unsteadily, as if on sea legs, hoping my friends would not smell what I could – the milky, earthy smell beneath the orange-flower water. Besides the tender, torn sensation in the lower half of my body, I was somewhat cast down in spirits – my heart ached at the loss of my child, and my eyes were pink slitted things that too were sore – for against my will I had spent much of the past week weeping. Being glad of the distraction that work would bring in this regard, I pasted on a feeble smile and tried to look cheerful.

'What's this!' cried Manners, leaping down from the stage, and coming to embrace me no sooner than I shuffled through the doors, half hunched over. 'Out of bed so soon! And even wearing a smile. Well, a grimace. See, I told you ladies. Ursula is one of the bravest women I know.'

'Did it live?' said Thruckle, her eyes rolling down my body.

'Oh aye,' I said. 'Alive and lusty as the day is long. She is out to nurse. I have named her Cassiopeia.'

'Of course you did,' said Manners. 'Halloo hallay for Cassie.'

'Will you not sit down,' said Thruckle. 'For you look fit to drop.'

'Sitting down,' I said, 'is just the thing I cannot do.'

Careby and Parrykin came onto the stage then, Parrykin with a roll of papers in his hand, looking consternated and pink about the jowls.

'Ah, there she is,' he said.

'Just in time,' said Careby. 'For he has written another one and it gets increasingly terrible the more he scratches at it.'

'Punk!' cried Parrykin, throwing the sheaf of papers down.

'I will do what I can,' I said. 'But is this a propitious time to say that I have something else here that we could try?' I rummaged about in the bundle I was carrying. 'I have made copies for you all. And many hours it took me, all the hours that I was laid up abed in fact. But I finished the last at the stroke of midnight last night, and so here I am.'

'What's this, imp?' said Manners, dancing a few steps across the pit. 'Ah, a new play. Who am I to be?'

'You shall play two parts, if you will, Manners, in turn: the first one being disguised as a villain, the second as a gallant.'

'Huzzah,' he said.

'Oh now I do not have a say in the casting neither?' said Parrykin, blowing out his cheeks and kicking a piece of scenery, which was hanging by a thread. It splintered.

'Forgive me, Parry. But there is something I wanted to ask you – will you... come out of retirement and play the father? 'Tis a mighty good role, for he is the kindest man, and all the audience will love him.'

'Well, I do not know,' huffed Parrykin. And then under his breath: 'I am ever being subdued by women!'

'Letty shall be the child,' I went on, 'and Sukey shall take the parts of the companion, and the mother-in-law, and for the latter she shall be aged and wear a false nose. And I shall need more actors, for the other parts – and the servants... well, perhaps you would all take it and read it and think upon it withal.'

Parrykin had his nose in the pages of his script. 'I do like this fellow,' he said. 'On reflection. A kind man. Very learned.'

'But what is it to be called, Urse? For there is no title page,' said Manners.

'Well, I have been dwelling on it, and could not decide,' I said. 'What think you all of *The Illumination of Ursula Flight*?'

'Fairly well,' said Careby. 'Apart from the bit where it has your name.'

'She is a moth to a candle when it comes to the limelight, sister,' nodded Thruckle. 'So the illumination part is apt.'

''Tis a story I have drawn from life, only I have changed the names, for all but my own.'

'By the beard of Juno, I love it,' said Manners. 'And I shall have to kiss you for it.'

Parrykin put down his papers and lifted his nose.

'It will do, I suppose,' he said. 'But what is this scene here? 'Tis not finished.'

'That is where I become a playwright, Parry. And I hope to end it with applause.'

❧

## GOOD LUCK CHARMS FOR
## OPENING NIGHT

A rabbit's-foot brooch pinned to my shoulder
A silver horseshoe on a chain
My beloved old writing book (in my pocket)
A note from all the company
A posy made up by Bunty with a four-leaf clover
A lock of my sweet daughter's hair, tied with a sea-green
   ribbon and pressed into my bosom – for now all of this is for
   her, and her alone.

❧

The smell of the hair irons roused me out of my reverie. I had been thinking on the play's epilogue, which, though it was the opening night, I was still making notes on in my script book, my hands splotched over with ink.

'Curses, I have frizzed it again,' said Thruckle, setting the instrument back on the grate. 'They will never think me a just-betrothed young maid at this rate.'

'I do not think it matters,' I said soothingly, 'for the words are the thing, and you know them off by heart. Here, I have made some changes to the final line; do you think you can get this pat in an hour?'

'Well, I will have to, I suppose,' she said, snatching the paper from me.

Parrykin came in then, with a scarlet face. ''Tis filling up, my dears, filling up! At this rate we will have a full house. 'Tis no wonder, for I have had the playbills plastered everywhere from Whitechapel to Whitefriars.'

'I expect they have all come to gawp at a lady playwright,' said Thruckle. 'For the bruits about town are that she is a famous whore, or else the runaway wife of a duke, or a nun come from a Flemish convent, or all of them put together.'

I laughed at this. 'How chagrined they will be to see it is only I. But I hope they may laugh at my trials and tribulations, for even I can see the humour in them now.'

❧

The sounds of the audience began to float backstage. I thought of all the rows of eyes that would be upon my play, and all the mouths that would chatter of it afterwards, and I began to feel the clammy sensation that used to grip me before I went on the stage to act. My throat was swollen and dry and I felt a swirling in my belly that had not been helped by the posset I had swallowed, made up by Bunty and with rather too much rum. I smoothed out my skirts. I was thankful that I had a new gown, and had sent for a French hair-dresser, who had primped me and powdered me where my shaking hands could not.

The boy appeared.

'Note for you, Mrs Bearwood – 'scuse me – Mrs Flight, from a gentleman. Shall I put it with the others or do you want it now?'

'I will read it, Dennis,' I said, taking it from it and breaking off the wax.

DEAREST,

Forgive me, my Ursula, but I could not keep away, though I tried.

I will come to you in the 'Tiring Room after the performance, if you will see me. I am so full of wonder and joy that you have written your story at last, as I always knew you would.

YOUR UNDESERVING & MOST CONTRITE,

SAMUEL.

❧

# XVII

# CELEBRATION

*In which the first night of my very own play unfolds*

How do I begin to describe my feelings as the curtain went up on the first night of the first play I had authored, under my very own name of Ursula Flight? It was a thing that I had been writing for so many years, from a child to a woman, not knowing what it would be; only that as I scratched each piece of me painstakingly onto the page, I had been comforted and protected by the familiar place that was my imagination. How strange it was now to hear those words – words that I had heard spoken in life – now changed as I heard them in the mouths of the company playing their parts. I chuckled as Mr Manners strode about the stage in a dull brown suit as Tyringham, and smiled with the audience as I saw Mrs Thruckle, without her wig and patches, sit by the side of Parrykin, who played my father, and conjugate her Latin verbs.

My whole body felt tight with the tension of not knowing how my tale would be received, and wishing to better gauge the reaction of the audience, I crept up to a box and peeked through the curtain, scanning the rows in the hope of a glimpse of my mother or Catherine or Percival or even Reginald, for I had cherished the hope that if my mother could not see her way past my shame, then one of my siblings, younger and more sympathetic to the age we lived in, might give in to their curiosity to find out what their elder sister had become. But if one of them was there, I did not spy them. Leaning against the side of the box, concealed by the blue velvet back curtain, I gave myself over to a daydream of my family and I come together again, my brothers now tall and broad, Catherine pretty – much prettier than I – and my mother's arms stretched out to pull me to her. I felt suddenly the acute pain of thinking that my mother should never see my daughter, or advise me on the tribulations of motherhood I knew were to come, and I felt a wave of sorrow rise up and threaten to engulf me.

The laughter of the audience pulled me back to where I was as Mrs Careby, as Sibeliah, spake her lines in a high, faltering way which had the flavour, if not the exact timbre, of the original. I pointed my face up towards the gallery to see if the 'prentices and wenches laughed as much as the citizens. Some did, some were engaged in chatter and flirtation, but there was one man who stood, his face mostly obscured by a cloak. I peered at him briefly, mildly curious as to what he was about and why he came to the playhouse, when he turned his head towards me – perhaps some movement of the audience had caught his attention – and I could see his face at last. Pale, bulbous of forehead, the weak chin, the heavy top lip with its black stripe of moustache. *Tyringham*, said my mind, though I did not want it to be so. My lost husband, Tyringham. Had he come to claim me back once more?

Though I knew he could not hurt me now, I found that I was tremoring about the hands, and shrank back into my curtain, for fear that he had glimpsed me (how foolish this instinct was, now I think of it, when my name was writ large on every playbill and poster, and I was on the stage too, in every word of the play), but he had not spied me – his attention now was on the stage. He did not laugh with the audience, as the man playing him sat in bed beside the woman playing me, but looked much surprised that there was humour in what was depicted there, and drooped his head, as if in thought. Feeling suddenly strange, I drew myself back in the curtain and slipped back down to the 'Tiring Room, where I might be alone and comfort myself with a cordial. The sounds of catcalls from the audience seeped through the walls as I sipped at my drink and thought of how I had come to this.

Presently, Parrykin pushed his way in, pulling off his wig and throwing it on the trunk.

'Oh well, it cannot be helped,' he said, looking very down in the mouth, and avoiding my eye. 'You tried your best, of that I am sure. They are booing out there, and a rotten cabbage has just landed on Mrs Careby's hat.'

'Oh,' I said falteringly, feeling my heart drop to my stomach. My worst fears had been realized. The play was not a good one and my daughter's future was no longer secured.

Just then Manners rushed in between scenes. 'Here she is, here she is!' he said, catching me up and leading me in a sort of caper, which did not suit my mood and made me stumble and fall against the prop cupboard. 'Did you see them all laughing, and crying some?' he said, seeming not to take in my melancholy.

I looked at him in confusion.

'Ah, you have ruined my joke, Manners,' said Parrykin, swatting at him. 'But p'raps it is best, for I could not keep it up.'

'I do not understand,' I said. 'I beg you – is it good or is it bad? I feel quite sick to my stomach.'

'I was joshing you, my dear,' said Parry, his expression now completely changed from the melancholic one it was before. 'Forgive me. I shall put it plainly: the play is a success! As a playwright myself of some years' standing, believe me I know the strangeness of this – indeed 'tis a surprise to me, in truth, for I thought your play good but—' He broke off. 'Are you not content?'

I looked up at him. 'Oh aye, I am. I just... cannot take it in.' I found that I was welling up.

The door swung open then and the boy called, 'Final dance and bows please, ladies and gents. Places for the bows.'

Mr Manners caught up my hand and pulled me with him, down the short passage to the side of the stage, with Parrykin close on our heels. In a sudden giddy spurt of joy, I went on with the company to join them in their closing ballet, they all a-smiles, and bowing before me. Even before the musicians were done, the sound of applause began to rise up from all of those in front of us. There was whistling too, and cries that I could not make out, and the stamping of feet.

The company took two bows, and then came cries of 'Author! Author!' taken up by so many voices I felt quite shy, but though I protested, Manners and Careby came and brought me onto the stage and stood back for me to take my own bow, and began clapping for me themselves. I made my curtsey as elegantly as I could muster, and only a very little shyly, and held my hand out to the company and to the musicians, but the clapping did not let up, but grew louder, and then the people began to rise from their seats, and I began to laugh despite myself at the clamour of the people who had liked my play.

Manners came and stood beside me as I gazed in wonder at the audience, who all now stood to applaud me.

'I cannot believe it,' I whispered.

Manners laughed himself and squeezed my arm. 'It's the women.'

'Thruckle and Careby?' I said.

'Nay, nay,' he said, gesturing out towards the rows of people, who still did not quieten. 'Look who it is that clap you the loudest and scream out for more! 'Tis the women, Urse. 'Tis they who call out and they who jump up from their seats to applaud. You have put them on the stage, Ursula. You have shown their plight as daughters and wives and mothers. You have told their story. And they love you for it.'

And it was then that, finally, I wept.

❦

My play was a resounding, uproarious, undisputed success! Parrykin went about saying that it would make us all rich, while Thruckle and Careby found themselves admitting that they never had heard such a clamour and 'twas plain there was a need for plays with many female parts, with pretty actresses to play them. I cannot remember much of what passed after I had taken my bows and retreated once again to the 'Tiring Room – there were many people come to congratulate us all, and there was wine, and a jig, and many posies come for me from admirers, and Parrykin declared that I was his discovery and he had known all along that I should be a great playwright, only being shy, I had taken much persuading. And then I remembered that Samuel had said he would come. I looked up from where I sat, wedged between two ladies on the costume chest, feeling suddenly strange at the thought of he who had been my love. I pushed my way through the throng to Bunty, who stood in the passageway, guarding the door like a lioness.

'Away now, gents,' she was saying to two fops who seemed the worse for drink. 'For actresses or nay, they is ladies and will not appreciate such language, and neither, I must say, do I.'

'Did a man come for me, Bunty? Tall, with brown eyes of a wicked sort?'

'There's many men who've come for you, and many have been sent away with a thick ear for their pains.'

'But this one in particular said he would call – he might have said his name was Hanbury.'

'Now then, half a tick,' said Mrs Bunty, eyeing me. 'There was one who was 'ere who was tall and brown and very handsome in the eyes, now I think 'pon it.'

'Where is he, Bunty?' I said, looking about me. 'Did he leave?'

'Aye,' she said. 'He could not tarry and since he could not get to see you privately, he said he had changed his mind about seeing you at all. Very strange and dithery a fellow he was.'

'Ah,' I said. 'No message then?'

'Well, he said: "Tell her I liked the play – very much." And he said: "Tell her I wholeheartedly beg her forgiveness – for everything."'

'That sounds about right,' I said.

'Who was it,' said Bunty. 'A sweetheart? Or a husband?'

'Nay, nay, just someone I used to know.'

I went back inside the room.

'Now, who will give me wine?' I cried.

They cheered.

# XVIII

# JUBILATION

*In which I enjoy a sunny afternoon*

I sat under the shade of a great oak tree, the whisper of a breeze lifting the leaves of its branches and letting them fall again. I was pleased that my daughter was growing strong in the country away from the dirt and disease of the city. Waltham Stow was a godly place of less than two hundred dwellings, most of them farms and manors, which sat aside a great forest and banked by the wending River Lea, which brought fresh water and fish to its villagers. The grasses grew high all around in the meadow where I had stolen away to be with my child, for it was my visiting day, and all was bright to me. Though it was not yet May, the weather was fine and warm, and I had taken off my shoes. My Cassie lay on a blanket beside me, freed rebelliously from her bonnet and shawl as soon as I had carried her from Mrs Fisher's cottage.

My daughter had grown fat in the seven months since her birth and I watched as her chubby little hands grasped at the sky, stroked the frosting of light down on the top of her scalp. I tickled the pudgy creases of her knees, her skin feather-light under my fingers. She kicked. I kissed her nose and chanted the song of nonsense noises that was our private language. She giggled. I shook my face in front of her and watched her bright brown eyes dart about in wonder – Samuel's eyes. I was glad that she had this of him, though she had nothing else. I had not asked for it. He did not know of the child we had created, and I would not tell him. I did not need him now.

I picked up my script book again and looked at it. The page was riven all over with crossings out, and blobs of ink. Parrykin had got hold of it and scribbled prop directions down one of the spines.

A paper fell out of my book.

March, 1684

Dear Sister,

I am thankful you have written to me, for I did not have your address, and thought, along with Mother, that you might be dead, or gone to a convent in Flanders. I am glad to hear that it is not so.

I am also happy to hear that you are a lady playwright, though I confess I do not know much about the theatre, my reading being not what it could be – you shall tell that from my poor hand, I think, and by the shortness of this letter, which has cost me some labour.

I told Mary you had written and I am to write this from her:

'I miss you my Ursula and send kisses to you, from me and my husband Ben and my two babbies. I have wondered all this time how you did and wished that you were happy. If you will write to me at The Cottage by the Chestnut, Little Oakham, I will get someone to read it for me, and write by return, Your Mary.'

Mary has looked after me, did you know that? Mother does not know I am writing, by the by...

Yes, as you ask, in a few years I shall be old enough to be promised to a man (I am ten! Which means you are nineteen!!!), but I do not think Mother would want me to leave her for a long while yet, not until I am grown up. She was so very ill after you had gone, you see – did you know? She spent my whole childhood abed it seems, though I was too little then to know about it. I only knew that the house was always dark and there was no laughter in it. But perhaps you will come back to us, and there will be, again.

Your loving sister,

Catherine

I put the book down and folded the paper inside. The words weren't coming today, though I had promised Parrykin a draft of my new play in but a week hence. I would have to stay up all night to finish it, but it would not do me any harm. *The Illumination of Ursula Flight* had been a success, still running; and with the King's Men snapping at my heels to write for them, Parrykin had had no choice but to pay me handsomely for it. So I had a fine set of rooms at Charing, and two servants now, who did the work of the house and prepared my meals, for which I blessed myself every day. I had a flirtation with Mr Manners and letters and posies from gallants still, and occasionally took my pleasure with them when I had the mind, but I did not fall in love with them, knowing my independence a thing too precious to give to just any man.

The country smells of earth and grass and meadowflowers were all around us, and I felt lazy with the first good heat of the year. I let my hands drift across the grass, looking out beyond the field to the trees whose bright green leaves rippled in the gentle breeze. A flock of swallows rose up from the thicket and wheeled in formation overhead and out of sight. The sun dappled across the folds of my baby's fat legs. I lay back onto the grass beside her and touched the wispy top of her head, feeling the cool of the earth as it pressed against my back through my gown. I looked up at the sky, bright blue between the tree branches. My daughter chuckled at the light glinting on her face and her little voice mingled with the cries of the birds. An idea for a play began to float into my mind. There would be a dashing heroine. And a journey. I would write it all down the very instant I returned home. I sighed. Somewhere in the distance, a church bell began to ring.

❧

# Acknowledgements

This novel was begun (and mostly written) whilst I was on the MA Creative Writing at Bath Spa and I am hugely grateful for the time, space and structure the course gave me to write, as well as the ancient splendour and shadowy corners of the campus at Corsham Court, Wiltshire, which proved ideal on-the-job inspiration for Tyringham's Turvey Hall.

So many professors at Bath Spa offered their support, encouragement and criticism. The largest part of my gratitude must go to my inspirational supervisor Tessa Hadley, for her ideas, understanding, advice and incitements to 'make better' – I am forever in her debt. Thanks also to Nathan Filer, Kylie Fitzpatrick, Richard Kerridge and Philip Hensher for their encouragement and support. For their generous critiquing, I especially send thanks to my fellow students, in particular Deb McCormick, Zoe Somerville and Molly Aitken.

It's one thing to write a novel, and another to get it to the final, final, FINAL draft, and for that reason I send my fondest thanks to my endlessly enthusiastic agent Hellie Ogden as well as to Will Francis, Emma Parry and all at Janklow & Nesbit. In the same vein, I am immensely grateful to the talented and dedicated team at my publisher Allen & Unwin, particularly my editor Sam Brown, for believing in Ursula and me from the start, as well as Kirsty Doole and Clare Drysdale. To Sophie Hutton-Squire, copy editor extraordinaire; thanks for all the red pen. The visual elements of this novel were hugely important to me from its very first breath, and I owe Elzo Durt big thanks for bringing my ideas as well as my cover to life in illustrative form.

Enormous thanks go to my friends and family for their interest and encouragement, and for allowing me to ignore them for a year while

I went to ground and wrote. Special mentions go to Nick Hills, who taught me the magic of an ideas book; to Mike and Tara Bennett for having me to stay while I wrote the middle bit; and to Mum and Dad, for your support, encouragement and love. Large swathes of the novel were written at my much-missed late mother-in-law Marie Antoinette Tivnan's house in Massachusetts, and I dedicate all the funny bits to her memory.

Finally, my biggest thanks of all go to my beloved husband Tom, who made me believe that I could. So I did.

Anna-Marie Crowhurst
London, October 2017